# A DEVIOUS WAR

*To Calin*

*Paul Stanley*

## PAUL STANLEY

# CHAPTER 1

---

# Shanghai May 2014

Ru Nuang was sitting at his desk going over the papers he had spent the past week setting. He sat back and smiled – that would sort the men from the boys. Each year for the past 5 years he had done the same, not that it was compulsory; in fact it had been suggested that he stopped, but he ignored them. Wrong yes, foolhardy most certainly, but he knew they had little choice but to accept his methods. He always produced the best results; the bosses were well aware of this and were more than happy to take the plaudits. Ru knew that a good fifty percent of his students would not make it by simply not having the brains, whilst a further thirty percent were lazy, thinking they had a right to do well. That was the problem these days, a great number of youngsters had it too easy, had inflated egos and thought the world owed them a good life for little return. Out of the remainder, there was a small minority who could be awakened and spurred on to make the extra effort; they were the ones he was targeting. They were the ones who gave his department and his bosses the glory and the recognition.

The exams were not for another 3 months but this test would show who would succeed, the ones that would be going home and those who might, just might, make the cut if they buckled down. Ru was a happy man, happy with his work as he pressed the "print" button on his computer.

At that moment a loud rap sounded at his door and his mood changed. He hated people knocking on the door; it brought back bad memories. He had instructed his students never on pain of something terrible to knock. If the door was closed, he was busy or with someone, so no need to disturb. If it was open, they could stick their head round the door, cough or do anything but never, never tap on that door.

It all stemmed from his childhood when his parents were living in Nanjing. His father was a carpenter and made a good living doing jobs for local government officials. He worked every day of the week, day and night. Whenever he was summoned, he went. His hard work was rewarded by being given a small 2-bedroom house on the outskirts of the city. It had a small garden where Ru used to play and meet a few of his neighbours and a lean-to as a workshop where his father kept his tools and wood. His mother was a seamstress and worked at the local laundry where she did most of the repairs and darning. Between them they had a good living by Chinese standards and Ru was well cared for. He went to the local school, played with his friends, watched TV and applied himself well in class.

This happy and easy life suddenly ended when, one evening, there was a loud knock on the door. His father went to see who was there, fully expecting some emergency but, to his surprise, was greeted by three policemen who promptly arrested him and carted him off to the local station. His mother was not allowed to follow, nor was she allowed to see him over the next few days; no one told them anything, they remained totally in the dark. Then, six days later, his father appeared at the door severely bruised and in great pain. He was put straight to bed by his wife; refusing to be seen by the doctor, he did not eat and barely had a sip of water. He died of internal bleeding and organ failure three days later. They buried him soon after, just he and his mother, no friends, no neighbours. His mother had lost her job and none of her friends spoke to her. A good, happy life turned to a nightmare.

A few weeks later, after his mother managed to obtain travel passes, they left, taking the few remaining belongings she had saved and hitched a ride on a truck. After many hours being tossed and bounced around, they arrived in a small town nestled beside a wide river, flanked by high hills covered in forest. It felt to Ru like the end of the earth and at first, he hated this new world. He missed his friends, the small garden and the dusty bustling streets of home. His mother immediately got down to finding a home and work; a new life was about to begin.

It was about three months after they had settled into their new life that his mother met a commercial traveller she had known from her old job. He gave her news from back home and that was when he dropped the bombshell. He told her that her dear beloved husband had been reported for plotting against the state by a jealous neighbour. Everyone knew it was a false accusation but, in a world where everyone is spied upon by friends and even family, the consequences of showing sympathy could have dire repercussions. Silence was key to a safe and long life. The revelations had shaken his mother and made her bitter. Just thinking of her dear, dear husband beaten and tortured for nothing, being abandoned by all their friends, had a great effect on her mental health. Ru soon discovered that she had changed, became harder; not that her love for her boy ever altered, he was her only reason for living. She kept herself very much to herself, made only a few acquaintances and lived a solitary life. She worked hard taking several jobs and spent nothing on herself; just making sure her son lacked for nothing. She soon looked much older than her 35 years. For the best part of ten years, she did not tell her son the true story, of how and why his father had died, shielding and protecting him the best she could.

Ru decided from the start that he would make the best of his new surroundings. He soon became used to the solitude of the hills and forests and became fascinated by nature. He spent hours watching and studying the fauna and was especially interested in plants and the diversity of nature. He borrowed books and read as much as he could. He was not particularly academic, but he did excel in biology and natural history, winning several prizes for best pupil in his year which made his mother extremely proud. As the years passed, young Ru joined the local youth committee and did what all good Chinese teenagers did, taking part in organised debates, socialising and doing sports. He enrolled in the area sports group where he learned and became a very useful table tennis player.

It was one evening, whilst relaxing, watching TV with his mother who was sewing at the table, that they heard the loud rap at the door. Startled, they both jumped at the noise, memories flooding back from the last time they had heard such a sound; his mother ashen and trembling nodded and told him to see who was there. His mind racing and in turmoil he went to answer the door. Standing before him were two middle-aged men he had never seen before, dressed in official suits. Both smiled and bowed, enquiring whether his mother was in; as she was, they would like to come in. He led them through to the parlour where they introduced themselves as members of the local education committee and said they had been sent by orders of their superior to discuss her son, Ru Nuang.

"Please take a seat. Would you like tea?" his mother enquired, fussing about the parlour to hide her panic. They nodded and sat watching her intensely. "We have been asked by our superior to come and talk about your son," said the thinner of the two men. "There have been reports from his school that your son has a special aptitude in biology and natural science; it was felt that these talents should be developed." Ru watched as the second man sat there grinning and wondered whether he could talk; he had not uttered a word since he first opened the door to them. He did not like him, he did not like those little beady eyes staring at him, watching him. The first one continued, "China is in need of good academics and always encourages its citizens to develop their talents". His mother by now had relaxed a bit and was sipping her tea although neither stranger had touched theirs. He continued, "it is the express wish of our superior, Mr Wong of the area educational committee, that your son attend university in Shanghai". He nodded and smiled profusely whilst No 2 remained silent. "Of course," he continued, before his mother could say anything, "thanks to the generosity of the State and our esteemed leaders, all costs would be covered, and you would not be expected to contribute anything. I am sure you are extremely grateful; it is the least we can do." A long silence followed while his mother digested what she had heard. Both men sat grinning. "I should also say," said No 1, "that you would be granted a travel pass twice a year so that you can visit your son, which again is a most generous offer made by the State".

Neither man had yet spoken or looked at Ru; the discussion on the future of his next few years was as if he was not in the room. His mother looked over at him and asked what he thought of the plan and whether he wanted to go. "With due respect Mrs Nuang, there is no decision to be made, there is no question what your son wants or does not want, he is going, and you and he, should be grateful that the State has singled him out and is giving him such a wonderful opportunity that millions of others would die for." No 2 nodded in agreement. Looking over to Ru, No 1 continued, "I suggest you now prepare your things; we leave early in the morning; we will be here at first daylight". They both got up in unison, bowed curtly and made their way out.

Once alone, they had both sat in silence before his mother burst into tears, the thought of losing her son had hit her. What would she do without her wonderful, kind and helpful boy, always there, always happy. He comforted her as best he could and held back his tears, tried not to show his emotions and his fear of leaving for a new life he was not prepared for. Neither slept and daybreak came all too fast. The two men appeared just as the sun was rising over the distant mountains, their impatience to get going clearly visible.

\* \* \*

Once he settled into his new surroundings time past relatively quickly. His first two years were, not as explained, at university, but at college, continuing his studies. He could not understand why they had to take him away from his mother and his local school, just to learn the exact same things as he had been. His mother wrote regularly and, like a dutiful son, he attempted to reply promptly, giving her news of what he was up to and life in the big city. He doubted his mother would be jealous; she was a country girl at heart and preferred to be alone rather than surrounded by hordes of people.

His accommodation was good, sharing a room with another boy and having a further four in the same apartment. Although they all got on, he did not mix much as he had little in common with them. He was the only one studying chemistry and biology and by far the brightest and hardest working. Apart from watching football on TV and occasionally spending an evening roaming the streets, they kept themselves very much to themselves.

At the end of the second year and following stressful exams Ru was given a place at university. His mother was delighted and managed to visit, a rare outing for her, and they spent a few days catching up and discovering the city. As they returned to his rooms that night they were greeted by Mr 1 and Mr 2 standing at the main door. Ru was surprised to see them, the last time he had set eyes on either of them was when they had left him, standing alone, at that very same door two years ago. Both men bowed. Mr 2 still had that fixed smile, but his eyes seemed to be colder and more expressionless than ever. They motioned that they wanted in and followed as soon as the door was opened.

"What brings you here?" asked Ru, "last time I saw you was when you escorted me here two years ago".

Mr 1 bowed slightly and turned to his mother. "Mrs Nuang, you must be very proud of your son, he has done very well, congratulations."

Why did they never look at him, wondered Ru? Back home when they came to fetch him, they spoke as if he was not there and again now, the same thing. He felt like making a comment but decided to keep quiet.

Mr 1 continued, still looking at his mother, "your son has done well thanks to the excellence of Chinese teaching. You will be pleased to learn that he now has a place at University, here in Shanghai, starting in a month". We will, of course, take care of finding him adequate accommodation and will let your son know when this has been done." He bowed slightly. "I suggest you both go back home for a couple of weeks and we will be in contact." They both got up, nodded, and left.

Time passed too fast and before long Ru was summoned to return and start his new life as a university student. He enjoyed his time, worked hard, played hard and made some good friends; a big difference from his previous years. He started playing table tennis again making one of the teams. He discovered the pleasures and heartache of first love but always stayed focused on his studies. The only dark point was the sudden death of his mother. He was not allowed to return home as exam time was fast approaching. He would miss her, missed her letters and occasional phone calls, missed her love and affection.

He qualified at the end of the 5th year with honours as top student, elated but saddened his mother could not be with him to celebrate his achievement.

Ru was about to take a few weeks break when the Director of the University called him to his office and offered him a full-time job as teacher of chemistry and biology. He would be given a couple of rooms, a decent salary and access to the various labs and the libraries. With no plans for his future Ru accepted instantly. From there on in that was his life, a life that he enjoyed and a life he grew into very rapidly. He spent hours arguing with the powers to be that the courses had to be adapted to modern times and to reflect the new Government policies. After months he got his way but not before upsetting several old school scholars. He spent many long nights working in the laboratories with a couple of the other teachers, experimenting and developing various techniques and even sending their discoveries to the Central Chinese Research Laboratory outside Beijing. They heard nothing back but nor did they expect to.

*   *   *

There was a second knock on the door and Ru scowled, wondering what student was stupid enough to go against his orders. "Enter," he bawled. The door opened to reveal a man he had never seen before. Dressed in a suit and tie, middle-aged with greying hair, he walked in and bowed slightly. "Most sorry to disturb you Mr Nuang but my name is Xin, Xin Lau. I have seen your director and he told me where to find you." Ru carried on scowling; he was not happy to be disturbed in the middle of his work and anyway, why did this man want to see him. Certainly not a student nor a scientist, he was too well groomed. He got up and greeted his guest, then showed him to a chair. Mr Lau took a few seconds seemingly weighing up the offer but, in the end, sat down and folded his hands on his knees. The two men locked eyes and a after what seemed ages his guest decided to speak.

Xin cleared his throat, "Mr Nuang, I have been sent by my Director in Beijing to invite you to come and meet him as soon as possible. I have cleared this with your superior and he has agreed." Ru continued to stare as the memories of 21 years ago flooded back. The same bland, although more elegantly dressed, civil servant requesting that he obey orders from some far-off authority with no real choice or possibility to refuse. Nevertheless, he was not just going to agree meekly.

"I appreciate you coming here, Mr Lau, but would like to see your credentials and the letter of authority from your superior," he spoke politely and knowing perfectly well that his guest had neither a letter nor the need for such. "Can you please tell me what this is all about?" he added.

Xin looked at him and smiled, that same expressionless, insincere smile they all had. "I am afraid I am not at liberty to say anything more; my orders were to meet you and escort you back to Beijing."

Ru shook his head, "how long will I be gone?" he enquired; "we have most important exams coming up and my presence here is vital to the students, the University and future of China". "I am pretty sure my superior will not be too pleased if I abandoned ship at this time."

Xin remained impassive, nodded and shrugged. "I am sure your superior understands very clearly that this surpasses anything you are doing for the University and that your presence in Beijing takes precedence." "Do not worry about what happens here, but please prepare to leave by tomorrow; we are booked on the 10.30 flight."

"How long will I be away for? What should I take?"

"I am afraid I do not know, Mr Nuang, that is up to my director, but may I suggest you take a suit and tie; I believe it may be appropriate."

A suit, tie, shirt! Ru did not have such things, never needed them. He could imagine what his student's reaction would be if walked into a lecture dressed like a penguin. "I don't own such a thing as a suit, let alone a tie. I thought that was for the decadent Westerners." Xin did not react or chose not to hear.

After Xin had left, Ru sat for a long while trying to make sense of this new development in his already turbulent life. After a while he made his way to the Directors office and requested to be seen. The reply came so promptly that there was no doubt that his visit was expected. He was ushered into the small, cluttered office. The desk was clear of all papers, unlike Ru's, with only a couple of photos, a diary and a pen. Files were neatly stacked on a table by the desk and the large bookcase was crammed with books. A few pictures of the University hung on the wall and, in pride of place, was the portrait of China's President flanked by two half sized Chinese flags.

The man was halfway across the room and greeted Ru warmly with a vigorous handshake. "Congratulations, Mr Nuang, you have done the University proud, and I am delighted your work has been recognised".

Ru looked at him puzzled. He was about to say something when the Director continued, "Ru, I can call you by your first name, can't I? What an honour you have bestowed on this place. We are so excited for you and for what you have brought to the University. Please come and sit down. Some tea?"

Ru made his way over to one of the small fake leather chairs whilst his boss poured two cups of green tea. "Thank you sir, but I do not understand what all this is about. I have been asked to go to Beijing tomorrow by someone I have never met. With exams due soon, I really don't think this is the right time for me to leave, even if it is only for a few days.

"Yes, you are right my boy, but this surpasses everything; we will just have to muddle through. Such a request to work at the Chines Central Research Laboratories is not something you can refuse and certainly not something we can oppose. It is such an honour for you and for us; thanks to you we will all benefit." He paused and sipped his tea, "to work with China's top scientists for the good of the Chinese Nation and our people is only for the few and must be grasped with both hands".

Ru stared at the man in disbelief. When he managed to find his voice, he croaked, "Director, I still don't really understand. I have done nothing extraordinary apart from sending findings of three small experiments we have done to the CCRL as is our duty, and not heard back from them. I doubt that my findings on why mice survive certain paralysing agents and frogs don't, is sufficient to send me to such an important research centre."

"It is not up to me or my duty to say why or why not you have been chosen; just accept it and do your best. You will meet many great brains and mix with some of the best scientists in the country. What you do with that is up to you but, what I am sure of, is that you will learn and progress rapidly. Embrace it and your life and that of millions will benefit."

Ru felt touched and for the first time liked the man sitting across the desk. "Do you know how long I will be gone for" he asked.

"You are leaving for good. Your new home and life will be wherever they send you, although I hope you will make time to come and visit us occasionally. You will always be welcome."

After a few more warm words of advice the Director rose and showed his guest to the door. "I suggest you go and prepare your things and pack your books, Mr Nuang, a new life awaits, and you must not be late; it's never good to be late, especially when the Nation is calling." On that he shook Ru's hand warmly, grinned and closed the door.

# CHAPTER 2

---

# Dorset, England 2017

James Horton stood at his study window gazing at the rain battering against the window. It had been wet for the past 2 days and nature was looking miserable and sodden under the continuous downpour. The clouds were racing low across the sky and a rainy mist obscured the sea. He stood sucking his empty pipe, his mind a million miles away. He jumped, startled, as the phone rang on his desk. Who could that possibly be, we wondered? He had few friends now that he was retired and had moved to his new home in the country. Retirement suited him and he certainly did not miss his old lifestyle.

He picked up and instantly recognised the lilt of the caller's voice.

"James, how are you; Sean Docherty here." The smooth voice gave the impression of a kindly, fatherly man who would do anything for you, which he was when not at work. In his day job he could be a cold, calculating and a hard soldier. Native of Belfast, Sean had spent many years as an undercover Special Branch informer infiltrating the IRA, passing invaluable information to London and in doing so saving many lives. Once the Good Friday agreement had been signed he moved to England and was given the job of monitoring drug cartels and dissident groups in the Far East. Well-travelled and speaking three languages, Sean knew how to turn on the charm or to be ruthless when necessary.

They had met by accident at an official reception and struck up an instant friendship. Both were sportsmen; James a cricketer, had played at County level and was passionate about the game. Sean was a rugby man who also played at the higher echelons of club and army. He was built like an ox and kept up his military fitness; at the age of 56 he still had an impressive physique and a big presence.

"Haven't seen you in ages. What are you up to these days James?"

"Well I I'm retired since last autumn but still do some odd jobs and write a few articles, but other than that, not a lot. Keeping myself occupied in the garden and watching the cricket pretty well sums up my life."

"In that case let's meet up; I may have a project for you and a bit of research."

Intrigued, James enquired what the project was. "Let's say," his friend continued, "I would prefer not to talk about it on the phone; never trust you aren't being taped. At least in the old days you knew Mrs O'Hara at the post office was listening and you made sure not to say anything, but now, with modern technology, it can track your movements and listen in to everything. If you aren't doing anything tomorrow, I can get the 9.17 and be with you by 11am." It certainly seemed to James that this was an order, nicely put, nevertheless an order with no possibility of refusal.

"Sounds great and I look forward to it. I'll come and pick you up from the station. I I'll be in the car park," he chirped. "I will get Mrs Horton to have some lunch ready, ;see you tomorrow". They exchanged a few further words and hung up.

He turned back to the window feeling much happier. What on earth did Sean want from him? It certainly sounded very business-like and secretive. He wasn't sure about all that telephone stuff and liked to think that here in Britain, it did not happen as a matter of course. He smiled, once a spook always a spook. Leaving his cosy study, he set off to warn his wife they would be having a guest the following day for lunch.

*   *   *

When James woke the next morning the sun was out and only a few remaining clouds dotted the sky. What a difference from the past few dreary days; it must be a good omen, he thought. Before leaving home, James checked the train was running to schedule and left in plenty of time. The trip would only take twenty minutes, but he liked to make sure he got to the station early. Finding a place not far from the main exit and with a good view, he sat and glanced through the paper. Nothing of interest in the news so he turned to the sports section and looked through the cricket scores. Bang on 11 he saw the London train pull in and a few minutes later a tall, well-built man appeared, dressed in grey flannels, a green tweed sports jacket, cream shirt and a very colourful green tie. James stepped out of the car and waved to the man, who came over with a wide grin on his face. "Sean, nice to see you again, you're looking great." Both men shook hands vigorously and got into the Jaguar.

"Well my friend, for a retiree you aren't looking bad at all, a bit greyer perhaps." Sean smiled and continued, "see your old county is struggling a bit, lost yesterday again," and he chuckled.

"Oh, shut up, it hasn't been that bad; yes, a couple of losses lately but we do have three players on International duty," retorted the driver. "Anyway, London Irish are not doing all that well either; what's your excuse?"

The banter carried on for a while longer before turning to more serious topics of the economy, Brexit and the US President. The drive through the country lanes was quiet and Sean sat looking out at the rolling scenery. He liked this part of England, but it was too far from London where he spent a lot of his time. He looked over to his friend and smiled, a typical middle-aged Englishman he thought, sucking on his empty pipe, a plain brown tweed jacket that had seen better days and a tweed trilby. In fact, he could have come straight out of one of those TV sitcoms. Sean knew that was as far as any comparison could go and that his friend was nothing but brilliant. Behind those grey eyes a great brain, razor sharp and crammed full of knowledge; witty also, but what Sean admired most about James was his grasp of economics, and how they affect nations, and how it has shaped the world for centuries.

He turned to his friend "Do you know, or have you heard of Professor Howard of Cambridge University?" he enquired in a serious tone. "He worked for the MOD at Porton Down for 10 years whilst still based in Cambridge, and now lives in St. Andrews, semi-retired and doesn't even play any golf."

"No, no idea who he is. Why, should I?"

"Not really but I thought you may have crossed paths at one those fancy evenings you used to attend; he seemed to be well in with the bigwigs."

James smiled. "You mean like the one where I first met you? How do you know him?"

"Well, I don't really know him. I was given his name when I had a meeting with the boss about a week ago and I made some enquiries. Seemingly he's brilliant and has done loads of work advising the army and government about chemical and biological warfare. I'm told he's a real boffin; doesn't play any sport so definitely not my type."

"Why do you ask?" enquired James.

"Later dear friend, all in good time. For now, I can't wait for a good cup of coffee; that stuff they serve on trains tastes like dishwater and they charge an arm and a leg."

James drew into the drive and parked in front of the garage. "Here we are, welcome to my humble pad. Come on in and meet the wife and we can get you that coffee."

"Not doing too badly for yourself, are you?" quipped Sean. "Here I was expecting a wee cottage with thatched roof and roses but hey! We have a mansion with gardens and lawns. Where are all the servants and gardeners?" he asked with a wry smile.

"No servants, no gardeners except for me, unless you call a fifteen-year-old lad once a week a gardener. Come on in."

Claire Horton was in her early sixties, petite, attractive and very bubbly; that was what had attracted James to her all those years ago. They met at a friend's party and it was love at first sight. She was studying languages at Exeter University and lived with her parents. Courtship was brief and they married a year later. She greeted Sean with a big smile and a warm handshake before ushering them into the study. The two men made their way over to a large leather sofa; the room was airy and bright, flanked on one side by a large bay window overlooking the gardens. A large partners desk and comfortable chair dominated the area. Floor to ceiling bookcases covered the other two sides and were crammed with books of all kinds. The wall behind where they sat had a couple of pictures and a few family photos as well as some of James, dressed in whites, holding a cricket trophy.

Sean looked round and took in the homely feeling, a long way from his own small bachelor pad back home. He envied his friend for his lifestyle, so different from his own itinerant, nomadic routine, never knowing where he was going to be from one day to the next. Because of that he had never married. Yes, he had had a few girlfriends and, way back, had a long running affair, but his constant postings abroad and the dangerous nature of his job made any long-term relationship impossible. His home reflected his life and his nature, it lacked the warmth of a woman's touch, but it was fine, he was used to it and it suited him, for the time being.

James pulled out his pipe, stuck it in his mouth and looked at his friend. "Well, what's this all about?" he enquired.

"You've never been to my place, have you James? Not a bit like this – you must, one day. I definitely think I prefer this, much warmer and friendlier." He paused, his eyes on one of the pictures, "when I retire I'll ask Mrs Horton to come and do the interior design, she clearly has a great touch".

James was about to ask his question again when his wife came in carrying a tray laden with biscuits and homemade baking. She set it down on the table in front of the two men and smiled, "some proper coffee as you requested, and I thought you might like to taste some scones I made earlier. There's cake also, just in case you still feel peckish. Lunch is at one thirty, so don't overdo it and don't let James have more than one scone; he needs to lose weight," she chirped.

"Get stuck in and don't believe what she says. I've not put a pound on in the past five years!" James poured them two cups of coffee and handed Sean a plate and serviette. "Right, what is all this about? You've not come down here to socialise, it's not your style."

Sean took a sip of the hot brew and bit into a scone. "What do you know about China?" he enquired.

"What do you mean? in what way?"

"Its economy my friend, its economy. I'm sure in all your years you've studied the evolution of its economy; I want you to tell me all about it."

James sucked on his pipe. "From when, how long have you got and in what context? I'm an economist and journalist, but my knowledge of China is pretty limited, so I really need to know what you want specifically; it's a vast subject."

Sean took another bite of scone and scratched the back of his head, "I've been working on an assignment for the past year. It started as a routine surveillance, monitoring calls, tracking e-mails and mobiles between Pakistan, the Taliban and the Chinese Triads. We had intel that the three were working together and coordinating large movements of drugs from Pakistan to Europe and other parts of the world. It was all going well - probably had about a month to go before I busted them. Then, a week ago I received a call from HQ, telling me to drop everything as they had a major tipoff about something far more worrying. As I say, this was last week and I was livid to say the least, all that time spending days, weeks getting to know the key players and partly infiltrating them, just to be told to stop. I was making real progress."

He sat back. "What I'd like to know," continued Sean, "is some good background on China's economy and economic policy since the 80's and you my friend, are the one that can help".

"Surely you can Google it," replied James, "it would be much quicker. What's it about?"

Sean sipped his coffee. "Yes I know, but you can read between the lines and can extrapolate better than I can and then you can explain things simply. I do not want a whole lot of crap, just your take on the facts put in layman's terms. I'm a simple guy. I can't tell you much now, but time is short."

"How long have I got?" asked James.

"Ideally four days. I would like to have your views by Friday. Oh, by the way, I hope you have nothing planned for tomorrow. We're meeting the Prof. in London for lunch, twelve thirty at the Savoy."

James laughed. "What do you mean we're meeting your boffin tomorrow; you never mentioned that. You want me to get up to speed on China's economy in three days and then tell me I have to spend the day travelling and making conversation to a stranger; you're crazy."

"Not a stranger," retorted Sean. "A very important scientist who, I hope, will be of help for both of us. Anyway, you can read up on the train; you have phone or iPad haven't you?"

James rolled his eyes and sucked harder on his empty pipe. "I get sick when I read on a train and I must sit facing forward."

Just as Sean was about to make a sarcastic remark there was a knock on the door and Mrs H popped her head around and announced lunch was ready.

They both got up, "well that's settled then, I'll meet you under the main clock at Euston station at twelve". Sean started to make his way to the door, "I'm looking forward to lunch, I I'm starving".

\* \* \*

After seeing Sean on to his train, James went and booked his ticket and seat for the next day. Back home he went into his office and started to work on his new task. He felt some excitement and silently thanked his friend for giving him a job to occupy his mind. That was the main problem with retirement; he had come to accept the mundane lifestyle and certainly did not miss the deadlines and hectic pace of his previous journalistic life, but he did miss having to use his brain. All very well reading, he loved his books on history, military battles or learning about the greats of cricket and doing the crossword, but it did not tax the grey cells and he certainly did not want to turn into doddery old bore.

The train pulled into Euston on time and he made his way to the clock where they met up. They then proceeded to the taxi rank and once settled in a cab Sean turned to him. "You look a bit pale and green under the gills my friend."

"Yes, started to get some reading done but I felt queasy pretty quickly and had to stop. Decided to have a sleep but some ghastly banker chap kept yelling down his phone. Someone did point out that it was a quiet carriage, but as usual, it made no difference and he kept wabbering on; so rude and tiresome".

"Have you got far with your research?" enquired Sean.

James looked over to him, "yes and no. I stayed up until three this morning but have mases more to get through. I don't like to say, but I will need more time, perhaps until next Wednesday?" he looked quizzically at Sean. "I know you're under pressure, but if you insisted on me coming up to town today and if you want a proper report, I do really need that extra time."

Sean sighed, "guess I was expecting a bit much from you and I know you wouldn't ask if it wasn't necessary," he grunted. "Alright, Wednesday it will be. I'll come down on the same train and you can fill me in." He looked over to James and, reading his mind, added, "no, you can't send it by e-mail. I told you, I don't trust anything like that. I'll come down and you can tell me everything you've learned over another of Mrs H's great lunches."

The cab drew up in the courtyard of the Savoy and the door was opened by a liveried doorman. As they entered James looked around and recalled the last time he had come here, some 25 years earlier. The place hadn't changed all that much, still opulent and grand. They made their way over to the iconic Simpson's Restaurant and were shown to their table. Sean's instructions must have been very precise - a good table, in a booth, in the corner and slightly obscured. A trade habit thought James as they made their way across the room. The dining room was busy with lunching businessmen and a few tourists.

"We will shortly be joined by a friend; please show him over when he arrives," Sean instructed the maître d. "We will wait until he arrives before we order drinks, thank you."

"This wasn't my idea," grunted Sean, "I would have preferred a small Italian bistro but our guest was insistent that he wanted to come here, so here we are".

Just then they noticed the head waiter coming over towards them closely followed by a tall lanky and rather dishevelled man. Sporting a greying goatee and a small pig tail, thick spectacles and dressed in a crumpled suit, he looked totally out of place in such surroundings. Both men got up to greet their guest and Sean introduced himself and then James.

"Good of you to meet us at such short notice Professor; we know how busy you are and that you are only down in London for a short time." James was impressed at the smooth talk from his friend.

"Well indeed, it is a bit of an inconvenience, but I had little choice – our mutual friend here seemed very insistent that I meet you," retorted the Professor.

Conversation over the beef was strained and difficult as the Professor did not seem to want to talk or volunteer any information. Despite James's and Sean's best efforts all they got were one syllable replies. At the end of the meal and after he had drained his glass, the Professor sat back, wiped his mouth, and started to get up. "It was nice meeting you gentlemen; thank you for a fine lunch. I'm in a hurry as I have a train to catch back up to Scotland; perhaps we could meet up in a week or so in St. Andrews, at my place, where we can discuss matters in peace and tranquillity." He stuck out his hand and turned to leave. "See you in a week's time, Wednesday, my place," he said over his shoulder.

The two men looked at one other. "Well, that went well," James commented. "A vast amount of food, two bottles of wine and nothing for it apart from a big fat bill."

"Ah don't be too downhearted," replied Sean. "Like me, he's obviously a suspicious and cautious person; the fact that he's invited us up to Scotland means he will open up, but not here. Don't fret, I'll make sure you're re-imbursed!"

"What do you mean I I'll get re-imbursed! Thought you were paying, damn it; it was your idea."

Sean roared with laughter, "Just joking. Should have seen your face."

James shook his head. "So, we are actually going to see him?" asked James.

"Oh yes, for sure. Next Wednesday, I'll book us on a flight up to Edinburgh and we can hire a car. During the drive you can tell me all you've learned – see you don't get away that lightly," Sean turned and winked.

As the pair made their way out Sean turned to his friend and clapped him on the back. "It's great to have you on board James; welcome to my murky world." They stepped into a waiting taxi that the commissionaire had hailed, "let's meet up Tuesday night at one of the airport hotels, that way we can take the first flight up. I'll book a couple of rooms for the Wednesday night so you can stay in London with me before returning to your country mansion the next day. I'm sure Mrs H will survive your absence for 2 nights; give her a bit of peace," he smiled.

# CHAPTER 3

# Washington

Hank Gobolsky sat in his cluttered office staring out at the far-off skyline. He was not in a good mood; he seldom was on a Monday but that day, even more so since his favourite team had lost the night before. He turned around and picked up a slim manilla folder and began to read. A few minutes later he slammed the file shut. "Carter," he roared.

A few seconds later a young, thin, bespectacled assistant came through the door.

"What the hell is this?" asked Hank tossing the file towards the young man who promptly dropped it.

"A secretary brought it down earlier this morning sir; told me to make sure you read it urgently."

Hank watched his aide retrieve the papers and put them back in order. "Urgent! my arse. Take it back to whoever sent it and tell them not to waste my time. What the hell do they think I care about a Brit scientist having lunch with a couple of guys in a fancy restaurant? Don't the London boys have anything better to do? Now, get the hell out of here."

He turned back and resumed looking out of the window. He shook his head; well, things have certainly changed. Sending a report about three unheard of dudes having lunch in a fancy hotel. A couple of toffs, and some scruffy retired lecturer - what a waste of his time. What they needed was a taste of the real life, of the past. His thoughts were suddenly interrupted by the buzzing on his telephone. He picked up. "Hank Gobolski" he growled.

"Hank. Brian here. Just wondering if you can come up to my office if you have a minute; there's something I need to talk to you about." The phone went dead.

Hank sighed. He was in trouble and he knew it. Brian Millento, his Director, very seldom invited anyone up to his office, especially his workers, unless it was to demote them or give them a major dressing down. He got up and walked through the small reception area where Carter was sitting busying himself and pointedly not looking up at his boss.

He announced himself to the very neat secretary and was immediately shown into the Director's office.

"Hank, good of you to come up so promptly," the director smiled and pointed to the chair across from the vast desk. "Now, I hear you didn't think much of the file I sent down earlier." Hank's stomach cramped up and a lump formed in his throat. He was about to speak but his boss held up his hand.

"Let me finish," he said, cold eyes boring into his victim. "When I send one of my operatives a file I expect it to be taken seriously. It may by a bit sketchy, but I am not in the habit of wasting my resources' time. If you don't want it or if you think you aren't capable, then by all means, tell me and I I'll hand it to someone more competent."

Hank sat silently before replying, "It's not..."

"I have not finished," interjected the director. From your past and your experience I had assumed you would take a bit more interest; you are good man Hank and I trust you." He picked up the file and handed it over, "now take it back and get down to work. I want a full report on those guys; who they are, what they do and what they are working on by the end of next week, you understand?"

Hank took the file and nodded. He rose and was halfway to the door when his boss spoke again, "I smell something big here, Hank; not sure what it is but I know you will get to the bottom of it". He winked and then added, "Oh, and be nice to that poor Carter, he's only young, just like you were once".

Back in his office Hank took the file and read it again. Sketchy was the word. Barely two pages long, it described a meeting between three Englishmen in a posh London restaurant a few days earlier. The only reason the London boys had been watching was, out of habit – the organisation kept tabs on current and ex scientists as well as businessmen, politicians, and a whole raft of normal looking citizens. It was routine. By all accounts someone there decided, in their wisdom, to track the scientist. He shook his head

"Carter, in here buddy."

The young aide appeared and stood at the door. "Come right in. Don't stand there, looks as if you're ready to bolt. Right, think I must apologise for earlier, I know you were just doing your job. Having said that, don't take my apology as a sign of weakness." He smiled. "I want you to take these papers and I want a full report on these guys by tomorrow morning, understand?" As an afterthought he shouted out, "No, forget about the report, I will deal with it myself". The aide nodded and left.

Hank picked up the phone and dialled; a few rings later a voice came on. "Yeah, Joe speaking."

"Hi Joe, its Hank, how's it going buddy. Doing anything interesting these days?" he enquired.

"Not really, taking a few days up in the cabin and fishing up in Maine."

"Right, I want you to drop all that and get your arse over to London pronto."

Joe laughed, "Hey you don't give me no orders, you're not my boss anymore and I'm having a great time up here, relaxing".

"It's no joke, I want you in London in two days' time and a report in person here by Thursday at the latest. I'm sending my young assistant up to Boston and he can hand over the file: usual dress for such a trip. See you back here on Thursday, and don't let me down. Cheers buddy, good luck."

Joe was about to say something, but the phone went dead. He sighed deeply; he was enjoying his fishing and beers. He could just ignore the request. No, he couldn't. For Hank to call him and be so forceful meant he may have something big on, and when Hank got that gut feeling Hank was normally right.

Hank smiled. He liked Joe, a go-getter and a good ally, always reliable. They had worked on a couple of assignments together and had got into some pretty hairy situations but they each knew they had one another's back when the chips were down. The last one was particularly scary, down in Nicaragua eighteen, twenty years ago? Hank had thought things were going fine but Joe had smelt a rat. Before he knew it a gun battle had erupted and Joe downed two gang members, saving his life. It was after that operation that he had been transferred to Washington and a desk job. At first, he was resentful but quickly admitted to himself that field work was not for him.

"Carter, in here and at the double," he roared. The young man appeared, looking more nervous than ever. "Stop shaking man, I'm not going to eat you. I got a job for you; get yourself on a flight tomorrow to Boston and be at the British Airways Business check-in desk 16.00. You are going to hand over a copy of this file to a man I know. He will be dressed in a navy business suit, red tie and a small badge of our national flag in his buttonhole. Make sure he gets it, then get yourself back here pronto. Understood?"

Carter nodded. "Yes sir, but I don't think I have sufficient cash to buy the ticket," he stammered.

"Just go up to personnel, give them this." He handed the young man a note.

"Thank you, sir. Is there any passcode I should know?"

Hank roared with laughter, "hell boy! What do you think we are; spies or something? No, my contact will recognise you. I've sent him your picture. Just hand him the file and get the hell back here".

# CHAPTER 4

# London

The air hostess leant over and touched Joe on the shoulder. "Mr Briggs, we're on our final approach; please put your seat in the upright position and ensure your table is folded away," she smiled sweetly. Joe stretched and got himself together. He had learned over the years to sleep anywhere and in any conditions. The flat bed of a BA flight was heaven compared to some places he had kipped down. He opened the shutter and peered out at dawn breaking over London. He felt a tingle of excitement at being back in the old, grey city where he had been stationed for five years and looked forward to the next few days.

He made sure he was off the plane first and headed straight to passport control, arriving just before a crowd of Japanese. He stepped up when beckoned and handed over his passport. The officer glanced at the open page, swiped the passport and looked up. "How long are you going to be in the UK for Mr Briggs?"

"Just three days, on a quick business trip," replied Joe.

"Staying in London or are you travelling on?"

"No, just staying here in town, meetings starting from lunch time today," said Joe and smiled.

"Well, that's fine, thank you, have a good stay."

Joe then made his way to the exit and across to the Heathrow Express. An hour later he was handed the key to his room on the 7th floor. He showered quickly and changed into some fresh clothes before making his way the short distance to the US Embassy in Grosvenor Square. He arrived at the front gate and was greeted by a marine on duty. After showing his passport he was allowed into the front hall and passed through security – lax was what he thought. Once done he marched over to the large reception desk and was greeted by a young receptionist with long straight hair and nails like talons painted with stars and stripes.

He smiled his best smile. "Good morning. Could you let the Second Commercial Attaché, Mr Sharps, know that Joe Briggs is here to see him?"

"Do you have an appointment sir?"

"No, I just flew in this morning, but I know he will see me."

She shook her head. "Sorry sir but if you don't have an appointment I can't call. I suggest you go online and fill in the request."

"Well perhaps you could try, just for me." said Joe; "simply say it's an old friend. I'm sure his secretary, Sally, will remember me".

"Sorry sir; as I say, go online and book an appointment. It's very easy".

"May I suggest – Beth – that you pick up the phone and call upstairs or you may find you'll be returning to Georgia sooner than you had planned." He looked at her through squinted eyes.

"Please don't threaten me sir or I will have to call security," she looked apprehensively at the man in front of her.

"I'm not threatening you, Beth, just suggesting that if you want to stay in London you should seriously think about making that call," he said soothingly.

Who was this man and who did he think he was, just demanding and expecting her to go against protocol? She was in two minds as to what to do but curiosity got the better of her. "How do you know I'm from Georgia?" she enquired.

Joe tapped his lapel and looked at the pin on her left breast pocket of the blazer, then pointed at the small desk flag behind her. "Pretty simple Beth, observation." He nodded.

After a few seconds thought she resigned herself and picked up the phone. "Morning Sally, its Beth at reception. I have a gentleman in reception; he has no appointment but is insisting on seeing Mr Sharps. I've tried to get him to go through the official channels, but he's not listening. He says his name is Joe Briggs." Her eyes popped wide open and her jaw dropped, "yes, sure I will. Immediately. Do you want me to bring him up myself?" she enquired before setting down the receiver.

She looked up at the visitor and smiled, "seems you are known, Mr Briggs; the Attaché will see you immediately".

Joe shrugged, "guess if you've worked here for five years, they kind of remember you". "No need to come along; I can remember the way, thank you Beth."

He was greeted by a middle-aged woman who got up from her desk and came over to shake his hand. "Welcome back Joe, nice to see you. Follow me. Bill is waiting for you."

She led him to an office where a plump balding fifty-something man was standing at the window. He turned around on hearing the door open and beamed widely. "Joe buddy, how are you? What brings you to London?" He motioned Joe to a chair across from his desk. "Thought you were retired so is this a social trip?"

"Semi-retired, and no, Bill it's official. Hank asked me to check out a real sketchy report your guys sent him a few days ago. Oh, yeah I nearly forgot –he says hi, hopes you and Sonja are still together."

Bill nodded. "Ah yes, the report about three guys meeting up in Simpson's; surprised Hank didn't use it as toilet paper," he laughed.

"He did at first but then the Boss got him by the balls and ordered him to take it seriously, so that's why I I'm here." He shook his head, "I just can't understand what or why your guys decided to put out such a crap report or why they even took an interest in these brits; are they terrorists or something?"

The Attaché sighed, "I know. Things are different from when you were here. Our hands are tied, we don't have the freedom you had, nor the experienced personnel. Budget cuts mean we have a bunch of kids playing at spies who have no idea of the real world and who have too many principals. Anyway, orders are that we have to keep tabs on all active and non-active scientist no matter who they are and where they come from; far more important than chasing the real bad guys who are plotting to blow people up."

Joe sat silent for a few seconds, "I know Billy, times have changed; I'm not blaming you. Look, I I'm here for just a couple of days so need to get on. Can I speak to your two guys?" he enquired.

"Sure, no problem, be my guest." He leaned over and pressed the intercom, "Sally get the two dudes who prepared file 15555 come to the conference room asap, thanks".

Twenty minutes later Joe was shown into a large airy room with a massive oval table surrounded by twelve chairs: each place had a blotter, A4 pad, a pen and bottle of water. Two young men remained sprawled on their chairs and chewing gum. They looked up as he walked in but did not bother standing or introducing themselves. Joe glowered at the pair.

"Joe Briggs," he said. "Nice to meet you. In my day I was told to stand up and introduce myself to a superior." The two men remained silent and stared at him.

"I've been sent here to check out the report you made a few days ago about three brits having lunch at Simpson's. Pretty sketchy to say the least, wouldn't you say?" He looked at the two men who stayed silent.

"Did you get photo ID?" he enquired. They shook their heads. "Any names, addresses?". Again, they shook their heads whilst resuming their chewing. "Do we know what they do or what they were meeting about?".

"We know one of them is a scientist, the old thin one, but have no ideas about the other two, nor why they were meeting."

Joe's patience was running thin. He clenched his jaw, "first things first guys, I I'm your superior, so you call me sir. Secondly, you stop chewing that damned gum when you talk to me and thirdly you sit up properly. I have no idea what they taught you back at training camp but it sure wasn't manners.".

Both men immediately sat up and stopped masticating. "Just in case you don't remember, you're working and representing the United States of America so get a grip and start acting like professionals. Now, I I'm here for a couple of days only, so need you guys to get out there and find answers to those questions I just asked. I want a full report within the next thirty-six hours; understand?"

The two youngsters got up, "we'll do our best sir, but it won't be easy".

Joe shook his head and sighed. God help us if that's the best America can produce. No, wrong; there are still great servants of the Nation, great spies and professionals, working tirelessly to protect this great country of ours and all its citizens around the world. Shame that these two had been posted in one the most important cities of the world. In his day you started from the bottom and cut your teeth in the back of beyond, you learned to use your instincts and your resources to survive, or you were killed. Now, it is seen to be unfair and even the CIA fears being sued; what did the Brits call the youth of today? Ah yes, snowflakes; very apt. He looked at his watch and got up; time to get to work.

Once outside the Embassy compound Joe hailed a taxi and asked to be taken to the Savoy. It must have been at least seven years since he was last there so held little hope, but the idea was worth a try. He made his way to the restaurant and was surprised to see the old maître D hovering at the door. As he approached the man looked up from his diary and immediately recognised the guest and beamed widely ,"Monsieur Briggs, how wonderful to see you again after all these years, are you back in London for long?" He normally didn't like Americans all that much but this one was different. A soft, polite man who enjoyed good food as well as good clarets, and who always tipped well.

"Emile, how are you? Not looking a day older," said Joe thrusting out an open hand out.

"Are you eating Monsieur?" enquired the head waiter. "I'm afraid your usual table has been taken. Had I known..." he left the sentence unfinished.

"Yes, I I'm starving and would just love some of your fabulous beef and a half bottle of claret," said Joe enthusiastically.

Once seated and with a glass of red poured, he turned to Emile. "Emile, I don't suppose you could help me. About a week ago you had three men in for lunch, they may have been sitting at a corner table and one of them sported goatee from what l understand, you don't possibly recall who they were do you".

Emile looked thoughtful. "Indeed Monsieur, I do remember three guests, especially one of the gentlemen - very strange, no dress sense and very fond of his wine. They sat over in the corner by special request. However, they may not be the gentlemen you are thinking of; we have many visitors and regulars."

"I'm pretty sure they wouldn't be regulars. Any name come to mind?" asked Joe. "Description even. The thing is, they could be connected to a scam and possibly fraud back in the US. My boss at the bank in New York got a tip off that they may be planning something here in London, so I I'm over to investigate."

"Let me have a think monsieur and I will let you know once you have finished your meal."

Joe savoured the beef; he had to admit it beat anything you could get back home, especially when washed down with several glasses of Emile's choice wine. As he was paying, Emile came over and leant over.

"If you are not in too much of a hurry Monsieur, I could meet you at 3.30 this afternoon at the staff entrance on the Embankment, the one with the black door. I may be able to help."

Joe pressed a large note into Emile's hand and thanked him. "Excellent lunch and wine. Thank you. I'll see you later".

"Oh Monsieur, you are too kind."

Having plenty of time before returning, Joe jumped into a cab and asked to be taken to Victoria station where he got out and strode down Wilton Street, before turning left into Gillingham Street. He could have got the taxi to drop him off at the door but needed the exercise after his big lunch. He turned into a small alleyway and stopped in front a faded green door. He peered at the various buttons until he found the name Aaron Goldberg and pressed the buzzer. A woman's voice crackled and he gave his name. A few seconds later the door clicked open and he started to climb the four flights of stairs. Aaron Goldberg's door was open, so he went in and was greeted by an ancient grey-haired old lady who simply nodded and beckoned him to follow her. He entered a small dusty and dark room where he found Aaron sitting stooped over a bench working on a necklace through a pair of magnifying glasses.

The old man did not look up. "What brings you here my boy?" came a gravelly voice.

"Good to see you Aaron. Not retired yet?" quipped Joe.

"You're a long time dead so no point in wasting what little time you have," came the reply.

"Still have your ear to the ground have you?" enquired the younger man.

"Depends what for."

"I'm in town for a couple of days, wanting to catch up with what's going on. Not terrorist or drug-wise but anything out of the ordinary." He kept his eyes on the old man. "Not interested either in any raids or robbery plans, just odd events."

As there was no reaction, he jotted down the hotel phone number in his room and left it on the small table by the desk. "I'm on a fishing trip, no real leads just a hunch, so if you hear anything leave a message at the hotel reception and I'll get back to you. The number's on the table."

As he turned to leave the old man croaked, "fishing trips don't come cheap, leave something with Elspeth and I will see what I can do".

Exiting the small office Joe pulled out a £50 pound note and left it on the table in front of the old lady. "For your favourite charity," he said smiling.

It was 3.40 when he arrived back at the Embankment and found the right door where he spotted the maître D patiently waiting. "So sorry Emile, forgot what the traffic is like."

"No problem monsieur, please follow me". He ushered Joe along several corridors and then knocked on one of the doors a couple of times before entering. A Sikh with a fine blue turban was sitting in front of a console with several screens above showing images of various parts of the hotel.

"This is the security centre, monsieur, for the hotel. If you tell Mandeep here what you're looking for he may be able to help. I'll sit and wait just over there."

"Thanks Emile. Never thought that such an iconic venue would be covered by CCTV." He introduced himself to Mandeep and explained what he was looking for. He was pointed to the desk where the Frenchman was sitting and within a few minutes the screen in front of them came to life and they settled down to watch. It wasn't long before two men were getting out of a cab and entering the hotel lobby, then they were picked up standing at the door of the restaurant. The camera showed them being shown to the corner table and Emile pointed excitedly.

"Are these the two you remember?" Joe enquired. Just then a third individual appeared.

"Oui, yes Monsieur, those are the three men. You can recognise the tall thin gentleman? He was the one who liked his drink". Emile continued, "you see the man in the middle? He was the one who made the reservation in the name of Flannigan and also asked for that table."

Joe sat back and smiled. "You've both been extremely helpful, I really appreciate it, thank you." Turning to the Sikh, "Mandeep, would it be possible to have picture of these guys?" The man nodded and went next door.

Joe thanked the Indian for his patience as he handed over the photos and, in exchange, Mandeep received a large note as they shook hands.

"It is a pleasure Mr Briggs; I am pleased we were able to help. Let us hope you can find them and stop them before they make any more trouble." He followed Emile out and at the door and pulled out another couple of notes.

"Non, non, monsieur, you have already left a good tip at lunch time; no need for this I assure you."

"Take it Emile, buy something for your long-suffering wife or take her out for dinner; she'll enjoy that." He grinned and patted his shoulder.

"Thank you again, Monsieur. Oh, I forgot, I asked Mandeep if he could delete your visit earlier today, no need for anyone to know," he winked.

Joe shook his head and as he turned, "Emile, you are one in a million".

\* \* \*

The late afternoon sun was warm, so Joe decided to walk back to the hotel following the river until he got to the Houses of Parliament. He then turned north and headed to his hotel. He pulled out his cell phone and called the two youngsters. "Hi, this Joe Briggs. How are you getting on with your investigation?"

"Not too well sir; we aren't getting very far."

"Right, change of plan. Meet me at QH at 8.30 tomorrow morning and we can go over things." The last thing he wanted was get into a conversation so quickly hung up. He then called a number he knew off by heart. "Hello Ann, its Joe, Joe Briggs."

The voice at the end sounded surprised, "well, well if it's not Snoopy himself. How the hell did they let you back in?" she enquired teasingly.

"Got in late last night and going back the day after tomorrow on the lunch time flight. Doing anything tonight?" he asked.

"Perhaps, perhaps not; what's the deal?" said the voice playfully.

"Dinner followed by a couple of drinks and then we'll see," he replied. "Meet you at your favourite place, 8pm and don't be late," he smiled, as he knew Ann was a stickler for being prompt. They hung up with no further words.

Once at the hotel, he checked for any messages, but Aaron Goldberg had not got back. It meant he had heard nothing or, more likely, the old crow was out of the game. He didn't grudge his "donation", it was always good to keep in with the Aaron's of this world and he had been a great asset a few years back.

The next morning, he woke just before the alarm and groaned; his head felt ready to burst and his tongue felt swollen and dry. Damn! At his age he should know better than to mix beer and wine followed by a few tequilas and anyway, everybody knew not to try to outdrink Ann. It had been a great evening with good food and great company; they reminisced, talked about old friends, and caught up with each other's lives. He liked Ann and she liked him, they enjoyed spending time together, going out to restaurants or to the cinema and they confided in each other, but that was as far as it went; more of a brotherly, sisterly relationship.

He got up and had a cold shower, brushed his teeth several times and swallowed a couple of aspirin. He stopped off at a Starbucks and picked up a coffee and bagel and made his way back to the Embassy. Once inside he made a point of saying hello to Beth and indicated he was going upstairs. She smiled back and nodded.

The secretary was expecting him and led him through to the conference room. "If I may say, you don't look that great Mr Briggs. Can I get you a coffee or a tea?" she asked.

"That would be fantastic; just a bit of jetlag, I'll be fine thanks." He knew she wouldn't believe him but he was damned if he was going to admit to being hungover.

The door opened and the two juniors walked in. "Good morning, sir," they said brightly.

"You're fifteen minutes late. I told you to be here at 8.30 and it's now 8.46," he growled. "I don't like being kept waiting. Understood?"

Both boys nodded and mumbled apologies.

"Right, what have you got for me?" he enquired.

"Well sir, nothing really, we couldn't trace the three men and we have no idea who they are."

Joe sighed, "how long have you been in London? In fact how long have been in the job?"

"Two years, sir, both in the job and in London."

"What I want to know is what the hell they taught you and what the fuck you've been doing here?" he said angrily. "You're in one of the most exciting cities in the world, in a job most of your colleagues would give their right hand for and you don't seem to have learned anything. A total waste of time and space." He looked at them hard and held his hand up.

"I've been here 24 hours and I I've traced these 3 guys, got photos of them and you, you who initiated this file can't even trace them. Can't have tried very hard. Where are your contacts?" He decided he was ranting a bit much so stopped and took a deep breath. He pushed the file over.

"Take this and make sure you get names for these three dudes by tomorrow morning. I know them, but I think it a good idea you find out yourselves. I'm on my way back at lunch time so e-mail them to me. He shook his head, "go, get off your arses, and do the job you're paid for".

They took the file and turned to leave.

"You could at least thank me for not firing you here and now. Make sure you get those names or I will have you transferred to Nigeria or Peru."

Was he getting old, or was it the hangover? No, the head was clear again and he felt fine so it must be age. Was he expecting too much? Not really. He recalled when he and Hank were that age, they were hungry, enthusiastic, looking for adventure and trouble, but this lot... ah, what the hell.

He stopped by Bill's office and brought him up to speed but spared giving his thoughts on the two boys. He then went down two floors and knocked on a door. A middle-aged man waved him in and he introduced himself. He briefly told him what he wanted. The man looked dubious but on hearing Bill's name he soon agreed.

"Should have a reply for you by close of office today," said the man.

"Great, that's really appreciated," said Joe. "Can I ask you to text me the result when you have it? I'll be on my way back first thing in the morning so won't have the time to come by."

The man nodded and Joe left. A whole day in London – what should he do? He decided to call Ann again and suggest they went to Richmond Park and have a picnic; he'd done what he had set out to do and knew he would get the answer he was looking for from his last conversation.

Just after 18.30 his phoned pinged and he glanced at it. He smiled. An hour later he rang the boys. "Got anything for me?" he asked, knowing what the reply was going to be.

"Well sir, we've asked but the department says it will be next week before they can give us a definite ID; they're very busy."

Joe sighed again, "as I told you, I know their names; took me a couple of hours. So, for your information they are a James Horton, Mike Flannigan and a Professor Howard. I also know their ages, marital status and home addresses - not difficult if you know who to ask and where to look. I suggest you two start looking for a new career, clearly you're not cut out for this job. We need keen, enthusiastic and resourceful guys which you have proved not to be. My advice is you get out soon before you end up at the bottom of the river." He hung up.

\* \* \*

## China

Ru was sitting by the window; he felt the sweat tricking down his back and his hands were clammy. He looked out at the land below, interspersed by a few fluffy clouds; it was his first time on a plane and he wasn't sure he liked it. Trains were fine; you were on the ground and you could see the countryside, but up here, with no buildings flashing past, no paddy fields with waving kids or bustling villages, it was different, and he admitted to himself he was scared. A hostess pushing a trolley of drinks smiled sweetly but he declined the offer of tea; he was not sure he would not spill the hot drink and he certainly didn't want to have to get up to the toilet.

Fifty minutes later the plane touched down and taxied to their final parking place. Ru heaved a sigh of relief as he stepped on to the gangway and made his way to the luggage collection. After picking up his suitcase, he made his way through the exit doors to be confronted by a wall of people and faces; following his fellow passengers he pushed his way through the crowd, eventually emerging into the vast bustling hall. He quickly spotted a woman dressed in a dark navy suit with burgundy trimmings and a hat, holding a board with his name. He went up to introduce himself, but she quickly interrupted him, "please follow me Mr Nuang". She turned around and marched off towards one of the main doors.

Outside the hot, humid air, hit him and he started to sweat again. He followed the short dumpy woman to a parked minibus and was ushered in. At least it was cooler in the vehicle, the air conditioning was on and he settled himself on one of the back seats. The door closed, and the hostess disappeared. Twenty minutes later she returned with two other passengers who smiled politely and nodded as they took their seats. The bus moved off; a new chapter in his life was about to begin.

# CHAPTER 5

## England

On the same day Joe Briggs has landing at Heathrow, James was on a train bound for Reading. After they pulled into the station, he made his way over to the Express Bus service heading for the airport and thirty minutes later was checking into his hotel. He freshened up, called his wife who seemed not the least up-set that he had gone away, and made his way down to the restaurant. After ordering a large gin and tonic and some food he settled down to read over his notes.

Earlier he had received a message from Sean saying he couldn't make it but would meet him at the departure gate at 7.15. At first James had been a bit disappointed as he had questions to ask and was also looking forward to having a good verbal sparring match with his old friend. By the time he went upstairs, he was happy with what he had achieved and could, pretty well reel off all the facts by heart.

The next morning James was waiting at the departure gate, the flight had been called and almost all the passengers had gone through. He was getting anxious and looked at his watch once more' Where is he? What's held him up? he wondered, then out of nowhere, he heard the soft lilt behind him.

"Been waiting long?" asked the voice. "Sorry, darned security took ages. Got stuck behind some man who was asked to practically undress; don't understand people who just think they can swan through with coats and jackets. Come on, we're late," he smiled.

The two men made their way to the plane and settled down in their seats. Once buckled in Sean turned to his friend, "sorry about last night, had a few urgent things to sort out from my last job".

"Oh! that's fine, I had an early night and re-read all my notes," replied James.

"Great, you can tell me everything once we're in the car; let's just keep conversation mundane for now. Tell me what's happening in the cricket world and I I'll talk about rugby".

\* \* \*

When they landed in Edinburgh the skies were cloudy with a chilly wind. They made their way over to the rental company and Sean handed over his driving licence. The formalities finished, the clerk handed over the contract and car keys. "You will find the car in section C, row 5, car park number 24. Have a safe trip, Mr Flannigan."

Sean nodded and hustled James away quickly. Seeing his friends quizzical look, he simply shrugged "No need to advertise our movements unnecessarily. Now, let's go and find the car."

James was going to ask what all that was about but decided it wasn't worth it; let Sean play his games, and he obviously loved playing games, making matters seem mysterious. They found their way out of the airport and were soon on the road heading north. As they crossed the Forth road bridge, they could see the beginnings of the new modern crossing. The day was improving; a watery sun started to emerge and the clouds were thinning. James turned to his driver, "what's the plan when we get to St. Andrews, then?" he enquired.

"Be nice to the dotty professor and see what we can wangle out of him. But first, what have you got for me?"

"Right," said James. "I've had a really good dig around and have lots of general information which could take most of the drive".

Sean interrupted. "Stop right there. Remember I just need the bare facts: the main facts, not the complete history. I have a simple mind and too much detail isn't good for me," he grinned.

"How far back do you want me to start?" asked James.

"As far back as you think I would be interested in and my brain cells can cope with, dear friend. Now please proceed."

James was silent for a moment whilst he decided what to say. "Well, if we go back to the 1980's that should be enough. In 1983 at the Annual General Conference, president Deng Xianping and the Council agreed to implement the Socialist Commodity Economy among other ideas on how to get China moving forward. The resolution was a big change of thinking as it was based on breaking away from the traditional view, contending that socialism and commodity economy are mutually exclusive. The resolution clearly pointed the way to turn enterprises into relatively independent socialist commodity producers, and that this kind of economy must consciously employ the law of value. It is a planned economy operating under a system of public ownership. It indicated the basic difference between such a socialist commodity economy and capitalism, and that the full development of commodity economy is a prerequisite for the modernisation of a new Chinese era."

Sean put his hand up. "Stop right there. You've lost me already."

James sighed, "I was just trying..." but he was interrupted.

"Just try harder to keep things simple; as I said, I have a small brain."

"Ok, well one of several points that came out over the next couple of years is that China also wanted to expand their influence throughout the world. They understood that you had to be a military powerhouse strong enough to scare any belligerent foe but that wasn't enough. The question was how to get more influence without actually taking over borders. They decided to go in by the back door and stealthily sabotage the international community in order to build a new world order'"

"Now you're talking," Sean smiled. "That's the sort of thing I understand; keep going along those lines."

"I'm pleased you are happy m'lord," retorted James sarcastically before continuing, "someone at the newly formed Ministry in charge of implementing the resolution hit on the idea that economic and physical aide to poverty stricken third world countries would be ideal. It would boost local construction and manufacturing capabilities, but at the same time, China would be seen to be helping and reaching out to the outside world. Big projects such as dams, irrigation and opening up mines in Africa would be perfect and would have the benefit of being a relatively cheap way of creating influence in a region which was mostly ignored by the West and the USSR." Sean was nodding.

"So, over the next decade a major push, both diplomatic and economic was undertaken resulting in a major boost to China's world standing, especially in Africa where they have practically bought their UN votes and have tremendous support. It also boosted manufacturing at home and the economy. Things in China started to move fast, and in 1992 Jiang Zemin coined the phrase – Socialist Market Economy – which was another way of saying, State owned enterprise".

They were now driving across country through rolling hills; the road wasn't busy, and they were making good progress. The weather too, was improving, with a warm sun. James continued, "the second point was that China's top brass understood that technology, and in particular electronics, was essential to any economy, and any country with an advanced electronics industry was going places."

"Thought the internet was banned in China?" Sean interrupted.

"Yes, it was and still is in a way. For the general populace it was important to keep them from getting too much information from the outside world, but they realised that they could not keep people completely cut off if they wanted to progress. It's very state controlled and even now most phones only work within China. Internet is still fully State controlled. By 2005 electronics industry made up over fifteen percent of the country's economic growth and firms such as Huawei, Skyworth, Konka and others are all major exporters. In fact, a couple of years ago they had the world's largest export share."

"Sounds about right," said Sean. "The bastards have taken over and control the damned lot, that's why I don't use phones too much, as you may have noticed. As I said the other day, they can trace you, listen in, hack, you name it, your life just is not private anymore. And it's not only the Chinese, Russians. Americans and our own Government, all bloody snooping, either trying to cause harm or being bloody nosy."

James nodded. They were approaching the outskirt of St. Andrews. "I could go on or do you want me to continue on the way home?" he asked.

"Anything else of importance?" asked Sean. "You said there were several points, or is that it."

"Well, there is a third point which I found interesting."

"Ok, let's hear it, but we are nearly there, so better be brief."

"One other major decision which was little publicised and mostly went unnoticed," continued James, "was that they decided to develop and encourage highly skilled experts to work on various forms of chemical and biological weapons. The Russians at the time were well advanced in the production of various of these agents, and the Chinese top brass decided to follow suit. Rightly, they took the view that having this kind of secret armament could be better used in case of a world conflict than the A bomb. Yes, they had to continue to develop and seem to be ready to use the atom bomb to deter and show they meant business, but they realised that chemical warfare was a better option, as it meant they could re-start life in a relatively short time compared with the total devastation of a nuclear war head."

"Makes perfect sense, and we could see if our friend here can help," said Sean.

"So, they embarked on building several research and manufacturing labs, sent students to the US, France and here to study – as they did with electronics, and are still doing – and soon had three big research centres working flat out."

"Where did you get all this from if it's secret; not the internet?" asked Sean.

"No, I have a friend, retired now, he worked on one of the big papers and did some research about this a few years ago; he got his information from his son's girlfriend who was Chinese and studying here at the time. She had been sent by her government as a budding student and swore him to silence, saying that if it got out, she would never have a job again and probably not live either. It was top secret and after all her efforts she didn't want to be in trouble."

"And is she still with your friend's son?"

"No, she qualified and went back to China. The lad was devastated and thought about following but she dissuaded him." James pointed, "the Old Course Hotel - ever played there?"

Sean shook his head. The voice on the Satnav was telling him to turn left at the next roundabout. Just as he was about to take the exit, a cyclist came in on the inside and he had to swerve to avoid him. "Bloody idiot," he screamed. The woman's voice on his route finder whined on, 'please take the next available exit, please take the next available exit, please take the fourth exit, please take the fourth exit.' "Oh shut up woman! that's what I'm doing," yelled Sean.

After a few minutes they turned down a small side street and stopped in front of no 23, a large semi- detached terrace house with a bright red door. Sean turned off the engine and sighed, "well here we are. That last point is very interesting' Let's see what the old professor knows and has to say about it. Leave the questioning to me; you make the small talk".

\* \* \*

They were greeted at the door by the professor who welcomed them and instructed them to follow him into the front room. James was amused at the old boys' attire: tartan plus fours with red socks and a white roll neck. Compared with the frumpy clothes he wore the last time this was positively flashy. "Are you going to play golf later?" he enquired.

"No, no, I don't play, but up here, I like to dress a bit more appropriately. Many think it eccentric and I like to go along with it. Tea or coffee for you gentlemen?"

James and Sean agreed on coffee, black - strong and no sugar. The professor disappeared and left them standing in the middle of the most cluttered room either of them had ever seen. Papers and magazines were everywhere along with a few files, and at least six large A4 pads. Soon their host re-appeared with a tray laden with three mugs and an assortment of biscuits. He shooed two large cats off the settee, removed a pile of journals and beckoned them to sit down. "I hope you don't mind; I I've booked a table at a fish restaurant near here for 1pm, hence the meagre offering of edibles. I trust you both like fish?"

Both nodded and thanked him.

"You very kindly looked after me in London, the least I can do is to reciprocate and introduce you to a couple of nice wines. So, what can I do to help you?"

Sean pursed his lips. "Well Professor, you may know that I work for a government department."

"MI6 I believe," interjected the professor.

"Yes. I was recently working on a case when I was suddenly pulled off it and summoned to my superiors who have asked me to investigate certain chemical laboratories in China. Now, I have no idea about chemicals or any factories, but they suggested I contacted you as you may be to help me."

The professor looked over to James. "Are you MI6 also?" he enquired.

Sean jumped in, "he's a very dear and long-standing friend, a semi-retired journalist with a great knowledge of economics and a good understanding of the Far East. You can rest assured, he is very discreet and yes, my superiors are aware of him being with me," he lied.

The Professor nodded and relaxed a bit. "What exactly do you want from me?"

"I believe you worked, and still do occasionally, at Porton Down; can I ask in what capacity?"

"I'm still on their books and get called in occasionally to give my opinion and my expertise on certain problems they face sometimes. In fact, I was down last week looking into a new, well new to the amateurs, Russian drug which they are supposed to be developing. Untraceable apparently and very lethal. You don't need much to kill a person."

"Were you able to help?" asked James.

"No, it's too early, but within a month or so we'll have got to the bottom of it. It will not be the first time the Russians have used lethal chemicals; look at Chechnya and, as you both no doubt recall, the Litvinenko case, or rather murder."

Both nodded; it had happened in 2006 when a Russian double agent died in London from a Polonium attack, just a pin prick given by a passer-by, so easy and so lethal. The experts had worked hard to save him but to no avail. The Russians of course had denied all knowledge, but it was proven in the end that it had been carried out by their security forces and instigated by Putin as revenge at the spy's double activities.

The professor carried on, "I would certainly not waste your time looking at China gentlemen, it's Russia that is the main threat".

"Professor, we have hard evidence that the Chinese have three research and development laboratories and that they have been working continuously in developing new warfare chemicals." Sean sat and watched the scientist carefully.

"Call me Edward, Mr Flannigan, and can I call you Mike?" he asked.

Sean nodded, "of course".

"Take my word for it, the Chinese are a long, long way from developing a cohesive and threatening programme. I strongly suggest you got back to your bosses and get them to focus on the real threat which is coming out of Moscow, and the laboratories in Panza, Serov and Lensk. They are the real threats, Mike."

James was looking out of the window pensively, "Professor".

"Edward, please, I prefer to be called Edward," interjected his host.

James nodded, "Edward, I hear what you say, but how do you explain SARS, Ebola and the like that came out of China and one of their laboratories, it was not denied by the Government".

"Personally, I don't believe that they did, but if so, the small and mostly ineffectual results shows that they are not in a position to produce anything really lethal," Edward replied.

"Not sure I can agree with the word ineffectual ,Professor: tens of thousands around the world died and they caused major problems, especially in Africa," James said nippily.

"Edward," Sean butted in and throwing a warning look at James, "you are probably right Edward, but you must agree that it's a possibility, nevertheless. China is an economic and military powerhouse and does have designs on world expansion. I can't see them not being interested in developing their own version of A-234, or a chemical weapon, even if it is only to protect themselves against the likes of Russia".

Edward thought for a moment "Yes, you're probably right in that respect, I hadn't really thought of it that way. Putting it in that context, you do have an argument, but still, I firmly believe they are light years away from developing anything significant".

"You must know or have heard of these laboratories in China," insisted James.

"Of course; it's our job. We, I, know of two small ones in the north of the country, but we've heard nothing of their work, nor have they produced anything substantial to our knowledge."

Sean, wanting to cool things down a bit, changed tack. "What about America?" he asked, "anything major happening over there".

"No not really" replied the professor; "as we all know they have their own labs but like us, they're more interested in prevention rather development. From the start of the Obama administration, it was made clear that all financial aid to such centres, just like the armed forces and space programme, would be cut very severely. The President did not wish to antagonise the other powers and wanted to show that America was open and non-aggressive. Although I totally agree with what he wanted to do; I do think he went too far."

"What about other European countries?" asked Sean.

"Like us, most are working to find preventive antidotes to the existing known chemicals and viruses. Sweden leads the way, with us in second position. Neither the Germans nor the French have the finance or the desire to develop such things. It's more the dictatorships and the authoritarians States who are at the forefront of development."

"Nevertheless, I would have thought even with a restricted budget our American friends would be actively in the game," interjected James.

Sean once again shot him a look which clearly told him to shut up.

"Probably they are in a small way, but as I said, they are more interested in finding antidotes and vaccines rather that creating new ones. Looking up at the clock on the mantlepiece he said, "now gentlemen, I suggest we make our way over to the restaurant for a spot of lunch." The professor rose and indicated the door.

*　　*　　*

Three hours later, on their way back to Edinburgh airport, James was gazing out of the car window; he turned to Sean. "What did you make of our meeting?" he enquired.

"I'm a bit bemused by out professor. I must admit, I don't really know what to make of him. A funny chap and pretty secretive."

"He was certainly defending the Chinese and laying the blame and accusing Moscow, I was surprised at how tetchy he was".

"You certainly wound him up' my friend, thought I'd told you to keep the conversation mundane," Sean grinned.

"I know; could not stop myself", said James. "Do you believe what he said about the Yanks? Surely they're one of the leaders in the game."

"Not sure what my next move is, Jamesie," Sean said musingly. "I'm not going to pursue Edward's idea of Russia; we know they're experts at this kind of thing. No, China is where we must dig."

After a big lunch James was feeling sleepy and nodded off for a few minutes; he woke with a start and turned to his friend who was in deep thought. "Sorry, I drifted off briefly."

Sean laughed, "You've been asleep for thirty-five minutes my dear chap, that's what comes of partaking in a large lunch and trying to compete with Edward in the wine drinking contest."

"Yes, I did have a touch too much of that very fine Sauvignon; must say he does know his wines."

"Ach just give me Guinness anytime, I'm Irish and have no time for wine; a good dram yes, but I've never been fussed about wine, especially white, too acid for my liking."

"No, seriously Jamesie I've been thinking." He looked over to his companion, "don't say it, I do occasionally," he grinned. "Think I'll take a short trip to China once I've contacted our office over there and they can tell me where these laboratories are situated; shouldn't be too difficult for them to do that. Just have a look round and try to get some idea of what is really happening".

"Think that is safe and worth it?" asked James.

"Nothing tried, nothing gained. You, my friend, could contact your mate again and see if his son knows the whereabout of his ex-girlfriend. I'd like to meet her when I'm over there, I feel she could point me in the right direction".

James nodded, "Ok I'll see what I can do and get back to you in a couple of days. She may not want to meet up as it appears she was pretty nervous and worried".

"You can assure the boy that I'll not put her in any danger, just meeting up with an old friend she made when over here studying. Even the Chinese snoops can't stop her doing that, especially these days."

James pointed ahead, "don't miss the airport turnoff or we'll miss our flight".

# CHAPTER 6

## Beijing

The drive from the airport was slow; traffic, once off the main highway, was heavy and the roads were congested with a mix of cars, trucks and cycles all vying for space. They turned down a small side street and stopped two hundred yards down in front of a dilapidated building. The sour woman driver opened the door and signalled Ru that was as far as he was going. She pointed to a door with a large bell and instructed him to ring it. Gathering up his belongings, he got down and decided not to bother thanking her and went over to the door she had indicated. He was about to push the buzzer when it opened and he was confronted by a small, dumpy man of about 50, dressed in loose trousers and a blue shirt, several buttons missing down the front. He bowed and showed Ru in. "You must be Mr Nuang; please come in, I was expecting you. Follow me please."

Ru followed his host up three flights of stairs onto a dark hallway, to the left there were two very tatty doors with paint peeling off. In front, a single door with a sign indicating it was the bathroom. The little man opened a door on their right and ushered Ru in. Smiling widely he bowed a short, brief bob and handed over a key; he then turned and departed, leaving Ru standing in the middle of a dark room that smelled of musty damp.

Once his eyes were adjusted to the darkness, Ru made his way over to the window and pulled up the shutter, opened the window

53

and looked out to the street below. It was noisy with masses of people jostling and going about their business. The smell of food wafting up from the multitude of stalls quickly filled his nostrils, which reminded him he had not eaten since last night. Nervous of the flight the next day, he had not fancied anything, but now, well his stomach was grumbling big time. He turned from the window and surveyed his bedroom. A small poky room, with a metal framed bed in one corner, a small side table with a lamp, a cheap chest of drawers, a metal chair and a single light bulb hanging from the ceiling made up his new residence. Whoever is paying for this is certainly not splashing out thought Ru. He inspected the bed, a single pillow with a thin blanket covering the sheet; he wondered when they had last been washed. A tired, grey looking towel was folded over the bottom rail. Ru doubted he could stick this out for long; if this is what they expected him to live in they were sorely mistaken. Either he was going to have to get himself a place, doubting he could afford it, or he would ask to be returned home, but living here - a big no.

He was on the verge of unpacking when he noticed an envelope on the side table addressed to him. Opening it, he scanned it and sighed in relief. The instruction told him that he would be picked up at 8.45am precisely in two days' time and that he would be taken to his new permanent residence. Feeling much happier he went to freshen up, spending the least possible time in the communal bathroom, before making his way down and out into the street. He strolled about looking at the shops and stalls before stopping to buy himself something to eat; it tasted good, incredibly good in fact. He spent the rest of the day exploring the neighbourhood, deciding that he preferred his native Shanghai. The people back home were more friendly, less rude and although a vast city, the pace seemed slower than here. He stayed out until late, delaying returning to his room for as long as possible. Sleep that night was fitful, the heat, the noise from both inside and coming from the street was something he had never experienced before; The metal bed dug into his body. The next morning, he woke early and was out by 8am. He bought himself a map of the city and spent the day exploring.

He got back late that night and noticed on arriving, that one of the doors across from his had been broken down. Raised voices and commotion came from inside the flat; he wondered what was going on when someone appeared and gabbled at him - "they broke down the old man's door and took most of his possessions just because he was a week late paying his rent," cried the man. "The bastard knew Chang had been ill and unable to work, but he still smashed his way in and stole his belongings. "If I had my way, he would be found in a ditch one day soon. It's not like he doesn't have enough with the rents he charges, and for what? A shitty little room, little heat and a couple of gas rings; thieving whore."

The man was clearly upset and Ru, not wishing to get involved, shrugged, and let himself into his room, making sure of locking the door. Not that that seemed to deter anyone he thought ruefully. He blessed his good fortune; another few hours and he would be away from this dump. Then a thought struck him – what if he was just being relocated to something similar; he felt his heart sink and he was overcome by sadness.

The next morning Ru was outside waiting, impatient to get away from this hell hole. Soon after 8.45 the bus came trundling down the street, honking its horn as it crept along. The same sour-faced woman was driving, but this time he nodded as he stepped into the vehicle. An hour later they arrived in front of an imposing building with guards at the door. As he alighted a man came forward to greet him. They made their way through to a vast imposing hall where he was subjected to a strict security search. A photo was taken of him before he was directed to a desk where he collected his pass. Apart from confirming Ru's name, the man had not uttered a word and as they were crossing the great hall Ru asked where they were going.

"This way, to the Director's office," mumbled his guide. "Leave your bags in this room, you can collect them later".

After following a maze of corridors and passing dozens of closed doors they eventually arrived in front of a door with a name plate on it and the guide knocked. The door was opened by a young man impeccably dressed in a suit and tie who ushered Ru in. The guide, who obvious knew the routine, turned and disappeared the way they had come. He was shown into a large office with a huge desk from behind which emerged a small, lean, balding man sporting a pair of thick spectacles. Dressed in a similar immaculate suite the man bowed and greeted his guest.

"Good morning Mr Nuang, my name is Tao Wey-Ming, I am the Director of the Chinese National Institute of Virology and Microbiology. We are, as you may be aware, a government body and are responsible to the National Council. We obey their orders and work on programmes that they, and they alone, decide and dictate."

Ru nodded and stayed silent.

"I trust you had a good journey," continued the Director, "and that your first couple of days in the Capital have been interesting. Always good to have time to explore and visits the sights," he smiled. "What did you think of Tiananmen Square? Were you impressed by the Summer Palace? And of course, the views from Jingshan Park are superb."

Ru was stunned but did not show his surprise. The bastards must have followed him, keeping tabs on him; he inwardly shook his head, nothing really changes he thought. "Yes, I think the Summer Palace was my favourite," he said at last.

"Good, now that you know your way around I suggest you settle into your new flat which we have provided for you and then tomorrow, I will introduce you to some colleagues with whom you will be working with. You have come very highly recommended, Mr Nuang, and with an excellent reputation, although sometimes a little confrontational, but if you can control that trait, I am sure you will make quick progress and will be a great asset to the State." He rang a bell and the young man re-appeared to show Ru out. "Please be in the great hall by 9am tomorrow morning at the latest," instructed the Director.

He was shown down different corridors and to a smaller lobby where he was re-united with his bags and then shown to a side door. The young man handed him a piece of paper with an address. "Turn right once you get on the main artery and follow the road for 3 blocks, turn left at MO Chi noodle bar and proceed for about 300 metres until you see a large block of flats on the right side of the street. Takes about twenty minutes". He was about to leave when Ru stopped him.

"What door do I come to tomorrow?" he enquired.

"Main entrance - once through security, cross the hall, pass under the row of flags and follow the corridors marked with a blue line; you will come to the Director's door and knock. I will be there; don't be late".

The walk to his new home didn't take long and he found it easily; entering he made his way over to the small office where a young woman was sitting behind a glass window. She got up and smiled a warm smile. Ru showed her the note and she nodded and disappeared to a filing cabinet. On returning she asked him to complete a form and contact details. He realised then that he had none, the only place he had called home was his old place in Shanghai. The young woman smiled again, "is this your first time in Beijing" she enquired. Ro nodded.

"It's an exciting place and I am sure you will enjoy it. Please read this leaflet - it explains all the rules of this building and what you should do in case of emergency," then handing him two keys she advised him, "the large one is for the main entrance between 11 at night and 6am, during the day it stays open. The other is your flat key. Just take the elevator, 4th floor, apartment 404". She bowed slightly. "Anything you need please come and see me."

Ru thanked her and made his way up to the fourth floor. On entering he was amazed at its size, a nice sitting area with a large window and a small kitchen diner; off to his left was a good-sized bedroom also with a nice window and a small en-suite shower room. He had never been in such a luxurious place; back at the University he was happy with his small bedsit with its minute bathroom, and he had been happy to share the common sitting area and kitchen with four other teachers. He went over and opened the window which looked out over a small courtyard; he could hear the noise of the city in the distance. He let out a small whoop of pleasure. He quickly went to unpack his belongings and the small box of books he had brought with him, then decided to have a good, long shower. He needed one to get rid of the city grime and the dirt from the other place. Feeling better and relaxed he went to flop on the bed.

He woke with a start, lost at first as to where he was. He looked at his watch, 5pm! After splashing his face with cold water, he felt like a new man. Once more that grumble of hunger returned. Before going out to get some shopping he went to the kitchen and was amazed that a small supply if essentials had been provided, he shook his head in disbelief. Did the Chinese government really look after their scientists in this manner. He didn't think so, but perhaps it was to lead him into a false sense of security. Well, he wasn't going to complain.

\* \* \*

The next few months were busy and passed quickly. He had been assigned to join a team in the nearby laboratory as junior to several established scientists and had been praised several times for his excellent work. He was quickly promoted through the ranks and today had just been told that he would be second in command of the small elite group. He was pleased with himself, pleased that he had managed to keep his mouth shut and pleased that he had managed to show his understanding of the work and not demonstrate too much initiative. Initiative was not appreciated. It was a fine balance; you certainly didn't wish to rile your superiors by showing them up. On a more personal note, he always liked someone with initiative and was always open to suggestions or new ideas, but overall, he knew it was best to keep a low profile if you wanted to advance.

On the way home that night he stopped off and bought some beer and noodles from MO Chi where he was now a regular customer; he preferred the prepared chicken Chow Mein which you had to cook yourself. After showering and changing he put on the food and opened a celebratory bottle. Just then there was a knock on the door. A tall young woman with long black hair and wide smile stood in front of him. "Hello, my name is Mei Lien. I live across at number 403," said a happy voice.

Ru looked at her in awe. He had only had one girlfriend in his life and this one was nothing like her, she was stunning. "Hi, I'm Ru," he stammered.

She stuck out a hand and he shook it. Her soft warm touch flummoxed Ru even more. "I know you have been here for a while now and I'm sorry I haven't come sooner to introduce myself," she said.

"No, no, my fault. I shouldn't have been so rude," mumbled Ru.

"Why not come over and have a drink; you can tell me all about yourself. If you have a few more bottles of beer it would help,", that large smile again, making Ru weak at the knees.

"Thanks, that would be great, I'll just go and fetch them."

As he followed her across the landing Ru couldn't help but notice her delicate shoulders, thin waist and long legs. A super star model he thought, or was he dreaming. He pinched himself, but no, there she was ushering him to the sitting area and pointing to a large chair.

"Sorry for the mess," she said, I've been at work all day and wasn't sure you would accept."

He looked round the room, it was just like his but with a feminine touch, more colour and some family photos; much more homely than his sparsely furnished flat. "Not at all, it's lovely. Have you been here for long?" he asked awkwardly.

"A year next month. Please tell me all about yourself, where you come from, what you do."

"Oh, I don't have such an exciting life, nor has it been glamourous."

"Rubbish," she interjected, "don't be so modest, come on now, tell me all".

"Where do you want me to start?" he asked.

"From the day you were born."

Ru took a deep breath and then to his embarrassment spent the next forty-five minutes recounting his life story. He told her everything expect the nature of his exact work. During that time Mei Lien just sat there, head cocked slightly and a faint smile dancing on her lips. She went from looking sad to pleased depending on what he had had said; finally, as he arrived at today's promotion she clapped. "What a fantastic life story and with such a great ending," she exclaimed, "but I'm sure it won't end here, I am certain you will go far".

He thanked her modestly and then asked for her story. She got up and went over to get another couple of beers and settling down, then started to tell him all about herself.

"My name in Mei Lien Chow and I was born twenty-nine years ago in a small town just east of here where my father and mother worked in the local factory. They were good people, good Chinese and good citizens, proud of their heritage and their country and what it has achieved. I went to the local school then progressed to higher education where I excelled at sciences and came first in my year."

She smiled that smile before continuing, "thanks to my grades I was sent to Uni, and after six months was nominated to be one of the select few to be sent to England to continue my studies in Sheffield".

Ru's eyes boggled and he gasped, "wow! that is something; makes my life very boring as I knew it was".

"No, not boring, I just got lucky," she replied. Before continuing she passed him a bottle, I spent four years in England and got my PhD in virology before I came back and was sent to work at the NIVM here in Beijing".

"What!" exclaimed Ru, "the building on Maliandao Nanjie . That's where I work".

They both looked at each other, "I don't believe it," she said finally, "you're also a virologist!".

Ru shook his head, "no, microbiologist. Tell me more about England and Oxford," he said.

"It was some of the best years of my life and really interesting. I had to learn English, but it was ok. I'm not perfect, but I manage pretty well. I got help from my boyfriend."

"Oh, is he here in Beijing?" asked Ru, disappointment in his voice.

"No, he was English. He did want to come over but couldn't get a visa in time and then found work in London as a journalist, so things fizzled out. A shame, he was a nice person," she said reflectively. "You should learn English. it's not all that hard apart from the pronunciation, some of the letters I still can't say properly. There are several places that do evening classes and I can…" She was about to continue when a smoke alarm rang out from across the hall. Ru jumped up, "oh no! noodles," he shouted as he rushed to the door closely followed by Mei Lien. His flat was full of smoke. He went to the stove and took off the pot and half threw it into the sink, Mei Lien went and opened the windows. "I completely forgot," he said. "I had just put these on when you knocked and well…." they both burst out laughing.

"You better go down and tell the office; I'll try to stop this thing," she said as she fanned the alarm.

Ru ran down the stairs meeting several concerned residents on the way. "No panic, just the kitchen pan and my dinner burning," he said several times. At the desk he was met by a frosty faced night caretaker. Eventually, after answering her many questions, she accepted his explanations and sent him back with a stern word of warning.

He found the girl had tidied up and was at the sink trying to clean the pan. She looked up and smiled. "There, all smoke free but I think you may have to invest in a new pot, this has to be thrown out". She turned and gave him a kiss before walking towards the door, "good night, Mr noodles," she said with a giggle.

It was the start of a deep and loving affair.

# CHAPTER 7

# Washington

The British Airways flight touched down at Dulles International and Joe, once again, was first off the plane. On his way to immigration, he called Hank and they arranged to meet at a small Italian restaurant they both liked.

Two hours later they were seated at a corner table with a bottle of Chianti. "Welcome back Joe. Good trip?" asked the boss.

"The flights went smoothly, and it was nice to be back in London; you know how much I enjoy that city."

"Did you find what we were looking for?" enquired Hank.

"Yep, but it was no thanks to the idiots over there. Never met such a bunch of ineffectual, useless and self-inflated nerds in all my life," he spat out. "You should really have a word with Brian and get him to go over and read the riot act." He shook his head, "bunch of snowflakes with no imagination".

Hank laughed, "you've always had colourful language Joe and, admit it, you do have exceptionally high standards".

"Bullshit," replied his friend. "There's standards and there's standards; the two dudes who came up with the report and who were assigned to me couldn't find their way out of a kids' playground, let alone work in one the most intriguing and sharp cities in the world. No, if that's what Uncle Sam is relying on to protect us, God help us! Tell you something for nothing; it took me no more than a day to find out who these three guys were, and my two punks were still picking their noses wondering what to do."

"Ok, ok calm down and have some more wine," interjected Hank.

"Promise you will go and talk to Brian. It's urgent," continued Joe after taking a large gulp. "It's not only the two idiots, but the entire lot have also lost their way, from security, who let me through with my gun, the receptionist, right up to Bill. He's been there too long with no one checking on him," he continued. "And yes, before you say anything, I am aware of the cuts the last President made, but it doesn't excuse being lax and letting the organisation and the country down."

Hank nodded. "Got any names for me."

"James Horton, Mike Flannigan and a Professor Howard. I set the two dudes the task of finding that simple fact out – nothing more. Now I I'm gone they'll sit back and continue scratching their balls".

They chatted a little longer before Hank promised, once again, to talk to the boss about London.

Joe decided he was going to have a relaxing day in town before flying back up to Boston. He was about to leave his hotel room when he got a call. "Joe, how you're feeling today, calmed down?" Hank's voice bellowed in his ear. "I've had a word with Brian as promised and he wants to see us both this afternoon, 3pm in his office."

"Thanks Hank, appreciate it, but I I'm going back up to Boston," he replied.

"No you're not buddy, you got me to speak to el supremo and now he wants you to tell him everything so, sorry, but your plans have just changed."

Joe let out a long slow sigh, "Ok, will be there, see you later". Hanging up he cursed; why did he have to open his big gob? At his age he should have learned to keep stum. He spent time doing errands he had listed and turned up at Hanks office ahead of schedule.

On the way up to the director's office Hank turned to his partner, "seems your big mouth has opened a can of worms; Brian is in a real panic. It also appears you're not the only one to raise concerns; someone in MI6, of all people, has been mumbling about the lack of professionalism." He shrugged his shoulders, "that's all I know".

The two men were immediately shown into the Director's office where they were greeted by Brian and the head of the CIA - John Pintaro, God himself.

The head came straight over and introduced himself which was pointless as both knew who he was but feigned surprise. "Thank you gentlemen for coming at such short notice," he continued before anyone could say anything. "Thought it best to come here rather than you making the trip to see me; less inquisitive eyes around here," he chuckled at his little joke. "Brian has filled me in with your concerns about London, Mr Briggs. I understand you have recently been there."

"Yes sir, got back yesterday afternoon."

"What took you there?" asked Pintaro.

"I was asked to go over by Hank to try and find out more about a very sketchy file some of the London boys had sent, sir. I just had to voice my concerns to Mr Gobolsky last night."

"What makes you think we are in danger?"

"Not in danger, Sir, just that I was over for 48 hours and I was shocked at the lax security at the Embassy and the total – I was going to say uselessness – how should I say…professionalism. As I say, I was there a short time and found everything I was asked for in a day whilst the two operatives I was given never got out of the starting blocks."

The supremo looked glum and paced the room. "To be frank it's not the first story I I've heard. Since the cuts, the service has lost its way and we no longer seem to have the right men over there. London, of all places, is where we should have some of our best operatives," his voice was getting louder. "We can't rely on the Brits to do our work, and I don't trust them to keep their mouths shut in time of crisis," he bellowed. He continued to pace, trying to calm down. "Is it still Bill Sharps?" he turned and glowered.

"Yes sir," they all answered at once.

"How long has he been in the post? Ten, twelve years?" it was a question, but he knew the answer.

"Coming up to twelve years sir," replied Hank.

Pintaro pursed his lips, paced some more before addressing Brian, "get him and his family back here soon as," he ordered. "Say that we had overlooked the length of service he's done; to make it up we are giving him a six-month sabbatical starting immediately. If he questions it, tell him I I've given the order and that I hinted at a possible promotion when it's over, that should pacify him," he turned and nodded.

Brian didn't look happy. "Are you sure that's wise John? He's done a good job and knows..." he broke off as his boss's glare bored right into him. "No problem. I I'll do it immediately," he continued. "Who do you have in mind as a replacement?"

John smiled. "A man who knows London, has proved himself repeatedly and a man we can all trust – a certain Jack Warren. We all know him. He's a good trouble shooter and a top-class operative, perfect for London." He turned to the three men. "Get him in Brian, today, and give him his papers. Gentlemen," he stuck out his hand, "good luck, and thank you Joe for alerting me to the situation; you've done great".

"Thank you, sir, I was only doing my job."

"Don't underestimate yourself; you are a real professional, resourceful and shrewd. Hank, you should be pleased to have a man like this on your team. Good luck."

After Pintaro had left the three men stayed silent for a while before Brian spoke, "come on guys, time to celebrate; drinks on me," and led the way out. No one uttered a word as they made their way out of the building; it was only once they were installed in a bar that Joe spoke.

"Hope you two aren't too disappointed, I know how much you wanted the job, Brian."

"Darn it, I would have been real pissed off five years ago but now, no, happy for another mug to have all the problems. Anyhow, I've never set foot in the place."

Joe turned to Hank, "what about you, boss?" he asked.

"Same here. A few years back I would have been real upset, but now, with Elie not doing too well and my parents needing more help, I sure wouldn't want to make the move." He looked over to Joe, "and what about you?"

"Yeah, like you guys, I would have been upset a few years back. No, now I just couldn't be arsed to spend time knocking sense into those idiots. Just looking forward to going back to my cabin and fishing." They lifted their glasses, "cheers, bottoms up".

Hank nodded, "forget the fishing Joe, I need a good guy to co-ordinate things here; it should be easy and not too taxing, perfect for you in your old age," he winked.

Joe shook his head, "No, I'm off fishing and that's final".

Brian ordered another three beers. "As I am boss to both of you, I I'm ordering you, Joe, to do as Hank has asked; if you don't, I'll personally make sure your life won't be worth living - clear?"

Joe shook his head and sighed resignedly, "when do I start".

"Now, this minute, so stop drinking on duty," he slapped Joe on the shoulder. "Oh, yeah, and you can have Carter as your assistant, he'll sure learn more from you than with Hank."

*   *   *

Ten days later Jack Warren was standing at the UK boarder immigration desk equipped with the necessary official United States papers advising the British authorities that he was the new Second Commercial Attaché. The official behind the screen scanned his passport, stamped his papers, and greeted the new Attaché to the United Kingdom, wishing him a very pleasant stay. He proceeded quickly through customs and was met in the arrivals hall by a military chauffeur who took his bags and led him to the waiting car. He was about to get in the front seat when the soldier held the back door open; Jack hesitantly stepped in. As a spy, you aren't used to being pampered and served on and he felt a bit uneasy. Hell, he thought, must get used to it, I I'm now in charge and I guess I've earned it.

The second Commercial Attaché does not get involved with trade and delegations - that is the first Attaché's job. Jack's title was just a cover story, an excuse for the CIA, and all other such services. Everyone knew it and all turned a blind eye. The Russians had more commercial Attaches than anyone and so it wasn't surprising that when things went wrong and countries decided to kick spies out, it was always the second or third commercial Attaches, along with those actively involved, that were sent home.

Over the following couple of weeks Jack worked fourteen-hour days, interviewing, firing, and reorganising the whole department. He made some major changes, upset a few and, with the help of the military, tightened up the Embassy's security procedures. Many in his department and in the building were well known to him and considered top class people; others like the two idiots Joe had dealt with were soon redeployed in far off and un-glamourous countries; they would either learn fast or sink. The Ambassador briefly met him and officially welcomed his new second Attaché; however, Jack was not the type of person he wanted to get to know too well or get cosy with. On Joe's suggestion, he moved Sally from being secretary and PA as well as being in command of the office. In a moment of weakness, he brought Beth from downstairs to replace her. At last, he was satisfied, with a few more minor tweaks here and there, especially on main security which he had tasked the military to operate, and a couple of field operators still to arrive, one of his main tasks had been accomplished. Now he could buckle down and get to work on the exciting stuff - that of finding out what was happening here in the city. Now for the fun and the real job, he just couldn't wait.

# CHAPTER 8

# England

James Horton woke early, the dawn chorus was in full swing and he turned to check the time, 4.45am. He sighed and turned over. After an hour of tossing and turning he got up leaving Mrs H purring contentedly, had a shower, dressed, and went to the kitchen where he made a pot of coffee. He had felt disturbed since the visit to Scotland. Despite Sean's assurance that he would be in contact in a couple of days, he had not heard from the Irishman. He had tried to call and left messages, but still a stony silence. More miffed at the lack of contact rather than being upset, he had to admit he had enjoyed the buzz of being involved in Sean's world. He sighed; spies will always be spies and they worked in mysterious ways, he thought. He walked round the garden enjoying the blooming flowers and breathing in the early morning air. How lucky he was to live in the country.

Later that morning he was half-way through painting the back fence whilst intently listening to the test match when his wife came out and called, "James, phone; it's your friend Sean". He dropped his brush and rushed to take the call.

"Sean, good to hear from you; thought I had misbehaved so much up in St. Andrews, that you had dropped me."

"For sure not, my friend," laughed the voice ,"just had a few loose ends to tie up from my previous job. Been working on reports which

I had to type up - you know the thing. Now all that is all sorted, I can concentrate on the task to hand."

"Can I be of any help," asked James.

"Yes. As I mentioned, I'm thinking of visiting China very soon and would like to meet that girl, just have a chat and see what she can tell me. Can you, through your friends' son, try and get me information on where I could possibly find her?" he continued.

"I can try; may be a bit difficult as it's been some time now, but I'll ask."

"Grand. Can you come up to London again, say Thursday? Bring your pj's and a toothbrush. Give the lovely Mrs H a break from looking after you," came the breezy voice.

"I would be delighted and hopefully I'll have the info you want. Where do you want me to stay?" enquired James.

"Somewhere not too far from Piccadilly suits me best. Let me know where and I'll call by and meet you about 7pm."

James replaced the received and felt much happier. He went out into the garden and his good mood faded rapidly - whilst on the phone to Sean, England had lost two cheap wickets and were now in deep trouble.

That evening he phoned his friend and explained that a colleague might be heading for China and was wondering if there was anyone in Beijing he could meet up with and use as a tour guide. Did his son, Harvey, still have the ex-girlfriend's contact details? Thank you, he would wait to hear back preferably before Thursday as he was meeting the chap that night. An hour later he had arranged to meet Harvey at Café Valerie for tea.

\* \* \*

Sean was sitting at his desk in a small office just off Jermyn Street; it was his headquarters for now and a place his boss liked him to work from. He was studying the latest files and numerous emails forwarded to him, which were deleted pretty much unread. One, however caught his eye. It was a note reporting that a new second commercial Attaché had taken his post at the US Embassy. Personnel changes were usual, but it was the name that had attracted his attention – Jack Warren – now that rang a bell. He sat for a while thinking hard. Where had he heard of that name, he knew it and it was nearly there but…yes, of course Lima, that's where it was. He'd been posted down there soon after the Good Friday Agreement to investigate the possible links between the IRA and drug barons in Peru. He'd bumped into this guy there. He couldn't really remember how or why they had met, but he did recall a Jack Warren. He was working under a different name but during a rather drunken night it came out. Like Sean, he was also looking into drug barons and their association with traffickers in Nicaragua. Interesting, he thought. What would he be doing here and why the sudden change. He would have to find out. In the distance Big Ben struck six.

Sean breezed in just before 7pm and found James sitting at the bar sipping a gin and tonic; he went over and sat by his friend as he ordered a Guinness. "Well, if it's not my old friend cricketing James. Hope that's the first one," he said jokingly.

James smiled and nodded, "I managed to speak…" he started.

"Not now my friend, later," interjected Sean, "all in good time, the night's young. Tell me what you've been up to".

They chatted over a couple of drinks before heading over to Walton's where Sean had booked a table. A couple of hours later feeling a bit mellow, James followed his friend across Piccadilly into Soho. "Where are we going?" he enquired.

"You'll see soon enough," Sean winked. They walked down several streets and entered a club where apparently Sean was known.

"I didn't realise you frequented this sort of place," quipped James. "Seems you're fairly well known." They were shown to a table in a corner and with a good view of the stage where a couple of girls were gyrating with hardly a stitch on. They ordered drinks.

"Part of a spy's workplace," said Sean nodding over to the stage. "Bet you'd like to be as supple as those two," he laughed. "Surprising who you see and what you discover in these sorts of dives. It's also more private." He nodded, "loud music, distractions, perfect not to be overheard and talk about confidential matters".

James couldn't take his eyes off one of the girls who was contorting herself in knots and was brought back to earth by a pat on the shoulder, "wake up Jamesie, we're not here to ogle. Start behaving or I'll tell the lovely Mrs H," Sean joked.

"Yes, sorry. I met my friend's son, Harvey, this afternoon, and he told me the girl is back in Beijing, working as a virologist in one of the State labs. Said he would try to find out which one and where she lives and would get back to me asap."

Sean nodded, "good work partner; did he tell you her name?"

"Mei Lien - which means beautiful lotus apparently - Mei Lien Chow."

"Pretty name. Hope she's as good-looking as her name sounds."

It was James turn, "now, now, no hanky-panky ideas from an old Irish spy please," and they both laughed. A bare breasted waitress came over to refill their glasses.

"I'm planning to go over there next week for a few days, visiting one of our offices in Hong Kong first. It would be great to meet up with this girl; see what she's doing and get the low-down on what's happening in her world."

"Doubt she will tell you anything even if she does know," replied James. "Remember she swore Harvey to secrecy."

"Yes, but she may loosen up once she's succumbed to my Irish charm; I'm sure she'll be more open than our good professor and, even if she's not, I may manage to get her to give me her views on the Russians and their work. We have four or five good people over there and I've already set them to work."

They both remained silent watching some more hip wiggling and pole dancing. Eventually Sean spoke again, "on a different note,

I discovered an interesting wee development which I must look into tomorrow. A new second commercial Attaché at the US Embassy has been appointed."

James looked at him. "What possibly could be so interesting about that?" he asked.

"You should know that most such people around the world are spies, James, so it means we have a new head here in London and I want to know why. The old one has been around for a while and we, in the service, got on with him ok; no great genius but he was open to sharing information. The funny thing is I think I know the new chap. I'm fairly sure we met in Peru many years ago"

James shrugged, "still don't understand why it's so interesting". At that moment two topless girls came up and were about to sit on their knees when, to James' relief, Sean shook his head and thanked them.

"That was a close shave" Sean laughed, "should have seen your face when she started to sit on your lap. Hey, hope I didn't speak out of turn, an old rogue like you. I should have let you decide, sorry," he continued shaking with mirth.

James shook his head. "Might have thought about it thirty years ago but now, the old ticker may not survive, but I am sure I could still show them a trick or two".

They finished their drinks and left. Walking through the streets back to Piccadilly they chatted happily before going their own way. Sean gave directions on how to find his office and they agreed to meet up at 10am next morning.

\* \* \*

James was standing outside a dusty grey door and pushed the buzzer next to a small, printed tag with WS Trading typed on it. The door clicked; third floor said a crackled voice. Folding his umbrella, he mounted the three flight of stairs and found Sean waiting.

"Come on in James, coffee or tea" he asked.

They went into a cluttered office with a dirty window looking out across to another grey, drab building where figures were sitting at their desks pouring over screens.

"Insurance company," said Sean as he came back. "Sleep well?" he enquired. Smiling he added, "Not too many wet dreams, I hope?"

James shook his head and ignored the jibe. "What's this WS Trading all about".

"Ach, just a cover name for one of the firm's many such places; you can't really have Sean Docherty, Spy, plastered all over the place can you?"

"So, what's the plan?" asked James between sips.

"I'm off to Hong Kong next week, meeting our people there and then I'll make my way to Beijing for a couple of days. By going to Hong Kong first, I'm allowed to travel into China on a three-day tourist visa, saving weeks of paperwork and prying into my background by the Chinese officials." Sean paused and continued, "I really hope I can meet up with this girl; got a gut feeling she could be very helpful."

"If I don't hear from Harvey by the week-end I'll phone him. When are you leaving exactly?"

"Hopefully Wednesday; that would be grand if you could chase him up." He looked over at James. "I have a task for you whilst I I'm away," he continued. "I want you to dig out as much information as you can on our Professor: where he studied, how he got his job, what his speciality is, how he gets his money, what his pollical leanings were and are, anything and everything? Use all those contacts of yours and your journalistic instincts."

"What are you thinking?"

"Just a gut feeling," replied Sean. "I always like to know my subjects. He was very keen to throw the book at the Russians, a bit too keen for me". He looked over to James, "I've done checks on you, know you better than you know yourself," he grinned.

"You bastard!" exclaimed James. "Think I'll start looking into you, Mr Docherty."

"Be my guest, but I bet you come up against a brick wall even if you find a wall. No, seriously, my life is an open book and quite simple – I'm just a plain ordinary spy. Now, haven't you got a train to catch and a lovely wife to go back to. Call me as soon as you get an address for the girl".

# CHAPTER 9

---

# China

Sean took the short flight to Amsterdam and booked into one of the airport hotels. Once he was installed in his bedroom he looked at his phone and saw a message from James giving him the address and contact number for the girl.

The following morning, he was at the KLM check-in desk in plenty of time and ambled around the vast airport, something he had always liked doing. Somehow the coffee and sandwiches not only looked more appetising but tasted better. He browsed the shops and eventually boarded his flight to Hong Kong. The hostess showed Mr Flaherty to his seat and offered him champagne which he politely declined for water.

Just over eleven and half hours later the jumbo touched down onto the tarmac of Hong Kong International, a massive sprawling airport boasting of some of the most up-to-date technology and finest shopping in the Far East, if not the world. Disembarking and immigration procedures were smooth and Sean - no, Mike - was impressed. The last time he had landed here it was at the old airport; he recalled how the planes coming into land flew just a few hundred feet above suburbs crammed with buildings and homes. He was glad to finally have a shower and fall into bed.

He woke with a start as the phone by his bed buzzed loudly. He picked up, "yes" he said drowsily.

"Mr Flaherty, you have a visitor waiting at reception," said a perky voice.

He looked at his watch confused, "what time is it?"

"9.30 am sir."

He jumped up, "tell them I'll be down in half an hour and thank you". Twenty-five minutes later after a cold shower and a shave he strode into the hotel lobby. A young man dressed in jeans and a white T-shirt came over.

"Mr Flaherty, Jimmy Wang. I am head of department here in Hong Kong."

"Pleased to meet you Jimmy and really sorry to be late - slept in."

"No problem sir, long flight and the time change, I hope all went smoothly."

Sean looked at the fresh young man and took a liking to him immediately. He had a bright face with dark, intense eyes set deep into a wide face and a strong mouth. From the file he had read on the plane, Jimmy was forty-one, born and bred in Hong Kong, studied political sciences in Sydney and joined the murky world of spying when he was twenty-eight. His decision followed the disappearance of his sister when visiting friends in mainland China. It transpired that she had been arrested on suspicions of being a subversive subject and died in jail awaiting trial. Since that day, Jimmy held an intense hatred of China and its ruthless government.

"Call me Mike," he said "and we'll get on just fine. Let's go and get a coffee, if we can get coffee in this country, can we?" he asked with a smile.

"Yes, of course. Follow me, I know a nice small place not far from here".

They chatted about Hong Kong, China and Australia and Jimmy confirmed most of what Sean already knew. A clever chap and resourceful too, he liked that. He also liked the dedication. Without dedication and flair you could never get far in their world. Eventually the man in front of him suggested they made their way to his office where they could continue their conversation and discuss the matter Sean had come all that way for.

Hoping onto an already jam-packed tram they trundled along, Jimmy all the time pointing out buildings or something of interest until eventually they reached a large intersection. They alighted and made their way through a couple of smaller streets, finally turning into a small side lane packed with stalls. They pushed their way past throngs of locals out shopping or sitting on make-shift stools sipping tea. Sean loved the feel and the buzz of the place, he liked souks and bazaars, the real life of a city or town. They were not always the safest places to frequent, as he knew from experience. He had come face to face with near death a couple of times in such locations but survived thanks to his instincts and training. They stopped at a door with a sign painted above it with the name JM Shipping written in both English and Cantonese. Sean smiled; the service certainly don't have much imagination when it comes to naming their special offices, he thought. Making their way up a couple of flights of stairs, they entered a bright, airy office, very modern and functional; it could have really been a shipping office.

"This is very impressive Jimmy," he said pointing to four men and three girls sitting at desks glued to screens. A large TV on one of the walls had a news channel on.

"Please, come into my office. Would you like tea? I'm afraid we don't have coffee, but I can get someone to go out and fetch one."

"No thanks, happy with a glass of water. How long have you been here?"

"Eight years; my predecessor was here for about ten. I have modernised the place," replied Jimmy. "When I took over it was very old fashioned, no computers and there were two secretaries who typed everything out," he continued with a smile and shake of the head. "These operatives spend their time monitoring China and its neighbours day in, day out."

"What are they looking for?"

"Everything from military movements, government and political decisions, research, trade, the lot, even down to monitoring the triads. We also keep tabs on what's happening in the far east of Russia and in North Korea."

"Pity I didn't know about you keeping an eye on the triads a few months back," retorted Sean," I was working on their links with the Taliban and South American gangs."

"You not on that anymore?"

"No, got pulled off and given this new assignment which is to look into chemical and biological labs up there in China," Sean pointed to the map on the wall. "See what they're up to. Not sure why but the boss seems to think something is brewing, you have any idea?"

Jimmy got up and went to the door calling one of the men sitting at a screen. A young lanky man appeared and smiled nicely. "This is Tony, he is monitoring all such activities and following any new discoveries, although it is hard when you are not physically on the ground." He made short introductions. "Perhaps, Mr Flannigan, you spend some time with Tony. I will leave you two alone. I will be next door if you need me."

For the next couple of hours Tony answered questions with precision, giving a clear picture of what was happening across the border. He kept things simple and factual, something Sean liked.

Eventually after grilling the man, Sean was satisfied he knew as much as he could and thanked Tony for his patience and understanding. They made their way out into the main office where Jimmy came over. "Everything ok?" he enquired.

Sean nodded, "first class, really excellent, most appreciated and I must thank you and Tony for sparing the time and being so patient".

"What's your next move Mr Flannigan?"

"Well, I'm not sure about you, but I'm starving, so would be happy to invite you and Tony for a bite to eat," his belly rumbled, they both laughed.

Jimmy looked at his watch. "Yes, that would be very nice. Could we wait an hour until the next shift comes, if your stomach allows?"

"Oh, for sure," said Sean, both surprised and a bit disappointed. "How many shifts do you have?"

"Three, Sir; the office is monitored 24/7. The two nightshifts have only 4 people and they mainly write up all the reports. It's also a good time for them to analyse what our little fat friend in Pyongyang is doing."

Sean nodded in appreciation. "All sounds very professional. I must admit I had no idea we had such a big operation here, and you run it all?"

"Yes, sir." It was said in a natural and humble way which struck Sean. "I don't want to be rude, but can I ask again what your plans are," he looked quizzically.

"I am hoping to go to Beijing and look around, but mainly meet a young lady who is currently working in one of the laboratories as a virologist. She studied in England and before leaving seemed keen to tell something but was scared stiff." He nodded towards Jimmy's office, "you go and do what you need to, I'll sit somewhere if I may and go over my notes."

An hour later four new faces entered the office, all young and all oriental in looks. After each of the outgoing crew had briefed his new colleague, Jimmy and Tony came over followed by a young woman.

"Well sir, we're ready, hand over has been completed. I hope you don't mind; I I've asked Pearl to join us; she could be of help to you."

Sean eyed up the girl with appreciation. Over a meal of fish and noodles they discussed what was happening in Hong Kong and the underlying unrest in the city which China and its meddling was stirring up. Sean was given an insight to what really was happening in North Korea, and he was shocked to hear the difference between reality and the sanitized media version. Eventually conversation came round to Sean's visit to Beijing . "Do you know where this scientist lives?" asked Pearl.

"No, that's a problem. The only thing my friend's son knows is that she works at the NIVM in Beijing but has no idea where she lives or a contact number."

"Ok, that is no problem Mr Flannigan; I can find her address easily. What is her name?" Pearl smiled back.

"She goes by the name of Mei Lien Chow and she is a virologist".

Pearl picked up her phone and dialled her counterpart at the office. A minute later she turned to Sean, "I will have the information tomorrow by lunch time. My colleague will start making enquiries tonight".

Jimmy nodded his appreciation and thanked her.

"Good, I think Mr Flannigan…".

"Mike," interrupted Sean.

"I think Mike," Jimmy continued, stressing the Mike, "that Pearl should go with you to Beijing; she could be your "guide" as needless to say, she speaks the language. Apart from that she knows the city well, having been our agent on the ground for three years."

Sean thought for a few seconds and pursed his lips. "Won't it be suspicious that I come with my own guide?" he queried. "And what happens if she is recognised?"

"I will take an earlier flight and meet you at the airport looking like a guide, and no worry if I am recognised, I'll be doing my "old" job of guiding."

Sean nodded. "Then that sounds a good plan. I'm leaving tomorrow afternoon on the 15.20 Cathay Pacific flight."

Jimmy interrupted, "where are you staying?" he asked.

"At the Park Plaza Wangfuging," answered Sean.

"Very nice and in a good position to sightsee," Pearl said. "I will stay with a friend a few miles away so that is no problem."

Jimmy smiled happily, "good, all sorted. May I suggest that Tony show you round our wonderful city now; he is an expert guide and knows some more… interesting places," he grinned.

"Sounds a plan but perhaps another time. I don't want to bother poor Tony any more than I have done and, besides, we have a busy schedule ahead."

"I would be delighted, any time Mr Flannigan. Come, I will show you back to your hotel."

They parted company with Jimmy and Pearl after Sean agreed to meet them at the office the next morning at 9.30.

# CHAPTER 10

# England

James was sitting at the kitchen table whilst lunch was being prepared. He had been busy that rainy morning doing odd jobs around the house. After three hours of getting annoyed and cursing, it had only confirmed his disliked and uselessness of DIY. It pleased his wife, and he would do anything in order not to be nagged at but, enough was enough, next time he would splash out and get a local joiner. He had planned to spend the afternoon watching cricket, but all games had been cancelled due to the weather; he was praying his better half would not think up any other jobs.

During lunch she asked if he had heard from Sean and he shook his head. He mumbled through a mouthful of ham and egg sandwich, that he was in Hong Kong and Beijing. Saying that, reminded him that he had work to do adding quickly, that he was going to be busy in his study all afternoon.

Retiring to his office with a mug of tea, he sat down and started googling. Nothing much of interest was found about the Professor other than when he was young; he had flirted with Communism, had participated in a few anti-nuclear protests - yes that figured - and was now a Labour supporter. Further research indicated that he had links to several research laboratories both in Russia and the US.

He worked for a few more hours making a couple of calls to some past colleagues, probing and questioning. One of his contacts in particular, was more than eager to impart his knowledge and views, and it became quickly apparent that he did not like the Professor one little bit; something to do with an article he had written about Edward, and a long-fought battle to have it stopped. His contact was only too happy to give James a raft of information and some astounding facts about the Professor. "Well, thank you so much for your time and the information, it is really interesting and will be very helpful for my article."

"Wish you luck; I just hope he doesn't put an injunction on you as he did with my article. A slippery chap and has loads to hide," said the voice at the end of the phone.

James confirmed that he would love to receive this information in writing and asked for it to be posted as soon as. He was deep in thought as he went over to pour himself a stiff Scotch. Probably best if he made a few more enquiries. There's no smoke without fire, but his contact did have an axe to grind, so before sitting down to type up his notes he needed to confirm a few facts. Sean would discard the information without any proof.

The next day James continued his research and delved deeper into the Professor's past and present activities. The more he looked, the more shocked he became. How come people didn't know? Surely it was common knowledge and if it was known, why did no one do anything about it? Not surprising he had slapped an injunction on his friend's piece.

At last, satisfied he had covered all angles, he typed up his notes. All he had to do was wait for his contact's report to drop through the letter box.

\* \* \*

## Beijing

Sean made his way through to the arrivals hall and was met by Pearl dressed in official guide uniform. She was holding up a sheet of paper with his name in capitals. They greeted as if they were meeting for the first time; she bowed slightly and gave her name, and he responded with a similar small bow. While making their way to the exit doors, both remained silent until they reached a minibus. She opened the door and helped her client with his bags before jumping in the vehicle and pulling out of the parking slot. Only then did she look into her rear-view mirror to speak. "What are your plans tonight, Mr Flannigan?"

A flutter of excitement came over him. "Firstly, call me Mike," he replied. "I was hoping we could have dinner together and get to know one another a bit better".

"Sounds a nice idea but it isn't possible; it would look wrong, and I could be recognised. Remember that CCTV cameras are everywhere and all hotel rooms given over to foreigners have bugs, so please be careful".

Sean nodded, "thanks for the tip, worse than in Moscow. So, what do you suggest?"

"We meet up at 9am tomorrow and we can take it from there. I will see you in the lobby," she smiled sweetly.

He made sure of being down in the hall in good time and found a chair offering a good view of the entrance door. He glanced around nonchalantly and counted six cameras, well hidden, and very discreet.

He spotted the minibus as it came sweeping into the hotel forecourt and made his way outside. He was struck by the heat but mostly by the acrid smell of pollution.

"Good morning, Pearl, very prompt indeed," he greeted her.

"Thank you, good time keeping is a trait of mine," she smiled. Once he had settled in his seat and they had pulled out, she continued. "We should do some sight-seeing this morning as you are a tourist, after all. We can go and see some gardens where we can talk."

There was a long silence while she concentrated and weaved her way in and out through the traffic. At last they reached a main artery and she resumed. "We have an address for miss Chow so we try and make contact with her around 6pm; that's about the time she returns home."

"Sounds like a good plan to me and I must say I am impressed by the way you all work," commented Sean. "We could do with some of that professionalism back home."

They spent the rest of the morning ambling around Jingshan Park, admiring the neat gardens and fine specimen trees. They chatted about life in Hong Kong and her time here in Beijing, only reverting to tourist language when anyone approached. She took him to a "typical" Chinese restaurant that catered for tourists before making their way over to the Summer Palace. The place was busy with tourists and locals enjoying the warm day. Pearl pointed out a couple who, seemingly acting as tourists, were secret police. She knew them by sight, still doing their tedious and boring job of keeping a close eye on the crowd. She steered him clear of a few more "local" tourists and by 4pm they decided to make their way back to their vehicle.

With all his years of training Sean had developed a keen sense of direction and quickly picked up the fact that Pearl was driving in the opposite direction to the hotel. "Where are we going?" he enquired.

"Back to where I'm staying, I'll change into normal clothes and we can pick up my friend's car."

They drove a few miles and came to a set of traffic lights where she told him to get out. "I will meet you at the tea house across the street, the one with the small bridge in front," she said. "Order some green tea and their homemade biscuits; I'll be with you in 20 minutes".

He got out and made his way across to the tea house, delightfully nestled among flowering trees. Despite it being in the centre of the city; the small garden was an oasis of peace and tranquillity. He ordered two teas and home biscuits and sat back relaxing. His thoughts drifted to Pearl; he was pleased to have her company and appreciated the local knowledge. As a spy he had been to too many dangerous countries but never to China. Here was different, creepy even, and he thanked the Lord he had someone with him who knew her job.

A young woman dressed in a summer floral dress, her long, dark, hair down to her shoulders, walked in and made her way towards him. It took him a few seconds to recognise Pearl, totally transformed from the dowdy guide he had left earlier. She took off her large sunglasses and sat down smiling at him. "You look surprised and shocked."

"I didn't recognise you," he stammered. "What a transformation, a different person completely."

"This is me," she exclaimed. "Back at the office I have my 'work look' but sometimes I like to be me, especially when I am with a fine man."

"I'm flattered, but I must point out I could be your father," they both laughed.

In a low voice she explained that they would go to Mei Lien's flat and hopefully manage to catch up with her. She told him that he should do most of the talking and that he should introduce her as his interpreter whilst he was in the city.

Thankfully they left in plenty of time. The trip to Mei Lien's apartment took longer than expected due to the heavy traffic at that hour. They battled through a throng of bicycles, cars, buses, and a mass of humans all vying for space. After a chaotic and hair-raising drive, they eventually arrived and managed to park just across the road from the building. They watched people come and go, a couple of aged men, a mother and baby and several smart young men entered the block of flats. At last, a young woman matching the description they had, turned up and let herself in. She walked confidently and was laden with groceries. They sat watching for a further fifteen minutes, giving the woman time to settle in before making their way into the building. They were promptly intercepted by the sullen woman coming out of a small booth. Pearl smiled sweetly, "Good afternoon, I am a friend of

Miss Chow and this gentleman knows her from her time in England. Could you tell us the number of her apartment please?"

The woman looked them up and down suspiciously and sniffed "4ᵗʰ floor, number 403" before returning to her booth.

They made their way over to the lift and Sean felt the caretaker's eyes boring into his back. Neither spoke. They knocked on the door and waited. After a minute it opened and a head peered through, "yes, what do you want" it asked.

Pearl turned on the charm again, "hello, I am Pearl, and this is Mr Flannigan from England".

Sean quickly took over, "yes, a friend of mine said you used to go out with his son, Harvey, and as I was visiting Beijing, he asked me to come and say hello".

Mei Lien's eye lit up. "You know Harvey?"

"No, his father; we served together in the army many years ago before he became a journalist,", he lied hoping she didn't know otherwise.

"Please come in,", she ushered them in making sure no one else had seen them. "This is a friend and colleague of mine, Ru Nuang".

They shook hands and sat on one of the two sofas. "Beer, tea? When did you arrive in Beijing?".

"Yesterday and I'm just staying a couple of days before flying to Hong Kong, I have business to do down there," replied Sean. "Pearl, here, is my guide and interpreter as my Chinese is non-existent. You speak excellent English."

"I am afraid I am a bit rusty, and my friend has only just started to learn so I will have to translate."

"So, tell me, how did you like your time in England?" asked Sean.

"Very much, it was a big change for me, but I learned a lot, apart from my studies. I was very sad to leave but I had no choice," she replied. "How is Harvey?"

"Good and doing well, he's followed in his fathers' footsteps and is climbing the ladder fast; not long before he becomes editor," he replied. He noted a sadness in her eyes; must have really been love. "So, what are you up to these days?"

"May I ask what your business is first?" she wasn't going to open up to an unknown even if they did claim to be friends with her ex-boyfriend, and more so with a Chinese supposedly interpreter/ tour guide. Everyone knew these people worked for the State and reported back on everything so, for now, she intended keeping the conversation as general as possible.

Sean instantly felt her reticence and weariness and threw a glance over to Pearl. Both knew what the girl was thinking, and both knew exactly what to do. The conversation continued seamlessly covering every day mundane subjects, Sean asking her about Beijing and taking the conversation back to her time in England. Picking her moment carefully, Pearl suggested that, as they both spoke such good English, she would take her leave and make some errands she needed urgently. They agreed that she would meet Sean outside the building in an hour. Sean inwardly smiled; that's my girl he thought, a good operative with keen instincts.

After she had left, Mei Lien visibly relaxed; she moved over closer to Ru and they spoke a few words and he nodded. She turned to Sean, "is your friend really an interpreter?"

Sean shook his head, "no, she works in Honk Kong with the people I do business with and offered to come and help me. She knows the city well and, as I have said, I don't speak the language."

"You see," continued Mei Lien, "here in China, all interpreters and guides are state workers and report to the police on everything. It is not safe to say anything and meetings with foreigners can cause much trouble."

"What about the woman downstairs?" enquired Sean.

She smiled, "once you have left, she will tell someone of your visit and you will be followed, even more than you have been. We will have an official come round soon, probably tomorrow, asking us questions and possibly making trouble," she sighed.

"Very sorry if I have caused you problems, just doing a friend a favour. Can I help in any way."

She shook her head. "You asked what I do," she continued. "My friend and I work in a research laboratory not far from here; I am virologist and Ru is a microbiologist; we work in the same building but in different departments."

"Is that for the University?"

"No, for the State. We analyse all the findings the two main research centres send in and then report to the National HQ; they then decide what is useful and has to be worked on further."

"I didn't know that the State had such a programme, I thought that happened only in Russia and the US."

She smiled, "Mr Flannigan, China has the largest and most advanced programme in the world; hundreds of millions of dollars are poured into research and development. It is little known by the outside world, but we also invest heavily in foreign laboratories and fund many worldwide projects. We are also the largest contributor to the WHO – World Health Organisation."

Sean shook his head, "I have a feeling that you shouldn't be telling me all this."

"We are currently looking into a couple of projects which, we understand, could be huge and potentially extremely important to China." She looked at the man beside her before continuing, "in fact, we are both being sent to oversee and report on a top-secret programme which has been developed and is ready for final testing".

Sean noticed Ru nudging the girl and she stopped. "Perhaps you should stop there, Miss Chow, before you say something you may regret."

"It worries me Mr Flannigan. I must get it off my chest. The initial analysis is extremely frightening. Of course, it is very flattering to be selected but at the same time I am very worried."

"About what"? asked Sean.

"About our safety and mine and Ru's future. If we disagree, find it is not what the military is hoping it is, or try to end the project, we could be striped of everything, lose our jobs and be sent to a 'rehabilitation' centre far away, perhaps even killed. If we give it the go-ahead then, potentially, it could have a devastating effect, worse than the atomic bomb."

"I'm sure it won't come to that," said Sean.

Mei Lien looked sceptic and shook her head. "No, from the initial reports we have read, it is a very lethal weapon and I am worried." She went silent and very thoughtful.

"When are you leaving for this job?"

"Soon. We will be told shortly."

He smiled sympathetically, " I have taken up enough of your time, I must be getting on". Sean stood up. "It was a pleasure meeting you both and thank you, I just hope my visit won't make trouble for either of you. Apart from saying hello to Harvey, do you wish me to tell him anything else?"

"Thank you. Just say hello, but please don't say anything I've told you to anyone."

He smiled, "of course not. Good luck and I'm sure it will all work out well for both of you." He turned and made his way to the door where he gently patted the girl's shoulder and handed her a piece of paper. "In case you need to get in contact with me or need help, call this number, it's Pearl's - she will know where I am and can help you, any time of day."

\*　　\*　　\*

As he reached the entrance hall Pearl appeared from a door behind him and followed him out. They didn't speak and made for the car. Once inside Sean looked over, "where were you hiding?"

"In a broom cupboard next to the small office."

"The sour old hag will have probably phoned and reported us; hope they don't give the two young ones too much grief".

Pearl shook her head. "She will not give trouble and there will not be any record of our visit".

Sean looked at her quizzically.

"It will be a day or so before they discover the woman has had an accident and, coincidently, the video tape had stopped working." She looked over to Sean. "Did you learn anything interesting?"

He nodded and then shook his head. "Huh! Glad you're on my side, I wouldn't like to cross you," he exclaimed. "The lassie let a whole lot of stuff out, but both are terrified for their future, poor kids. It seems that they are extremely well qualified and very much sought after; so much so, they are being sent out of town to report on a major discovery in some laboratory. From what I gather, this chemical or whatever it is could kill off half the world population. When you get back to base could you check that out?"

"Sure, did they say where and what it was."

Sean shook his head.

# CHAPTER 11

# London

Jack had spent the last couple of days digging into old files in the hope of finding out more about the three Englishmen at the Savoy. He had managed to find just one, an Irishman going by the name of Docherty with an alias of Flannigan. Ex-soldier / informer during the troubles in Ulster, now working for MI6. Flannigan - now that was a name he'd heard of. For several hours he'd sat trying to recall where he had heard of that name before but eventually gave up. Nothing much was found out about the retired journalist but a bit of digging on the internet proved interesting. He called Sally in and asked her to start a couple of files, one on the retired journalist and the other on the professor. He liked Beth, his new secretary, but for certain things the older woman was more reliable and more discreet. He was about to make a phone call when, in a flash, he remembered the name Flannigan. He let out a yell of triumph. The brain is incredible, you spend hours trying to think of someone and then, for no reason, it comes to you.

Of course, it was that guy he had bumped into one evening in Peru; they had got terribly drunk and both had talked more than they should have. He was working on some drug cartels just like himself and they compared notes but after that night had lost contact. Wonder what he's working on now; surely the professor was not into narcotics although anything was possible these days. As for that Horton dude he doubted very much if he knew the difference between aspirin and crack. He turned his mind to Mike Flannigan and read the sketchy file once again but drew a blank. Ok, he would have to try and make contact somehow.

The cab dropped him off at the Savoy and he ambled through the foyer, then across to the restaurant where he found Emile.

"Bonjour Monsieur, you are back in London again. Mr Briggs not with you?"

"No, he had to return to the bank but I am here for the foreseeable future, which is very nice, just like old times. Would you have a table for one?"

"Of course, Monsieur, your usual one is free. I believe Mr Briggs, your colleagues at the bank was looking into a couple of gentlemen; any news of the people you were looking for?" he enquired.

"Still working on it but at least they haven't attempted to defraud another bank, yet. To let you in on a secret, I have managed to trace two of them but am still looking for the person who made the booking. I believe you and your security man were most helpful".

"I'm afraid I cannot help you this time, he left no contact details and I think he called from a land line and it came direct to the restaurant number."

"No problem Emile. You've already been extremely helpful." Jack was disappointed, he had hoped that Flannigan would have left a number and was surprised Emile had not asked for one. Back to square one then.

Returning to the office he spent the next three hours googling and reading up on the professor. He knew it was him by the grainy CCTV photo Joe had left - although it was a bit fuzzy, you couldn't mistake the features. He sat back in amazement, shocked in fact. Was all this known to Flannigan? Was he onto something? must have been, no agent of his experience would not know; or could he? He had to find out. Picking up the phone he called one of his new, young assistants to find the Irishman asap.

*    *    *

On returning to London, Sean immediately contacted James and reported that he had met the girl and had an hour or so with her. He instructed his friend to phone Harvey and pass on her best wishes, love or whatever ex-girlfriends pass on.

"Did you find out anything" asked his friend eagerly.

"Aye, certainly did, but I am not going to tell you over the phone. You know me. What about you? Get anything on the prof."

"Yep, but I'm not going to tell you anything over the phone; you know me" quipped James.

There was a laugh at the other end, "Ok, touché. What about we meet later this week, my office and we can catch up. You might want to stay over and we could check out that club again," he chuckled.

"Ha! very funny! But yes, Ok, what about tomorrow? I could be up for 11am."

"See you then my friend, with or without your night things."

James spent the rest of the day getting his file on the Prof in some sort of order and went over his notes again. The more he re-read what he had learned, the more he aghast and shocked he became. Could it all be right he wondered. He was sure Sean would find holes in his report and tear it to pieces, but he had checked and re-checked and was confident.

The next day, just after 11.30 he was sitting in Sean's office, a fine cup of steaming coffee in his hand. "Well, how did it go?" he enquired.

"Very good and, as I told you, I met the lassie and her boyfriend. Nice kids although he doesn't speak English. Did you speak to Harvey?"

"I did, and he was delighted you managed to catch up with her. How did you find out where she lived?"

"Easy my friend, with the contacts I have, it took under 24 hours." They chatted a few minutes before Sean asked what he had found out.

James pulled out a file from his battered old briefcase and handed it over. "You'll never believe what I found out, I still can't".

Sean took the file, "well, I certainly know what I'm going to buy you for Christmas," he nodded over to the limp bag. "A new briefcase, that one is in a very sorry state, how long have you had it, since school?" he chuckled. For the next ten minutes there was silence while Sean read the report. He showed no reaction, not a flicker and James couldn't tell what his friend was thinking. Eventually Sean put down the file and looked up, "wow, you've done a fantastic job. Although it hurts me to say it, even better or at least, as good as I could".

"I've checked and re-checked the facts, and I'm still not sure it is all accurate or true."

"It reads true my friend, and that contact of yours certainly seems to know what he's talking about. Pretty shocking, frightening even, but true, for that I am one hundred percent sure".

"Well, I still think you should get someone else to check it," said James. "I just can't believe a person like the professor, in his position, can get away with it and not be found out.".

"They are smart, believe me, and they have the gift of the gab. Like me, they have kissed the blarney stone and how to turn on the charm but, unlike me, they use its powers in the wrong way" he winked. "It could fit in with what I found out in China but how, I'm not sure yet".

They continued to discuss at length various points with James arguing that he still couldn't believe his contacts story fully. The man had an axe to grind after all, making his allegations dubious. Sean disagreed and pointed out many facets and possibilities proving the contact right. In the end neither could agree so, ending the discussion, Sean looked over. "Right Jamesie! you must be starving, I know I am, let's get some lunch". He stood up, "I know this little Italian not far from here, great salads but even better Chianti. No girls I am afraid, but you can't have everything!"

On their way over Sean rested his hand on his friend shoulder, "well done my friend, I'm really very grateful for what you've done so far, and the time you have put into it, so, lunch is on me".

Over a meal of salad and pizza washed down with some excellent wine they chatted about cricket, rugby, and life in general. In true Sean style nothing was mentioned of their business; he just excused himself and made a brief phone call. They didn't make their way back to the office but hoped on the tube and made their way south, getting off at the National Theatre. From there they walked briskly to a large imposing building occupied by MI6 Head Quarters. "Sorry James, I am going to have to ask you to wait here, way too complicated for you to come in. I'll meet you in forty- five minutes over there, in that café, the one with yellow parasols".

Sean made his way quickly to the third floor and, after a few minutes wait, was shown to a meeting room. A young 30 something man with a mop of floppy fair hair greeted him and pointed to a chair. "What can I do for you today?" came a low raspy voice.

Sean liked the man, trusted him, and felt sorry for him when he spoke. He had been shot in the neck whilst on a mission in Iraq and by some miracle had survived. After several operation and months of rehabilitation he had managed to regain some sort of voice, but the croaky rasp was there for life.

"I'm wondering whether you could look into a certain professor Howard, semi-retired. He has worked at Oxford and helps occasionally at Porton Down, advising on chemicals used in warfare and such like. You have a mate that works there, no?"

The young man nodded. "What do you want to know about him?"

"Everything, from when he left working for the University right up to now. What sector of chemical he specialises in, where else he works, who he sees, the lot. I understand he advises the military and the Government, but I want to know in what capacity and who decided he was the best man."

"Hm, don't see any problem with that; it 'll take a few days as we have a couple of people off but I'll get Charly to help me, he's a wizard at digging up peoples' lives and dissecting them. I'll call my mate and see what he can tell me".

"Much appreciated my friend, just let me know when I should call back to collect the file". They parted with a warm handshake. Sean was always amazed at how taciturn the man was, ok, he had his problem, but even before he had been injured, he was a person of few words, the essentials and no more.

He found James sitting on the terrace reading a paper and joined him for a coffee. "What do you want to do tonight?".

"Thought I would go back home, take the 6.15 train".

"No, no! that will get you in too late. Check into the hotel and we can have some fun, have a couple of pints of Guinness, hit the town. What d'you say? Oh! I've got it, you left your pj's at home," he teased.

"True, I don't have a toothbrush or any spare underclothes; anyway, I don't think there is any more for me to do here at present."

"Rubbish man! Just a few beers and we can catch up some more. Been a long time since we had a good chin wag. I'll even phone Mrs H if you're too scared to".

"That's the last thing I want you to do! no I will. Ok, then, but not a late night".

It was just gone 10pm when James checked into the hotel equipped with some toiletries and a new pair of underpants and socks purchased at the nearby M&S. He had phoned his wife who, as usual, took everything in her stride and simply hoped they would have a good night and she would see him sometime tomorrow. He decided to shower and then lay on the bed, tired and a little fuzzy from the drinks. He must have dropped off and was awoken by his mobile buzzing. Sean, he sighed and turned it off, he was too tired to start chatting right now. A few seconds later the phone went again, he answered it.

"James, have you seen the news?" came an excited voice. "Turn your TV on to BBC News, now, hurry".

James did as he was told but it took him a few minutes to work out all the fancy buttons. Eventually he was tuned in. It took him a couple of seconds to focus on what the presenter was saying. "What's all this about?" he asked.

"There's been a poison attack in Salisbury. It seems it happened earlier today, a Russian spy and his daughter, still just alive but it's touch and go." He paused, glued to the screen, "this is just what we're looking into James. Our professor could be telling us the truth after all. The Russians are not all nice and innocent. Anyway, we can't do anything now so get some sleep, night".

James lay there watching the developments for a while, all sleep banished. It was a long night of tossing and turning. At 7am, frustrated, he got up and dressed. He could make the 8.15am if he got going soon.

As he walked into the lobby the familiar figure of his friend appeared, grinning and full of the joys of life. "Well, by god! You can wake early!" he exclaimed. "Did you watch the rest of the news? I did".

They made their way over to the breakfast area and sat at a quite table with steaming hot drinks.

"What is all this about?" asked James.

"Well, old Skripal worked for us as a double agent and was found out. We eventually made a deal and exchanged him for a couple of their guys and he's been living a quiet life ever since. The girl is his daughter, just came back from Moscow where she was visiting relatives."

"But why kill him; presumably, they were happy with the exchange, and why now?"

"Putin was never happy and the whole thing was agreed without his blessing. So, my guess is that he's got a couple of his trusted hitmen to bump the old boy off; serves as a warning to others that they will never be safe."

"Why not just shoot the man?"

"Too messy and too obvious. Doing it this way gives the killers time to get away, probably already on a plane back to Moscow. Now, I reckon the stuff is something called Novichok. It's lethal; can kill thousands of innocent people so the authorities could have a big problem".

"How do you know all this; is it new?" asked James.

"No, developed many years ago during the cold war; the Russians had developed this as THE chemical weapon. For the past few years they have always claimed to have destroyed all of their stock; my foot, as if they would! I can't say for sure, but knowing them as we do, I bet, if it's not that, it's something very, very similar."

James was silent, going over what he had just heard.

"I think James, you should go back home now; there's nothing you or I can do, I guess my mate I saw yesterday will be ever slightly so busy. I will call once I know more".

The train was just starting to slow down when James' phone rang. It was Sean. "I was right!" said the voice. "My gut feelings are very rarely wrong. As I said earlier, you may not hear from me for a while but don't fret; we'll resume our work once all this settles down. Talk to you soon and look after Mrs H; tell her I am looking forward to having another one of her lunches".

# CHAPTER 12

# London

Sean, after taking the week-end off, was back in his little office and mused what a different set up WS Trading was to the office in Hong Kong. He inwardly shrugged; that was life, he was happy with his lot. Although good at man management and giving orders he much preferred to work on his own. Besides, he was hopeless with computers and the thought of sitting all day looking at a screen and trawling through information was most definitely not for him.

His thoughts turned to China and to the professor; he picked up the file and started reading what James had given him. Suddenly he remembered about the new man over at the US Embassy. He looked up the number he had jotted on a pad and dialled. A clipped voice came on after 3 rings. "Good morning, US Embassy, how can I help?"

"Ah, good morning, my name is Mike Flannigan. I wonder if you could put me through to the second commercial attaché please?"

"Can you spell your name please and tell me what you want?"

He spelled the name out and repeated his request adding, "Mr Warren and I have met a few years ago and I would just like to meet up with him again now he is in London".

"One moment please, I will put you on hold." The phone clicked and some jazz music came on.

The minutes ticked by and Sean was beginning to wonder if the voice had forgotten about him when suddenly it returned, "you are through".

"Good Morning Mr Flannigan, my name is Jack Warren; what can I do for you?"

"Good morning, thank you for taking my call," started Sean. "I read that you have recently taken up the post here in London and wondered whether we have not met before. I think, perhaps, in Lima".

There was a short silence, then a chuckle. "Well hell, if you are the guy I think I met down there it's a miracle you remember anything."

"For sure, that makes two of us. I seem to recall you were as bad as me," retorted Sean.

"Those damned local cocktails. That mixed with that piss they call beer, gee! I'll remember the next morning until the day I die. So, what can I do for you?"

"Just wondering if we could meet and catch up, for old times' sake. Have a proper beer."

"Yeah, sounds good, but I detest your warm sludge you call bitter as much as I hated that other stuff. When can you manage?" asked Jack.

"What about Friday after work; we can have a civilised drink and then go and have a meal?" Sean suggested.

"You're on. Where do you want to meet?"

"What about El Greco, on Portman Road, say 6pm?"

"Great, see you then. And, hey, thanks for calling, looking forward to seeing you again," the phone went dead.

\* \* \*

Sean was sitting at the bar of the El Greco when Jack Warren walked in. They both recognised each other immediately and shook hands warmly.

"Good to see you again, Mr Flannigan."

"Likewise, call me Mike. It's not as if we're complete strangers. Welcome to London."

"Thanks, always loved this place. I was posted here a few years back, just after the South American trip; so, I'm not totally a stranger. What are you up to these days, still chasing drug barons?"

"Sort of," replied Sean. "Working on various things, and you?"

"Thought you would be hot on the trail of these Russians who are causing all the fuss. Not good. Those bastards sure have balls; never liked that Putin, dangerous dude and a real thug."

"No, not on that; I certainly agree though about Putin," replied Sean. "What about you, still undercover?"

"Guess so, as you see I'm the new second Attaché, been promoted of sorts. Another one?" pointing to the empty Guinness glass.

They discussed the situation around the world, the new President and Brexit, reminisced about old- times and back to the Salisbury attack. "Did you ever get anywhere with those drug barons?" asked Jack.

"Yep, we managed to dismantle a fairly big operation about a year after we met. Thought we'd made real progress, especially over here and in Holland but as always, it's a drop in the ocean. You stop one lot, another pops up,". Sean sighed.

"Sure, I remember there was a bit of gun battle, very unlike you Brits, in a small port in Venezuela. Our then President didn't want to get involved, scared of upsetting the locals and the image the US were no longer world policeman."

Sean nodded, "and you, get your guys?"

"Did we heck! Two years of hard work, time, money and resources and when the fish was on the hook the White House vetoed it and put a stop to the final stage. Didn't want to look bad and lose the Mexican vote. At the same time, they decided to cut the agency's funding by thirty percent; balls man - utter balls!".

Later, over diner, Sean decided to toss the bait. "Do you know anything about Chinese chemical and biological weapons?"

Jack shook his head, "not really, no. Why are you asking?"

"Just wondering."

"Spit it out buddy; you began, you can't stop now!"

Sean smiled, "well, I'm working on something, un-officially, and looking into how big the industry is over there. Seems that they are well advanced and have a major programme, but it's all very hush, hush."

"Funny you say that. I've been looking into a tip off we received a couple of months back. Not anything to do with the Chinese I may say". Jack looked at Sean closer but didn't see any change in his expression. "You know a couple of guys called James Horton and a Professor Howard?"

Sean shook his head.

"You sure? Coz I have CCTV footage of you and those two leaving Simpson's in the Strand." He looked quizzically at Sean under his eyebrows.

There was a long silence before Sean replied. "Why don't we talk about this somewhere quiet, my office or yours, too many people here and we've had a few."

Jack smiled. "Fine by me; what about tomorrow, your place, say 11am."

When in town, Saturday mornings were normally when Sean went to the gym, did his weekly shop and his washing before watching rugby or sport. A chill-out day. This day he was in his office early, tidying up and putting some sort of order to his desk. He had spent most of the previous night deciding what and how he was going to deal with his visitor. Eventually he had a plan, go with the flow, it always worked best. The doorbell rang at 11am sharp and he pressed the buzzer.

He greeted Jack and, after making coffee, they sat down in the small room. "Apologies for the less than salubrious office, it's all I've been given."

"Fine by me. Trust there's no bugs or you aren't recording?"

"Have some faith Jack, our departments doesn't work like that and I, certainly wouldn't."

"Ok, I guess we're batting for the same side and it's in our mutual benefit to work and trust one another. Why not cut the bull; you know I know, our names are working names so what about if we dropped all that and revert to who we really are?" He continued, "you know I'm CIA, moved to shake up our somewhat under-performing guys over here. My real name is James Williams but I go under the name of Jack Warren; can I ask you to call me Jack, it's been so long since I've used my real name I no longer answer to it. Come from Boston originally, made my way up through the ranks after leaving the army; must have seen something in me, but I'm still trying to figure what it is," he chuckled. "What about you?"

"I was given the name of Sean Docherty, born in Northern Ireland, I served as an undercover agent, then moved to my present position within MI6, chasing drug barons and monitoring dissident groups through the Middle and Far East."

"Good to meet you properly Sean," and Jack thrust his big hand out. "Now, tell me what you were up to at the Savoy?"

"I like a man who goes straight to the point," smiled Sean. "We had a tip off that China is producing and developing chemical weapons on a big scale and I've been tasked to look into it. I've just recently returned from a visit there and, although it's early days yet, I'm convinced there is something to it."

"Ok, what about the two guys you were with?"

"James Horton is an old friend, retired journalist, particularly good at digging things up, trawling through the internet, all that stuff; has lots of contacts. I have unofficially drafted him in to help. My boss set up the meeting with the professor who, I was told, knows all about chemicals, microbiology and such. He worked at Oxford University and now advises the Government and the military establishment."

"What's he say about this Novichok theory, guess you've asked him?" interjected Jack.

"Not a lot. James and I went to see him; he spent most of the time defending the Russians and accusing China of being the real bad guys. Must say, we are both convinced he was holding back."

Jack chuckled, "don't blame him. I wouldn't open up to a retired journalist and a spy."

"Interestingly," continued Sean, "he's had nothing to do with finding out what was used in Salisbury".

"Sure sounds weird. Being adviser to your government, as you say he is, means he should have taken the lead."

Sean took a sip of cold coffee. "James has found out a whole lot of very interesting stuff on the man which one of my colleagues is looking into." He passed over the file to Jack. "Take a look but it goes no further, ok."

While Jack read through the file Sean watched carefully. Not a flicker, not a twitch, a real pro and very good at his job he thought to himself. Normally, with most people, as good they could be, there was a slight flicker of the eye, eyebrow or in the jaw but with this man, nothing; he was impressed.

Closing the file and looking up Jack shook his head, "it's pretty damning and bloody scary. Thanks for this; not often someone you don't really know gives you this sort of information. He sounded truly thankful and appreciative. "What now?"

"As I said, I have a chap back at base looking into it and hope to get his verdict soon."

Jack hesitated a second before plucking up the courage, "it seems the US could possibly be implicated somewhat; I sure would appreciate if you kept me in the loop."

Sean smiled, "I wouldn't have shown you the file if I didn't trust you. Of course, and I would even go so far as to suggest we work on this together. But ONLY you and me, it's too sensitive to get others involved."

"Sounds fine by me. I can make enquiries back home and see what I can dig up. To tell you the truth, my ex-boss, well, my boss actually, sent me a file and requested I check things out. That's why I've been looking into the three of you. It was just routine because we have a policy to keep tabs on all active and retired scientists. Hence the questions. Must have been fate that threw us together." He looked at Sean closely, who shrugged.

"Wondered why all the questions and you were not surprised to hear me on the phone."

Jack continued, "you remember a guy called Joe Briggs? He was here a few years back."

Sean frowned and thought a moment. "Can't say I do but I was away a lot in those days. Why? what's he got to do with all this?"

"Nothing, nothing at all except that he's the one who found out who you were and got the CCTV footage. He is working on the case back in Washington."

"That's fine. We're in this for the long haul and will need all the help we can get. Make sure both of our governments are aware of the situation and sing from the same hymn sheet."

They exchanged mobile numbers but agreed that most communication would be face to face, another point Sean liked about Jack. Like him, his American counterpart avoided phones or e-mails as much as possible.

# CHAPTER 13

---

# Washington

Hank Gobolsky was sitting at his desk sifting through papers when his phone buzzed. "Jack's on line one," said a smooth voice.

"Put him through." A second later the line clicked, "Hi, Jack, how you doing buddy? Been a long time; thought you were locked up in the Tower of London!".

"Good to hear you too Hank. I'm fine, just been busy. You know me, been discovering the delights of the city and the fishing," he chuckled. "No, seriously, I've been pretty busy with the reorganisation and have been equally busy working on the file you gave me."

"Found anything?"

"Yeah, in fact that's why I'm calling; though I might come over and see you and bring you up to speed."

"Just send a message - coming from the Embassy it will be encrypted; or don't you trust that now?".

"Yes and no. Would prefer to talk to you face to face; it's kind a sensitive."

"Ok, ok," came the amused voice. Hank knew how much Jack distrusted messages and phones. "I know the real reason is that you're craving for a big, fat juice American T-bone steak".

Jack laughed, "I'll fly out on Sunday, see you on Monday about 9am".

\* \* \*

Jack made his way across the park enjoying the warm sun, happy to be back on home soil. Not that he didn't like London, he loved it, loved the oldness, the mixture of culture and the special buzz he had always found there. Yes, the brits were a bit quirky, they had different ideas and many did not understand the American way of thinking but, overall, he was a relaxed and happy man when in the city.

On entering the big lobby hall, he was greeted by two security officers who recognised him immediately, gave a smart salute and a polite request for him to hand over his phone and go through security. He made his way to Hank's office where he was met by a new secretary he did not know.

"Good morning, Mr Warren. Mr Gobolsky is expecting you; please follow me." She led him down the corridor he knew well and knocked.

"Welcome back stranger." They clapped one another on the shoulders and sat down. The secretary returned immediately with two mugs of coffee and a couple of muffins.

"Ok, tell me all about your new life, enjoying it?"

"You know how much I like London Hank, must thank you again for getting me the post, without your subtle arm twisting and hinting, Pintaro would never have thought of me."

"Best man for the job Jack, no denying it. I knew you could do it and so far, I have been proved right. The boss told me recently he had a call from the Ambassador himself commenting on what you have done in such a short time."

"Not sure whether that is good or bad," replied Jack. "He sure is a cold fish and I guarantee he doesn't like agents like us; avoids me like the plague."

"Who does, buddy, who does!", they both laughed.

Over the couple of hours Jack talked through everything he had learned from Sean; telling him that they were now working unofficially together on the case. "Tell you Hank, this is big, very big and could have massive implications around the world."

"Is this Mike Flannigan trustworthy?" enquired Hank.

"One hundred percent, one of us and sure good at his job, one of the best. I've checked him out myself which wasn't easy as he doesn't leave traces but, by luck, we had met in South America by accident, when I was working on the Spinaro gang."

"What about his side kick, the journalist?".

"No problem there. Ex-journalist as I've said, a friend of Mike's. He was highly regarded when in full time work for his investigative acumen. Mike trusts him a hundred percent and that's fine by me."

Hank sat back and steepled his fingers while he thought. This was, by all accounts, going to be a tricky investigation and diplomacy, as well as secrecy, was essential. "You've done great buddy, real great; who do you think we should call in on this side, any ideas?"

"Good question but I thought Joe had been brought in. With all the cuts and the pensioning off of the old guard, we don't have a big choice," sighed Jack.

"Yeah, Joe was ordered to help but I was thinking more of who would lead the investigations over here."

They were silent a short while before Jack spoke, " I know, got the perfect guy".

"Who?"

"You."

Hank laughed, "me, don't think so. I've been desk bound and out of field operations for years".

"Don't laugh, you are ideal. Ok, you may be a bit rusty, but you know everyone that counts here in Washington, you're recognised and know how to get insider info. Oh yes! you also have my full trust," he grinned.

"Very kind of you," smirked Hank. "Not sure though. Do I really want to go back to field work at my age and to start upsetting people in high positions. I have my pension to think of, and anyway, no one ever takes me seriously."

"Don't be like that; you're perfect and you'll enjoy it. You always enjoyed a challenge, and in this case, we really do need experience and discretion. The least people working on it the better. Who better than THE number 3 in this organisation? You don't need to tell anyone, they'll never notice."

Hank sat deep in thought, scratching his chin and passed a hand through his thinning hair. "No," he said eventually. "You're right, no one will ever notice that's for sure. It would be fun and yeah, I could do it, but I would prefer Joe to take the lead! I can't think of anyone good enough or discrete enough. I'll co-ordinate things from here, from my desk. We need someone to do it and that is my forte now. Joe loves getting under peoples' skin and ferreting about; this case is right up his street."

"Are you sure he'll accept. You know how he likes the retired life now."

Hanks smiled, "he's sort of on the case already, we gave him the job the day we appointed you for London; but only in a low-key capacity, checking facts, that's all".

"Fantastic, just like old times," grinned Jack. "You might want to warn Brian though, just in case he finds out."

Hank shook his head, "no, ignorance is bliss we'll keep Brian well out of it for now. You know what he's like, the least he knows the better".

"OK, we'll name it Operation Opium. Drugs, labs... In answer to your quizzical look Jack."

"Now that's settled what about the T-bone you promised me? I'm starving, not eaten anything since I was flying at 35.000 feet across the pond yesterday."

On the way to the door Hank stopped and turned to his friend, "I'm a happy guy; with you and Joe working together and taking the lead, suits me down to the ground. Jack, I'll make you number uno, Joe can be number two."

"Covering your ass already," Jack laughed. "Ok, but only if you pay for lunch."

∗   ∗   ∗

The next day Hank arrived back in his office, tired and grumpy. He hadn't slept a wink that night, going over and over what he and Jack had discussed and agreed the previous day. It was not going to be easy and could be politically sensitive. Furthermore, the White Sox had lost again and that always made him moody. The phone rang on his desk and he picked up.

"Hank? Brian here, can you come up to my office, now." The line went dead, and Hank sighed deeply. Now what did the bastard want? The last time he had such a call he was in trouble for ignoring the file he was now working on. "Carter!" he roared. The young man appeared at the door.

"You haven't forgotten to give me a file to read, have you?"

No, sir, the last one was last week, the one about a possible terror attack in Atlanta".

"Thanks, that's what I thought. How you getting on with Briggs?".

He got up and made his way to the floor above. He had read the file, concluded his investigation, and sent up a report to his boss the previous day. He relaxed slightly and took a deep breath. He was shown into Brian Millentos' office and was beckoned to a seat across the wide desk.

"Thanks for coming so quickly Hank. Just wanted to ask you if there was any news of Jack and how he's getting on."

"Jack's doing fine, settled in well and has got the department working more efficiently now. Wasn't easy but he seems happy with the new set up".

"Good, good, always knew I had made the right choice. He's a good man, reliable."

Hank inwardly smiled. As usual Brian was taking the credit; it didn't bother him, he was used to it. Let the little man bask in glory. "Did you get my report about Atlanta?"

"Yes, excellent! Any news on that?"

"As I said in the file," he answered pointedly, "we found out who was behind it. Pretty easy. Made a couple of arrests, two students with neo-Nazi ideas who wanted to prove something or other. They'll be sent to a psychiatric hospital for assessment and then to trial, probably looking at five years."

"Well done, thanks. Oh, Hank, what's happened about that file you ignored a few months ago? anything come of it?"

"Jack is working on something. It seems the Chinese have a chemical weapons programme and he is investigating. Not easy, but that's his forte. I'll keep you posted of any developments".

"Thanks, Hank, appreciate it".

\* \* \*

Walking past his aide, Hank nodded, "Carter, come through, shut the door".

The young man hovered awkwardly until told to sit down. "Right, from now on, you are going to be working under Joe Briggs on a very sensitive case, so no official files understood. No talking to anyone about it; it's top secret and if anything gets out of this office, I'll feed your balls to the jackals. I stress, discretion, discretion, discretion, understood. You report to me and Joe Briggs, no one else."

Carter gulped and nodded.

"I'm still your boss but you do exactly as Joe tells you; it's a great opportunity to learn from one of best. He has asked me to get you to drawn up a list of all companies and laboratories based here in the US who are involved in research and producing chemicals, mainly those who have a microbiological and virology centre. Forget for now the petrochemicals. Can you do that?"

"Yes sir. "I guess there will be quite a few".

Hank nodded, "that's why I'm asking you son. Don't mess this up – go over everything twice, this is your break. I want that list by the end of the week."

"Thank you sir, you can rely on me."

"Right, get your ass out of here and get to work. Remember, no file, nothing left on computers and NO talking. Oh, one other thing – if Joe Briggs gives you instructions you drop everything."

Hank swung his chair round and faced the window, looking down to a wide avenue, deep in thought. An hour later he had a plan and picked up the phone.

# CHAPTER 14

---

# Beijing

It had been seven weeks since the visit of the Englishman and the Chinese woman. Ru and Mei Lien had gotten closer, living part time in his flat, part time across the corridor. He much preferred staying at her place, it was cosier, and it felt comfortable. At first, they were worried about what the neighbours would say but it seemed no one was interested. Ru's English was improving fast thanks to his three times a week classes and Mei Lien's insistence they only spoke it in the evenings. They were happy and both found each other's company easy and relaxed. Although both worked in the same rambling building, it was rare that they met up during the day. Evening times were spent catching up and comparing notes, bouncing ideas off each other. They had decided, from the beginning not to show their affection at work or to meet during their lunch break. Safer to remain flat neighbours in public, not lovers.

They had not yet been sent to report on the new findings as there was some un-specified problem; an imminent researcher had been dispatched to investigate. They had been assured that once everything was back on track they would be called upon. All very vague and both were beginning to think that a decision had been made not to involve them.

That night, Ru came back from his class and, as he opened the door, his nose filled with aroma of some delicious cooking. He went over to the girl he loved and kissed her gently and gave her a big cuddle. He realised every day that he loved her more and more; how lucky he was to have such a beautiful and intelligent woman. He had never dreamt his life would turn out the way it had.

Releasing her and kicking off his shoes he turned, "I was just thinking, have you heard from your English boyfriend?"

She shook her head, "Ex-boyfriend! No, but I don't care. I have a far nicer and more handsome lover now," she said and smiled.

Ru continued, "don't you think it a bit strange how things have turned out since our foreign guest paid us a visit; we have heard nothing from anyone". They sat down and dug into a wok full of his favourite stew. "Firstly, the grumpy Mrs Wong was found dead in the outside toilet and no one has come to question us about that, nor have they come to ask who our visitors were. Then, the other day, we got some fancy story why we have not been sent to check on this new project," he looked up at the goddess across from him.

"You're right. Although never in a good mood, I can't see why the caretaker should take her own life, hang herself? Most odd." They went silent before she resumed, "I can't understand how the video had stopped working that afternoon either; the old bag spent her life glued to it and would have been quick to phone the authorities and report the fault. You don't think the girl had something to do with it, do you?"

Ru shook his head, "must be co-incidence. I don't believe in such things as you know, but I just cannot see why or for what reasons they would bump her off and make it look like a suicide". He shook his head, "no, she must have been in a bad way mentally, probably turned the video off without thinking or for her own good reason".

"The official line is that she took her own life because of stress." They both laughed.

"Stress! What do they make up. The old bag didn't know the word," Ru wiped his mouth. "Wow, that was fantastic, I'm going to have to go on a diet; you cook too well".

"I like chubby men," she giggled. "Funny that no one from the authorities came to ask us if we knew or heard anything," she continued seriously. "Surely someone must have seen two strangers, especially as one was European."

Ru thought a minute, "not really; who really wants to get involved with the police, more questioning, suspicions. Anyway, I can't see many people feeling the loss of the old hag; she certainly didn't endear herself to anyone".

"What about the delay in the project? What do you make of that?"

"Not sure, but from what I gleaned, there is a problem. A few calculations went awry and matters have stalled. That's the official story at least and the reason Huai and his team have been sent. Speed things up and try to sort out the mess; you know how the authorities up high hate delays."

"That's clear then, if professor Huai is on the case, we aren't needed. They would certainly not send two young budding scientists to check up on such an imminent brain. Shame! I was looking forward to it," she said in a dreamy tone. "You think it has to do with what happened here?"

"Think of it as a positive," said Ru. "We can spend our two week summer break together, go to the seaside or to some romantic place and spend our time making love."

"You have a one-track mind," she giggled, "but I like the idea".

"Before we go to bed and I ravish you, have you still got the number the Englishman gave us?"

She shook her head, "no, I destroyed it. I didn't want anyone finding it if they came to interrogate us or look round the flat".

"Shame! We could have tried to find out what really happened."

\* \* \*

## Hong Kong

Ru was feeling uncomfortable, the plane was full and overheated, he just could not get used to flying. He couldn't understand how people could enjoy such an alien form of transport. As the plane descended, bouncing through the clouds, he began to sweat feeling it trickle down his back. He looked round at Mei Lien and admired her calmness. Sitting there, cool, reading her magazine, she didn't seem to notice the turbulence or heat; he took her hand and she looked up, smiled, and nestled into him.

"You ever been to Hong Kong?" she asked. "You know, we could have taken the train. I just didn't realise who much you disliked flying, I'm sorry".

He shook his head, "I'm fine, just not used to jetting around like you are. Anyway, the train takes too long. Like this, it's just over in three hours."

As they emerged through the clouds she pointed out of the window, "look, what a fantastic view, all those boats and skyscrapers".

He gingerly leant over her, conscious of his clamminess and looked out. The view was great but all he could think of was that in a few minutes they would be on firm ground. She looked at him and kissed him gently, "nearly there!"

After checking in to their hotel and freshening up they went out to explore. Ru bought a guide and sat at a bar with a beer planning the next few days. Tonight, out for a good European meal; Mei Lien wanted Ru to taste a different cuisine. Tomorrow, take a boat trip and explore the bustling sea front with, perhaps a little shopping. After that a trip to Aberdeen and up to the top of the mountain by cable-car. He was looking forward to discovering a new world.

The next day the clouds had lifted, the humidity was nearly as bad as back home. They made their way to the ferry and spent the morning taking in the Honk Kong skyline from the water, followed by lunch, then along the seafront to the end of Kowloon peninsula. In the evening they dined in a restaurant atop one of the towers. Ru discovered other tastes and textures and had to admit Western cuisine, although very different, was palatable. The one thing he did not enjoy was sitting right by the window. The view was stupendous but looking down to the streets forty-five floors below, made his legs shake. Mei Lien had suggested they moved but he declined.

They visited Aberdeen on the other side of the island, enjoying the hustle and bustle of the markets and old streets. They ate fresh fish on one of the numerous boat restaurants and spent hours watching the traders haggle and barter with their clients. They returned exhausted and retired early and made love. It was the first time they both felt relaxed, not worried the neighbours would hear.

Feeling refreshed the next morning Mei Lien decided it was time for some serious shopping, something Ru, most definitely did not like the sound of. He suggested she went off and did her thing while he would spend the time exploring the small side streets nearby. They arranged to meet back at the hotel at twelve.

The morning was spent in heaven, a girl's best dream, visiting the big stores, looking at items she could not get in Beijing and spending a small fortune on clothes, handbags and shoes. It took her back to the days she was in England visiting the big stores in Oxford Street. Back at the hotel she felt guilty - all that money spent, more than she had budgeted for but, well, she never really treated herself too much. She worked hard and spent little, so why not? Besides, it was not all for her. She had purchased several T-shirts and jeans for Ru, as well as a few good quality shirts; she was fed up with those cheap things he had that frayed and faded after a couple of washes.

Ru gasped when he saw all the bags, "what have you been up to?" he exclaimed. "You've bought a whole shop! Must have cost a fortune."

"Yes I know, I did go a little mad, but most of the clothes were in the sale and you can't get things like this back home. Look, I've got you these; see I didn't forget you."

"Thanks. I love them, especially the jeans, they must have cost you an arm and a leg." He kissed her. "I love you and I'm not cross or upset it's just that I have never seen so many bags. I think we'll need to buy another case for going back home," he chuckled.

After changing they made their way to the Ngong Ping Cable Car. At the top they admired the breath taking views of the peaks of Lantau Island and across the South China Sea, sparking in the sunlight. They walked round the impressive Tian Tan Giant Buddha and strolled the small streets of the touristy village. Standing once again at the foot of the statue Ru turned to Mei Lien and kissed her. Pulling away from her he looked deep into her eyes and took one of her hands. He fumbled in his pocket, then placed a small box in her free hand. "Mei Lien Chow, I love you more than anyone I have loved before. Will you marry me?"

Her eyes filled with tears and she hugged him tightly. Looking up into his eyes she smiled, "I love you also with all my heart. Yes, it would be an honour to have you as a husband. I could not wish for anyone nicer, kinder or better". She opened the small box and gasped ,"Is that the one I liked on the first day, the one in that window?" Putting it on she exclaimed excitedly, "and it fits, perfectly". She kissed him and held him even tighter. "Oh, Ru, we'll make a wonderful couple, have lots of children - well, one or two. Thank you."

They sat on a bench looking out across the sea, his arm round her shoulder, silent, each contemplating the future they had promised one another. Her head was on his shoulder and he looked down, "when should we get married? Two, three months' time?"

"I would say sooner but perhaps we should wait a year, save up and try to get a nicer flat."

"You spent three month wages this morning," he said jokingly. "Perhaps you're right, we should save up first." As an afterthought, "guess we should tell your parents. Do you think they will object?"

"No, not when I tell them what a wonderful, kind, and intelligent man you are."

They fell silent again before she chuckled, "life is funny, had it not been for you burning the pan of noodles we would not be sitting here, and I would not be the future Mrs Nuang".

They sat for a long time, chatting and making plans, eventually strolling over back to the cable car. Halfway across the square they heard a voice calling out. Not thinking it was aimed at them they ignored it. "Hello, Mr Nuang, hello," the voice was closer. Stopping they turned to see a slim, elegant woman dressed in a floral dress, large sunglasses and a summer hat.

"Mr Nuang, Miss Chow, what a coincidence, we met at your flat in Beijing. Do you remember?"

How could they not. Ru smiled politely, "yes, of course. You were with the Englishman." He glanced at his fiancée.

"This is my husband. What are you doing in Hong Kong? You should have let me know," Pearl said introducing a slim man with broad features.

"Yes, what a coincidence. I must admit I I've lost the number your English friend gave me and did not know how to contact you," lied Mei Lien. "We are here for a few days on vacation, our first time."

"When are you going back to Beijing?" asked Pearl.

"Another day and then we must go home. Hong Kong, is fantastic but very expensive," said Ru.

"What are you doing tonight? We would love to invite you for diner but understand if you prefer to be alone".

The young couple looked at one another and replied in unison, "that's very kind of you, yes, we would like that very much".

The four made their way down the mountain. Pearl and the man pointing out places of interest as well as giving their guests the history of the colony. They parted and the future Mr & Mrs Nuang agreed to be in the hotel lobby for 7.30pm.

Back in their room Ru looked at his fiancée, "was that coincidence or was that planned? Must say I never felt someone was following us and I would have spotted that dress".

"I thought you had eyes only for me," she winked. "No, I'm sure that it was pure chance and I must say I don't think I would have recognised her either, even if she was wearing the same dress."

Ru remained sceptical; a scientist, he never believed in chance, everything had an order and a purpose, but he kept silent. "What do you think I should wear?" he asked.

"Those new jeans and that blue shirt I bought this morning." She came out of the bathroom and went over to the cupboard taking out two dresses. Turning she lifted them up, "this or this?" she asked.

Seeing her naked Ru just nodded, "If I had a choice, neither. I would just love to take you to bed and make a baby," he grinned. He pointed to the one in her left hand. "Hurry up and get dressed before I do something I shouldn't!"

The evening went smoothly, conversation was relaxed and flowing. Both Pearl and her "husband" proved to be interesting and amusing. They were excited when told of the engagement and immediately champagne was ordered to celebrate the occasion. No one spoke about the meeting in Beijing and Pearl never touched on the young couple's work. Driving back to the hotel she turned round, "we are both working tomorrow, so I am really sorry, we can't show you around but if you need any advice please ask".

As they got out of the car Mei Lien was handed a note, "here, take this, my details are on it, please feel free to call me anytime, night or day".

Back in the room Ru flopped on the bed. "Must say, and I hate to admit it, I enjoyed the evening and the company. You looked stunning, very sexy." He put out his arms and pulled her to him.

"Have you changed your mind about it not being a coincidence?"

He was struggling to undo her dress buttons, "that fizzy stuff".

"Champagne," she interrupted, "really nice and the proper thing, I loved it".

"Not really my taste. It certainly hampers finger movement," he giggled, still fumbling trying to undo the last button. "And it makes you burp a lot," he chuckled.

"Perhaps it has something to do with the 2 bottles we had and that wine," she unfastened the last clasp and wriggled out of her dress. "Now don't fall asleep on me."

# CHAPTER 15

# London – December 2018

Sean was sitting in his small office feeling morose. It hadn't stopped raining for the past three days and the days were dark and gloomy - 2.30pm and all the lights were switched on. To crown it all, it was Friday 15, his birthday. There he was, alone and contemplating the start of his fifty sixth year on this earth. Where had the years gone? What had he achieved? He opened a draw in his desk and pulled out a photo of his parents and his sister going back to when they were all alive. He would not change his professional life; the soldiering, the spying, all that he loved. It had, and was giving him, a purpose. It had taught him to be a team player, a leader, to fight and to use his instincts and mental faculties, to survive. The part of his life he did not like was the killing. Yes, he needed to do that in order to help his companions or save lives and the people he was paid to protect. From a young age he had lived with death, natural or otherwise. It had made him hard, uncaring sometimes, and that was a side of his persona he disliked. No wonder he wasn't married.

He looked down at the faded photo taken when he was about ten years old. A large family gathering taken at his uncle's home in County Antrim. His grandmother had died of cancer as did his aunt. His uncle was found a few months later tied to a lamp post, a bullet through the head. It was alleged the IRA was responsible but no one could prove it. His youngest sister, Kathleen, was killed in a bomb explosion whilst out on a shopping trip with a girlfriend. That day was for ever etched in his mind. His poor mother never got over the shock and took her own life two years later. His father found solace in the bottle and died of cirrhosis of the liver. The day he learnt his sister had died he vowed to fight, to do anything to stop further killings and to make the bastards responsible pay. That's why killing became part of his life, each time he was about to pull the trigger he thought of his sister and her needless death.

He was frustrated that the job in hand had stalled. Since the meeting with the American, everything had gone quiet. He had tried to phone him a couple of times but never got through, nor did he have any return calls. He was annoyed with himself; why had he got involved and opened up to that man, someone he hardly knew; he should have known better. The guy had probably found out a whole lot of things and was keeping him in the dark - traitor, he thought. Typical yank, self-centred idiot; well that was last time he was going to rely on outside help or try and be friendly. Try to be nice and what do you get - a slap in the face; he was annoyed by his own stupidity. At the same time, he was equally disappointed that his contact at MI6 had not come up with anything new; nothing more than James had found out. Hong Kong had gone cold and silent. Nothing was advancing, no progress and that was really getting to him. He was a man who liked action and all the avenues he had been working on and investigating had led to nowhere.

He sighed, putting the photo back in its place in the drawer. He looked out across to the next building where the office workers were warming up for the annual ritual of the office Christmas Party. The girls were all dressed up in their finery, the lads loosening up with a few beers. He was abruptly brought back to earth by the phone ringing; he picked up.

"Happy Birthday dear boy,, said a chirpy voice. "Sorry, forgot your office address so couldn't send a card. I didn't send a text or e-mail as I know you would hate the world knowing your age."

His mood lightened immediately. "James! Thank you. Really kind of you to think of me and, yes, you're right, I'm not prepared to divulge my age to all those bad guys out there.

"What have you been up to? Seems ages since we last talked. How's the investigation going?"

"Jamesie, I too must apologise; I 've certainly not been a good partner. To tell you the truth things have stagnated big time. No one seems to be talking to me and everything has stalled."

"Gosh, that is frustrating. Nothing from that American chap of yours?"

"No, the bastard has probably found things out but is keeping it to himself; our cousins across the pond are like that, they like to keep the glory to themselves; take and give little. They don't trust us."

"I'm surprised. By what you said, he seemed a nice fellow and not like that at all. What about your contacts in Hong Kong?"

"Nothing there either. That's more difficult to understand."

James paused a second, "suppose the powers up on high haven't put a block on things, do you? Or the professor has found out and put pressure on your bosses?"

"You're thinking like a spy, James, my man," chuckled Sean. "Learning to be suspicious, I like it. No, nothing like that. If any pressure had been brought to bear, or if the file had been closed, I would have been told. They don't like their people sitting idle."

"On a different note, what are your plans for Christmas?" asked James.

"Oh, nothing. Thought about going up to the flat in Oxfordshire but I can't be bothered getting someone to clean it. I'll stay here, have a few beers and an M&S ready meal."

"Oh no you will not!" came an insistent voice. "Come down and spend a few days with us. We have plenty of room and I can educate you on the finer side of life, like wine and port."

"That's a mighty fine offer Jamesie, but I don't want to trouble you or Mrs H. What about your grand-children? I'm not too good with kids."

"They're coming down for New Year so no need to play Father Christmas or charades."

"Well…."

"Perfect, that's settled; let me know what train you're catching, and I'll come and pick you up. Say the 23rd, mid- afternoon. See you then and we're looking forward to your company." The phone went dead.

Sean smiled. Now, there was a friend indeed. Thinking of it, probably the only real friend he had and could rely on. Looking at his watch he decided 4.30pm was a good time to start celebrating his birthday. He was about to get up when the phone rang again.

\* \* \*

Jack was at his desk shuffling papers about aimlessly. He looked out at the weather, the pouring rain battering against the window. Typical London weather for the time of year he thought. He was not looking forward to the coming evening, the Embassy Christmas bash where all head of departments were expected to attend, be merry and pretend they all got on. The Ambassador and his wife would be attending, making small talk and faking interest and bonhomie; why on earth did they persist in the charade. Protocol had it that men sported tuxedos, wives or girlfriends dressed in evening gowns, so stupid and a total waste of time.

He was about to put away a well-thumbed file when he felt a pang of guilt. He sat back and scratched his head. What would the Englishman, or rather the Irishman think of him? There was a man, a colleague of sorts, who had trusted him and fed him highly sensitive and important information, and how did he repay him? By his silence. It wasn't all his fault; things had dried up and as much as he wanted to, he did not find anything new on China's chemical war developments.

Hank and Joe's enquiries had not proved very fruitful, and he had not heard from his boss for over a month.

Had he done right to entrust them with such a task. Perhaps Hank's relative inexperience had simply closed doors and warned people to put up shutters. Jack could have kicked himself for being such a fool, he hadn't followed one of his golden rules; never entrust anyone or anybody with anything sensitive, and if you want results, do it yourself. On the other hand, Joe was on the case, so perhaps it wasn't Hanks' fault. He looked at his watch – 4.30pm, two hours before he had to dress up and act the happy spy. He picked up the phone.

\* \* \*

## West of England

The train pulled into the station on time and disgorged a throng of passengers all making their way home for Christmas. Sean stepped down and buttoned up his coat; an icy wind cut through the air catching the back of his throat. He made his way to the main hall where he found James standing by the book stall.

"Sean, great to see you. Have a good journey down?" he enquired grasping his friends' hand.

As usual conversation was easy and the banter good. Sean was relieved that his friend was not upset at his silence for the past couple of months. At the cottage they were greeted by the lovely Claire and shown inside.

"Please come in and make yourself at home. Tea, or would you prefer a whisky?" she asked. "James will show you up to the guest bedroom later unless you want to freshen up first."

"Tea would be lovely, and any chance of one of those scones? I've not eaten and been saving up," he smiled.

Both men made their way to the study where a large log fire was roaring and they settled down in the cosy chairs. The rest of afternoon and evening was spend chatting about sport and world affairs, eating Mrs H's delicious food and sampling a couple of bottles of excellent burgundy. Even though Sean was not overly fond of wine, he had to admit to enjoying the one poured by his host.

The next morning after breakfast James suggested they went for a walk, blow the cobwebs away and get out of his wife's way. The wind was still cold and cutting but was forgotten when conversation turned to the professor and the findings that James had un-earthed over the past few weeks. Sean was gobsmacked to learn that his friend had been hard at work and his guilt quickly returned.

Back in the study, James handed him a file. "Sorry, I've not told you about this earlier, but I wasn't sure how to get it to you, or if you were still working on the case."

Sean read through it with growing excitement and amazement. "This is extraordinary. Where on earth did you find all this?"

"Hours of trawling through the internet, reading articles and making phone calls to my friend who was gagged."

"You haven't told anyone have you?"

James shook his head.

Looking over at the door he continued in a hushed voice, "Jamesie, this is explosive stuff and potentially dangerous for you and Claire if it ever gets out".

"What do you mean?"

Sean looked at his friend, "If it falls into the wrong hands or people find out what you have uncovered, it's not only a gagging order you'll get. These kinds of people are ruthless and anything that threatens their cosy, lucrative business, is dealt with swiftly and by any means".

James smiled, "well, I'm relying on you to protect me; that's your business after all. No, seriously, I wasn't born yesterday, I fully understand the situation and my mind is made up."

Sean was silent for a long while. Eventually he looked up, "don't think badly of me, you know how much I appreciate your help and friendship, but I think it best if I continue on my own. I would hate if anything bad came of you both and would never forgive myself. I value your input, you know that don't you, but if all this is true, then I would seriously advise you to walk away from the enquiry now."

"In for a penny, in for a pound. Unless you order me, I'm in this with you all the way, for good or for worse. I appreciate your concern Sean, and value your advice, but I've already talked things over with Claire and she agrees, this is a cause worth fighting."

"You've told Claire? What have you said?" Sean was shocked.

"Of course, that's what couples do – talk. I had no one else to discuss this with. You had disappeared, and I realised it was a massive find with all the risks that came along with it. She told me to talk to you after Christmas but now seems a better time."

Once again guilt flooded over Sean, how could he have been so lax at keeping in touch with his one and only friend. He may have lost heart but James had certainly kept going. He understood the reason the man wanted to be part of it after all he had done, but did he really, truly, understand the dangers?

"I'm sorry I I've not been in contact, I feel really bad about it, James. It's just that I had lost the motivation. I must be getting too old for this game."

"Old! my foot, look at me, twelve years your senior and still rearing to go. Bring it on I say!".

Sean laughed, "Ok, but understand that if you want out at any time, you are free to walk away. I wouldn't blame you. By the way, did I tell you the American phoned me, just after you called the other day? Like me, he hasn't got anywhere; his contacts are as useless as mine, apart from you! Wait until I show him this, he'll wet himself."

The rest of the afternoon was spent sipping a fine malt and planning their next move; both looked forward to 2019 with eager anticipation.

# CHAPTER 16

## January 2019

James made his way to London and was met at Paddington Station by Sean. It was cold with a thin wind slicing through the throngs of passengers milling around the station. They wished each other a Happy New Year before making their way quickly over to the Heathrow Express where they found a relatively calm coach and settled down for the short trip to the airport.

"Thanks a million James for the wonderful Christmas. I haven't had such fun and enjoyment for a long time." Sean turned and tapped his friend on the arm, "really great and I don't know how you keep so slim with Claire being such a good cook."

"It was our pleasure and, yes, we also had great fun. It was a perfect way to spend Christmas without the grandchildren."

"I hate to admit it, I kind of got to like wine now, at least the stuff you produced," he grinned.

"Only the best for a good friend. You seemed to take a liking to the port also."

"Yeah, that's a killer! What was it? 1985 Taylors?"

"1977," replied James.

As the train pulled out of the station and they looked out of the window, Sean turned to his friend, "Hope you have your thermals, Jamesie, it's going to be cold".

"I have indeed, and I have everything on the list you sent, like the good boy I am!" he said sarcastically. "Anyway, why are we having this big meeting in Reykjavik, in the middle of winter?"

"When I spoke to our American friend, we decided that it would be best to meet in a neutral place, far away from prying eyes and ears. Don't want to be recognised; especially since his boss in Washington will be joining us. Seems that their side have been doing some research also and have discovered some new info just recently."

"Ever been to Iceland before Sean? I've always wanted to go but never at this time of year. You realise it gets light at 10am and dark again just after 2pm?"

"Yep, that way you won't be recognised," Sean chuckled. "And Jamesie, sorry, there are no topless bars," nudging his friend.

After landing, Sean turned to James, "best we stop at the duty free before going through customs and get a couple of bottles; things here are more than expensive. I'll let you choose the wine, I'll do the malt. We have time, the Amsterdam flight is due in half an hour."

They waited in the busy arrivals hall until Sean spotted Jack coming through the sliding doors accompanied by a thick set man dressed as if he was going to the arctic. After introductions they made their way to the taxi rank and, finding a minibus, settled down for the half hour drive into town centre. Little was said apart from small talk. They checked in at the Odinsve Hotel, a stone's throw away from the famous and impressive, although stark, Hallgrimskirkja Cathedral.

As James was unpacking, his phone rang. "Want to come along for a dram?" came Sean's voice, "Room 335," and he hung up. Over a glass of Glenmorangie they discussed the next day and Sean re-assured his friend that everything would be fine. James was anxious; he didn't know what to expect and the thought of sitting with three professional spies and being part of serious discussions relating to top a secret matters made him nervous.

Sean soothingly turned to his friend after pouring him another drink, "just relax, they're not going to eat you and, anyway, you know more and have greater knowledge of the situation than any of them. Don't worry, I'm here to protect you, big brother!"

They spent the evening in Jack and Hank's company and James was introduced to a third American, a Joe Briggs. The three Americans were laid back, enjoying the banter and simply asked James a few questions about his past and teased him endlessly about the game of cricket.

The next morning after a typical Icelandic breakfast, they gathered in the hotel's conference room and got to work. Jack opened the conversation and got right to the point. "James, I understand you have found out quite a bit about our professor. Can you please give us everything you have?"

James glanced over to Sean who flickered his eyes and gave a slight nod.

"Well gentlemen, it seems that Professor Edward Howard is playing several fields, and is a very nimble and agile operator. As you know he was educated in Manchester before being accepted at Cambridge University with top grades. There he excelled in chemistry and biology and left with a PHD and honours. It's all in the file." They nodded and he continued, "It seems that he had extreme left-wing tendencies and was highly involved with the UK Communist party but, after several years, moved away and joined the Labour Party."

"Like a lot of young people of his era," interjected Sean.

"He managed to get a job as head scientist at Porton Down and for many years was the British Government's Chief Adviser. He was then transferred back to Cambridge about six years ago and took up a place as head of Department, but I've been unable to find out why."

"Sure seems odd," interjected Hank scratching his nose.

"Well, yes and no," continued James. "From what I gather he got a bit too big for his boots and started demanding a bigger salary and insisting on enlarging his team while at the same time refusing to divulge any findings unless the Government paid him a 'bonus'., that sort of thing".

Jack snorted, "sure way of upsetting your political backers and Government in any country, but he did keep his position as advisor, that's the bit I don't understand".

"I think they had no other choice, for some reason, they do trust and admire him. Anyway, back at Cambridge he met up with a couple of old Uni pals who re-kindled his left-wing feelings. "James looked around and they nodded to continue. "One of his new friends was a chap by the name of Francis Baker - you may have heard of him." They all nodded.

"He's the guy who was caught passing on photos of military installations in the UK and Afghanistan to the Russians," Sean sneered. "A nasty piece of work; claimed he'd been set up by us and made a scapegoat, lot of rubbish. He's behind bars now and if I had anything to do with it, he would be six feet under."

"Would have thought that being involved with a guy like that would be enough to make any Government department suspicious," said Hank. "Anyway, sorry James, please carry on".

"Soon after Francis' arrest, the Professor attended a world seminar in St. Petersburg organised by the Swiss pharmaceutical company, Roche, to discuss possible antidotes for new viruses. Much discussion was to do with how best to regulate any new findings falling into the wrong hands. He was one of the main speakers". James took a sip of water before continuing, "a couple of months after his return he quit his post in Cambridge and took up a position as head scientist and Chairman of a newly formed research laboratory based outside London." He looked over to Sean and continued, "this new centre was called Star Laboratories and, you guessed it, was financed by Moscow".

The three men shook their heads. "Unbelievable. He goes to a conference in Russia, and a few months later he jacks in his high-profile job at Cambridge to take up a new career working for the ruskies," interrupted Jack. "Did you guys know any of this?"

Sean shook his head. "The first I or MI6 ever heard about it was when James told me just before Christmas. We're looking into it now and I expect a report when we get back".

Hank grunted, "why and how come you were suddenly asked to look into the Chinese connection, what brought that on? Why were we kept in the dark?".

Sean's features darkened a little, "you haven't been kept in the dark. Ask Jack. Now, let James finish and I will answer any questions afterwards". Hank shrugged.

"This new laboratory was only a smoke screen; it's main aim was to operate covertly and enable the Professor to pass on information gathered at Porton Down and around Europe. Report on any new drugs and antidotes that could affect the Russian chemical weapons programme. Take the Salisbury attack last year. Being at the forefront of Government operations the professor knew what was happening and how we were progressing with finding out what killed the Skripals; we're pretty sure he kept Moscow well informed of our findings."

"You mean to say the guy is a fucking double agent working for the Russians, and he's still in there!". What sort of fucking idiots are you?" roared Hank.

"Hey, Hank, calm down," soothed Jack. "James here has nothing to do with it." Turning to James and smiling, "sorry, he's never been good at keeping cool, that's why he has a desk job! please, continue".

"I must point out" said James, "Star Laboratories have offices in Paris, Frankfurt and Atlanta, all run by the professor although, from all accounts, London and Atlanta are the main ones".

Hank blushed slightly, "Nah, don't believe that, must be a different company. It would have been flagged up in our search we've undertaken of all labs and research centres based in the States."

"I can assure you," continued James, "it is the same. It has six employees and the chap in charge is an American; the only difference is that they are more focussed on disinformation and are extremely commercial".

There was a silence while everyone digested the information. James decided to plough on, he was on a roll. "The good professor hasn't stopped there and seems to enjoy playing several hands at once. Not content with helping the Russians. he is also very closely associated with the Chinese."

"The file touched on that but didn't say how much. Is that why you were brought in Sean?" said Hank testily.

"Not really, I was working on drug dealing by the Triads when I was assigned this case," replied Sean. "As you know, the Chinese are investing heavily in overseas telecon and software companies, that is happening in the United Kingdom and across Europe and on your side. Over the past few years, they've bought into most industries, especially in pharmaceutical and chemical companies."

James nodded "They've purchased two research laboratories recently in Britain: one in Leeds and one just outside Glasgow. As well as in England, you must be aware that they own three laboratories in the United States."

Jack looked across to Hank and Joe who shook their heads. "First I've heard of this. Who are they?"

Sean butted in, "Sunshine Technologies in Florida, SACS Laboratories in Texas and Beacon Pharmaceuticals in California, all 100% Chinese owned".

Hank looked glum. "Yeah! Knew about Sunshine and SACS, small outfits but they're home owned".

Sean continued, "both were purchased in 2017: Beacon has been Chinese since 2015 and all three have as Vice President a certain Professor Edward Howard, all three are 100% financed by Beijing".

Sean couldn't resist adding, "you must have known that Hank!" giving a wink to Jack.

"Ok, ok, sorry guys for losing it earlier; I admit we're as bad as you lot."

They called a break and returned thirty minutes later with fresh coffee and some Danish pastries. Jack turned to Sean, "so what have you got on the Chinese? You went over there, no?"

"Not a lot in fact" started Sean. "Our office in Hong Kong has been monitoring events but nothing eye-catching has come to light. As it says in the file, I met with a couple of young scientists, but it was more a speculative meeting, didn't find out much and it turns out they're pretty low grade."

"Sorry to interrupt," said James, "you do know that the Chinese have doubled their contribution to the WTO over the past 2 years and have had a big say in who the new president would be?"

"Yep, we knew about the financing," said Jack, "we suspected they had a major part in the choice of the new incumbent."

Hank chipped in, "did you know some of our top military and scientists have been invited to visit one of the main laboratories in China. It's in the name of good will and world co-operation – if you believe in all that bull".

"Had heard a rumour," replied Sean. "I know the UK government isn't going; would be good to know more about and who is involved."

The meeting went on for another couple of hours before it was decided to reconvene back in Iceland in a few weeks' time. Both parties had a long list of points to follow up and check out. All agreed that secrecy was key. The three Americans left for the airport whilst the British pair stayed on overnight.

\* \* \*

## Beijing

After returning from Hong Kong, Ru and Mei Lien decided to move in together and to openly advertise their relationship. It was going to be impossible to hide their love and the fact that they were going to get married. The new guardian was unimpressed when Ru told him he was going to move across the corridor and grudgingly handed him the papers to fill in. He did not like the fact that they were going to co-habitat whilst unmarried. Ru pointed out that nothing in the law forbade them and that was how the world was going. The old man shrugged and grunted, "just don't make trouble or noise or I I'll have you both thrown out of here".

They both continued to work in their separate departments but now met up during lunch break. Ru continued with his evening classes and with Mei Lien's help, was now fluent in English.

It was a bright sunny day with an icy cold wind blowing. As they left the flat both pulled their coats close around their bodies and bent their heads into the wind, scarves firmly wrapped over their faces. At the main door they kissed and parted to their respective laboratories.

\* \* \*

Ru was at his desk, deep at work, when the head of department called him over. "You're wanted in the Director's office, now!"

It was the first time he had seen the Director since his first day at the Institute and Ru was puzzled. Walking through the long corridors, his brain raced. What could it be about? Was it his work? No, he was doing fine, keeping head down and mouth shut; he was proud that he had not questioned anything for some time. Was it to do with Mei Lien? Perhaps the old concierge had reported them to the authorities; it was well-known they did not take well at scientists being close and, specially, co-habitating. They had made no trouble, were quiet, so it couldn't be any complaints from the old man. He shuddered, surely not about the foreigners visiting? That was months ago. Their trip to Hong Kong? No, unless they had been spotted with their new friends. Or was it that they had found out about Mei Lien's big shopping spree and thought they were involved in something illegal; if that was the case, they were both in trouble; deep trouble.

He turned the corner and stopped dead. At the Director's door the secretary was talking to Mei Lien. She spotted him and waved nervously. "Hi," she said in a little voice, "this is a surprise".

The secretary knocked on the door of Director Tao Wey-Ming and entered immediately, closely followed by the two scientists. Once the door had closed and they were left alone, Tao Wey-Ming waved them to a couple of chairs and motioned them to sit down.

"Thank you for coming so quickly," he started. "I know you are both very busy and, by the way, my colleagues and I are most satisfied with your work."

Both silently sighed in relief.

"Thank you, Director," croaked Ru.

"I'm sorry we have not yet been able to send you to Lanzhou but unfortunately things have not gone to plan. Eminent Professor Huai is working hard to put things right; it will be some time before we can send you to help with the final tests". He smiled and nodded. "I understand you both speak English fluently."

Mei Lien nodded and Ru added, "Miss Chow is far more proficient than I am, I only started a year ago".

"Very modest Mr Nuang and very nice of you but, by all accounts, you can hold a proper and difficult conversation. Your teacher at night school speaks very highly of you."

Ru sat silently – what don't they know? - he thought.

"What I am about to tell you is top secret," continued Wey-Ming. "The Chinese government have invited several eminent American scientists and military experts to come over and visit one of our laboratories. This way we hope to prove to the world that we are serious about doing our part in helping curb rogue states developing dangerous weapons of mass destruction." He looked at the young couple intently. "We need trusted scientist with fluent English to act as interpreters and to send out the right sort of message. Of course, if you can find out what they are doing, even better. You both, for your expertise, discretion and mastery of the language, have been selected. It is of course, a very big honour and you should be extremely proud to be chosen."

The young scientist sat in silence digesting what they had just been told. Ru was the first to speak. "Thank you very much Director, it certainly is a great honour. We will do our best to obtain as much information as possible. We are both very appreciative of the trust you and the Government are showing us. When is this meeting to take place?"

"Next month, on the 15th, at our laboratory in Wuhan. It's the smallest and least important centre but will give the impression that we are serious. Again, I must remind you, this is a sensitive matter and no one, absolutely no one, should know or suspect anything, you understand".

They both nodded. "Can I ask who the other of our scientist will be?" Mei Lien asked.

"There will be no one from here, just the Director of the laboratory in Wuhan, Mr Chi Tao and yourselves; you will have to go there a couple of days before and get to learn about all the projects. We don't deem it necessary to take our top scientist away from their highly important work. Tao Wey-Ming stood up signalling the end of the meeting. As they reached door he spoke again, "discretion is key, do not talk to anyone, and do not tell anyone where you are going. I will make all necessary travel arrangements and let you know in due course when you will leave."

Outside in the corridor the secretary looked at them with pity. Obviously, he thought they were in trouble and had been hauled up in front of his boss for a dressing down or worse. He looked puzzled as the young couple made their way back giggling, arm in arm.

\* \* \*

Back at the flat the atmosphere was electric; both Ru and Mei Lien were on a high as they closed the door, and they threw their arms around each other. "Wow what a day," she exclaimed.

"Certainly was,", said Ru. "I don't know about you but when I got the message to go to the Director's office my knees went weak, and my stomach felt like someone had stabbed me."

"I was sure we were in trouble; couldn't make up my mind if it had to do with our visitors or going to Hong Kong. Deep down I knew it was not to tell us we were being sent to check on the tests".

"It's all very secret and we will have to be ultra-cautious who we see and what we do. They will be watching us like hawks so we must ensure we don't meet with anyone."

"I just pray Pearl or anyone like that doesn't call on us, or ring," she said worriedly.

"Don't think about it and stress yourself too much; all will be fine.". He took her in his arms and kissed her.

# CHAPTER 17

# Washington

Jack had decided to take a few days off and returned to Washington with Hank and Joe. The visit served two purposes: have a few days back on home soil and follow up on his colleagues' progress. He didn't like the Brits getting the better of him and had to try to get things moving. He made the decision after the first day of the meeting, not that he distrusted his "boss" and friend, just that he needed to inject some impetus into the investigation, especially after what they had just learned. His companions were oblivious to the real reason of the sudden change and were simply happy to have their old pal as a travel companion.

Hank marched into his office and, waving Carter to follow, slammed the door behind them. "What the fuck are you playing at Carter?" he roared. "I told you to go through your findings with a fine-tooth comb and ensure you did not miss anything."

"I did sir, trawled through every file I could find and checked everything, as you asked."

"Well, why the hell did you not tell me about the three Chinese owned laboratories. I had to be told about them by the Brits and pretend I knew; made me look a bloody incompetent fool and it's all your damned fault, it's just not good enough."

"I'm sorry but..."

"Just get the hell out of here," roared Hank.

At that moment Jack walked in and looked at both men. "Hey, calm down and lay off the poor boy; sure he did his best". Turning to Carter he nodded towards the door. The aide couldn't get out quick enough.

"It's bloody well not good enough, he's fucking useless."

Jack shook his head. "The trouble with you Hank is that you expect too much. Just remember; you were his age and a trainee at one stage, cut him some slack."

Hank looked glum. "How did we miss the fact that three, not one, not two but three of our most prominent research centres are Chinese owned?" His eyes gleamed and his cheeks were flushed, "someone had to know," he blurted out.

"Right, and no offence to you, but it would be a good idea to let Joe get on with his job and stop interfering." Hank remained silent. "I know you want to do your best but let the man do his job; cut him some slack, too. He's been around for years, has masses of investigative experience and is discreet. I trust him and so do you. As for Carter, he's not your problem - leave him to Joe".

Hank sat silently for a while before giving out a sigh, guess I've lost it Jack, thought I still had it but all this has proved I'm only good at a desk job, even then I'm not very good." He looked over to his friend, "you know, I was excited at first, but as time went on and no one wanted to talk to me, I got frustrated and lost heart".

"Nah, don't say that Hank. You were, and are, a great operator, way better than me. I was good at the heavy stuff, the shoot-outs. You were always better when it came to smooth talking your way out of a situation," he smiled.

Hank snorted. "Yeh, well somebody had to do it, you were never a smarmy bastard, subtlety was never your forte. Planning was mine".

Jack nodded in agreement. "Get on the blower to Joe and get him in. We should work on a proper plan of action. You, my friend, your task in all this, is to collate all the info and sit behind that desk checking the facts. Leave the poor Carter kid to Joe and stop yelling at him."

"Thought I was the boss here, not you! You're right though, I've been behind a desk for too long - best part of ten years - and have got good at reports, but obviously not checking things; must get my act together." He picked up the phone and dialled Joe's number.

An hour later the three men were deep in discussion. "Sounds pretty scary; sure the hell don't like the thought all these places being in foreign hands."

Hank leaned forward and cracked his fingers "we, I, want you to look into all these research laboratories, especially the three mentioned, and find out as much as possible. Names of the people who run them, who works there and how exactly they are financed; anything and everything."

"We all agree that looking into the professor and his involvement comes as a priority, so start with those three and see where it leads; you may discover other strings to his bow," Jack continued.

Joe nodded, "that shouldn't be too difficult and will only take a week or so, I'll get started straight away. I'll keep you both posted."

They all rose and started to make their way to the door when Jack put his hand on Joe's shoulder. "Give young Carter a break; don't be like Hank."

Joe looked quizzically, "what do you mean?"

"Just trust him, help him; don't take him for granted."

"I don't ,but he's useless. Why are these youngsters so darned inept?"

"Not useless, just green, inexperienced, that's all. Hank isn't the best teacher and has no patience and I think it would do the boy some good to be with a true professional," he winked.

Joe shrugged, "Yeah, ok. Don't seem to have any option, do I? But I ain't being a nursemaid if it gets rough."

"Great, that's solved." Turning to Hank ,"look, this will give the boy some proper training and you - you will avoid getting yourself a heart attack".

That night Jack flew out of Washington back to London, his planned break forgotten.

\* \* \*

## London

Sean walked out of the monthly briefing along with the other twenty operatives working in different departments and on other cases. At these meetings the "Boss" gave them the low down on any up-coming concerns, and everyone had to give a short presentation, describing any progress made with their particular operation. Further discussion would then be held face to face with the man at the helm. Nothing dramatically new was on the horizon and most of the meeting was taken up by the continued high terrorist threat in London and other large UK cities. Sean did not expand much on what he was working on, playing down the operation and keeping things vague. He did not have enough to get everyone excited and set off alarm bells, well at least not for now. He made his way over to his friend with the raspy voice and asked if he could share his office for the rest of the day.

The young man nodded, "sorry, I I've not been able to find anything for you, just been so busy with the Salisbury case" he said apologetically. "On a brighter note, it seems that particular problem is nearing its end, so if you would like me to look into anything I would be more than happy."

"That would be great. The investigation has stalled a bit, but we've found out more about the professor; another pair of eyes and ears would be great."

Sean sat at one of the spare desks and switched on the computer. He trawled through the numerous e-mails, deleting most without reading them. One especially caught his eye and he clicked the "open" button with anticipation; it came from his new friend, Jimmy, head of the Hong Kong office. A quick scan and he leant back and sighed, then sat up as he continued to glance through the report. The mail advised him that Ru and Mei Lien had been in Hong Kong and contact had been made by Pearl who had "accidently" bumped into the couple. She had learned of their planned break from her Beijing contact. They had the couple followed from the minute they landed and were confident they had no suspicion it had been set up. The message continued by saying that both scientists were to be married and that they were being sent to Wuhan as main interpreters for the forthcoming visit by the American delegation.

Now, that was interesting! His excitement grew as he read on. According to the contact, both were going to test some new discovery at the plant in Lanzhou but unforeseen problems and delays had postponed this. It was hoped to send them there soon after. He wondered if Jack knew this. The message also stated that China was going to use the American visit as a major media coup to show the world that they were open and willing to co-operate. Sean looked up and was about to tell his colleague when his mobile rang. Glancing at it, he quickly picked up, "James, my old friend, this is a surprise, I was just about to phone you".

"More of a surprise for me. Thought you never answered your mobile; going soft in your old age," he chuckled.

`Interesting stuff has come through from our people in Hong Kong; think it's worth we get together for a catch up. Tomorrow? Fine - usual time at the office," and he hung up.

James was left holding a dead phone. He shook his head and sighed; London here we come again.

Sean looked over to the man across the desk, "do you know anything, or have you heard about a visit by the Americans to China in the next few weeks"?

The man shook his head.

"Could you find out from your contact on the US desk who the Americans are sending; that would be a great help."

A rasped, "no problem" came back.

Returning to his e-mail Sean wrote a reply thanking Jimmy for his up-date.

\* \* \*

Jack's plane landed early. He made his way to the Embassy by his own means as the Icelandic and Washington visit had been unofficial and off the record.

The morning was taken up with paperwork and chairing a meeting of his team. The main theme of the day was possible terrorist attacks on London and, most probably, New York. The word of the day was to be vigilant; he was expecting to put everyone on amber alert later that day after reports from two of his main agents. Washington was advised. Internet and radio Intercepts were pointing to increasing violence, and vigilance was paramount. Practically his entire force was now working night and day on the potential threat and both nations were about to be put on high alert; something very nasty was brewing. It was past 5pm when the phone rang and he heard Joe's voice, "Jack, got some news, are you on a secure line?"

After confirmation that all was safe Joe continued, "found out who the American team is to visit China," he said excitedly.

"Gee, you don't waste time do you Joe," exclaimed an astonished Jack.

"Easy when you know who to ask and how to ask," came the southern drawl. "Got a pen and paper?"

"Right, there are three Generals which is nothing surprising, three scientists working for the OSRD and two independent scientists chosen by that organisation. The three OSDR guys are well known and advise the Government on the stance the US should take in case of an outbreak of SARS for example."

"Anyone, we know?" asked Jack.

"No, none are on the radar but what is really interesting are that the two other guys, the independents, one works for Beacon Pharmaceuticals and the other for SACS Laboratories".

"What!" croaked Jack, "You must be joking. Are you sure?"

"One hundred percent, both owned by the Chinese."

Jack was at a loss for words. "Hey, you still there, buddy?" asked Joe.

"Yeah, sorry, just digesting what I've just heard.

"Ok, will call you again when I have anything else, and, hey! I'll wire you over confirmation of the names asap."

Jack sat in his chair for a long time before picking up the phone and dialling Sean's number.

\* \* \*

James sat across the desk, a large mug of steaming coffee in his hand, listening to Sean's new discoveries. "It's incredible," continued Sean, "a man like the professor with so many hands in so many pots. Wonder how he managed to get himself and his buddy on to the tour".

"Money," said James, "just money my friend, bribes I guess, he can afford it".

"What do you mean, he can afford it?"

"Well, he's on 250K a year retainer from the Government as an advisor, add a further £250.000 salary from his two UK laboratories; he can certainly afford a few thousand in the right places".

"How do you know all that?" asked Sean incredulously.

"Ah, well, you see, I've this friendly accountant who is semi-retired like me, used to work for a big city out-fit, I happened to ask him how I would find out about such things, and he offered to help. It took him about a week."

"You and your friends and contacts! A quiet chap like you. Who would believe it!"

James ignored the dig and continued, "he also told me that it wouldn't surprise him if he wasn't being paid other monies into an off-shore company".

"Why did he think that?"

"It seems his little abode up in St. Andrews is not the only place he owns: he has a big flat here in London and he owns a villa in Spain, one in the south of France and a pad in Florida. Even with a mortgage it's difficult to see how he can afford these places on what he earns."

Sean sat silently for a while before picking up the phone, "I'm going to call one of my contacts at HMRC and see what he can find out".

"Oh, you have contacts, too!"

Sean stuck his tongue out and screwed up his nose. After a lengthy conversation he replaced the phone in its cradle, "there, that's done. Should take a day or two and then we should know if you're right or not. Use him occasionally when we're working on drug gangs," he mentioned off-hand.

# CHAPTER 18

# China

Ru and Mei Lien walked arm in arm; they manoeuvred their way across the wide avenue avoiding the onrush of traffic and bikes before making for the massive gates that lead into the research centre. At the main door they were met, to their surprise, by Wang, the Director's secretary. He summoned them over and led them to a secluded corner of the vast hall. He handed them an envelope and in a melodramatic hushed voice, "Miss Chow, Mr Nuang, here are your tickets for your trip; you are leaving tonight so the Director has asked me to tell you to take the day off to prepare". He bowed slightly and continued, "I'm to remind you not to tell anyone where you are going or what you are doing. You will not need to sign in and you do not require any further papers, all is here in the envelope". He turned and was about to leave when Ru spoke.

"How long will we be gone? Who do we meet when we get there?" he asked.

Wang simply shrugged, "it's all in there," pointing to the large manilla folder Ru was holding.

The young couple looked at each other perplexed but excited. Back at the flat they opened the file and read through it. From the information given they had a couple of seats booked on a train leaving for Wuhan that evening; the journey would take just over fourteen hours. On arrival they were to proceed to the Hotel Imperial before making their way to the Laboratory to meet its director at 4pm sharp. Also included in the envelope was sufficient cash to see them over their stay. By all accounts they were going to be away for a week. Watching Mei Lien count the money and divide it between them Ru looked at her, "now, that is not for shopping and buying new clothes," he grinned.

She stuck her tongue out at him and grimaced, "not much hope finding anything of quality in that dump".

They spent the rest of the day packing and sorting the apartment, then decided to go and buy some food as if, by chance, anything was provided on the train, it would be inedible.

After arriving at the station in plenty of time and settling into their hard, uncomfortable seats, they prepared themselves for the fourteen-hour journey. Before the train pulled out a woman, whos' age was difficult to guess, and a man, who they presumed was her husband, came and sat in the seats beside them. Nothing was said, there was no reaction to Ru and Mei Lien's greeting; it was as if the pair did not exist. Fine by Ru, he did not want to get into a discussion or answer any questions. His future wife, however, was put out and mouthed her contempt.

Shortly after the train pulled out of the station the ticket controller, a large, sour-faced woman, appeared and demanded to see tickets and passes. She glanced quickly at the old couple's papers and stuck out her hand for Ru and Mei Lien's. She looked dubiously at the two tickets proffered by the young woman and scrutinised both credentials with a disapproving look. "How come you're in this carriage," she eventually asked; "It's reserved for officials and special guests." She turned the paper over and over and shook her head, "this doesn't look right. I I'm calling security".

Mei Lien and Ru looked at each other and noticed the older couple were studiously reading. Eventually Ru retrieved the manilla envelope from his case and pulled out the Directors' official letter, headed and typed on Chinese National Institute of Virology and Microbiology paper. It advised whoever concerned that Mr Ru Nuang and Miss Mei Lien Chow were on official business. The fat woman was not convinced but hesitated, weighing up whether to call her superior and be praised if her suspicions were right, or demoted, lose her job even, if she was wrong. Eventually she opted to accept that these two could stay and reluctantly handed back their papers. She would, nevertheless, make some discreet enquiries, just in case.

Left alone in the company of the couple Ru and Mei Lien settled in for a long, uncomfortable night. Dawn was breaking when the train suddenly came to a halt in the middle of vast fields. People woke and peered out only to be greeted by miles of green and lush landscape. They stayed there for a good forty to fifty minutes before the train slowly started to inch its way forward. Two hours later they limped their way into the station and came to a grinding halt. No one had been told anything and when the older woman had asked the controller she shrugged and moved on.

Ru and Mei Lien headed quickly to the exit and grabbed the first motorised rickshaw available. Being so late they decided to head straight to the laboratory which was on the outskirts of the city. Like in Beijing, the streets were busy with a mass of trucks, buses, cyclists and people all jostling for position. It was not a nice place, no nice buildings, just large concrete blocks, soulless and grey. Eventually they pulled up outside an imposing modern complex protected and surrounded by iron railings. The main entrance was guarded by two ferocious looking guards you definitely didn't want to get on the wrong side of. Handing over their papers to one of the soldiers, they waited until he emerged from the small hut. His colleague, a particularly ill-tempered looking man, kept a close eye on the two visitors. At last, soldier number one came out and nodded. Handing back the papers he pointed to a large glass door.

The lobby was a vast marble hall covered by a massive glass dome in the centre, the walls were decorated with symbols and fake mathematical figures supposedly representing research. Making their way over to the desk they were intercepted by a tall, thin man sporting an impeccable suit, his thinning hair neatly combed back. As he approached, he stuck out his hand and, with a broad smile and a cheery voice greeted them. "You must be Miss Chow and Mr Nuang; welcome to Wuhan and to my institute of research. My name is professor Chi Tao and I am the director of this place."

Introductions over Ru bowed slightly, "nice to meet you professor; please excuse us, we are a little early, but our train was over two hours late and we didn't think we had time to go to the hotel first".

"No problem at all Mr Nuang. You came by train," he said sounding surprised.

"Yes, our director has very kindly organised everything, we are extremely grateful to him".

Chi Tao laughed out loud, his voice echoing around the hall. "Grateful! You are too kind. The mean dog! –he is a good friend of mine by the way - was just thinking of how much he can save so that he can pocket the difference. How long did it take?"

"Just short of seventeen hours," Mei Lien replied, "and on very hard seats," she smiled.

"Terrible, just terrible. I will have a word with him. You must be exhausted, so I suggest you go to the hotel, freshen up and get some rest; be back here tomorrow for 8am." Remembering something he added, "what cesspit has he booked you into?"

"Hotel Imperial," said Mei Lien.

"Oh, that's not bad, sounds better than it is. You shouldn't get bitten too much," he grinned. "Do you know where our American guests are staying?"

Both shook their heads, "no we weren't told".

Before parting he led them over to the desk and handed them a couple of badges and a sheet of paper. "This is for tomorrow, show the badges and papers to the guards and they 'll let you in with no problem." He took them to the main door and bade them farewell.

The next morning the pair were in the hall well on time and waited for Chi Tao to come and meet them. The Centre was busy with throngs of workers arriving for their shifts. Mei Lien turned to Ru "nice place. I like it and so different to where we are; I'm really looking forward to our tour".

Just then the director came striding towards them. "Well, I must say you are both looking much better this morning. I trust you had a good night's rest. Come, follow me," he said jovially.

Two hours later they arrived back in the lobby having been shown round every part of the research centre. "Let's go to the canteen and have some tea. We can chat about the next few days and I will try to answer your questions." Chi Tao and Mei Lien made their way over to a table while Ru went to get the refreshments. "I'm sorry, but I never, or as rarely as possible, have people in my office. I always eat and have my tea here, with everyone else. I expect to do the same with all my visitors. I like to be open and approachable and don't like secrets."

Mei Lien nodded politely. "But surely some things are too sensitive to discuss here where everyone can hear?"

"Nothing should be too secretive but if there is a problem or, as you say sensitive, I prefer to discuss it in the lab or my office with all concerned present. Research related topics stay in the laboratories, always!" he said pointedly. "I don't discuss private lives or individuals, that's not my domain. If there is a problem with one my researchers or any of my workers, it is taken up by the Centre's HR department and its director."

Ru arrived with the tray and sat down. Chi Tao turned to him, "Mr Nuang, our visitors will be landing tomorrow and are expected here the following day at 10am. I understand you are both fluent in English, something I am not, so I will be relying on you greatly. I am also told that you are both very highly regarded scientists", he paused and smiled. "So, I will require you to explain to our American friends what our work consists of here in Wuhan, sufficiently for them to know and feel we are being open and helpful, but guarding from giving them too much. A difficult juggling exercise when you are with experienced peers."

"What sort of thing are you going to show them?" asked Ru.

"We have several experiments going on at present, mostly involving genetics and viruses, but they are small and relatively un-important. "However," he continued "there is one which is slightly different; this is taking place in block 6 but we are not going anywhere near there; it is far too sensitive. If asked, you can tell them it is closed for maintenance between experiments. All the personnel have been given two days off and told to stay away."

There was a short silence before Mei Lien spoke ,"how many of your scientists will be coming round with us?"

"None. You are the only ones. The scientists in the labs have been given specific instructions not to talk; anything said to them or by them must go through you. I repeat, none of them are to speak unless it is in Chinese and through you".

"Do we know how many visitors are expected?" asked Ru.

"Nine Americans and five of our people from Beijing, my deputy and myself, that way things are even."

"Can I ask who the people from Beijing are?" asked Mei Lien.

"They are all government officials. We must put on a good show and make it look as if we mean business. Of course, there will be the media, but they will remain in the entrance hall once the official photoshoot has taken place and await our return for more pictures."

All three were in no doubt that all of the officials would be from the secret police or some such organisation. You can't have foreign visitors and leave them alone with locals, that would be far too dangerous. Both Ru and Mei Lien asked further questions relating to the work and what they would be showing. Both were handed notes of the experiments which they had to memorise and were instructed to speak and act as if they worked at the centre. Finally, after an hour or so and several more pots of tea, Chi Tao got up, signalling the end of the meeting.

On the way back to his office he was composing his report to Beijing on the two scientists. He liked them, liked them a lot. They were both intelligent and articulate but what he liked most was the openness and enthusiasm; so refreshing. He had to be careful not to be too gushing. He was trying to figure how to get then transferred permanently to his department.

\* \* \*

Security was tight when Ru and Mei Lien arrived the next morning. Both had slept badly, worried they would not be up to the task. Positioning themselves just behind the laboratory's three directors and a couple of local officials, they waited at the door of the vast lobby. A cavalcade of vehicles soon appeared, the American and Chinese flag fixed on either front wing. Stopping in front of the building the drivers jumped out and held open the doors.

# CHAPTER 19

# London

Another e-mail from Jimmy in Hong Kong, this time it was short. *Your two scientists have arrived in Wuhan Tuesday. American delegation landed there this afternoon. Two extra visitors on list, last minute additions, will find out who.*

Sean sat back and wondered who the two extra scientists were. Ok, Jack had told him that someone from Beacon and SACS had been included. Who were they and who arranged the last-minute change? It would not be taken well in China and they would have to get someone to attend also. In China it was equal numbers or even better, one more for them, never the other way round.

He turned his attention to the thin file in front of him. His contact at HMRC had had it couriered over that morning. James's friend was right, the professor had indeed several properties of high value, all owned by an offshore company based in Panama. He was a director and managed these properties for a third party and everyone was in doubt as to who that party was. The problem was how to prove it. The professor did not seem to be receiving any extra payments for his work and there was no paper trace leading to him. The contact was going to dig deeper, but it could take time.

Sean's e-mail pinged and he looked over – Jimmy again. *The extra members of the delegation are a Professor Edward Howard of SACS*

*Laboratories in Texas and John Freeman of Star Laboratories, England. Let me know if you need anything else.*

Sean sat up, eyes boggling. It had flashed through his mind but had discarded it quickly, convinced that the members of the party would all be US scientists and not some English professor and his side kick. He picked up the phone.

"James! thought you should be first to know; you and your friend are totally right; our professor is involved in those properties through a Panamanian company. He's a director and manages the operations although no payments are made to him directly. My contact at HMRC is delving deeper."

"That was quick," replied James. "I have something else, also. My friend, the ex-bank manager, has a nephew working high up in Barclays and they just happened to be chatting about money laundering, when his nephew told him about a client. The man, a professor, had received not long ago a payment of £500.000 and, by that afternoon, the amount had been transferred out again; the bank is investigating but he is a long-standing client. I have asked if he could get a name and more information; did not tell him of course what we are working on, just said I was writing a book about money laundering".

"Well done, Jamesie, you're turning out to be a top investigator; let me know as soon as you hear anything. Just received an e-mail from our Hong Kong office that your son's ex-girlfriend and her fiancé have arrived in Wuhan and,", he paused a second, "here is the biggie - we have a name for the two extra delegates that joined at the last minute". Again, he paused a few seconds for effect, "guess who it is? Yes - our friend Edward Howard. Not only that but the second person, it seems is John Freeman who works for Star Laboratories."

There was a long whistle followed by a short silence. "How the hell did they get themselves invited? The man must have some mighty contacts."

"For sure he must, I'm wondering if that payment you just mentioned, has anything to do with it.".

"I'll try to push things along with my banker friend,", said James. "Think it is getting urgent we get a proper picture."

"That would be a great help Jamesie, things are moving fast. It may be an idea if you came up to London again and we meet our American friend."

"No problem, just let me know when. By the way Sean, I I'm most surprised at you; for a man who hates telephones you seem to be using it a lot these days, not to mention e-mail," said James sarcastically.

"Needs must my friend, needs must. I hate doing it but, as we don't have pigeons anymore and you don't have an encrypted line, I have no choice. Come up as soon as possible, early preferably."

Sean picked up his mobile and rang Jack's private phone. "Think we should meet tomorrow; things are moving fast and lots of goodies are emerging. James is travelling up first thing in the morning."

They agreed to meet at Sean's office at 11.30am.

\* \* \*

## Washington

Hank sat at his desk reading through the report that had come through from Joe. It was detailed and had a list of all research centres and laboratories based in the US. At least thirty more names had been added with addresses, contact details and a description of the sort of work they did. Amazing, he thought; how did the man manage to produce such a comprehensive list in such a short space of time. He felt depressed. How come he and Carter could not? A sense of failure hung over him once again and his mood darkened. Should he give up, resign, retire to the cabin he had up in the Blue Mountains. Almost thirty years of operations chasing bad guys, of risking his life and a great deal more here in the office; he had paid his dues, it was time to go. Then he thought of Jack and now Joe, both slightly older and both still going strong and still with the same enthusiasm; how did they do it? What drove them he wondered? He would dearly love to know the secret. His thoughts were rudely interrupted by the buzz of his phone. He looked down and sighed.

"Hi Brian, how's it going?" he enquired.

"Just wondering what news you have of operation opium, if any?" came the cool, aloof voice.

"It's going well, we're gathering lots of information and are getting a good picture. Seems the Chinese are big players, bigger than we thought."

"How's Jack doing in London? Haven't heard a peep from him since he left."

"Fine, busy and liaising with me. Did you know the Chinese have invited a delegation from here to visit one of their laboratories?"

"Yes, have known that for some time, although", he hesitated slightly, " I don't know who's on the list; happening soon I think".

"It's happening now, Brain. Shame you didn't tell me; it would have been nice to know."

"Sorry, slipped my mind. Ok, well done, keep up the good work and keep me posted." The phone went dead.

Hank shook his head; "pig headed bastard," he said under his breath. Slipped his mind indeed! What kind of boss forgets to tell his second in command info like that. "Bastard," he repeated. The phone buzzed again - it was Joe.

"Got something interesting and pretty disturbing. Need to see you urgently, Hank, but not at the office."

They met an hour later in Hanks' house and settled down at the kitchen table.

"What's up Joe? You sounded pretty secretive and cagey on the phone."

"I was digging around the three labs owned by the Chinese and came up with several things which are curious, to say the least. Firstly, all three are run by the same man, an English professor by the name of Edward Howard. He apparently runs these companies on behalf of the Chinese and gets paid a small salary. However, he is known for his lavish lifestyle, and has expensive houses and condos in Florida, Texas and California".

"How did you find that out?" asked Hank.

"Easy, although none of them are in his name; they all belong to a real estate corporation that is ultimately owned by a trust based in the Bahamas. The beneficiary of the trust is, again, a certain Edward Howard, resident of the United Kingdom. My guess is that the Chinese pay his main salary and other "dividends" into the trust."

"Can we prove any of it?"

"Am sure that if we inform the IRS they should be able to come up with a case. Problem is, I don't have any contacts there. Not sure either if they can do anything as he is a British citizen."

"Let's talk to Jack first and work out a plan of action and then I'll call my contact at the IRS," replied Hank.

"Another point, and this is a sensitive one; the professor is extremely friendly with Frank Campese who sits on all 3 of the boards."

"THE Frank Campese, vice president of the Senate Committee for Research?" said Hank incredulously.

"Yep, that's the man. Seems he is employed as a PR man and spends a lot of time promoting the various vaccines these labs produce."

"Thought they were only research labs."

"Those three are but they are all connected to BND Pharmaceuticals who, as you know, produce more than half the vaccines sold here in the US."

"Are you telling me that the Chinese also own BND?" squeaked Hank.

Joe nodded. "Fully financed and owned. Clever though, because BND is owned by a venture capital outfit in Japan who in turn is owned by the Chinese State."

Hanks was silent for a minute before shaking his head, "sure makes sense, when you think of it. And yes, in fact I have heard Frank on TV, promoting and banging on about how important it is to buy from BND and support a great American corporation."

"Wouldn't mind betting he's being paid handsomely too. Haven't had time to dig there yet but will get to work on it."

"Fantastic work Joe, I'll contact Jack and put him the picture."

They parted and Hank made his way back to the office feeling like a happy man.

\* \* \*

## London

All three men were sitting in the small, cramped office and Jack had perched himself on the corner of Sean's desk.

Jack was the first to speak. "Had a call from Hank last night, big developments and news, all about your professor but it goes further than that." He then proceeded to tell them what Joe had found out.

"It all ties in with what James has found out, seems he is working on several fronts. You know he is in China with your delegation? I also learnt that he is accompanied by a John Freeman who is his side kick in Star Laboratories based here in the UK."

Jack got up and paced the small office, "what about we all meet up again, sooner rather than later? There's so much stuff we need to sit round a table and bring it all together, decide how to proceed. Shame we can't do it over the phone but it's not safe."

"Thinking of another visit to Iceland? It's closer for Hank and it's neutral ground," suggest Sean.

"Yeah, sounds good. Will get Joe to join us also, and I hope you can make it, James."

James nodded his agreement.

"Great, let's all meet up there on Friday so we can be back in the office Monday. Same routes for everyone and same hotel?"

They all agreed. Sean suggested they went across the road to the small Italian and have some lunch. Both James and Jack nodded enthusiastically.

Outside the restaurant Sean turned to his friend, "you Ok to come Jamesie? I know we are asking a lot from you. Remember what I said. Any time you want out, just say. We'll all understand."

"Looking forward to it and more than happy to come along," replied James. "Anything you want me to do or look into between now and then?"

"Not really, just try and get some more info on those transactions. Meet you at Heathrow Friday morning. I'll book the flights and the hotel. After all you've done, it's the least the Firm can do."

\* \* \*

Three days later they were all sitting round the table in the Odinsve Hotel conference room. After summing up what was known Sean turned to the man sitting on his right. "Joe, have you anything new?" he enquired.

"Yeah! As you know, I found out that the Vice President of the Senate Committee for Research, Frank Campese, is employed as a PR man for one of our leading manufacturers of vaccines in the US. BND is owned indirectly by the Chinese and for several years Frank has been pushing their products and ensuring that other, probably better vaccines made in the UK or France are discredited. Of course, he gets paid handsomely for this - not directly, his official salary is US$ 40.000 - but through an off-shore Panamanian company called REALXA Inc. He looked round the table before continuing, "I've asked Hank's contact at the IRS to have a discrete look into this and give me more information; it should only take a week or so."

Sean nodded, "seems to follow a pattern". He turned to his friend, "James, here has some new information also".

"Well, like you, I've been looking into our professor and it seems that he too, gets paid through an off-shore trust. The other day a friend of mine told me his son, who works at Barclays noticed, not for the first time, a large sum entering his account and then a few hours later it was transferred out. It seems the trust is set up in Panama and has himself as sole beneficiary. After some delving it transpired that the funds came from the National Bank of China branch in London." The others nodded in approving style. "Just yesterday, my friend called me to say the same Barclay account had been credited with a further US$ 250.000 and 200k had been moved on to the same account in Panama."

"Busy guy this professor of yours," Hank chipped in.

James nodded, "Yes, but what is interesting, is that the latest funds came from the Novotny Bank in London".

There was a long silence. Jack found his voice first. "You mean he's also being paid by the Russians? for what?"

James continued, "Certainly, we know he works for them as well," he looked over at Hank, "I told you at our last meeting. The prof is involved in three labs ultimately owned and financed by the Russians and it seems these payments are made regularly every two months. Up until now the bank has never questioned these as they have been going on for years."

Sean interjected, "a few months back we went to talk to the prof up in Scotland and we asked him about what he knew about the Chinese. He was emphatic they were out of the picture and totally adamant the

Russians were the baddies, and all the time he has been working for them. It makes sense now we know all this other stuff."

"The bastard is playing a double game," said Hank grimly, "hope he gets what he deserves".

"Do we know if they are all in contact with each other?" asked Jack.

Sean scratched his nose, "too early to say but I wouldn't be surprised. What is certain, they are all playing a big game and for big cash."

"I have some more news too," Joe butted in. "One of my sources told me that there could be a second US official implicated; don't know his name yet or if he is actually involved, but it seems Frank has been in contact with him and that they are both actively obstructing any ideas or new vaccines coming out of the UK and Europe. My contact believes this person is placed high up in the US hierarchy and will let me know asap."

"Any hints to who he or she is?" asked Jack.

Joe shook his head, "no, only heard a couple of days ago; too early yet, but it won't be long until my contact finds out".

Hank exhaled a deep, long sigh. "So, what we're going to do?" he enquired.

Sean took the question quickly, "It's too early to do anything, and if we want to find out more, we'll have to let them run and see where it leads. In the meantime, I suggest we keep a close eye on all of them and especially keep tabs on their financial transactions."

"Agree," said Jack. "We don't have enough on them yet, but things seem to be moving fast. Let's see what the IRS and your revenue people come up with. That way we can hope to pick them up on tax evasion and money laundering at the very least."

They all nodded their approval. James who had kept silent for much of the discussion cleared his throat, "I would just love to know what the prof is doing in China and how he got invited. I can't help thinking that one of your team, either a scientist or a military is involved also." He saw Hank's jaw tighten and that he was about to jump up and start one of his rants so put up his hand and quickly continued, "no, I am not accusing anyone, and I I'm sure I'm barking up the wrong tree, it is just a gut feeling I have, sorry."

Hank sat back and stared ,"Ok, but I don't go by gut feelings, as you well know, just facts and I sure as hell don't like to be told one of our military or politicians is involved in such shady shenanigans."

James nodded and smiled. "Just for general information, I can tell you John Freeman sits on SAGE, the Governments Advisory Board, who collate all the known information and advises the UK Government what to do and how to react in case of serious epidemics such as SARS and the like. He is apparently very widely listened to."

"Well gentlemen, Jack picked up, "I think we are progressing, and I must thank everyone for their work, in particular, you, who is, sorry James, not a professional but is excelling himself. Without him we would not be here now."

All agreed and gave a muted applause. "Now, time to get back to work and see what we can find out. Most important of all we must keep communicating and passing on all new info."

Sean, Jack and James spent the evening at a fish restaurant in the centre of town and drew up a master board of all known facts with names and connections. It was easier to get a picture when it was set out in black and white. By the time they returned to their hotel all three had a clear idea of the scale of the problem.

# CHAPTER 20

# Wuhan

The visiting party were greeted by their hosts; Ru and Mei Lien getting to work immediately with their translation duties. Both found it hard at first understanding the American accent but soon tuned in. Photo opportunities completed, the visitors were ushered into the large entrance hall and offered tea and light refreshments. Everyone was playing the game - fake joviality, poor jokes, and small conversation -until it was time to start the tour.

Mei Lien had noticed that one of the guests seemed to hang back, spoke little, and didn't mix much with the others. She also noted that both extra visitors had English accents and kept themselves slightly apart from the Americans. One in particular, the professor, was dressed in slightly shabbier clothes; his ill-fitting jacket, ever so slightly frayed shirt and his gormless look seemed at odds with the rest of the group. She took an instant dislike to him.

The tour took forever, the Chinese keen to show their counterparts all the various laboratories and at pains to give the impression of passing as much information as possible. Questions were asked and answered, heads nodded. Ru watched all the acting and simulated interest from both sides and could not but wonder whether the foreigners believed, or were interested in, any of it. The military may have been taken in, but the scientists surely knew they were being sold a dummy. It was obvious that the hosts were at great pains to show openness but divulged little. Eventually, the delegations arrived outside laboratory no 6. It was explained that this was closed for maintenance and deep cleaning as, a previous experiment conducted there had finished and as per Chinese efficiency, everything had to be disinfected before new research began. They were asked, not surprisingly, what had been the research and both Ru and Mei Lien explained it was to do with testing a vaccine to stop transmission of disease between Panda Bears which had been requested by the WWF. Yes, something had been found and results would soon be published and shared worldwide. The guests nodded their appreciation for such a worthy cause and complemented the Director.

Finally, both delegations arrived back in the vast entrance hall and after more photo opportunities, handshakes and bowing the visitors were ushered out to the waiting cars. All looked forward to meeting once again the next day when they would attend a conference organised by the WHO.

Chi Tao, The Director, came over and smiled broadly at the two young scientists. "Congratulations and my profound thanks for your hard work today, you did an excellent job. I was told by several of the Americans that you were excellent, and they appreciated your clear explanations." He beamed again.

Ru and Mei Lien bowed slightly, but both doubted his story as he did not speak a word of English and neither had seen him utter a word. Nevertheless, they were pleased at his subtle praises. "We are pleased you are happy with our work and enjoyed it very much," they lied. Both were exhausted and had found the whole thing farcical and a waste of time. "What time do you require us to be on duty tomorrow?" Ru enquired.

"You have the day off; you are not needed at the conference as the proceedings will be translated in all the delegates language - over thirty. I suggest you come back here the day after at say, 8.30 am." He continued ,"and you can start your new work in laboratory 6".

Ru and Mei Lien looked at him in puzzled shock. "Director, we are scheduled to return to Beijing; we were only here for the three days."

Chi Toa laughed, "yes, yes, indeed you were, but I have managed to change all that". He looked at each of them in turn and beamed ,"I have asked for your transfer here on a permanent basis to look into some exciting work being carried out in no 6; it is extremely sensitive. Unfortunately, the lead scientist has fallen ill and will not be back for some time." He smiled triumphantly.

"Sorry Director, we don't understand," said Ru. "No one has told us anything and we have nowhere to stay and don't have any of our equipment."

Mei Lien added, "our passes are only valid another two days and we have very few clothes or cash".

"Don't worry young lady, I have arranged everything. Beijing will issue you with a long-term pass and this establishment will see to it that you have sufficient money to live off and buy some new clothes. Your accommodation has been sorted also; a nice small apartment, very close to here." He bowed his head briefly." As for your equipment, it is on the way and should be with you late tomorrow afternoon. I am so looking forward to having two bright scientists working in my centre."

Ru and Mei Lien muttered their appreciation and thanked Chi Tao for his help and told him how they looked forward to the challenge.

\*    \*    \*

## Hong Kong

Jimmy Wang was sitting at his desk when the phone rang. A familiar voice came on and he cocked his head.

"Good afternoon cousin how are things at home? Grandmother is well as expected," the voice was matter of fact.

"Excellent, I'm glad grandmother's health is holding, thank you."

The voice on the other end continued, "just to let you know the shipment due out today is remaining in Wuhan, and I believe it will be some time before we can send the goods".

Jimmy was surprised but did not change his voice. "That's a shame. I will cancel the container but there will be a cost of course. Do you know the reason?"

"It seems the goods need to be inspected and worked on more in the factory and have not passed the final inspection. I fully understand there will be a cost involved. Send me the invoice when you have it."

"Very well and thanks for letting me know; please keep me up-dated on progress and if you have any news."

"I will. Talk soon, and please send grandmother my best wishes." The phone went dead.

What was happening wondered Jimmy. He did not like sudden changes; mostly they were warnings of bad things to come. Did the two young scientists mess up and had now been demoted? Surely not. he knew they had been asked to act as translators for the American visit. Had they messed up or shown too much interest in them. He was suddenly worried. He swung round to his computer and typed an e-mail to Sean.

\* \* \*

Sean's phoned pinged indicating he had a new e-mail. He read the message from Jimmy. *The two translators are not returning to Beijing, seems they have been told to stay in Wuhan, not sure why, but don't like it. Will keep you posted.*

Sean did not like the development either and wondered, like Jimmy, why the sudden change. He could do nothing but wait to see what his friend in Hong Kong could find out. He let Jack, Hank and James know.

\* \* \*

## Wuhan

Ru and Mei Lien spent that night discussing the turn of events. Neither were happy, and both wondered why the change of plan. They certainly did not believe for a second the story of the sick head scientist and both were suspicious.

"God I hate this place," said Mei Lien. "It's noisy, dirty and a dump; no proper shops and I dread to think where they are putting us."

"Don't fret, I'm sure it has nothing to do with the tour; just old Chi Toa playing bigwigs and playing politics."

"I don't like people playing politics with our lives, it never ends well, and you know it," she retorted.

"Well, it can't be for ever and when all this is over, I promise, I will take you back to Hong Kong so you can buy your wedding dress," he smiled. He took her hands and looked her deep in the eyes, "I love you Mei Lien, more than anything and I will do everything possible to make our stay here as enjoyable, and short, as possible."

She kissed him and nestled up to him. Tomorrow they were moving into the apartment, then a new job, back to normality, but it was not normality. She fell asleep in his arms.

They moved into their new temporary home, or so they hoped it would be, and both were pleasantly surprised at how nice it was. A large airy and bright living room/ kitchen, a good-sized bedroom and a functional bathroom which could have dated back to the 80s. They dumped their meagre belongings and headed for the shops to buy some much need essentials. As Mei Lien had predicted, the stores were full of cheap clothing at relatively expensive prices and the choice was uninspiring. Ru soon got fed up with trawling through the shops and suggested he go and explore, but that was firmly vetoed by his young wife to be. He sighed, resigned, and spent the next few hours getting more and more miserable and ratty.

Both rose early the following morning and were at the research centre for 8.30 as instructed. They were met by the director's secretary who led them to his office where they were warmly greeted by Chi Tao who showed them to a couple of chairs.

"Miss Chow, Mr Nuang, welcome. We will shortly make our way to laboratory No 6 where I will introduce you to the small team working on a top-secret project. As indicated, the professor in charge is indisposed and unable to continue; he has cancer of the throat, so you will be taking over as head of project. I trust you are happy to both be in charge?" he asked with a smile.

Both nodded and grinned at each other. "Of course, Sir, we are deeply sorry to hear about the professor's illness and very honoured you have chosen us to continue his work. We only hope we will be up to the mark," said Ru.

"I have full confidence in both of you. I must say I was worried about who would be able to take over; the team are good but there are no natural leaders, nor has anyone got much experience. You, along with your qualifications, are just what is needed for this task. Now, let's get down to the laboratory and get started". As they left the room Chi Tao turned and in a semi-hushed voice, "I hope you will not have too much trouble; inevitably there may be some suspicion or jealousy, but I'm sure you can sort that out".

They entered laboratory No 6 and were greeted by six pairs of curious eyes. The director made the introductions and showed the pair around their new place of work. "Before I leave, may I remind you that this is a top-secret project. Your job is to finish assessing the data before undertaking final trials and analysis; you have four months to do this. I will leave you to get to know your team and be brought up to date on the project".

After Chi Tao had left Ru and Mei Ling sat down and had a long discussion with the other scientists, explaining what had happened and how they had come to be sitting there. All seemed to accept their reason and soon were bringing the pair up to scratch.

\*   \*   \*

## Hong Kong

Jimmy picked up his phone and once again heard the voice of his contact.

"Hello cousin, how are things at home? Is grandmother still well?"

"Grandmother is feeling much better, thank you. I wanted to up-date you on the shipment," continued the voice. "The goods have been kept at the factory and will be used for testing and further development. We do not know how long this will take or when they will be ready to be exported."

"That's great news, I would be interested to hear how the testing goes and any results. Once you have these please let me know and I will arrange a container and ship."

"A lot is happening here, and I want to keep tabs on the testing and production of the new batch. I will say hello to grandmother for you."

"Great, keep in touch and take care." The phone went dead. Jimmy sat a while thinking and then called Pearl over.

"Just had a call from Tim in Wuhan; seems the young couple have been asked to stay and carry out tests on a new project."

"You want me to go up there and double check?"

He nodded. "Not that I don't trust him, quite the opposite, but you may be able to get closer to the work place and find out what is happening. Avoid, at all cost, contact with him or the two lovers."

She nodded, "I'll be on my way tomorrow, stay three or four days and get back".

"Good, let him know your movements." Jimmy then sent another e-mail giving Sean the up-to-date situation.

# CHAPTER 21

# China

Following the official visit to the laboratory and conference, Edward Howard and John Freeman decide to travel back home separately from the Americans. They had some particularly important private business to see to. They spent the day walking around Wuhan discussing their next move, smiling as they spotted two figures shadowing their every move. Finally, after spending time in a tea house in deep conversation they separated and went their own way.

John Freeman boarded a flight for Vancouver via Shanghai from where he would travel on to Panama before returning to the UK.

Edward Howard was relaxed. He trusted his old friend John implicitly and had suggested that his partner go and check up on their finances and expected payments in person. It never harmed to put in an appearance and remind the faceless lawyers and bankers in Panama what their client looked like occasionally; just to remind them you were alive and well. For his part, he would fly home via Delhi and Moscow. He felt it was time to turn up the pressure on the Russians. After all the hard work and sensitive information they had provided their masters in the Kremlin, it was about time they got recompensed handsomely. For too long now, he and John had covered up and diverted attention to all the murders, successful or botched, undertaken by the President. Time now for some serious talking. With game changing information he was about to tell them, he felt more than confident. Sitting back in his First Class seat, he closed his eyes and smiled to himself.

*   *   *

## Wuhan

As soon as the plane doors had been opened, Pearl made a hasty exit. Once in the main arrivals concourse she headed for the Ladies and found an empty cubicle. She had decided to travel under her own name; her story, if required, was that she was visiting her aged relative. She doubted anyone would question her motive for her visit. Once safely locked in, she quickly changed into a pair of cheap jeans, and pulled on a drab top and a fake leather jacket. She took out her large sunglasses – the fake Gucci ones she had bought in a Hong Kong market – and placed a face mask over nose and mouth. Nothing unusual with that, lots of Chinese wear them to protect them from the smog. She took off the name tag from her bag and replaced it with her new name and swapped the SIM card in her phone to a new one she had purchased before boarding.

She emerged from the cubicle, washed her hands, checked herself in the mirror and walked out heading for the taxi rank. She gave the cab driver the address a block away from her hotel, got in and sat back. She went over her plan. It was simple. Once checked into her hotel, she would head for the laboratory that had hosted the Americans and check out the lay of the ground. She would watch as the scientists and workers left and hopefully, with luck, she would see her two targets and follow them until they led her to where they lived. Jimmy had told her not to contact them, but she had decided to ignore that order. She took out her phone and rang a number.

On the third ring a voice came on and she was quick to talk first, "hello cousin, hope you and grandmother are well. Just to say I'm in Wuhan on a surprise visit as I'm concerned about her health."

"Grandmother is feeling much better and delighted with your decision to come; I'm sure your visit will do her a lot of good. Where are you staying? I'll come and pick you up."

"That's very kind. Can you be at the Asia Hotel for 7.30pm?"

"I will be there. Grandmother will be delighted to see you."

The taxi eventually dropped Pearl off at her destination and once he had driven off, she turned and walked the short distance to check into the Asia Hotel.

After a quick wash, followed by a careful room inspection, she left and headed for the nearest metro station. Twenty-five minutes later she was standing across from the large imposing building housing the research centre and laboratories. She ambled down the street getting her bearings and timed her return for 5pm. She sat down on a bench which offered a good view of the imposing building surrounded by an impressive iron fence, taking note that the main entrance was heavily guarded, as were the three other entrances she had seen.

People began to trickle out, most headed for the metro station, a few jumped on bikes or took the bus. She was confident that her targets would emerge from the main gate, the back and side entrances being mainly for deliveries and menial staff. Pearl was amazed at the number of scientists and people that must work in the place; she had always thought it one of the smaller, lesser important centres.

She was beginning to lose hope when she spotted two figures who she recognised exiting the gates arm in arm; no mistaking the two lovers. She slowly got up from her bench and ambled in their direction, keeping a safe distance. They made their way to the metro and Pearl only just managed to squeeze on to the carriage at the very last moment. After two stops they got off and she followed them for a few minutes until she saw them entering an apartment building. Waiting until they were well inside, she slowly walked on by, noting the number and address. Hesitating, she returned and entered. There was no caretaker or desk, so she went to the large bank of post boxes and quickly found the name Nuang with a number 22 beside it. Smiling she left the building and headed back to the Asia Hotel.

At 7.30pm on the dot a car pulled up and honked its horn. Pearl peered in through the open door and immediately recognised her contact and jumped in.

The driver was a man in his late 50's, jet black hair and a smiling face. Dressed casually he exuded friendliness but behind this relaxed demeanour the deep, cold eyes, showed another person, someone who was calculating, someone who did not flinch at facing danger, a professional spy and killer. As they pulled out into the traffic he turned to his passenger. "Well, you didn't take long to find our targets and discover where they live, I'm impressed!"

Pearl inclined her head and gave a faint smile "how do you know I found them?" she asked.

"I was in the square behind you all the time you were sitting there. Picked you up arriving, walking away down the main street, then returning. It did not take much to figure out you were not a tourist."

"Impressive" she acknowledged. Deep down she was furious with herself. How did she not spot him? Had she been so obvious? "Did you follow me to the flat?"

"No, once I saw you were trailing them and entered the Metro station I knew where you were going so left you to it. "Did you get the flat number?"

She nodded. "How long have you been following them?" she enquired.

"Since they left Beijing, me and my partner were on the train, sitting next to them during the whole journey. They nearly didn't make it."

"How do you mean".

"The conductor, a grumpy, fat biddy did not believe they were entitled to travel in that carriage and almost threw them off. Luckily, the lad produced the official papers stating the reason of the trip. She wasn't convinced but let them stay."

"Why are they staying? We thought they were here just for the American visit."

"It seems that the director has taken a shine to them. Sees them as his ticket to promotion and better things."

"How do you know all that?" Pearl was curious. Tim was good and certainly worked fast.

"My partner got a job in the canteen. Old Chi Tao, the director, loves his tea and always takes it in the canteen. He wants to be thought of as one of the workers. She overheard him talk to the couple and make a phone call, presumably to Beijing, requesting they stayed to oversee a project they are working on."

"You know how long they are likely to stay and what this project is?"

"Have no idea what they are doing. Security, apart from at the gate, is pretty lax but not that bad. I suppose they're staying until they have finished the job in hand. Our brief is to keep track of them and report back."

"I would dearly like to know what it is."

"We do know that they are working in lab No 6, which was closed for the American visit."

"Interesting; must be something pretty important."

"What do you want to eat? You must be starving. There's an ok place not far from here, food is passable; the city hasn't much to offer."

They spent the evening chatting and getting to know each other. Pearl was impressed by the man; he knew his job and was good at it. Born in Hong Kong, he was sent to England to finish his education and whilst there joined the army. He was transferred to Hong Kong and served until the hand over in 1997. He was recruited by the British

Intelligence and after his training he volunteered to be stationed in Beijing. He kept his deep dislike of the Chinese secret but, like so many, his feelings evolved to hatred after a family member was falsely imprisoned and died. The only way he knew to extract justice was to spy on and harm the Chinese machine as much as he could.

Over a cup of tea, he looked up and asked, "what's you plan now you know where they work and live?".

"I want to meet them, and I want to find out what they are working on," Pearl replied.

"Bad idea, very bad idea. The last thing you or they want is for anyone to contact them and put them in danger. Remember this is China, not Hong Kong. There are spies and snitches everywhere. If anyone gets wind of you, or me in fact, these two could be in big danger."

Pearl was silent for a while, thinking back to their meeting with Sean; she had to admit he was right. Jimmy had also instructed her not to make contact.

"What do you think we should do?"

"I think you should return tomorrow, after you have seen your 'Grandmother', and let us continue surveillance. I promise I'll report back regularly and contact you or Jimmy immediately.

Something new happens, we will report, don't worry." He looked over to her and continued, "there's a flight back at 3pm so what about I pick you up at 9am outside the hotel and we go visit Grandmother, at least then we have a proper story, any prying eyes or eavesdropping can report back that indeed you have visited her."

She had to agree with him; no one was safe in this country, and no doubt it would already have been reported that they had been seen together. Better play the game and leave the man to his job. She nodded her agreement.

As they were approaching the Asia Hotel he turned to her, "I know you have taken precautions so don't take this badly, but please do not ring Jimmy, even on your new SIM card. Flush it down the toilet before boarding."

The next morning Pearl was picked up and they drove through to the other side of the city. The area was depressed and crammed with workshops and small factories. He turned down a grit lane and stopped outside a small, faded building. "Come and meet Grandmother," he said cheerily. They entered a dark room where an old hunched up lady sat gently rocking on a chair in the corner of the room. A woman hovered in the background.

"Grandmother meet your niece, you remember Pearl, don't you?". The old woman remained impassive, staring into space.

"Grandmother is nearly blind, hard of hearing and has dementia so she will not remember you or your visit," said the woman. "She does not really know who I am, and I'm her daughter."

Pearl approached the old woman, kissed her and squeezed her hands.

After a few minutes, the woman whispered, "why don't you come through and have some tea, it's too soon to leave but it's a waste of time staying with her, she doesn't know you, and has already forgotten".

They made their way through to a small kitchen which doubled up as sitting area and the woman busied herself making tea. Over the next hour they chatted and made conversation. Eventually she rose, "I think you can go now, no one will be suspicious".

As they made their way to the door Pearl glanced through to the room and had a last look at the old lady, still hunched up and looking into space; she felt sad. As they bade the woman good-bye, Tim slipped an envelope into the woman's hand and patted her on the shoulder, "I will be back soon".

Once in the car and back on the main street Pearl turned to him and asked, "who is she? How do you know her?"

He shook his head. "A long story but I met the old lady's husband when I first started, up in Beijing, he invited me down here a couple of times but then we lost touch. I learned he had been killed in a drugs operation ten years ago, so since then I made a point of checking up on them both." There was a silence, "that's the daughter if you are wondering".

"How long has the mother been like that" asked Pearl.

"Five, six years I guess. I help out as much as I can, more now since I'm in Wuhan. It's a good cover and the daughter was very good at helping us find digs."

Pearl was looking out of the window ."This is not the way to the airport."

"No, I'll drop you off at the station and you can get the airport bus, it's safer that way and I have work to do."

"Thank you for your help and good luck. Keep in touch and if you need anything just contact Jimmy."

As she got out, he leant across, "good to meet you and don't worry about me, I'm a big boy and can look after myself. Say hi to Jimmy and tell him I'll keep him posted". After a brief pause, he added and grinned, "have a safe journey and don't talk to any strangers".

*　　*　　*

Mei Lien and Ru entered their apartment and immediately embraced, kissing passionately. "Oh! I love you, Mr Nuang," she whispered.

As they parted, she turned to him, "do we really have to stay until the end? I hate it here. All those creepy people in the lab looking at us and whispering, I can't stand them."

"We don't have much choice," he replied. "Must agree with you, they are an odd bunch and obviously jealous as hell that we've been put in charge of the testing."

"How quickly do you think we can get it done by?" she enquired.

"Three, four months at the earliest. It will be another couple of weeks until we get up to speed and then probably a couple of months of trials and tests."

She sighed. "I'm going for a shower and a change; you can start dinner."

# CHAPTER 22

---

# England

Professor Edward Howard was feeling extremely pleased with himself. Life was panning out just as he had hoped. He was happy with the way his meetings over the past few days had gone. Yes, a most profitable couple of weeks; time to plan the next few months. Spend a week visiting his laboratories, followed by a few days in St. Andrews, then take the next month off. Where should he head for, that was the question.

He stepped out of the limousine and headed for the BA First Class desk. His flight was in two hours, plenty of time to relax in the executive lounge and work on his next move.

He had fallen asleep somewhere over Germany and was rudely awoken by a cold hand touching his arm. The stewardess told him to put his seat in the upright position and to ensure the table was folded away. He looked out and gazed blearily at the suburbs of South London. He had a headache and wasn't feeling too good; a feeling of nausea came over him. Once the plane had landed and come to a stop and the doors were opened, he followed his fellow travellers up the aisle and weaved his way down the long, endless corridor. Gosh, he wasn't feeling good. Entering the gents, he went to a cubicle and was sick. Head pounding, he splashed cold water over his face. He located a couple of aspirin he always kept in his briefcase and swallowed them, adjusted his jacket, before heading out to join the stream of passengers making their way to emigration. He staggered slightly a couple of times and thought that perhaps the five glasses of champagne as well as several, of that rather good Rioja, had perhaps been a mistake.

The queue at passport control was horrendous. All this waiting and shuffling about was the downfall of flying, it didn't matter if you travelled first or cattle class, in the end everyone one ended up equal. There and then he made an executive decision, in future he would fly by private jet. His thumping head was easing slightly but the jostling and noise did not help his mood, especially that family with the screaming kid. They were at the gate in Moscow and the child was bawling then; on the plane he vaguely heard it somewhere in the back and now it was in front of him, still bawling. At long last he passed through control and made his way to pick up his bag. Still feeling unwell he was irritated that, even after so long, the luggage was just beginning to trickle in.

Retrieving his case, he proceeded to exit into the main hall. He stopped off to buy a paper and a bottle of water, and as he turned to leave, he bumped into a young man who apologised profusely. Feeling slightly more human he headed for the Heathrow Express. The train was about half full and he easily found a seat by the window and settled down. A few minutes later, a young executive came and sat next to him, he recognised the man as the one he had recently bumped into and nodded slightly. The train was filling up fast and was about to close its doors when a large woman struggled in with a massive suitcase. She staggered and nearly fell into the young man's lap. He took evasive action by leaning over towards Edward.

Twenty-five minutes later the train pulled into Paddington. For security, no one is let back on to the train until the guards have made a quick security check. As the official made his way through the carriage, he noticed a man slumped in his seat. On closer inspection it soon became apparent the passenger was dead.

\* \* \*

Sean sat down, a can of Guinness in his hand, ready to watch the news. It was always the same old thing, no matter what channel you watched. Always bad, always blown out of all proportion and mainly one sided, biased against the Government of the day and, more and more, against Western ideals and values.

One of the headlines made him sit up – an eminent professor, close advisor to the Government had been found dead on the Heathrow Express at Paddington. The special correspondent then came on to say that Professor Edward Howard had been found slumped in his seat at Paddington. It was too early to say the cause of death but that he had recently arrived from Moscow. He continued in a melodramatic voice, "Professor Howard had also attended a conference in Wuhan, hosted by WHO and was on his way back to report to the Minister for Health".

His mobile rang and he quickly answered, "James, you're calling about the news, aren't you!".

"Yes, I am, what do you make of it. You think the Russians have done a Skripal on him?"

"Not sure, too early to say but not impossible. He was playing games with them and was returning from Moscow so, perhaps they had a falling out."

"What do we do next?" asked James.

"Sit tight and watch developments. I'll make enquiries in the morning and hopefully get some insider info and, oh! Jamesie, don't forget if you want out just say it."

"Certainly not yet. Keep me posted."

Sean then called Jack and they discussed the situation at some length. Both agreed to make enquiries the following day and compare notes later in the evening.

\* \* \*

## Washington

Hank and Joe were sitting on a park bench facing the monument; the afternoon sun was warm for the time of year. "Have you heard the news Joe? Seems our Professor Howard was found dead in a train carriage in London. He was returning from Moscow."

"Darned awkward of him; why did he do that?".

"Don't think he chose to die Joe. Jack says he and Sean think he was eliminated, probably by the ruskies, you know what they're like."

"You think they didn't like his being in China? Thought that would be of interest to them. Shame we can't talk to him now," he grunted.

"Any news on Frank or this other chap who was on the trip, Freeman?"

"Not yet, the IRS are investigating but you know what it's like getting anything out of that lot, all take and no give unless it suits them. I'll keep plugging away."

After a few minutes pause Joe continued, "by the way, did you watch CNN last night?"

Hank shook his head.

"Apparently a French lab has found a treatment for SARS and EBOLA which works fantastically; it's cheap, reliable and doesn't mess up people's health. Frank was on, spouting vigorously, saying it was useless, advocating the only way is to use the vaccine developed by SACS Laboratories and produced by BND. It seems that he's managed to persuade AMA, the American Medical Association, to use nothing but the vaccine and to discredit the French treatment. Buy American and rely on American technology and expertise, all that crap."

Joe's phone buzzed and he looked at the screen; he got up and walked away. Hank looked after him annoyed and wondering what was going on. The conversation was animated, and Joe was pacing around like a hungry lion. Eventually, after much gesticulation and more pacing he came back. His mood sombre and he did not look a happy man.

"What's the matter?" enquired Hank.

"Got to go, meet you tonight at 7pm, Carlo's on the corner of K and 20<sup>th</sup> Street." He was off before Hank could utter a word.

Hank sat there, glowering after his friend. What was he up to? It pissed him off that no one talked to him, acted as if he was of no consequence. He was head of department after all but was treated like some young rookie. He clenched his fist, he should either resign or bring them all in and give them a dressing down, remind them who was boss and demand respect. Yes, that's what he should do, shower of self-important bastards. He got up and made his way back to the office. On the way he decided not to go that night; Joe should know better, he needed reminding of his position.

Just after 7pm Hank walked into Carlo's, the place was busy with customers, waiters rushing around, shouts from the kitchen, the atmosphere was typically Italian. He spotted Joe sitting at a table in the back, slightly apart from the rest of the patrons, a glass of red wine in hand. He smiled as Hank pulled out a chair and nodded to the beer, "ordered this for you, hope you're ok with it?".

Hank sat down and nodded. He had decided not to come but then, when the time came, had changed his mind. You never know, it might be important and even if he was cross and hurt, he had to be professional. Earlier, on the way over, he had decided to tell Joe how he felt and tell him, in a diplomatic way, how disappointed he was. A waiter came up with the menus and asked if they needed a top up.

"Right…" Joe started but was interrupted by Hank.

"I want to talk first Joe," as he put up his hand to stop his friend. "We've worked together for more years than I care to remember, we've been through lots, and you know how much I respect you Joe, but I was pissed off this afternoon at the way you excluded me and spoke to me. Old friends yes, but I'm still your boss so deserve a bit more respect."

Joe looked across the table, a hurt expression on his face. "Sure, didn't mean to be rude or disrespectful Hank. You know me, I'd do anything for you, even gave up my semi-retirement and fishing trip, so hey, what's up buddy?"

"That's just it, Joe, I'm your buddy when we aren't working but your boss when we are, and I think you forget that sometimes. You're a great operator, the best, but I sure need to be shown some respect, kept in the loop, and not just when you or anyone else feels like it."

"Well, I am sorry if you feel like that, again, certainly didn't mean it. Anyway, what's brought all this on?"

Hank sighed and sat back. "Apology accepted; no hard feelings?".

Joe shook his head. "Still want to know what all this is about."

Hank was silent a moment. "Not sure, think I'm past all this, been in the trade too long, getting old and tired. Seems I am always the last to know and I've lost my mojo. Take young Carter for example, I couldn't seem to get through to him; asked him to do a job which proved to be half done and didn't check it myself properly. Then you come along and managed to treble the info in no time."

"Ok, you might not be the best people's person, but you were top class in the field and a good leader. Carter's ok, not the brightest kid, just needs looking after, that's all."

Hank nodded, "Guess you're right. That's why Jack gets posted to London as the blue-eyed boy and I' am stuck behind my desk here."

"You said you were pleased and supported his posting; why did you not say anything?" retorted Joe.

"Didn't want to cause a scene in front of everyone. Don't get me wrong, Jack is a fine guy and has all the skills I lack so, yes, he was the right choice. Would just have liked to be asked that's all."

There was a long silence whilst the waiter brought more drinks and took their order. When he had left Hank looked up , "it's just that no one ever thinks of telling me stuff. Take Brian, I know he's a self-important idiot, but just the other day when he asked me how the project was going and I told him about the Chinese visit by our boys, he turned round and told me he knew. Did it occur to him to tell me?

No! Stuff old Hank, he can find it out himself, make an idiot of himself. Made me feel crap, as if I should have known."

"Ah! talking of Brian, I've some big news. Don't get all huffy with me ok, only just learned about it." He looked at Hank and smiled. "That was my contact on the phone this afternoon."

"Go on, spit it out," said Hank.

"I had to go check a few facts first and that's why I suggested we meet tonight; you know me, never take anything for granted. Sorry, no dig at you! It seems that Brian is also in on the game and was instrumental in getting Frank appointed to the board and being their PR man; that's why he knew about who was going to China."

Hank looked at his friend with a blank expression, mouth open. Eventually he found his voice. "What the fuck are you telling me, Joe? No, you must be wrong, the CIA's second in command involved and implicated in such a thing. No, I don't believe it."

"I can assure you Hank, every bit is true, we have proof, records of meetings between the two, phone calls and e-mails. The only thing is I have no idea how to proceed and who we should go to."

There was another long silence as Hank tried to unscramble all he had been told. He tried to make sense of the situation. He sat back and looked at his friend. "Joe, we can't do anything without being a thousand percent sure. If we're wrong our careers are finished, no pensions and probably we'll be sent to jail. If you're right, then its nuclear stuff with ramifications I just don't want to think about. Who's your contact?"

My contact is a she and works very close to Brian, so you can guess who it is. It seems she's had concerns for some time about various goings on but didn't know who to talk to."

"How do you know her?"

"She's worked her way up the ladder and was regularly promoted. Was married to a good friend of mine who worked in Central America, Nicaragua, a real hard guy, not afraid of confrontation until one day he met with a bullet in the back. I first met her at his funeral, never knew he was married. We started chatting about the firm and that's when I learned she was Brian's under-secretary. Soon after the funeral she was promoted as his personal secretary and confidante." Hank looked surprised, "Maggy! Are you sure she has no grudge against Brian and the department? After all her husband must have been sent to Nicaragua by him; then he got himself killed in the line of duty."

"No, she's not like that; knew all along the dangers and the possibility of him not returning home. Both are, were dedicated to the job, and she fully understood what the consequences could be."

"Any romance or hidden infatuations? Advances by Brian or been spurned?"

"You'll have to ask her yourself. I suggest you chat to her and make your own decision."

Hank shook his head and looked down at his plate of pasta getting cold. Neither man had touched their meal. "Would she agree to talk?"

"Yep, think she would be very happy to get things off her chest and get some guidance."

"Ok Joe, set up a meeting, somewhere quiet and discreet. But only you and me, understood!"

Joe, nodded.

# CHAPTER 23

# London

Sean's mobile buzzed and he glanced at the number on the screen. By now he recognised it immediately and picked up.

"Jack, how's life my friend?"

Jack came straight to the point. "Listen, there's been big developments back home and our friends there think we should take a trip over to see them, pronto".

"Sounds intriguing; any clues?"

"Can't say but they've scheduled a family get together for Thursday next week and you and James are cordially invited. We'll organise accommodation and arrange to have you met. Just let me know your time of arrival."

"Ok, will do. Good timing as I have a funeral on Wednesday. Oh, by the way, I got a few more details about the recent events but I'll tell you when we meet." The phone went dead.

James was sitting in his study when he got the call giving him the news of their impending trip to the States. Sean gave him details of his flight and clear instructions on what to do when he got to the destination; they were not travelling together for some reason, but he knew better than to ask why. He made his way to the kitchen and told his wife who simply looked up, smiled, and told him to take care. It always amazed him how relaxed she was, never questioning, never moaning. Smiling, he bent over and kissed her on the cheek.

\* \* \*

## Washington

Hank knocked on the red door and pressed the buzzer. He looked up and down the street. Being Sunday, it was quiet with no traffic; a couple of kids were playing on their skateboards and a faint sound of music came from a few gardens down.

The door was opened by a woman in her 60's, well dressed in jeans and a sparkly top. She smiled broadly, "Hi, you must be Hank, come on in. I'm Sandy, a friend of Joe's". Hank couldn't help seeing the woman take a quick glance up and down the street. They made their way through to the back garden where Joe was busy at a barbecue, a bottle of beer in his hand.

"Hank, welcome to my humble home, or rather Sandy's". He turned to a tall woman with blonde hair wearing summer print trousers and a t-shirt, "and you know Maggy, don't you?".

They both nodded and shook hands. "Yes, I've met Mr Gobolsky several times; thank you for coming today".

The four chatted for a while watching Joe cook the steaks; the atmosphere was relaxed but there was an undertone, a slight strain in the conversation and they all knew this was only a preliminary to the real reason for the meeting. Eventually after clearing up, Sandy turned to the others, "If you're done, I'll leave you guys to have your talk; I'll be in the kitchen if you need anything."

They waited until she was indoors before Hank opened the discussion. "Maggy, I really appreciate you coming today, I know it must be difficult but Joe tells me you have some things you want to tell us."

Maggy took a few minutes to gather her thoughts and cleared her voice. She started from the time of her husbands' funeral and went through the past six years, clearly explaining her rise and promotion to becoming Brian's secretary and PR. Pulling out a large file from her bag, she handed it over to Hank, "you will find records of all meetings held by Mr Milento and Mr Campese either in my boss's office or outside, copies of e-mails and a record of their phone conversations made from or to the office".

Hank took the file and glanced through it. "That's quite a file Maggy; it must have taken you a while to put it together. Were you not worried it would be discovered?"

Maggy looked at the man as if he was mad but kept her thoughts to herself. Shaking her head she replied in a firm voice, "not at all sir, these are copies of e-mails and as everything comes past me it is not difficult. Mr Milento insists I attend all meetings and take notes and it is policy, as you know, that every phone call is recorded".

Hank sighed and took a deep breath. "Now tell me Maggy, what's your motive. In my experience there's always a case of someone spurned or jealous; what are you after? To avenge the death of your husband?"

If Maggy was hurt or upset she kept her cool, not showing any emotion and not rising to the glaring insinuations. She had known that this was going to be asked, or at least suspected, but it didn't worry her. She glanced at Joe before turning back to Hank and looked him in the eye. In a slightly harsher tone than she had wanted, she replied, "there is nothing behind this, Mr Gobolsky. My husband died doing what he loved, we both knew the dangers and I accepted that he might be killed or injured at any time. I'm not jealous, nor do I have any secret desires for Mr Milento or anyone else in the department. He has not made any advances, nor has he behaved inappropriately. I have no gripes against the CIA or the Government." She continued to keep a steady eye on Hank before resuming, "my only wish is to do the right thing and I do not believe that, in his position and as second in command at the CIA my boss, Mr Milento, should be involved in shady dealings and being paid to help promote certain private enterprises. To me that is akin to treason."

Joe stepped in and with a nod of the head and a smile, tried to smooth things over. "I am sure Maggy that Hank was not accusing you of anything, just interested to know why you started keeping these files. In our experience, secretaries or PAs normally come forward because they felt the boss has tried to take advantage of them or because they have been overlooked."

She smiled, "I know Mr Gobolsky is only doing his job and I would have been surprised if he hadn't asked. I just don't like seeing people in high places and in very important jobs, work against the best interest of the country."

"What do you mean by that?" Hank interjected. "When did all this start?"

Maggy pursed her lips, "about two years ago. Mr Campese was at a reception and he and Mr Milento were introduced, or rather Mr Campese introduced himself. They spent a long time chatting and the next day I was asked to arrange a meeting. It's all in the file."

"I'm sure it is but I like to hear things first hand, to get a spoken version, it helps me understand.".

Maggy continued. "There were regular meetings after that, either at the office or in Mr Campese's office and most of the time the subject was the same, how to promote certain US laboratories and research centres. Mr Campese was adamant that the Europeans were gaining ground on the US and he wanted to halt this."

"Nothing wrong in wanting to promote American companies; did they speak of any laboratories in particular?" asked Joe.

"Yes, he was mainly wanting to promote two which he claimed could compete with the foreign centres."

"Any names?" asked Hank.

"SACS Laboratories and Beacon Pharmaceuticals, the two Mr Campese represents. When the US military were recently invited by the Chinese to visit one of their plants, Mr Campese was insistent that representatives from these two companies go along. That is when he asked my boss to arrange things."

"To arrange things? what does that mean?"

"To get himself and two of the directors invited and to arrange for the visas. About a week later Mr Campese was invited to come to the office where he was told that all three had been invited and all the necessary papers had been processed. As requested these two gentlemen, one from SACS, the other from Beacon, were supposed to be high ranked scientists in these organisation. The odd thing however, was that they were both foreign, British citizens. Maggy hesitated before continuing, "Mr Campese handed my boss a thick envelope and winked, telling him it was a little thank you for his troubles".

"You don't happen to know what was in this envelope or what it contained? Or get a photo of this handover?"

Maggy smiled. "No, no photos, they're not that stupid. I couldn't be sure of what was in the envelope but it was thick, and the boss seemed delighted. It wasn't the first time; it's occurred several times before, after Mr Millento had sorted and facilitated other trips or arranged meetings."

Hank was amazed, "you mean to say that these…these packages were handed over in front of you!"

Maggy nodded.

There was a long silence before Hank shook his head, leaning back he grimaced. "Incredible, the balls these guys have, just incredible. Thank you Maggy, think that's enough for now, I'll read through your file and get back if I have any other questions."

"I know I don't have to say it, but please be careful. I would hate it to fall into the wrong hands."

Hank laughed, "no worries there, I'll look after them as if my life depends on it, don't you worry. If this goes further, you do know things could get nasty, don't you?".

She nodded, "I know and have thought of that. I'm prepared to lose my job and my pension if it helps to stop this kind of treason."

"Very brave lady! I just hope it will be nothing more than that." He looked up at Joe. "Perhaps when, or if, things come out, it may be an idea Maggy takes a holiday up at your cabin in Maine." He looked back at the proud woman, "you do know that you will be called as a witness and it won't be nice; my initial questioning earlier will look like a kid's game. These guys will dredge up all the dirt they can find, question you in every detail and insinuate all kinds of things, not nice things. Your name will be dragged through the gutter."

Maggy nodded, "I know, I 'am not afraid".

# CHAPTER 24

# Wuhan

The past few weeks had not been easy, and both Ru and Mei Lien had worked hard settling in, as well as getting to know their colleagues. In spite of their best efforts, the feeling of suspicion and jealousy had not disappeared; it hung over the lab like a dark, thundery cloud, ready to erupt at any moment.

Ru had sat down with every member of the team and gone through their file, digging, probing into their knowledge and expertise. Some were open, others reticent and reserved, but none of them fully opened-up and it was made clear to the young couple they were not welcome.

Mei Lien had taken it upon herself to try and befriend the two female scientists, but it had proved harder than she had expected. She tried to play the good cop whilst Ru took a harder, more ruthless line in the hope of gaining some sort of control. He had set out weekly deadlines and insisted all tests and calculations were double, treble checked.

Once these had been done, he and Mei Lien went over them again and when satisfied signed off the paperwork for animal tests to begin. It was like sailing against a gale in very choppy seas. Each evening they got back to their flat late and exhausted.

On returning home that night Mei Lien dropped her bag on the floor and flopped on to the couch before bursting into tears. Ru went over and cuddled her. "I really don't think I can go back on Monday," she said between sniffs. "I've tried to be nice and patient, but all I get in return is silence or whispering behind my back. I have to repeat my request two or three times before anything gets done; it's not fair." She wiped her eyes and sighed. "Can't we just go back to Beijing and let them all get on with it?"

Ru stroked her hair and held her in his arms. "I know, I know, it's hard and they are making life difficult but we must stick it out. We have made tremendous progress over the past month in spite of them and it would not look good if we asked to leave now.".

She was silent for a long while before getting up, "what do you want to eat?".

"Don't be like that, you know I' am right and we can't leave. Even if we did get sent back, what future would there be? Certainly no job like we have now, more like a move to some back office pushing papers around; you know how it works".

She busied herself in the kitchen and didn't answer. Finally, she placed a bowl of noodles and duck on the table. "Better eat while it's hot; I'm going to bed".

It was their first argument and Ru had no idea what to do or say. He sat there in silence, unsure whether he should follow her or not. He decided to leave her alone; he had never seen her in that kind of state before. After a long while he got up and put the food away in the fridge, went to the bathroom and found himself a spare blanket.

He lay on the couch, his mind in turmoil until he drifted off into a fitful sleep, punctuated by wild dreams of a dragon with Mei Lien's face chasing him around a mountain, and creepy looking individuals, brandishing syringes trying to put him in a cage. He woke with a start, sweat pouring and breathing heavily. He sat up, turned the light on and stretched. His back was aching and he had a stiff neck. He glanced at his watch, 4.30am; yawning he got up and padded to the bathroom. He decided to have a shower ,then dress, and went back to the lounge. Jotting down a note, he left it on the kitchen top near the kettle, put on his thick jacket and picked up his briefcase.

It was still dark when he let himself out into the deserted street. A cold, biting wind hit him in the face. He walked briskly to the metro station and jumped on the first train heading East. He was alone in the carriage and his mind drifted back to the last evening. He understood Mei Lien's feelings; he didn't like the place either, but they had little choice. They had to stick it out and finish the work they had been sent to do. Why was she like that, was it something he had said or done? No, although he had little experience of women, he put it down to tiredness and probably the time of the month. He would buy her flowers or something on his way home.

Crossing the large, deserted square, he mused at how China was changing. Saturday morning, 5.30am; in the old days, when he was a boy, life would be in full swing with workers going to work, and traders would be setting up their stalls or hawking their goods. He remembered how his father worked seven days a week and all hours of the day; how his mother used to get up at 4am in the morning to get his lunch ready before going to the laundry, leaving him strict instructions not to be late for school. Now, people expected the weekend off; even the beggars started later. He approached the main gate and tapped on the guardhouse window. A bleary-eyed young man poked his head round the door looking surprised to see anyone. Ru flashed his ID at the youngster who nodded and opened the gate.

He made his way to Lab. No 6, punched in the security code and the door unlocked. Switching on the lights he looked around. It was eerily quiet, just the low hum of the air-conditioning and newly turned-on neon bulbs. The rows of desks and work tops were empty and spotlessly clean, the computers were turned off, it was as if no one was working there. He made his way across to the far door and went through to the adjoining room. His eyes adjusted to the dim blue light and his nose picked up the faint odour of chemicals mixed with the smell of animal.

He walked round slowly, looking carefully at every tank and cage. He checked monitors, graphs and temperature charts. Most occupants were asleep, some woke wondering why their slumber had been disrupted and others, such as the two pigs and the monkey, snorted and screamed their displeasure.

Returning to his desk he switched on the computer and logged in. He spent the next couple of hours analysing the data recorded in the room next door and then correlated all the information with previous figures and results. He stretched and rubbed his stiff neck before returning to the screen. He re-started all the calculation and analysis once again followed by a third time. Disturbed, he got up and paced round the room, thinking, sorting, and trying to make sense of what he had, or thought he had, discovered. He didn't like it, yet at the same time he was excited. Eventually he went back to the screen and made sure everything was copied and saved both on his computer and on the USB stick. Retrieving the small device, he went over to his and Mei Lien's safe and locked it in. As directors of the project, they had been given a fire-proof safe where all data had to be kept.

The young guard had been replaced by an older man who looked surprise to see Ru coming out of the building. Ru signed the register and looked up at the old man, "couldn't sleep so came in earlier for a few hours. You might like to remind the young lad that everyone should sign in". He nodded and headed for the station.

He found a florist and bought a nice bunch of lilies, Mei Lien's favourite, and a small box of coconut sweets.

He found her in the kitchen making tea and she looked round as he walked in, "where have you been?" she enquired.

"Went to the lab. Couldn't sleep on that damned sofa so decided to go and check on a few things. Here these are for you."

She smiled. "Thanks, but what have you got to say sorry for. It was my fault. I didn't mean to get cross. Think it was tiredness, I've been feeling off for a few days".

"Oh, why did you not tell me? What sort of feeling?"

"Not sure, just off, headache, itchy skin and I am not hungry".

Ru looked worried. "Think you should go to the clinic on Monday before coming to work, it's not like you to be ill."

She walked over to Ru and gave him a hug and a long kiss. "Thanks for these, you needn't have."

They sat down on the sofa and opened the box of sweets which Ru attacked with gusto. "I'm not sure, but I think we're on to something big, very big and I'm not certain I like it," said Ru. "I went through a whole lot of calculations and analysis this morning and unless I'm wrong, we can confirm a massive discovery, or rather, a massive invention."

She looked at him excited, "what is it?"

"No, not now, I'm in need of sleep and a rest. We can talk more later, and we can work on it Monday, after you have been to the doctor."

"You little toad, getting me all excited and then not wanting to tell me, that's not fair and quite out of order. Come on tell me."

"No, it's too complicated and I'm still very unsure. I would prefer to go over it with you at the lab, with all the data in front of us." He leaned over and kissed her, "for now, I want a comfy bed, cuddle up to my lovely girl-friend and have a couple of hours sleep".

\* \* \*

## Hong Kong

Jimmy Wang was sitting at his desk reading through reports received overnight. He liked to go through everything ensuring nothing was missed or omitted before sending the information back to England. He trusted his team implicitly; they were some of the best analytical brains in the business and he had their full loyalty. Each one had been hand-picked and trained by him. They came from a wide range of ethnic backgrounds and education, but all had one thing in common, they wanted to protect Western values and liberties. They hated communism and dictatorships, their only aim and goal in life was that they wanted to make the world a safer place. Many, like him, had had bad experiences, or knew of suffering of friends and family in the hands of tyrants.

He made a few notes and edited a couple of things on the report from Pyongyang. The US President had had a meeting, the first, with the little fat podgy one, and it had all gone rather well to the upmost chagrin of the world press. For some reason they hated the President and his open, frank speech, his doing what he had promised to do and his hard stance towards the dangerous and belligerent nations. No pussy footing around and trying to appease, just say it as it is, just the sort of person Jimmy liked.

He got up and made his way over to the coffee machine before walking round the office where he stopped and spoke to each of his operatives. He spent time discussing various events in the Far East before making his way over to Pearl. He had recently made her his second in command, a position she deserved and one that all members of his team were happy with. He sat down and sipped his coffee.

"Have you heard the news from Beijing?"

She shook her head. "Not since last night, no."

"It's not good. Seems that at the executive meeting yesterday and last night, it was decided to put pressure on Hong Kong and accelerate our return to their rule. They've issued a statement saying that new laws will be brought into effect within a month and have clearly ordered Carrie Lam to implement the new rules immediately or they will take direct action."

Pearl grimaced, "not good indeed, in fact that's terrible news. Have you alerted London?"

He handed a couple of typed sheets. "Have a look at this; think you should read through it and give me your take on the situation, they'll take it more seriously coming from both of us." He watched her read through his notes before continuing. "I'm afraid you're right; this could mean a rather unsettled time for our city and province. Can't see many people taking this lightly." He paused before carrying on, "we should probably draft in a few of our overseas operators, we need people on the ground and first-hand reports, things are going to get nasty".

He turned and called everyone to attention. "Guys! listen up, I'm calling code 2, big events and possible big trouble will occur in town soon; Pearl will fill you in, but for now, I want each of you to call in at least one of your agents and fast. I want everyone to be here in two days' time, understood?"

There was a murmur and nodding with a few worried faces. Half an hour later Pearl had finished briefing everyone and there was flurry of activity and a renewed air of determination; all understood the implications and immediately were on a war footing.

Later that afternoon Pearl went over to Jimmy's desk. She looked worried.

"What is it? You look as if you've seen a ghost."

"Bad or rather concerning news again! Seems that our friends in Beijing were pretty busy last night planning and plotting."

Jimmy was silent.

"You know we have an insider, a secretary, close to the President. Seems that he picked up news that China wants to start a World War."

"What!" Jimmy jumped up. "The guy must have misunderstood or been drunk."

Pearl held up her hand. "Sit down and calm down, it's not quite that bad. They have more sense than to start a military war. No, it'll be a more devious war, underhand and far less open. Sounds as if they've hit on the idea that, in order to save the deepening troubled economy, they should try and undermine and wreck the world economies."

"How are they planning on doing that? To take on the US, Europe, India and Japan is total madness. We all know they've been trying to infiltrate the Western economy through the electronics door, but I just can't see how else they can do it."

"I know and like you, I don't understand. Thought I'd better let you know and put you in the picture."

Jimmy sat a long time in silence biting his fingernails. Eventually he looked up, "thanks. I want you to personally keep an eye on this one and try and find out more. Is this coming from our usual source?"

She nodded. "Yes, he's been in situ for three years and has always given accurate and pertinent information; you know that".

He did. It was he himself who managed to recruit the man and place him as a junior, but through hard work and being clever, his source managed to work his way up to the top. "Good, see what else he can offer. Worth a quick visit?"

"Bit too risky, for his sake don't you think?"

Jimmy sat staring at his screen before pushing his chair back. No, he had to get more facts before sending his report. With the sketchy details he had, London would just laugh and think he had gone nuts. He stayed on late that night studying the reports and formulating a plan. He greeted the night shift and put them in the picture giving them the same instructions as for the day crew. There were a few questions which he answered.

He eventually glanced up at the battery of clocks on the wall of the main office and noted it was ten past midnight local time. He had one last task to do before going home. He made his way back to his office and closing the door, something he did only in a crisis, he picked up the phone and dialled a number.

\*　　\*　　\*

# Beijing

The woman was woken from a deep sleep by the sound of a phone buzzing. She stretched and yawned before turning over. The phone stopped only to re-start a few seconds later. Turning on the light she glanced at her clock – 1am – who on earth would call at this time of night. She sighed and answered it abruptly.

The voice at the other end was chirpy, which annoyed her even more but as it continued, she recognised the caller and sat up in bed, tense and alert. She listened intently, nodding to herself and making mental notes. The voice at the other end ended the call abruptly and the phone went dead.

She sat there silently going over what she had heard before turning off the light. Lying in the dark, her mind was racing, any idea of further sleep banished from her thoughts. An hour later she got up, washed, dressed and went through to the kitchen. Sitting at the table nursing her tea she watched the clock tick by until it was 6am and time to get started.

# CHAPTER 25

# Washington

James walked out into the arrivals hall and was confronted by a sea of bodies dressed in all manner of ways. Most were smiling, looking forward to meeting friends or loved ones; others were dressed in dark suits, drivers mainly, meeting businessmen or politicians. As he made his way through the throng a face he knew appeared out of nowhere and greeted him with a broad smile.

"Hey James! Good to see you! Have a good flight?" asked Joe.

They shook hands and Joe ushered his friend through the vast hall and out towards the car park. It was James' first time in Washington, he was excited to visit the hub and heart of America's government. Joe kept up a constant commentary and, to James' surprise, told him how much he hated the place. "A darned awful dump, dangerous and full of self-important egoistical bastards is my opinion. Every time I visit, I count the days before I can leave," he exclaimed.

"Well, it all looks fine by me; the heart of America's politics and the heart of the free world. I must say though, I did read it has some pretty rough places and you have to be careful."

"Too right," said Joe. "Heart of the free world and good old US of A but also a hive of intrigue and shenanigans. Loads of jealousy and people jostling for position, trying to make a name for themselves and a quick buck."

James chuckled, "think that's the same in every country and in all political circles. What's that over on the skyline?"

"Ah! that's the top of the Lincoln Memorial, just to the right of that is The Capitol and behind that is where we work from - you can't see it and would walk past without noticing it. Unlike your fancy HQ on the Thames, we work out of a place resembling a rabbit warren."

"Thought you operated from a vast building bristling with antenna and high tech. devices."

"Yeah! The CIA operate out of Langley, Virginia but our section is based here, and we are sort of hidden and rather forgotten, unknown. High command lords it up there but our branch is supposed to operate on the QT. Given special jobs or ops no one else wants."

"Where are we staying and what's the programme? Sean didn't tell me anything; in fact, l thought he was going to meet me at the airport."

Joe shook his head, "typical! They get you to come all the way over here and don't tell you nothing." Ok, not far now, just a couple miles". As he was talking, they turned off the highway and headed into one of the poorer districts of the city. They passed dilapidated buildings covered in graffiti, the streets strewn with rubbish and many residents sitting on the front steps, staring at them menacingly from under hoodies and caps.

"Where on earth are you taking me?" enquired James, now concerned for their safety.

"Just showing you the more salubrious part of town, James. Don't worry I'm not leaving you here; just to show you that Washington DC is not all glitz and glamour." As they continued on their way leaving the ghetto behind, James relaxed slightly. After a further five minutes they entered a more friendly suburb and turned into a wide street flanked by neat houses nestled behind hedges and fences. They stopped outside a bungalow with a bright blue door and a well-manicured garden. "Ok, James here we are; you can breathe easy now; come and meet auntie Beth."

James looked at Joe, eyebrow raised, "and who is auntie Beth?".

"Come on in and I'll introduce you to her." They got out of the car and made their way up the path and Joe pushed the buzzer.

The bell had hardly stopped ringing when the door was opened, and they were greeted by a young, muscular woman who James' judged to be in her early thirties. She smiled broadly at Joe and, turning to James, stuck out her hand. "Hi, you must be James; I've heard a lot about you."

James took the proffered hand and nodded. "Pleased to meet you, but a bit concerned that you've heard so much about me; can I ask you don't believe any of it?"

She beckoned them in and took them through to the sitting room. The house was bright and airy but sparsely furnished, just the minimum of decoration with little in the way of chairs or tables. James felt it was functional but cold and unlived-in.

Beth turned to her guests, "can I get either of you anything - tea, coffee, or something stronger?"

James's eyes brightened, "well, as you're asking, do you have any whisky? It's been a long day and it's after 6pm, I hate to break a habit of a life-time."

Joe chuckled loudly. "I like it James, well done on you, I'll join you with a beer." Turning to Beth, "why don't you show our guest to his room and I'll fix us those drinks. Water, no ice?"

James nodded and went after the young woman.

He was shown to his bedroom which was equally as neat and tidy, again functional and with no frills, with a door leading to an adjoining en-suite bathroom. "I'll leave you to freshen up, come through when you're ready; if you need anything, just shout. The woman smiled and left. James looked round the room., He didn't like the décor, too plain and clinical for his liking, but it was fine for the couple of days he was going to be staying and, a vital point, it was spotlessly clean.

They were sitting in a couple of the deep armchairs nursing their drinks when James asked what time Sean would be arriving.

"Guess he should have landed a few hours ago." Seeing the look on James' face Joe continued, "he's not staying here, not sure where they've taken him, but we will meet him tomorrow".

James looked even more puzzled. "Thought he said he was meeting me at the airport."

"Yeh, that was the plan, but it changed. We decided it would be better if we split up, you and me here, Sean and Hank somewhere else, just in case."

"Just in case what?"

"Always best to be safe. We are all working on very sensitive stuff, and you never know who may be listening or snooping". He grinned, "top up?"

James was slightly anxious and totally lost. He nodded and held out his glass. "Not sure that I fully comprehend; What is so dangerous?" he asked watching the drink being poured.

"As Sean has always said, you're free to walk away at any time and we wouldn't blame you". Joe handed over the replenished tumbler. "This thing we are working on has developed big time, as you know. The prof topping himself or being murdered is one thing, but over here we're on to something major and much more delicate; you will understand tomorrow, if you're still wanting to continue."

James nodded. "Of course I'm still wanting to stay, you don't think I've come so far just to flee the minute things get a bit hairy, do you?"

"Is this a safe house?" asked James.

"It is, and Sean is in another across town. As I say, things are very delicate, and we must be careful."

"Who is auntie Beth?" James nodded towards the kitchen.

"Here to protect us," grinned Joe. "Make sure we behave and don't get up to any mischief. Right. Time for bed. You've had a long day and we need to be fresh for tomorrow. Breakfast at 8am but don't expect anything fancy; cooking is not Beth's forte, she's just about ok with toast and makes a mean coffee,", Joe said lightly.

*   *   *

James woke early, he'd slept like a log and was feeling refreshed. Making his way to the kitchen he found Joe and Beth already sitting at the table holding steaming mugs of coffee. They greeted James like a long-lost friend and Beth made him some tea - he hated coffee. He could not but notice the gun strapped to both his hosts, and nodded towards them, "do I need one?"

Joe shook his head and smiled.

Half an hour later they were sitting in the back of the car while Beth navigated the morning traffic. Joe kept up a continuous commentary on the buildings and places of interest. "Don't know how good you are at your job but you're a fine tour guide," quipped James. "Feel I know Washington DC already."

They turned in to an underground garage beneath a drab building; James was not sure where they were but was not in the least concerned. He trusted Joe and the more he spent time with him, the more he liked him.

They took the elevator and stepped out into a modern lobby covered in a thick piled carpet. A large desk flanked the back wall where two National flags stood proudly along with the CIA Emblem. The young man behind the desk looked up and greeted them with a bright smile showing a set of very white teeth. "Good morning gentlemen, please follow me; the others have already arrived."

As both men followed the receptionist, James noticed that Beth stayed behind and remembered what Joe had said the previous night. The young man stopped at a door marked with a conference sign and "occupied" in red; he knocked sharply and showed them in.

Sean, and Hank rose from their chairs and went over to greet James with warm handshakes. After the usual small banter about flights and if he was being well looked after, Hank turned to introduce the woman whom James had immediately noticed on entry. "James, this is Maggy, Maggy this is Sean's associate James Horton from England."

James shook Maggy's proffered hand and noticed the firm grip; she looked him straight in the eyes and held his gaze. They were then shown to chairs around the large oval table and James selected one facing the window which offered him a view of Washington's skyline. A couple of minutes later Jack breezed in making his apologies.

At the end of three hours of interrogation, probing and cajoling Maggy, with Sean interjecting occasionally with a question of his own, the meeting ended. All six got up to stretch their legs , the thanked Maggy for her help and openness. She was seen out into the corridor where, just by a miracle, one of the biggest and strongly built men James had ever seen, appeared from nowhere.

Sporting a gun tucked under his right arm, he smiled brightly and gestured to the woman to follow. As they left, she turned and thanked them all one final time.

James turned to Sean "Now, that is a well-built fellow if ever I saw one, a monster".

They all agreed as Hank replied. "A good man for a vitally important witness. He'll be with her 24/7 from now on; certainly, one of the best protection officers we have - smells trouble long before it happens. Right any one for the restroom?"

Twenty minutes later they were back in their places and Jack set the conversation going. They discussed every point, every possibility, and every outcome at length. James mainly stayed silent feeling out of his depth but flattered that they regularly turned to him for his in-put. Finally, it was decided to hold fire for a couple more weeks until Hank and Joe had made further investigations and hopefully dug up more facts and proof of ill-doings. Maggy had been told to report sick and was sent to a safe house along with the burly protection officer for as long as it would take.

Dusk was falling when Sean moved the conversation on to something new. "As you know, I attended the professor's funeral the other day. A quiet affair with only a few of his cronies and I guess a couple of people from one of the labs, but no one of consequence. However, no sign of Freeman and I did notice a man lurking behind the other gravestones trying to look inconspicuous. He certainly didn't make a good job of it and I managed to get a photo of him. Turns out he was a Russian from the London Embassy."

"Guess he was just making sure the poor sod was being buried," said Joe.

Jack told them he decided not to go as Sean was there and it would have been a bit obvious.

"I managed to get a copy of the pathology report," continued Sean. "As we all guessed, he did not die of natural causes. The guys at Porton Down have still got the body and doing further tests but it's widely believed he was poisoned with the substance Novachok, same as the Skripals."

"The ruskies strike again!" said Hank.

"Did you say the pathologists still have the body" asked James. "Thought you said you went to the funeral!"

Sean nodded with a grin, "I certainly did, and his buddies all paid their respects, except they didn't know the coffin had stones in it, not Professor Howard. The press was sent a statement telling them that Professor Howard had died of natural causes and that his funeral had taken place. It was the best way forward and stopped them speculating. The Russians are not sure what we know, so It was best all round."

The others nodded their agreement while James stayed silent, his mind racing and in turmoil.

"The Inland Revenue has started an investigation into his affairs and his ties with a Panamanian Company, but we did ask for them not to divulge anything about his involvement with the Russians or Chinese," continued Sean. "We also requested that they don't look too hard into the laboratories in England or Scotland; no need for us to advertise that we're harbouring sensitive work in two major labs which are foreign owned. "

Hank sat back and scratched his balding head. "Seems there's a whole lot of things going on that could form part of a larger International plot. It's time we tried to put all the pieces of this puzzle together and decide what to do before it gets out of hand."

"How do you do that?" asked James. "Who would believe us, or rather, believe you chaps?"

"We'll have to go direct to the top but that's going to be difficult, on our side anyway, as some could, as we suspect, be implicated," said Joe.

Hank cleared his throat. "Probably one of the best ways would be for you, Sean and James, to go to your Embassy here and have a word with the Ambassador, see what he can do."

Sean shook his head. "No, it will have to come from high up in the Firm; no one is going to listen to me or a retired journalist, especially as he's not known to anyone in the organisation. I'll have a chat with the boss back home, see what he thinks. It's got to a stage where he needs to be informed in any case and it would be better if it came from him".

"He's not implicated, is he?" asked Hank.

"Not that I know. He's a good man, dedicated to his job. Can't stand politicians and their short sightedness. As I see things, it's you guys who have the problem."

They were all silent before Jack suggested it was time to break up, "been a long day and we all need to go home and think things over". He turned to Sean, "when are you guys going back?".

"Tomorrow afternoon, James is on the BA flight at 3.30 and I fly out on KLM via Amsterdam at 4pm."

"Right, let's meet up in the morning, 9am sharp, here, and we can coordinate plans as much as possible."

On the way back Joe suggested they stopped and got a carry out. He turned round to look at James in the back seat. "As I said this morning, I trust Beth to shoot anyone at any distance in the dark, but I wouldn't trust her cooking, and not to poison us," he chuckled.

\* \* \*

Sean was sitting in the small lounge, a beer in his hand, looking at his messages. He had a raft of e-mails and two missed calls. The e-mails were all run of the mill reports except the most important one being from the scientists at Porton Down confirming that the Prof. had been poisoned. They had found a small pinprick just above his left elbow made by a needle. They also confirmed that the substance was a new nerve agent. He knew that the body would now be kept for a couple of months in a secret mortuary in case it was needed again, after that time, if everyone was satisfied, it would be taken to a crematorium for disposal.

He looked at the two missed calls, both from the same number which he did not recognise but, by the code, knew came from Hong Kong. He pushed the re-dial button and waited. After a pause and several screeching noises, he heard the ring tone.

"Morning Mike," came the chirpy voice, "thanks for calling back; how are you?".

"Hope I'm not waking you, not sure what time it is at your end," he said worried it was half-way through the night. "It's 11pm here and my maths aren't good enough to work out the hour difference.

"Not at all. 7am in cloudy Hong Kong and I'm just on my way to the office. Look, we have a huge shipment, a really big job which involves several vessels. Can you come over urgently to help?"

Sean immediately understood something important was on or had happened and knew better than to ask. Jimmy would not have called him from an unknown mobile a couple of hours ago or spoken in riddles if it wasn't urgent. "I'm in Washington DC at the moment sorting out a contract and going home tomorrow; could come out in a few days' time."

"No, we need you here as soon as possible. Can you get a flight first thing in the morning? Text me the flight number and I'll be at the airport to meet you." The phone went dead.

Hank walked in and found Sean gazing at his phone. "What's the problem buddy, got a spooky call?"

"Yes, sort of did. Need your help Hank." He explained briefly his conversation, omitting to tell his host the full details.

Hank nodded and picked up his mobile and dialled the office number. Fifteen minutes later Sean was booked on the 9.45am American Airlines flight to LA and then a Cathy Pacific flight to Hong Kong.

"Thanks Hank, much appreciated. Can you look after James? Just say I had a call from HQ and had to go back early. Best not to tell him I'm flying in the opposite direction!"

"He's in good hands. Don't worry, although knowing him it won't be long before he twigs. Mike Flannigan, hey! Not a bad cover name."

Sean shook his head, "I'm known as Mike Flannigan in the Firm and on the street; what's yours?"

"Hank, pure and simply Hank. Haven't been a field worker for years, paper pushers don't need to hide their identity".

"Sound a bit bitter," said Sean.

Hank ignored the last comment and handed over another beer.

# CHAPTER 26

# Wuhan

It had been a difficult couple of days with Mei Lien not improving and Ru getting more and more concerned. She had a fever and had developed belly ache and a loss of taste. Ru was hesitant to tell her about his findings and didn't want to worry her further. Eventually he phoned the laboratory's medical department and asked to speak to a doctor. Everyone was away and the voice at the other end of the line pointedly reminded the caller it was Sunday before hanging up. Ru slammed down the receiver and sighed, what has the country come to? He made his way back to the bedroom and was relieved to see Mei Lien asleep.

The next morning Ru ordered a taxi to take them to the clinic. His fiancée was looking ghostly white and gaunt. At reception he was told to wait in the hall as they showed the patient through. He paced up and down, still with plenty of time before starting his shift, but what on earth were they doing? After an interminable long wait the door opened and a nurse walked down the corridor with Mai Lien trying to keep up; he jumped up and hurried across to meet them.

"Just food poisoning," said Mei Lien before he could say anything. She smiled weakly. "Must have been the fish we had the other night, thought it smelt funny; told you I never trusted that woman in the market, she's shifty and for ever trying to sell you out of date stuff."

Ru held up his hand. "Sorry, sorry, I was in a rush. Oh, I feel terrible! How come I was alright?" He turned to the nurse, "are you sure it was nothing else, nothing more sinister? How can a piece of fish make anyone so ill?"

The nurse shrugged, "people react differently to things. Your lady friend should go home and rest for a day, then she'll be fine." She promptly turned and left them.

"Thank you," Ru called out after her sarcastically. He turned to Mei Lien, "I'll nip over to the lab and explain I can't make it today; stay here and I'll be back to take you home".

She put her hand on his arm, "no, go to work. I'm fine and will survive," she smiled. He pulled out some notes and handed them over to her, "here take these and get a taxi, it will be quicker".

Shaking her head, she pushed the proffered hand away. "I'm ok, promise. Now go, don't be late or we'll both be in trouble. Just say I have female problems and that I 'll be back in tomorrow." Ru turned and left reluctantly.

Back at his desk he quickly checked the overnight data before calling the team together for the Monday morning briefing. Thirty minutes later everyone knew what their tasks were to be for that week and set about the work given. There were a few mutterings, still, after all this time, several of the older scientists were unhappy at being told what to do by a younger member, but Ru had got used to the situation and ignored the moaning. He turned his attention to the figures and data collected over the weekend. Poring over the calculations, checking the test tube results again, before beginning a new analysis. By mid-afternoon he was convinced he was right, and he didn't like what he had discovered.

Returning home that evening, he found his fiancée sitting at the table in her bright kimono top which they had bought in Hong Kong, wrapped tightly around her. She looked up as he entered and smiled. "You're early for once."

"Had to get back to see you, I've been concerned all day, how are you feeling?" He noticed she had got the colour back in her cheeks and the gauntness had gone.

"Just fine, had a great sleep when I got back followed by a lovely shower, back to normal," she smiled.

He kissed her lightly on the head and went over to the fridge where he pulled out a bottle of beer. As he returned, she frowned. "What's up, you look terrible, don't say you have stomach poisoning now?" Ru shook his head and sat down heavily on the settee.

He spent the next hour, explaining in great detail what he thought they had discovered, how he arrived at his conclusions and many of his concerns.

"Are you sure, absolutely one hundred percent sure you have covered everything" she asked.

He nodded, "I was going to tell you on Saturday when I got back but you were too ill. In fact, I thought you may have been in contact with one of the chemicals, or worse, you had caught something from one of the animals. I haven't told anyone yet. I wanted you to go over the data with me first, then we need to do some further tests. I tell you, I don't like it, don't like it one little bit." He looked glum and a deep frown was set across his forehead making him look older than his thirty-five years.

"Relax, I'm sure it's not as bad as you think; we can go over everything again tomorrow and once that is done, we can order further tests to just to make sure."

\* \* \*

## Beijing

There was a dampness to the morning and chilly wind blew down the street. The woman looked up at the skies – it's going to rain by ten – she said to herself. Making her way through the narrow alleyways that criss-crossed the city she eventually came to the wanted bridge.

Glancing around she slipped under the arch, her footsteps echoing, and made her way to a small crack at the far end. Looking around again, she inserted her hand and retrieved a small envelope wrapped in plastic. She did not open it, just took it, and slipped it into her blouse and buttoned up her coat. Returning the way she had come, she took care when emerging, picking up a few pebbles and made a scene of skipping them into the water. No one took any notice so, after a few minutes, she made her way up to the street and headed north. She walked briskly, stopping several times to look at shop windows, checking no one was following her. She felt a few spots of rain on her cheek and looked up at a clock hanging over a bus stop - 10.03 - not bad she thought and smiled. A few minutes later she got on a bus, sat down, and looked out of the window, still no one following.

Two stops later a small, bent old man got on and came to sit next to her. He grinned a toothless grin and nodding to the sky, "going to be a wet day. Have you the time?"

She fumbled inside her coat and pulled out a small pocket watch, pretending to look at it, she replied without looking at him, "10.50".

"No, it can't be; can I see please?" She showed him the watch and as he was peering at it his hand accidently knocked it out of her palm. They both stooped to pick it up, "Oh! I am so very sorry, how careless of me; I hope it's ok". They fussed around for a minute before retrieving the watch. Rising, the woman looked at it, shook it and listened to it, "it's all right, no harm done; please don't worry" before immediately getting up. "Excuse me, it's my stop. Thank you and don't worry, no damage done." She got off and headed away without a look back, discreetly fastened up her top blouse button.

She made her way into a nearby department store and looked round, admiring the handbags and scarves she couldn't afford. Having spent time and ensuring no one was watching her she headed for the ladies' toilet. Locking herself in a cubicle she pulled out a small package from her coat pocket and opened it. She peered in and inspected a small round object stuck to a sheet of paper with a cryptic note. She read the scrawl before flushing it down the toilet then, carefully replaced the disc in a small plastic pouch and stuffed it back into her coat pocket. She checked herself in the mirror and returned to her browsing.

She made a small purchased before leaving the store and headed back to the nearest bus stop. Checking, stopping several times to browse the street stalls, she remained alert. Just before arriving at her destination, she purchased a bunch of over-priced orange flowers – they didn't smell, they never did nowadays – and thanked the stall holder profusely before proceeded on her way. Arriving at the bus stop she took a seat, placed the bunch beside her and waited for the No 75. She was soon joined by a plump lady laden with bags. The woman did not want to make conversation with the new arrival, so took out her phone and pretended to be busy. Eventually the No 75 arrived and she held on until the very last second before jumping up and dashing toward the closing door. Her companion looked at the flowers and started to call out, waving them, but it was too late, the doors closed, the bus slowly picked up speed. She looked back and saw the plump lady pick out the plastic pouch from the centre of the bunch and quickly put it in her handbag, leaving the flowers on the bench.

\*　　\*　　\*


## Hong Kong

Jimmy was waiting in the Arrivals Hall when Sean emerged from the glass sliding doors. They shook hands briefly before proceeding to the station. It was only when they were in the sanctuary of a quiet carriage, did they begin talking . "Welcome back to Hong Kong. I must thank you for coming out so soon but things here are going to get nasty, and I need to explain first-hand what's happening".

Sean had noticed an anxiety in Jimmy's face and demeanour which he did not have the previous time. "I'm all yours", but Jimmy was silent and continued to gaze out of the window, watching a jumbo jet come into land.

Eventually he turned and smiled, "sorry I was away with my thoughts. Before I explain why I got you over here, I think it best you have an early night and some rest; you've had a long flight and must be well jet lagged."

Sean was relieved and would have agreed instantly but shook his head. He felt exhausted and rather smelly, he couldn't wait to have a good long shower. "No, come to the hotel and wait for me while I change, then we can go to the office and you can then tell me what's troubling you." He'd been summoned urgently, so no point in delaying matters.

An hour later he joined his friend waiting in the hall. He looked happier and more relaxed. They made their way over to the office and as soon as they had finished greeting the team, headed into Jimmy's office.

"Lots of developments both here and in Beijing," Jimmy started. "Firstly, I'll fill you in on how your young scientists are getting on." He then spent the next hour carefully relating all their movements and their progress. "It seems," he continued, "that they are on the verge of discovering something special, we aren't sure what, but it is suggested that it is a vaccine of some kind, which is a long way from the supposed chemical agent first thought. We aren't sure for what purpose it will serve but our people are monitoring things." He looked up at Sean who was listening intently.

"That would make sense. I've just been in Washington, as you know, and it is widely speculated that the Americans, or rather a couple of research labs over there which are owned and financed by the Chinese, are also excited by a new jab." He paused for a second, "like you, we and our American friends are not sure what it's for, but the two centres have a couple of senior politicians plugging the merits of their vaccine. Surprising though, that both the Chinese and American laboratories are competing in such a way. Anyway, it's all getting pretty hairy and extremely sensitive; the CIA are investigating".

Jimmy shook his head. "American politicians involved with the Chinese! I certainly don't believe that for one minute! Anyone who came to the show the other week?" he enquired.

They were interrupted by a knock on the door and a young man walked in, a couple of sheets of paper in his hand, which he handed to Jimmy. "Think you should see this boss, not good news." Jimmy thanked him and the aide left immediately. He read the report quickly before handing it over to Sean. "This is the other matter I wanted to talk to you about. We heard a few days ago that the powers that be in Beijing had decided to pressurise Hong Kong and get the colony back to full home rule. It seems they are going to impose new laws which will take away a lot of our self-determination and will do this by putting pressure on our puppet leader. Looks as if it has started already." He nodded at the sheets in Sean's hands.

Sean read through the report and looked up, "how did you get this? Has as it come straight from Beijing?".

Jimmy nodded, "yes, it has. We have agents well placed and this came in half an hour ago".

"How did it get here?" enquired Sean.

His host just giggled and shook his head, "that, you really have no need to know. Trust me, it is all one hundred percent accurate. Our agents up there are taking enormous risks. All hand-picked by myself and trained by your guys back in England". He pursed his lips, "I've ordered several more agents to come back to Hong Kong, things are going to get nasty".

"What do you mean by nasty?".

"There are plans for mass demos and un-rest, Hong Kong people don't like being told what to do, and certainly do not want to lose their semi-independence. They don't want to be even more under Beijing rule than they are already." He paused, "we need the world, especially the

West and America, to kick up a fuss, and we need the Prime Minister and the UK Governments' help".

"Send your report to London and tell them what really is happening. You don't need me; I can't help".

"That's where you're wrong. I need you to talk to the bosses and explain the situation, I don't trust our communication lines, even the encrypted ones". Jimmy got up and started pacing, "I know it sounds stupid or paranoic, I've got a feeling that our messages to and from London could be intercepted. It's highly unlikely but we can't take the chance. I have no proof, but the last things I want is to let anyone know we have this information. I've tightened up our security and changed all our codes but even so, I'm worried." He continued to pace up and down, "I trust you Mike, so I'm asking you to go back and tell the boss what is happening, stress it's not just a hunch but a fact and they, as well as the PM, have to start planning a response, and plan fast".

Sean watched the young man prowl about like a caged tiger. "Ok, I will, promise, however I need to know everything you know and more. Are you sure you are not overreacting and panicking for nothing?".

Jimmy shook his head and shrugged. "Maybe you're right, maybe I'm being stupid and over cautious, but I can't help it. Knowing that lot, you can never be too sure".

For the following couple of hours, they discussed the situation and various scenarios. Jimmy told Sean everything they knew and his take on the situation, and they analysed various outcomes this crisis could lead to. At last, Sean had enough information but was still unsure how he would present it. That would come he had a twelve-hour flight ahead of him to work on that.

The next morning Jimmy was at the hotel to take his friend back to the airport. It was a grey wet morning, the clouds hung over the hills and people scuttled around dodging the puddles. As they neared the airport the rain turned to a monsoon, lighting lit up the sky, and it was hard to tell it was 11am. Between avoiding the rapidly growing floods on the road and peering through frantically working windscreen wipers, Jimmy gave Sean an up-date on the overnight news. It looked as if the first mass demonstration would take place a week from now, on the following Sunday; local social media was buzzing. "I have several of my men going to be among the crowd, always good to mingle".

Sean nodded. "Can you keep me posted on developments with events in Wuhan?"

"Sure, no problem. I receive regular reports from our agents, and they will advise me when they know anything new." There was a pause before he continued, "how do you want me to communicate with you?".

Sean looked at him, "you certainly don't trust communications do you! Although I'm not a fan, probably e-mail is best, just make it innocuous and general banter about friends and family, I'll pick up you're meaning. Shame we're too far for pigeons".

As they reached the drop off zone Jimmy looked up at the dark sky. "Can't see any planes coming or going," he pointed out. "Airport could be closed. Wait here until I find out before you get soaked." A few minutes later it was confirmed all flights were cancelled and there would be at least an eighteen-hour delay for all UK out-bound flights. "No point sitting here for that length of time, we'll go back to the office and monitor things from there."

\* \* \*

## England

James collected his bag and was making his way to the exit when two policemen approached him. "Mr Horton, please follow us." James was taken aback and in a total panic but followed meekly. What did they want? They were certainly not border control, he had no duty free and, to his knowledge, no illegal substances. He had heard of people being set up and spending years in jail but that was more in South America or the far East. They reached a door where he was ushered in.

A young woman stood up and smiled. "Welcome back Mr Horton, apologies if we worried you but Mr Flannigan has asked us to meet you as he had to change his plans."

For a moment James was lost, then remembered Sean worked under a different name. He was about to open his mouth when the young woman continued, "I've been asked to accompany you to the train station and make sure you are alright. Mr Flannigan apologises and will be back in a few days when he will contact you."

She moved to the door and ushered him out; the two policemen disappeared. She marched him over to a waiting car and opened the door.

An hour later he was sitting in a First Class carriage heading for home, still totally bewildered at what had just happened. The woman did not speak much unless it was to talk about the weather and asked if he enjoyed his trip to Washington. She smiled politely when he had asked about Sean's, sorry Mike Flannigan's, whereabouts so he was none the wiser. He settled down and fell asleep.

# CHAPTER 27

# Wuhan

Ru and Mei Lien spent most of the day at their desks pouring over data and figures; they spoke non- stop, making comments and asking each other questions. The other scientists left them to it, the two kids could play at being busy, they were working. There was no love between the parties and jealousy was getting worse. Sometime in the late afternoon Ru sat back and nodded to Mei Lien to follow him outside. Once alone, they walked the vast corridors discussing in hushed tones what to do next.

"I think it is time we go and tell the Director" said Mei Lien. "We can't keep this under wraps for much longer".

"Totally agree but how to tell him? And should we do further tests on different animals first?"

"That's not a bad idea, we could set up the tests now and ask to see him tomorrow." She nodded towards the door of the lab, "I don't want that lot getting there first. Yes, they made the initial work, but you and I have driven it forwards and are the only two who really understand what is at stake."

Ru had to agree. "You go and see the boss's secretary and make an appointment and I'll get the final tests set up. They parted and Ru took a deep breath before entering lab No 6. He called over all the scientists and gave his instructions. They mumbled their agreement and for the first time he noticed a slight lightening of their mood. Pointing to a couple of the younger members he instructed them to organise delivery of a fresh set of animals. A monkey, several mice, a couple of small birds, chickens and, why not? -a cat. The grumpy looks soon returned when he told everyone all had to be prepared immediately and no one was to leave until the animals' pens and cages had been disinfected and cleaned, even if that meant staying on late.

Mei Lien got back soon after and whispered in his ear that they had a meeting first thing the next morning, apparently the director had been expecting their request. The lab was a hive of activity, each member working on their assigned tasks. Some preparing the various test tubes and monitors required; others preparing the animal lab. They worked silently with efficiency even if it wasn't done enthusiastically. By 8pm Ru decided to send them all home as he could not stand the poisonous atmosphere. He and Mei Lien busied themselves with last touches and checks. Satisfied each animal had been given their injection and that everything was ready and to their liking, Lab no 6 was closed and locked up.

Neither slept well that night, a combination of excitement and nerves. Ru especially was worried; he did not like what he knew was going to be the outcome of the final checks and in the early hours of the morning he woke Mei Lien from her light sleep. They discussed his thoughts and Mei Lien slowly came round to understanding what her future husband was saying. A deep furrow and concern came over her as she sat up in bed nursing a mug of tea. "Do you think we should stop everything now?" she asked tentatively.

Ru shook his head, "too late, everyone knows about it and the Director is expecting us in a few hours' time - no, we continue". He paused, "I'm not sure how or what to say to his nibs and how far we should warn him".

They fell silent for a long while, both deep in their own thoughts.

At the appointed time they were both standing outside the office waiting to be shown in. Mei Lien felt sick and Ru's mouth was dry as sandpaper. At last, after what seemed ages, the secretary rose from his seat and beckoned them to follow.

"Welcome, good to see you after so long. I understand you have some news." Professor Chi Tao Xing, Director of the Chinese National Research Laboratory in Wuhan pointed to a couple of chairs. He smiled, "now, what have you got for me".

Ru cleared his throat, "Professor, we think we are on the brink of a major discovery. At present, from last night in fact, we have started some new tests on fresh animals. The first results, if all goes well, should be available in ten to twelve days."

The director beamed, "this sounds exciting and most interesting. I did hear that my scientists were onto something big; they are an exceptional bunch, much under-rated". He grinned. "I'm sure they have taught you a great deal."

The hairs on the back of Ru's neck bristled and he dug his nails into the palm of his right hand. It took Mei Lien to speak out first. "Oh, they certainly are an extremely talented group and of course it has been edifying for us. We've learned a lot, especially how people work differently here from Beijing. May I say that we also, have done a lot of work and have often stayed on late and worked most weekends."

Chi Tao expression remained impassive whilst his beady eyes turned cold and bored into her as he nodded slightly, "I am absolutely sure dear lady, that you and your future husband, have worked equally hard but nonetheless, you are only here as final experts; the main work has been carried out by my scientists".

Ru decided it was time to move on and express his fears. "Director, I don't mean to put a dampener on the excellent work done by your fine scientists, but feel I must warn you, if, as we suspect, the outcome of the test are as we anticipate, this could mean China has created an extremely dangerous and lethal weapon. I am sure I do not need to tell you the utmost care will have to be taken."

Chi Tao sat looking at the two of them for a long time. "Thank you for warning me. However, I'm sure we are all capable of taking care of matters." He paused for a while before getting up, "I will not detain you any longer. You have a great deal of work to be done. Let me know when you get these final results."

Ru held his ground and continued. "Sir, I'm not sure you fully understand how dangerous these findings could be and…"

He was stopped by the director holding up a hand and rising from his seat. "Thank you, Mr Nuang, but I'm very capable of comprehending what you have said." He proceeded to usher the two out and quickly closed the door.

Once out of ear shot of the secretary, Mei Lien turned to Ru, "well, I don't think that went too well, the pompous, big headed slob. Did you hear? No thanks for our dedication and putting up with that shower of pen pushers. If it wasn't for you, and your insistence to re-configure the basic make-up of the compound, they would be nowhere." She stomped on, her steps echoing down the corridor. "The fat-faced toad had the nerve to defend that idle bunch and dismiss your warning with contempt, the fat pig!"

Ru put his arm round her shoulders, "I just love it when you get angry, your language is so colourful and you get a lovely flush in your cheeks. Come on, I agree with everything you say, but we mustn't let that "fat pig" upset us; we have work to do and a bunch of pen pushers to sort out."

\* \* \*

As soon as the two youngsters had left, Chi Tao went back to his desk and picked up the phone. He dialled a number by-passing his secretary and waited for the caller at the other end to pick up. His excitement was intense, thoughts of promotion and national recognition racing through his brain. Eventually, someone picked up, "Good morning, Government Offices".

Chi Tao cleared his throat, "good morning, this is Professor Chi Tao, director of science and virology at the National Research Laboratories in Wuhan. Can you please put me through to the Minister for Science and Technology; it is urgent." There was a pause followed by various clicks before he heard the voice he wanted.

\* \* \*

The woman was busy making tea when her mobile rang; she glanced at it before picking up. "The parcel has been delivered, hope you like it," and the phone went dead. She quickly turned off the kettle before putting on her coat and was out in the street heading for the bridge a few minutes later.

The next few hours went quickly. She followed her well-practiced routine, stopping frequently, checking, making sure no one was following. At last, on the way back to the bus stop she took a final look round before entering a tea house and emerged a few minutes later with a large packet of biscuits. Being distracted, she almost missed her bus again and just made it, but only after having carefully left her last purchase on the bench close to the old lady who had come to sit next to her. As the bus rumbled off, she glanced back and smiled.

# CHAPTER 28

---

# Hong Kong

The rain had turned into a full-blown typhoon the likes of which Sean had never seen before. It was clear that he was not going anywhere that day so asked Jimmy to book him into the hotel for another night. They sat chatting, listening to the hum of activity, to the numerous TV screens giving out the news from around the Far East. On the far side of the room things were quieter, three men and one woman were hunched over their desks with earphones on. They scribbled, turned a dial here and there and sipped numerous cups of tea.

Sean nodded towards them. "What are they listening into?".

"Listening to our friends across the border, the girl is tuned into North Korea, we managed to hook up to one of the military channels." He shook his head, "they never seem to think about changing frequency, always the same, has been for three years now".

"You think they know you are listening and are feeding mis-information?"

Jimmy shook his head, "no, everything we hear and pick up comes true. We knew about the nuclear test blast that went wrong last year at the same time as the brass over there did."

He continued, "apart from listening in they're getting coded reports from our agents on the ground". "See, young Lu over there," he pointed at a young man with a ponytail. "He's monitoring Beijing and Shanghai and is the one that heard about the forthcoming plans for

Hong Kong. The man next to him is the one who has been detailed to pick up information on your scientists and monitoring Wuhan."

Sean nodded, "must be pretty intensive and exciting at the same time".

"Yes and no. Lot of the time it is boring stuff but the real hard thing is to remain alert, to pick up on the slightest of insinuations or change of language. Many things are slipped in, what seems, normal conversation; they're not idiots but professionals, like us."

"Think I prefer my job; never been a desk man, I like the action, the danger of field work. What happens when they get something?"

"They report to Pearl or me, give a clear detailed transcript with as much detail as possible so that we can decide what to do".

They chatted and watched for the next few hours. A few reports were brought to Jimmy which he read and handed over to his British counterpart. Sean noticed that Jimmy was always extremely polite, thanking each agent, encouraging them. He never took them for granted. He liked the atmosphere in that office, just wished there was the same back home at HQ.

It was nearing 6pm when Jimmy looked up, "hungry?" he enquired. "Why don't I take you back to the hotel and then we can go and have a bite to eat?"

At the hotel reception they were advised that the weather was set to remain the same for the next 48 hours. The attentive receptionist busied himself juggling the full hotel, to accommodate Sean for two extra nights without having to change rooms. He assured him he would manage to get him on the first flight back to London.

Pearl joined them for a meal on the 32$^{nd}$ floor of the hotel overlooking the bay below. The wind and rain battered the floor to ceiling windows making any request for a window table pointless, there was nothing to see except for drops of water racing down the glass panels. Over dinner, conversation flowed easily, Sean relating a couple of his favourite stories and some lighter moments he had experienced in the field. The two locals were good listeners, and both had a sharp sense of humour, something Sean appreciated. They loved it when he put on his Irish accent; Jimmy trying to imitate it made them all laugh. It was getting to midnight when they left, agreeing that Pearl would pick Sean up just after 9am the next morning.

In his dreams Sean heard a church bell. He was battling some mysterious enemy mixed up with racing a car up a mountain pass. Somewhere deep in the subconsciousness of his brain told him the ringing sound was not a dream. He opened an eye, switched on the bedside light, and looked at his watch – 2.47am; who would be calling him at this hour? He picked up his mobile but didn't recognise the number. He was about to switch off when his instincts told him to answer. "Hello." he muttered.

"Sorry to wake you at this hour," said the voice at the other end.

"Is that you Jimmy?" asked Sean now fully awake.

"Yes, sorry, thought I should let you know we've had news from our friends; there have been some big developments. I'll meet you in the lobby in forty-five minutes."

Sean jumped out of bed and got dressed. He was feeling a little fuzzy after the copious amount of whisky they had consumed at the table, good Malt, but even the best in great quantities can make your mouth taste like sandpaper.

He was waiting in the lobby when a car pulled up and Jimmy waved him over. "Sorry to get you out of bed but we must get to the office. How are you feeling?"

Sean looked across at the young man. "Should you be driving? I'm sure you were keeping up with me."

Jimmy grinned and pulled out onto the empty street. "Got lots of practice when I was studying in England."

"That's no excuse or alibi my friend. What's so urgent that you got me out of my pit at this un-godly hour?"

Jimmy was silent for a minute before replying, "two developments. The first is news from Wuhan, the second from Beijing confirming the first and giving us more details on the plans for Hong Kong". They continued in silence before Jimmy looked over, "It must be fate that your flight was cancelled; fate plays a big part in our culture, did you know that?".

As they entered the office they were met by a middle-aged man with straggly, lanky hair and sporting a goatee. He ushered them through to Jimmy's office and closed the door.

Once settled in his chair Jimmy introduced the man as Coogan, chief of his night shift. Coogan then produced a sheaf of papers which he handed over for his boss to read. Once he had gone over them, Jimmy passed them over to Sean who was amazed at the amount of detail these reports contained. Jimmy then spent the next thirty minutes grilling his chief, questioning and probing until he was satisfied that all the information had been set out. He looked up, "well done, excellent work; you were absolutely right to call me in". Pursing his lips, he continued, "what do the team make of it?"

"Concerned Jimmy, very concerned, especially about what is going to happen here in the city."

"What about the news from Wuhan?"

Coogan shrugged, "don't have many thoughts about that, but it must be big for Beijing to get so excited about. No, what I'm worried about, is what is going to happen to Hong Kong; I bet my last dollar the world will just sit back and do nothing, mark my words."

There was a long pause before Coogan decided it was time to go back and continue his work. "Call me if you need me."

The next hours was spent reading and discussing the recent events.

"Yep, I think you're right Jimmy, fate has been good to us. What would you say if I decided to pay a visit to our two friends, get the up-to-date situation direct from the horse's mouth so to speak. The only problem is this damned typhoon, how long do they typically last?"

Jimmy shrugged. "As long as they do," he smiled. "You could get the train if you didn't want to wait."

"Are they running?"

"Oh yes, the typhoon is only over Hong Kong, once you go north, through the mountains, it's just a storm. In fact, if you wanted, you could fly home from Wuhan."

Sean thought a moment before replying. "Ok, I'll take the train, but I won't go home; once I find out what's happening I'll come back and report. You can tell me again what you want me to tell my people back home when I return to London. When is the first train?"

"Slowly my friend, slowly," Jimmy held up his hand. "You are not going anywhere without Pearl, and without us setting things up first."

"You seem to forget my friend, I have spent my life as a field operator, I can look after myself, I don't need a nanny or a chaperone." Sean regretted his tome immediately, "sorry, didn't mean it like that; for sure, it's your operation now and you are in charge, but I can look after myself".

"Thank you, and no offence taken. It would be way too dangerous for you, and them, to meet in public or even at their flat; things have changed a lot since your first visit, but one thing for certain has not. State surveillance is just as part of everyday life as ever, and our two will be under heavy scrutiny after what we've learnt. I'll get Pearl to organise the meeting and she can escort you."

"Fair dos Jimmy, I appreciate it and, sorry again. Of course, you're right my friend."

"I'll check it out but I think there's a train at 2.30pm, that will get you in about 4pm the next day, I'll get you both booked on it. In the meantime, I suggest you go back to the hotel, get some sleep and check out in the morning. I'll ask Pearl to come in immediately and you can meet her back here at about 1.30."

Sean nodded, "sounds a good plan boss but what about a visa?".

"Leave that to us, I have an idea."

\* \* \*

## Wuhan

Ru and Mei Lien spent the next couple of days working sixteen-hour shifts; they wanted to make sure that everything went smoothly but mostly, they wanted to keep tabs on their team. The closer the big day approached, the more paranoic they became, especially Ru. He didn't trust any of them, especially the very junior member, Lu Ching, who's position was more a goffer than a scientist. His shifty eyes, his slouching, and his constant sneaking about got on his nerves. Had he been planted there as a spy or was he just creepy; Ru couldn't make his mind up. All he knew was that he disliked the man intensely and the atmosphere in the lab was toxic; he didn't like it one little bit.

They were sitting in the canteen one afternoon, the first break they had taken since arriving that morning, enjoying the peace and relaxation they never thought the great hall could offer them.

Mei Lien was about to stand up and leave when the old cleaner came over to clear the table, something Mei Lien had never seen before. As she picked up the cups and flipped a dirty cloth over the table, she pushed a piece of paper inter Mei Lien's hand, patted her on the arm and returned to the counter.

Passing the toilets Mei Lien told Ru to wait for her whilst she visited the ladies. After checking all the other cubicles, she locked herself in the furthest away one. She read the note and re-read over again to make sure she had understood it correctly, her mind racing. Someone entered the cubicle next door and she hurriedly stuffed the note into her pocket. She felt the sweat trickle down the back of her neck and held her breath. Eventually the occupant flushed the toilet and left, she let out a big sigh of relief. She read the note a couple of times more before tossing it into the toilet and pulled the chain.

Back in the corridor she went straight to Ru, "we need to talk but not here. Can we go home?" she panted.

Ru looked at her in puzzlement, "tell me, what is it?"

"No, it can wait, I don't want to say anything in this place". Ru looked at her and shook his head, women he thought!

Once in the safety of their flat Mei Lien pulled her lover over and started to whisper. "Why are you whispering?" asked Ru. "You're really acting strange since the tea break; what's wrong with you?"

Mei Lien continued in a hushed tone. "I'm scared we might be overheard, or the place is bugged."

"Have you gone completely mad; our home bugged!" he shook his head. "Are you sure you haven't been inhaling some sort of gas or taken one of those drugs at the lab; our home bugged!" He tried to move away but she held him tight.

"Did you see the old cleaner at the canteen? She slipped me a note as we were leaving," she whispered, her lips a few inches from Ru's ear. "I read it when I was in the toilet. It was well written, too well for an old cleaner; anyway, it said that someone wants to meet us in a secret place and more details will follow. We have to go back to the canteen tomorrow between 3 and 4pm." She moved away and looked at Ru.

He remained silent for a long time, eventually he shook his head. "I don't understand. Who would want to meet us secretly and what for?" He continued, "unless it is something to do with work and in that case, I certainly don't like it".

"I'm scared," said Mai Lien as she cuddled into him.

He folded his arms round her, "It can't be the authorities, they wouldn't be so secret, simply summon us or arrest us; no, it must be someone else but who?" He shuddered and felt sick at the thought that had entered his mind.

"What's wrong?" asked Mei Lien as she felt Ru's tremor.

"Nothing, no nothing, don't worry." Looking down at her he knew he had to tell her, "it must be the Triads or local mafia; who else could it be? I bet it's one of those no gooders at the lab that is involved, most probably that slimy Lu Chin. I knew he was a bad one from the start." They fell silent for a long time before Ru spoke again, "it must be one of the Triads, he's told them of our work, and now they are trying to muscle in before anyone else".

* * *

The next day was probably the most difficult one they had ever spent. Suspicious and worried, they kept themselves busy and avoided contact with the others as much as possible. The trials were going according to plan. The tests results continued to worry Ru more and more, he did not like what he saw and nor did Mei Lien. Both understood the possible implications of the discovery, especially if they fell into the wrong hands. The thought of that brough back memories of the previous evening and, as agreed, they did not impart any of their concerns or fears to the other scientists. They were pretty sure one or two of them may have a good idea of what they were working on but doubted, very much, any of them cared or even considered the possible consequences.

It was mid-afternoon when they made their way back to the canteen and sat down at a table by the window. The old cleaner was nowhere to be seen. They spent a tense half-hour sipping tea and looking around. "Well, that was a waste of time," Ru muttered as they rose and headed for the exit. Just as they were approaching the main door Mei Lien felt a tug on her arm and saw the old cleaner by her side, "lady, you forgot this on the table," she handed over an envelope and bowed slightly. Mei Lien was about to thank her, but the old hag had left.

Mei Lien once again entered the toilet and locked herself in a cubicle. She opened the envelope with trembling hands and read the neatly written instructions. She memorised each word before flushing it down the toilet, pulling the lever twice to make sure it was well on its way.

Back in the lab it was difficult to concentrate but she managed to keep going. Ru was anxious and it showed; he was curt with several of their colleagues who came up asking him to check certain details, and barked orders to Lu Chin. At last, and not a minute too early, it was time to go home.

# CHAPTER 29

---

# Dorset

James woke to the buzz of his phone on his bedside table. He turned and switched on the light. His clock indicated 6.05am; who on earth would call him at this time of day? His wife Claire rolled over and mumble something before going back to sleep. James picked up the phone. Sean's distinctive lilt came over, "top of the morning to you Jamesie, how are you today?" asked the breezy voice.

"What time do you call this? I was fine, tucked up in my cosy bed, enjoying a lovely dream until I was rudely awoken," he retorted.

"Ah, sorry, must have got the time difference wrong," came the jovial voice. "How is the delightful Mrs H, hope I didn't disturb anything," he enquired.

James ignored the last sentence. "Where are you and what are you doing?"

"I'm in Hong Kong, had a few things to do, a last-minute change of plan. In fact, I'll be here for a few more days and wondered whether you could meet me in Washington next Monday? You'll be re-imbursed of course."

"I am sure I can find time for another cross Atlantic visit in my busy schedule. How long will I be staying?"

"Not sure, get an open ticket. I'll ask our friends to arrange accommodation and they will meet you at the airport."

"Well, are you going to tell me what you are doing in Hong Kong, or am I going to be kept in the dark?" asked James.

"Kept in the dark my friend, for sure you know how I hate talking on the phone. I'll fill you in when we meet. Must go. Enjoy your bedtime with Mrs H. and see you in a few days."

"Don't be rude and have a good time," his voice trailed off as he heard the sound of the line cutting out before he had finished.

\* \* \*

## Washington

Hank was busy finalising a report he was due to send up to Brian Millento. He was struggling to make it sound like they were making good progress but to not divulge what they knew of his boss' involvement. He was on his third draft when his phone rang and he saw it was Sean.

"Hi buddy, how's it going?" he opened up.

"Just to let you know that I shall be returning to see you a week today; have asked James to join us, so can you organise accommodation and a meeting party?"

"Sure, sure, no problem. I guess you have news; you want the others?"

A minute later he put down the phone and got back to his draft. Satisfied at last, he buzzed for his secretary and handed over the sealed envelope. He rubbed his hands in excitement, if Sean was returning so soon it could only mean he had some more news. He picked up the phone and put Joe in the picture.

"Good timing boss, I was about to ring you. Can you meet me for a pizza after work, usual place?"

He had barely hung up when his desk phone buzzed again, it was Brian.

"Well done Hank, great report and really happy you're making progress. The boss will be delighted." Hank just grunted and waited for the next sentence he knew was coming. "You could have expanded a bit with names etc…can you do that and fill me in now?"

"Not exactly Brian, as you can see the investigation is at a critical stage. It's not that I don't trust you, as my boss, of course I do, but it could put some of our people in danger if anything got out. I just don't want to jeopardise anything or anyone at this stage."

There was a silence at the other end; he could imagine Brian's expression and practically hear his brain working. Brian sighed deeply, "fine, but I'll need to have names very soon, you can't expect me to fob John off for ever. I'm supposed to be in charge and he ain't going to like it if I tell him I can't trust him or I don't know".

Yeah, Hank thought. Bet you want to take the glory and find out how much we know, but over my dead body. "Ok, give me a couple of weeks and by then I'll be in position to tell you."

There was a grunt and Brian snapped back his agreement before putting down the phone . Hank sat back in his chair, sweat trickling down his face, he closed his eyes and prayed he hadn't given any hint of their suspicions.

He looked at his watch; another hour before he met Joe. He didn't really feel in the mood, would much rather go home and watch a game with a can of beer. He sighed again, a deep long sigh; how long before he could retire? He could hand in his resignation and leave them to sort out this mess. He dismissed the idea at once, and getting up, he left the office.

He arrived early at the restaurant and found a quiet table in the corner and ordered a beer. He sat watching the other customers enjoying their evening – the two lovers making sweet talk, all totally unaware of the plotting and scheming going on a few blocks away; he sighed again and took a long gulp of his drink. He waited patiently; Joe was late, and that wasn't like him. For some reason it made him feel anxious and irritated. He finished his drink and ordered another.

Twenty minute later Joe marched in, a broad smile on his face. "Sorry, Hank, for being late, I know you hate waiting." He called over the waiter and ordered two beers before settling himself down. "Got some news. Have you heard from Jack?"

Hank shook his head. "Should I have".

Joe didn't want to tell the man in front of him, that the head of London operations had phoned himself rather than his boss. "Got a call from him saying he tried you but couldn't get through. Anyway, he had a call from Sean who sounded really excited and wants to come back here next Sunday. Asked if we could arrange accommodation and meet James."

Hank looked puzzled. "Never got a call. Did speak to Sean though, asked me to do the same. When did he try? he asked, but was met with a shrug of the shoulders.

Joe continued before Hank had time to say anything else. "Seems there are major developments in China on several fronts; he didn't say much but implied that things could turn nasty."

"Ok, I'll sort things out for James, same as last time I guess. Is that all you got me out here for, nothing else to tell me?" he asked. "What kind of nasty? Say something for god's sake!"

"Don't sound so pissed off, of course that's not all," Joe looked hurt and changed the subject. "Had another chat with Maggy earlier today".

"You did what!" hissed Hank, his jaw clenched. "You know we agreed we shouldn't meet with her unless I agreed first, and only in my presence. What the hell are you playing at?" he glowered at his friend across the table.

Joe held up his hand, "ok, ok I know, but I had to get confirmation on a couple of things and I thought you would be fine with it - sorry".

"Thought I'd be fine with it! Joe must I remind you again, I'm your boss and what I say goes. It's the second time recently. What's got into you?"

There was silence whilst the waiter brought their pizza and a couple more glasses of beer.

"Look boss, I heard through the grapevine that Maggy had a friend who works as a secretary at the White House and is very much liked by the President." He looked over to Hank who was munching on a slice of his pizza looking very unhappy. "It turns out that this friend is used by the President whenever he wants anything done privately."

"Where's this going Joe? It had better be good or you're going to find out who is the boss; in fact I might just feed you to Brian."

Joe ignored the threat and continued, "look, if this thing is as big as we think it is and we don't want anyone in the department to know, why don't we try and go direct to the President? We can use Maggy's friend and see if she can arrange a meeting?"

Hank nearly choked on his beer, "you really think the President will agree to sit down with a couple of low life agents and entertain us in the Oval Office! What the fuck are you on?"

"I know it sounds stupid but think about it; he has major problems with the Chinese and doesn't trust them an inch, rightly so. If we can convince him that the Chinese are developing a chemical or biological or whatever weapon and we have something of National importance, he might just go for it."

"You've lost it buddy, totally lost it. Think it's time you went back to your place and took up fishing again."

Joe was about to continue but thought better of it. He shrugged, "Ok, you're the boss. I'll leave in the morning," he smiled and winked. Hank glowered at him and carried on eating.

"By the way, your friend Carter, not a bad lad but he's too weak for the job, needs to be toughened up if he's to continue. Got the modern disease of many of his generation."

"Knew it. What is the modern disease?" asked Hank.

"Soft, flippy flabby and, as Horton would say, he's a snowflake; thinks everyone must be given a chance, you can't say anything for fear of up-setting them and you must be politically correct. All bullshit, but he keeps on pulling me up over comments I make and the way I talk."

Hank's expression changed instantly, and he began to laugh his low rumble laugh, a laugh only he managed to produce. "I can just imagine the two of you." He paused to wipe away a tear, "what'd you suggest we do? Perhaps I should assign him to you on a permanent basis. Yeah, that's what I 'll do if you don't start respecting my orders," he chuckled.

"You do that, and I'll never talk to you again. On a serious note, I'll keep him under my control until we wrap up this case; don't need any unhappy agent blabbing, he doesn't know much but...

He looked over to his boss, "after that, it's up to you. You either fire him or send him some place like Angola where he'll learn what the real world is really like. You know what he told me the other day? Thought we should have more female and transgender agents; that we're discriminating".

"I'm sure you agreed with him whole heartedly. Guess he has a point. I should take that up with Brian."

Joe shook his head, "Yeah, you do that; it'll really help your career prospects. To answer your question, I did give it to him both barrels. Poor kid just sat there white as a sheet, never heard anyone speaking in such a way. You know me, don't hold back." He looked up and took a sip from his new glass. "Told him to open his eyes and get his facts right before spewing garbage. Pointed out to him some of our best agents are female and are worth ten of the likes of him."

\* \* \*

## Wuhan

Both Ru and Mei Lien stayed on late, they needed peace and quiet to go over the week's results and didn't want to have snooping eyes scrutinizing their every movement. Happy with being able to talk freely, they worked on until tiredness took its toll.

Both slept badly and rose early next day. Ru checked his watch several times before calling to Mei Lien it was time to go. Today was the day; they had decided to follow the instructions that had been passed on to them by the cleaner. They weren't sure why and both were worried, but after talking things over the night before they had decided they had to go, even if it was foolhardy. Unsure of what trap or the consequences lay ahead, they had decided the best thing was to go along and see. As Mei Lien pointed out, if they didn't go it was most likely their hosts would come and look for them, and if that was the case, then the outcome might not be so good. Either way things looked grim.

Following instructions, they spent an hour travelling East through the city heading for a poor district, half-slum, half-rural and crammed with small factories and sweatshops. Getting of the bus they looked round at the dusty, empty street. No one was to be seen but they suspected dozens of eyes would be peering through blinds. Mei Lien shivered as she looked around and took Ru's out-stretched hand. They made their way down a narrow side lane and, as instructed, entered a small garden through a red gate. The house was a single storey building with flaking walls surrounded by a small, neat garden. Taking a deep breath Ru looked at Mei Lien, "into the dragons' mouth," he whispered and lifted his hand to knock.

The door opened before he had time to make contact and a slim, neat woman stood in front of them. She smiled and bowed politely. "Welcome, please come in." She ushered them along a dim corridor passing an open door; Mei Lien glanced in and noticed an old woman sitting hunched in a chair, sleeping, her mouth open; she shivered. The kitchen was small and doubled up as a sitting room. It was bright with a round wooden table in the centre. A woman and a man were sitting sipping tea and immediately got up to greet them. Ru and Mei Lien were surprised and relieved to see the Englishman and the woman.

The door closed and the four were left alone. Pearl waved them to a chair and offered them tea. She poured herself another cup and re-filled Sean's.

"We are so pleased you decided to come, we were worried that you might have decided to ignore the invitation," she sat down. "You no doubt remember our friend from England", she turned and smiled at Sean. "We must apologise for the manner of the invitation, we wanted to speak to you but didn't wish to arouse suspicion or put you in danger." She looked across at both of the visitors. "Are you married yet?" she enquired. "It seems such a long time ago since we accidently met you in Hong Kong."

"No, not yet, still just engaged. We hope to get married next year," replied Mei Lien.

"And are you still living in the same flat?" Pearl continued knowing perfectly well they had moved.

"No, it was a bit small, the Centre has kindly supplied a larger one, handy for work. Its free apart from the electricity." Mei Lien giggled nervously.

"The Chinese Government is particularly good like that," continued Pearl. "You must be doing very well and be important to receive such generous benefits."

Ru nodded.

"We hear through the Hong Kong press that the laboratory is about to make a revolutionary discovery."

Both scientists froze, and a worried frown came over them. "I don't know where you've heard that, but it is incorrect," blurted Ru.

"Oh!" Pearl looked surprised. "Just shows you can never trust the media," she smiled.

There was an awkward silence before Sean spoke for the first time. "The American labs have developed great vaccines lately and we read in the papers back home that China is doing the same, it's certainly very encouraging to hear that both nations are working on such good causes. I also read that the WHO conference went very well."

Again, Ru nodded. "Yes, it is encouraging as you say. I only wish all of it was true."

She looked over to him before taking over. "You are right, there have been some great advances and we are close to producing, not a vaccine, but a very dangerous weapon which, in the wrong hands could be a disaster for the world," she spluttered out.

Sean and Pearl remained impassive. "I thought you were working in a laboratory, not an arms factory," continued Sean lightly.

"We are indeed, here in Wuhan. Our research laboratory has been working on this for a couple of years. Things were slow at the beginning, and we were brought in to try and advance matters which we have. Unfortunately, I fear we've gone too far." Ru looked at Mei Lien and his head slumped.

There was silence for a long while, Pearl was the first to speak and her tone was soothing, "I am sure all will be fine; you're worrying yourselves needlessly. How far forward are you in the production of this... weapon?"

Mel Lien took over once more, "on the final trial stages, we should know within the next few weeks. We're now testing the third set of animals, all new, different ones. After we've completed all the lab tests and analysis on the new animals, we'll then know for sure if our findings are right. We're using mice, cats, chickens, a monkey and a couple of birds. Each set was carefully checked before starting, to ensure they were healthy and clean of any infections first. We're now on the last batch of results.".

She looked pleadingly at the two foreigners. "Please don't tell anyone; our lives depend on it. If it ever gets out that we have spoken to you, we could be in deadly danger."

"Not could be – will be," Ru stressed. Looking up, "I think it time we left," he added.

They parted company, Pearl assuring them of their discretion. The woman walked them down to the main street in silence, then, as a passer-by approached, she said in a louder than normal voice, "It was so kind of you to come and see me; I receive very few visitors nowadays, my time is so taken up caring for my mother".

She saw them onto the bus and waved them off.

Ru and Mei Lien found a seat away from the other passengers and breathed a deep sigh of relief. They were silent for most of the trip back.

\* \* \*

Sean and Pearl waited until the woman returned and relayed what they had been told. It was clear the two young scientists were working on something big and were petrified. Neither were clued up enough on science and they felt helpless; without Ru and his girl opening up further, they would remain in the dark.

# CHAPTER 30

---

# Hong Kong

That evening Jimmy received a cryptic note from Pearl giving an outline of the meeting and was disappointed. He had hoped for more but, it was early days yet ,and he felt, deep down, that things had only just begun. He turned his attention to the more pressing matter of the future of Hong Kong and the massive march which was being planned. The weather had improved, and the note indicated that Pearl and Mike were going to fly back early the next morning.

\* \* \*

## Wuhan

Back at the flat Ru and Mei Lien flopped down on the sofa and both started to speak at the same time.

"Not sure" Ru talked over his fiancée, "that we should have said as much as we did. We don't really know them; they were fishing".

Mei Lien shrugged.

"I know, you're right, but it just came out, sorry. You don't think they could help us, do you?" he continued after a long pause. "They may know people who could warn the powers in the West of the dangers."

Ru shook his head.

"No, my darling. They are working for the West, and they are agents or spies. I always knew they were not just friends of your ex; it was an excuse to meet us, to try and subvert us. The only question is, how dangerous are they to your and my future. They certainly don't care about us; these people have no feelings, so it depends how far they want to go in order to find out what we are working on."

Mei Lien started to sob "I'm so sorry, I really didn't mean to put us in such a situation".

He comforted her as best he could, and they spent the rest of the evening watching TV.

Ru woke early the next morning. he had slept badly tossing and turning, thinking over the meeting of the previous day. He rolled over and kissed Mei Lien who stirred. "What time is it?" she asked between yawns and a big stretch.

He got up, "just gone 5.30, I'm going through to the kitchen".

A few minutes later she joined him and they sat sipping steaming mugs of tea. "I've been thinking," he started, "we should call the girl and the foreigner and ask to talk to them again; It's the best way, you're right, they are the only ones that can help us".

She looked at him dubiously, "that's a change of heart; last night you said they were spies and foreign agents with no feelings and out to do us in".

"I'm still convinced they are," he nodded, "but somehow, I think they can help us, or at least advise us. You have the phone number – let's call them first thing before they leave".

They talked, changing their minds several times but eventually Mei Lien picked up her phone and dialled Pearl's number. She waited, listening to the continuous beeps until she heard the message advising that the caller was unavailable. She hung up

"Are you sure you have the right number?" he asked.

Mei Lien nodded, "look" and she handed him her phone. "I entered it in my contacts last time we met them in Hong Kong."

Ru looked shocked, "you stupid girl, what if you lost it or the police took it away!".

"I put it under one of my uncles' name; he died a while ago so they can't ask him. I'll try again in an hour or so".

They went out for a long walk; the flat felt claustrophobic, and both needed some fresh air. It was mid-day when Mei Lien tried again and once more, she got no response. "Typical of these Westerners," Ru mumbled morosely, "all talk and bluster, and empty promises. We should have known better". He got up and started pacing the room.

Mei Lien suddenly jumped up and ran through to the bedroom. She came back waving a scrap of paper, "look what I found," she waved the note under Ru's nose. "I only just remembered the woman had also given me this, it's her home number," she said excitedly.

Ru looked suspiciously at the number, "I don't like the idea of calling a landline in Hong Kong, you know what you hear, every call is monitored; it will come back and haunt us".

She shrugged. "Up to you; you know best".

They sat in silence for a long time, Ru's mind racing and in a turmoil. At last, he picked up the phone and dialled. A few rings later he heard a male voice ,"JM Shipping, how can I help". Alarmed, Ru immediately ended the call. He turned to Mei Lien, "must have the wrong number, it was a man's voice in some shipping company".

She looked puzzled and looked at the numbers again. "It's definitely the number and you dialled it right; try again, may have got a crossed line."

He shook his head, "no, once is enough. I knew it was a bad idea. I'm going out. Do you need anything?" he asked

She closed her eyes and her head slumped as she turned away from him. She kept silent, knowing he was in a mood and worried. No need to make things worse. She made sure he was in the street before trying the mobile number once more; still she was greeted with the same message. Plucking up courage she dialled the second number. On the third ring someone picked up, a man, "JM Shipping, how can I help?".

She spoke softly, almost a whisper, and asked for Pearl. As she uttered the name she panicked and ended the call. She sat back breathing heavily and a feeling of nausea came over her.

Ru returned in a better mood; his spirits restored. "I've been thinking, we can do this on our own, we don't need any foreigners' help. First thing on Monday we check the results, then we go and talk to Chi Tao and give him all the facts, show him the data. He's a pompous old fool but he is a scientist, so will understand what we are saying." He looked down at Mei Lien before continuing, "we must absolutely warn him again of the dangers; after that, well, the decision is his".

"Can we trust him to take the right action and not use it as a means to his promotion. I doubt he will listen to us; remember the last time".

Ru took her face in her hands, "we have no other choice. That way, we have done our work, have given our professional opinion and completed our job."

She smiled, "and we can leave this dump and go back to Beijing. Yes I like it, in fact, I love your plan".

*　*　*

## Hong Kong

Jimmy was puzzled and sat looking at the man standing at the door. "You say the same number rang twice. The first time the caller rang off when you answered and the second time just after mentioning Pearl's name."

The man nodded, "it was a woman, very soft voiced. Sounded scared and a bit panicky. It was like she changed her mind. I managed to trace both calls to a mobile in China, most likely in the region of Wuhan but can't be sure".

Jimmy thanked the man and told him he would take over from there. He would ask Pearl when she got back shortly.

*　*　*

The traffic from the airport was heavy and as they neared the city it got horrendous, with long queues and delays. Pearl tried to take as many back roads and streets as possible, but still the congestions were something to be seen. Police and ambulances were everywhere. The news on the car radio reported that the demonstration was gathering pace and police were expecting fifty thousand people. They warned the residents to stay at home.

Two and a half hours after leaving the airport Pearl pulled into a small underground car park. "That was interesting," she said.

She got out of the car followed by Sean and they made their way across the street, entering the offices of JW Shipping. They were greeted by Jimmy who led them straight into his office. "Coffee, tea?" he asked.

"Tea for me, but first, I need the loo! Two and a half hours it took us, it's mayhem out there."

Jimmy nodded to the TV, "media is reporting fifty thousand but it's more like double or treble that. The authorities have been completely taken by surprise".

Pearl returned a few minutes later, "Ah that's better, what news have you got?"

Jimmy gave them a rundown of the situation in town and how tensions were rising steadily. "The demo should be finished by 6pm but my guys are reporting that there are plans for it to continue through the night and all day tomorrow. The Government has totally miscalculated the mood." He took a sip of tea, "how did your visit go?"

"Fine, we met up with the two of them. Mike is a bit disappointed they didn't speak more, but it wasn't surprising."

"The girl seemed keen and willing. The boy spoke more than he should and clammed-up. Both were scared stiff," said Sean.

Jimmy nodded and thanked them. "We had a bit of a surprise earlier," he nodded over to one the desks. "Young David had a couple of phones calls, both presumably from the same person, but each time the phone call was ended within seconds. He says it was a girl's voice." He picked up a sheet of paper, "he managed to trace the mobile to somewhere in China, Wuhan area precisely".

Both Pearl and Sean looked at each other. Pearl leant over and took the sheet of paper Jimmy was handing over, "you recognise it?" he asked.

Pearl shook her head, "no, but there's only one-person I gave this number to who lives in Wuhan". She rummaged through her bag and pulled out her mobile. Inserting the sim card, she waited until it up-dated. Two missed calls, both from the same number Jimmy had given her. "It must be from Mei Lien. I wonder what she wants."

Sean hesitated, "to speak to us," he ventured grinning.

Pearl pressed the re-dial button and waited for the connection to be made. The voice at the other end sounded hesitant, but before it could say anything Pearl butted in, "Mei Lien, this is your aunt Pearl, you tried to phone me, I was travelling and didn't have a signal".

There was a palpable sigh of relief from the other end. "Oh, thank you for calling back, it's nothing urgent but we were hoping to talk to you about an idea we have." The girl learns fast thought Pearl. "Where are you?"

Pearl told her that she and uncle had just returned home. The voice sounded disappointed. Sensing the situation, she quickly added, "we're not able to come back soon, but if it's urgent I can see what we can arrange".

Mei Lien agreed to wait until she heard from her "aunt" and thanked her. Just before hanging up Pearl slipped in, "you know, one of the best things to do if you have a problem, is to go to the canteen and have some tea, it's surprising how things can fall into place with a good pot. Make sure of doing that next time you're at work". She hoped the young woman would understand her message; it was worth a try.

Mei Lien came off the phone all excited. She called out to Ru. He was at the same time cross, happy and relieved. He had told her to forget about contacting the foreigners but softened when she told him the woman had phoned back. When Mei Lien told him about the last message, he agreed that it was a coded message. Scratching the back of his neck he asked, "what do we do now? I still don't like it, I don't like it at all; one error and we spend the rest of our lives in prison, or worse. On the other hand, it could be, literally a life changer".

They both sat in deep thought for a long while. At last Mei Lien broke the silence, "we can play it by ear; we can go to the canteen on Monday and see if anything happens. If the old hag doesn't turn up or give us anything, we go to see Chi Tao".

Ru had to agree it made sense but remained uneasy. "I think we do as you suggest, but I also think we should go and tell him. It's only fair, and we must cover our backs. That way no one can accuse us of hiding anything or committing treason."

*　*　*

Back at the office in Hong Kong, the three of them sat mulling over their next move. Jimmy was desperate for Sean to go back to London and report the situation to his superior. At the same time, things were moving at a pace up in Wuhan. Pearl pointed out that Mike could not go back to Wuhan without getting a new visa and she did not recommend going through the recent process. A new one would take at least a week. Finally, it was decided that he would fly back to London that night, report to his boss and return to Hong Kong a few days after. Jimmy suggested that if he could use another name, it would be easier to re-enter China on a seventy-two-hour visitors' visa. During that time Pearl would monitor developments in China.

# CHAPTER 31

# London

Jack had not heard from Sean since returning from Washington; he wondered what the man was up to. Last he knew, Sean was heading for Hong Kong, for reasons only Sean knew. He picked up the phone and called James.

The phone was answered by a softly spoken woman who asked for his name and a few seconds later James's unmistakable voice came on the line.

"Is that you Jack?"

"Afternoon James, sorry to disturb you, but you wouldn't know where Sean is, would you?" He tried to put on his best English accent as he always did when talking to James.

"Not the foggiest. Hoped you knew more than me," came the chirpy voice. "Last I heard he was off to Hong Kong; woke me up in the middle of the night, well early morning to be truthful. Ordered me to go back to Washington to meet you all. Going up to Heathrow later tonight."

"What flight are you on?" asked Jack. "I'm on American Airlines leaving at 10am".

"BA at 11.30; I like to support our national carrier,", there was a slight giggle.

"Ok, I'll see you over there and make sure someone meets you. Safe journey". He hung up still puzzled as to the whereabouts of his English counterpart.

*  *  *

Jack was sitting in the back of one of the Embassy pool cars on his way to the airport when his phone rang. It was Sean.

"Hey stranger, where are you?"

"Just about to board a plane for Heathrow; and you?"

"On my way to Washington as we agreed. Why the hell are you flying back here?" he asked slightly annoyed.

"Too long to explain but need to see you the minute I get in. The Washington meeting can wait a couple of days. I've been trying to get hold of James to stop him, with no luck. Can you try? I'm due to land at 10.45am UK time tomorrow morning; I suggest we meet at my office at 1.30pm. And bring James with you. Must rush, see you". The phone went dead. Jack was left looking at his mobile with ever growing puzzlement. He told his driver to drop him off at Terminal 5 and wait for him.

Arriving at British Airways terminal, he made quick progress to the departure hall and then to the gate just before security. He was in luck, only one of the two was open. It was not long before he spotted James striding towards him dressed in a new tweed jacket, his tatty old briefcase in hand.

The older man looked startled at the sight of the American and they shook hands warm. "Don't tell me you missed your plane?"

"No, got a call from Sean, he's cancelled the meeting for now. Wants to meet us tomorrow at his office." He shook his head, "don't ask, I have no idea."

"How bloody inconsiderate of him. I was looking forward to another few days with you chaps." They both laughed. "How can I get my bag back, do you know?"

Forty minutes later Jack was escorting his English friend back to the car. On their way into town Jack booked James into a hotel not far from his flat. "Why don't we meet up tonight and have a relaxed meal. It's been a while since I've had an evening out."

\* \* \*

## Wuhan

Ru and Mei Lien woke at daybreak. Again, both had slept fitfully; neither could concentrate. Ru seemed more nervous than Mei Lien, who went about her morning chores as if she had no worries in the world. They arrived at the laboratory early, before the rest of the team, and set to work analysing the week-end data. They inspected the animals and looked them over carefully, making notes. By 8.15am laboratory No 6 was a hive of activity. Ru asked the animals be checked over one last time. "Make sure you take final readings, blood samples and every small detail noted," he ordered. After all this was done the group would sit down and go through the findings one last time. It was going to be a busy morning. Pouring over their microscopes Ru and Mei Lien worked continuously, occasionally altering their notes. The more Ru looked at the results, the more he did not like what he saw. He sat back and closed his eyes, was it time to end the project, to tell everyone to go home and tell Tao Chi they were quitting?

Mei Lien came over and put her hand on his shoulder, "I'm going to the canteen, want to come?" she asked quietly.

He shook his head and looked her in the eyes, "no, you go, I have too much to think about. You know what all this means, I'm not sure I want to stop, or if we should continue".

Mei Lien knew he was thinking the same as her, but she dared not to enter the conversation for fear of them making the wrong, hasty, decision. Quitting would be morally the easier option, but the consequences for both of them would be unthinkable. No, they would have to continue whatever the outcome but here, in laboratory No 6, was not the right place to take that decision.

She made her way to the canteen. At the door she stopped and hesitated, took a deep breath and proceeded to the counter. She found a seat away from the other patrons and looked around. The old cleaner was nowhere to be seen; she relaxed slightly but felt annoyed. Why did she put herself through all this stress? A voice in her mind told her to get up and leave before it was too late. She sat nursing her cup of tea looking into space, her mind a whirl of thoughts.

Minutes slipped by and still the old woman had not appeared, time to get back to the lab. She sighed and was about to get up when her contact appeared from nowhere and begun wiping the table. As she flicked a dirty cloth over the chair next to Mei Lien, she placed a small piece of paper on the girl's lap. She was gone as quickly as she had arrived.

Making the now regular visit to the toilet, Mei Lien locked herself once again in a cubicle and read the precisely written note. After memorising every word, she flushed it down the toilet. They would have a lot to talk about when they got back home tonight.

She stopped by the Director's office and asked the Secretary to book them an appointment first thing in the morning, stressing it was most urgent . He nodded and told her his boss would meet them at the laboratory at 9am.

Returning to the lab she found Ru still sitting at his desk, papers and notes all around him. He looked even more miserable than when she had left. She went over to him and put an arm around his shoulder before taking a seat beside him. Looking into his eyes she saw sadness mixed with fear, he looked as if he could cry.

They went over more data and peered through several microscopes. She soon understood why he was looking as he was; even sitting down her knees started to shake and she felt a sudden wave of nausea come over her. She turned to him, "I think it's time we went home, we have big decisions to make and here is not the place."

He looked around the laboratory at the other scientist. Most were sitting around chatting, their task done for the day. He clapped his hands and cleared his throat. "Ladies, Gentlemen. I would like to thank you for your hard work today. It has been a busy one and we have almost completed our research. Miss Chow and I would like to thank you for your hard work and dedication, what you have achieved will make a big difference and will ensure the gratitude of all the Chinese people". There were a few nods. "Once you have finished tidying your desks and benches you are free to go home. We will lock up." There was a sudden brightening of the mood. "Most probably tomorrow morning our director will be visiting, so please be prompt and ready. Good night."

They watched as the scientists busied themselves and left. Ru turned to his partner with a shake of the head, "incredible, not one asked about the results. Do you think they have any idea what we've come up with? With what they have produced?"

\* \* \*

## London

The plane from Hong Kong landed early so, with an hour to spare, Sean decided to drop by his flat for a shower and a change of clothes. He arrived at his office just as the figures of James and Jack came ambling down the street. He greeted them and showed them in. Switching on the kettle he apologised for the late change of plan.

"We had a most enjoyable evening last night. Jack was a great host and very amusing as well as interesting".

Sean looked round and grinned, "I forgot to tell you Jack, James is partial to Soho and it's delights, especially the Gas Light nightclub".

James raised his eyes to the sky, "enough of that, you're in no place to talk about an old man in such a manner".

Jack was enjoying the banter but was too anxious to get the news. "As James said, we had a great night, never thought he knew so much about so many things. Sorry, didn't mean to be rude and, I'm now an expert on spin and bouncers in cricket. Now, tell us what's all this about, you seemed all hyped up yesterday."

Sean poured himself and the American each a mug of coffee and handed over tea to James. He went round and sat down behind his desk. "There are two big developments; the first is our case." He then proceeded to tell them about the meeting with Ru and Mei Lien and that, following his return to Hong Kong, they made contact for a second meeting. "Seems they are extremely concerned at what they're working on and, at the same time, they're petrified about their safety."

"Did they tell you what this thing was?" Jack interrupted.

Sean shook his head. "From what we understood they've invented or made, a dangerous chemical weapon which could be catastrophic if wrongly used, but nothing more. Both realised they had said too much and clammed up."

"Armament! I thought they worked in a lab not a weapons factory," Jack looked worried and concerned at the same time. "This is an all-new ball game."

Shaking his head Sean continued, "no, it's nothing to do with bombs or rockets. It is most definitely chemical related, a gas or something like that is my guess".

They fell silent a while, each in his own thoughts. James was the first to talk, "either way it doesn't sound good; wonder what else they want to tell you now. What's the second thing?"

"Riots in Hong Kong. Our office there warned me over a week ago things were going to get bad. They picked up that the Chinese Government want more control over Hong Kong and are tightening up all sorts of laws. This has been met by fury by the locals who have taken to the streets. People there are worried the West will sit back and just watch, whist Beijing takes over the colony once again. They had a massive march at the week-end as you may have seen."

"The news did show a brief clip of a march but said it was a demo about climate change. Thought the agreement for semi autonomy has a fair few years to go," said James.

"That's just it; it has, but the Chinese want to change that. They know that if they ask, they won't get it, so they're putting pressure on the local Government to push these laws through quickly. Typical media controlled by the Chinese, and their misinformation department is working overtime. With the help of the ever so compliant western press and TV they hope to go in by the back door."

"What do you suggest we can do?" asked Jack.

"I have a meeting with the boss later this afternoon, as well as telling him about the new chemical threat, I've been asked to get him to talk to the Prime Minister and update him on the latest attempt by Beijing. Everyone in Hong Kong, including our office, are petrified the West will sit back and ignore the situation. Can you talk to your Ambassador Jack and request he warns the powers in Washington?"

"I can try. It won't go down well. The thought of you Brits beating us with info like that will go down like a lead balloon."

"Just try; use your influence. You can say we have a big set up in the colony, which is true; and you have never been strong in that area, which is true again. It's important the West condemns the action taken by China which amounts to a power grab."

Jack nodded, "I'll do my best, I promise".

"Good, thanks, I appreciate it. I plan to return to Hong Kong tomorrow; I need to be on the ground for both things. Why don't you and James fly to Washington and bring everyone up to speed."

"You still want us to go? Why?" asked James.

"You represent me and the service Jamesie. You know all the facts, have met all the gang over there and,", he looked over to Jack, "I think they trust you and your judgement."

Jack smiled, "at the same time we like you! I'll sort things over there James; you change your ticket."

Sean looked at his watch. "Gentlemen, I've a meeting to go to, as you do Jack". He nodded over, "I'll give you both a ring in the morning before I leave".

Forty-five minutes later Sean marched into HQ. After going through security, he made his way up to the 6th floor and was immediately shown into the head of service.

# CHAPTER 32

# Wuhan

When Chi Tao marched into lab No 6 closely followed by Ru and Mei Lien, he was feeling excited and confident. His research centre was about to be catapulted into the lime-light and be recognised as one of the top laboratories in China. No longer the poor relation, no more sneering, no more contempt, no more sniggering by other larger, more renowned centres. With what his scientists had achieved, by what he was going to show all those pompous, self-important colleagues in Handan and Lanzhou, life was going to change, and change big time. He relished the thought of getting his invitation to Beijing, to meeting the President, to being recognised, not to mention all the perks that would go with his new-found status.

As he entered everyone stood up and bowed to acknowledge his position. He grinned broadly and nodded his head. In his very soon newly-found position, no need to go through with everyday niceties. He gestured to Ru to show him to his desk and smiled sweetly at Mei Lien. In a flourish he took his seat in front of the computer and waited for Ru and Mei Lien to take a seat either side of him.

Before settling down he turned to the room and in a grave tone, began a short speech he had previously made up. He thanked everyone for their efforts and the great work carried out, congratulating not only them, but the Centre for such a wonderful achievement. Heads nodded, smiles all round greeted his words. In an over acted flourish, he swivelled his chair and took his place in front of the screen.

In a hushed tone Ru and Mei Lien explained the process undertaken from the start, going through at length the vast amount of data and results accumulated over the months. Peering through microscopes they talked the boss through the different permutations compiled. Chi Tao was an experienced scientist in his own right and quickly picked up on everything he was shown. As time went by his demeanour and expression changed. His questions went from a loud confident voice to a mere whisper. Eventually he sat back, slumped in his chair looking as if he had seen a ghost. He sat for a long time, expressionless and gazing into space, so much so that the gathered scientists became uneasy. One even started to come forward to see if the director was still alive only to be quickly waved away by Mei Lien. After what seemed a lifetime, Chi Tao swivelled his chair around slowly and faced the room. In a small voice he dismissed the scientists telling them to go home; his office would be in contact. Surprised and worried looks stared back at him; slowly they began to gather their coats and trickle out of the laboratory. A few murmurs but no comments, no questions. He motioned to Ru and Mei Lien to stay.

Once the room was empty, he turned to the pair and frowned. "Are you absolutely sure these results are correct, no mistakes, no miscalculations," he looked at them intently.

"We're sure, Director. You've seen the data, you've seen the results through the microscope, the various mutations and constants, there is no mistake". Ru continued, "Director, we did try to warn you the other day; please excuse us if we did not come over more forcibly, we were both very nervous".

Chi Tao remained silent and simply nodded. His mind was racing. Although delighted, he was by no means ecstatic at the discovery and breakthrough; he understood full well the dire consequences of their work should it be misused. Yes, he thought, this is a game changer, for him, the Centre and for the Country, but how to announce it and to warn his superiors. How to ensure the very people who worked on this programme keep silent. He looked up at the two young people standing in front of him. "I never imagined , in my wildest dreams, that anything like this could be created and I certainly didn't believe you the other day. I don't blame you; you did your best."

He rose and started to pace around the room. "How much do you think this lot know?" he asked, waving his hand at empty chairs and desks.

Ru was first to speak, "we believe they understand that something big has been found but they don't realise how big, nor the significance or dangers. Most have been working individually on different aspects with different data; we 're the only two to have seen everything together." He looked at Mei Lien who took over, "It's only in the latest tests that everyone has worked together. We don't believe they have sufficient understanding of all the other components to be able to piece together the result."

Chi Tao suddenly seemed happier. "We must ensure they never see these - understood? They are too sensitive and dangerous. I will ensure that everyone is redeployed in other departments, possibly even in different centres."

Ru and Mei Lien nodded. "Will they not get suspicious, Director?"

"Chinese people are always suspicious, especially scientists, you know that. But they also know that if they want to carry on working, then they obey, no questions asked."

"Do you have, or know any of the porters?" Seeing them nod he continued, "get them to deep clean and disinfect this place twice over. Get the vet to dispose of the animals and stress they are to be cremated."

Both nodded but before they could say anything he continued. "I want all these results and the data brought to me tomorrow. All the files, calculations and drafts, everything; make sure you don't forget anything and bring them in person."

Ru cleared his throat, "It will be done sir and you shall have everything in the morning. What time should we be there?"

"First thing – 8.00am, I'll clear my diary. We have much to discuss."

"Just one other matter sir, what are your plans for us?"

Chi Tao smiled a thin, strained smile, "all in good time, all in good time". He turned and left closing the door carefully behind him.

\*　　\*　　\*

## London

Back in his small office Sean slumped in his chair. By gum he was tired. The events of the past few days and travelling had caught up with him; he closed his eyes. He was rudely awoken by the shrill ring of the phone on his desk. He looked bleary eyed at the wall clock indicating 10.30pm – he had been asleep four hours. He picked up the phone.

"Sean, my friend, sounds as if I've woken you up," came Jack's voice.

"For sure you have but thanks, without your call I would have slept till morning. Did you manage to see the Ambassador?"

"Sure did. The pompous ass gave me ten minutes of his precious time before dismissing me to go to a party."

"Guess he gets his priorities right, "joked Sean. "I had a long session with the boss. Extremely interested in our case and I've to send him a full report before I leave tomorrow. Guess I won't be sleeping much more tonight. He will also schedule an emergency meeting with the Foreign Secretary and advise him to take the riots seriously. Like us, he certainly does not like developments over in the province.

"The ass upstairs dismissed both things out of hand. Said America couldn't get involved in Chinese affairs and cast doubt over your claims. As for the chemical thing, he just laughed and told me to get proof or stop wasting my time."

"So, all in all, not a very lucrative ten minutes. What are you going to do now?" Jack paused, "unlike you, I'm going home to pack and then have a nice sleep in a comfy bed."

"You bastard! I'll call you when I land in Hong Kong."

\* \* \*

## Washington

Hank had finalised arrangements for the forthcoming visit and meeting. He had managed to contact Joe and asked him to meet James and put him up in the same safehouse as last time. He went through the latest files and re-read the notes Jack had sent him relating to their case. Nothing had been said about the riots. Jack had considered that a separate matter and still needed to make his own enquiries.

Sitting at his desk mulling over the latest news Hank jotted down a few ideas; he would talk to the others about them and get their opinion. On second thoughts, why ask the others? He was the boss, the man in charge of this operation, so why act like a junior; time to take responsibility and show leadership. Yes, that's it, take leadership, something he hadn't done much of lately. He picked up the phone.

A deep growl came from the other end of the line and grunted when Hank asked to speak to Maggy. She came on sounding chirpy, "evening Mr Gobolsky, what can I do for you?"

"I've been thinking, Maggy, would you be ok going back to work? It's just that with you away we have no one to report back on what's happening."

There was a long silence before Maggy replied, "I'm sure I could manage Mr Gobolsky. When asking for leave I gave the excuse that my aunt was ill and needed care, but I'm sure she's recovered by now."

"Much appreciated. I suggest you go back in a few days' time. We'll keep watch on you, so no need to worry."

"Thank you. I can look after myself and will contact you if anything new develops. Yes, I'm looking forward to going back. As much as I enjoyed the rest and Tony's company, idleness doesn't suit me".

"Take care Maggy and, thanks again." He rang off; he was a happy man.

\* \* \*

The next day James was met by Joe, and they made their way to the safe house. Beth was on duty waiting for them. As soon as he'd freshened up, he made his way to the lounge and was greeted with a large malt. A carry out meal of chicken stir-fry was delivered and he picked away at it; it was not his favourite, and in any case, he was not hungry after all the food he'd been given on the flight. Noting that Joe had cleaned his plate in record time he offered him the rest of his. The evening passed by chatting about sport and the latest news, nothing was mentioned about the business he had come over for.

As usual breakfast was coffee, or in his case tea, and a rather burnt piece of toast. Joe was certainly right; Beth was not a cook. They made their way over to the office and were shown into the meeting room, followed soon after by Jack; there was no sign of Hank. Ten minutes passed and both Americans were getting edgy when, eventually the door swung open, and a smiling Hank appeared. He greeted everyone and thanked them for coming. Everyone noted there was no mention of him being late or an apology, but they didn't say anything.

Hank was the first to speak. "Good of you to come but I'm not sure that there's much to talk about since Sean isn't here."

"Well, in fact, there is Hank; both James and myself will fill you in. Things have moved on and at a considerably pace. Sean, as you know, is on his way back to Hong Kong and will bring us up to date once he gets there."

Hank shrugged slightly, "still think it's a waste of time but carry on".

For the next hour James and Jack took them through the new developments, Joe interrupting a couple of times with questions. "So, there you have it," concluded Jack; "our ambassador dismisses both our reports off hand and the British Minister is - "thinking" about it".

James had been silent for a while, he listened to Jack's lengthy and detailed report, he had nothing further to add. He put up his hand to speak, "It's a big shame Sean isn't here, as he could have tried to get to speak to our ambassador. I'm still unsure how anyone of us can get involved or help?"

There was silence until Joe spoke. "With respect, I don't think Sean could have done any more; he's done as much as he can. I am sure his boss would have suggested the idea to the politicians in London, and my guess is, they turned it down. I like your thought of contacting the Embassy here; your ambassador seems a switched-on sort of person. You know it's a woman, don't you? You could try James, with your charms who knows, no harm in asking. On the other hand, I doubt they will entertain you, let alone believe you."

Hank decided it was good time to give them the news and cleared his throat. "Guys, I spoke to Maggy yesterday and asked her to go back to work. We need someone on the inside."

"You what!" screamed Joe and Jack in unison.

"You heard. I've asked Maggy to go back later this week; she was happy to do so. Told her we would be watching her back."

"Have you gone totally mad. The woman is a sitting target, one slip and she's toast – and so are we." Jack looked appalled, "we agreed no decisions would be taken without consultation with the group first".

Hank looked at him. "Are you upset because you're worried about her or because I took a decision, I'm the boss and have a right to do things without asking you."

Joe couldn't believe what he had just heard, but remained silent.

James stepped in, "seems the decision has been taken and if Maggy is happy then, why not? You, we, need someone to report back. She could also try to get her friend to get us a meeting with the President as was suggested last time."

There was a long silence before Joe spoke. "Always the diplomat James, you should enter the diplomatic corps," he grinned.

"Absolutely not! Can't imagine anything worse than to rub shoulders all day long with politicians. The idea I would be seen is fanciful, unless it was with Sean or someone from the Firm, so we can forget the idea of me visiting the Embassy. Have you any news of Mr Millento and Mr Campese?"

Hank shook his head, "No, that's why I've asked Maggy to go back," he grunted.

Jack was about to say something when the phone rang. Hank picked up and looked over at the other three; "Sean".

*   *   *

## London

The Foreign Secretary was sitting at his desk when Sean's boss walked in. He greeted his guest and waved him to a chair. He listened silently, hands clasped under his chin, to the third highest ranking executive in MI6. He had only met the man a couple of times but had heard first class reports from the head of the Firm; thus, he took the events being described seriously. His visitor finished up, "and that, Foreign Secretary, is the situation and conclusions we have reached. I do believe both events are extremely volatile and present a major risk to the UK".

"Thank you for an excellent and very concise report. As you say it seems that the events in Hong Kong are worrying and I will be sure to report these to the Prime Minister. Likewise, the development at this laboratory is equally concerning." He paused before resuming, "where is your man at present?"

"Should be back in Hong Kong, sir; he flew out yesterday morning."

"Did I hear you say there was a second agent working with him?"

"Not exactly an agent, Sir - a retired journalist come professor, a friend of his, has been helping him from the start and has been extremely helpful and useful."

"Do you trust him?"

"I don't know the man, but my agent is adamant he is absolutely trustworthy. In fact, the man is in Washington at present representing him at a meeting with our American counterparts."

"Can you trust them? That's more to the point," said the Foreign Secretary grinning.

"Yes Sir, we can. Ever since they've found out about two high up officials in Washington being involved, they're more than keen to work with us."

"What's his name, this retired journalist?"

"James Horton".

"And he's there now. You know how long for? Do we have any contact details?"

The Foreign Secretary pursed his lips and scribbled a couple of notes on his pad. "I will let our ambassador know of the situation and will suggest he has a meeting with this Mr Horton, sooner rather than later. It's important she is made fully aware of the situation, especially as our cousins are involved. Please contact your agent or the Americans to warn him. Let him know the Ambassador's secretary will be contacting him shortly."

He got up from his desk signalling that the meeting was over. "I will inform the PM immediately. Keep me posted at all times."

# CHAPTER 33

# Hong Kong

Despite the long flight and jet lag, Sean made his way straight to the office. Knowing Jimmy was under pressure he had sent a message saying that he would make his own way into town and had warned him, that he was travelling under the name of Sean Docherty. He did not mention that was his real name.

He was greeted by Pearl who showed him to Jimmy's office where they sat down for a catchup. It had only been 4 days since he had left but it seemed an age ago. Pearl advised that his tourist visa was in hand and that, all being well, they could fly up to Wuhan in a couple of days. Checking one of the clocks on the wall he decided it was time to call Washington, he excused himself and was shown to a small room just off the main office. He watched as Pearl went to her desk and Jimmy slowly walk round and talked, one by one, to each of his operatives.

He heard Hanks' voice, "Sean, great to hear from you buddy". He shuddered, if ever he hated anything more, it was being called buddy; he bit his tongue. Hank then proceeded to give him an up-date and the news that they had made the decision to have Maggy go back to work. Sean's jaw dropped and he was about to say something when the voice the at other end continued. "James was suggesting that you get back here and go meet your ambassador, put her in the picture - what do you think?"

As nicely as possible Sean explained that was an impossibility, that an audience like that had to be set by London and that he had more urgent business in China. His last words to Hank were to tell James to behave himself and not to lead Joe astray.

\* \* \*

## Washington

Hank had no need to relay the conversation as they were on loudspeaker; he was simply relieved the call had ended when James gave his reply.

They stayed on for a while longer, discussing what exactly the Chinese had created, and speculated on how far they had actually got. The phone in James's pocket rang and he jumped, blushing, he looked embarrassed. "Sorry, thought I'd turned it off." He fumbled and looked at the number, a puzzled look came over his face. "Seems you have nuisance calls over here, too. A local number that I've never seen before," he passed it Joe who shook his head. The caller hung up just as James was about to answer. A few seconds later it rang again.

Joe stuck his hand out, "here, give it me, I love to wind these guys up and waste their time". He took the phone and answered. He waited for the caller to speak; always wait to see how they open – from the intro you can learn how to start messing them around. He listened, smiled and nodded, "Yeh! and I'm Santa Claus. No, Mr Hairton is not available. Sorry, you got the wrong name and number," he hung up. Turning to the others, "said they were from the British Embassy, couldn't even get your name right". He paused and suddenly looked sheepish and worried, "Shit, it may really have been them. How the hell did they get your number?"

James shrugged. His phone rang for a third time. Hesitantly he looked at the screen which displayed the same number; he answered. A few nods of the head, a yes here and there, a confirmation of a time and venue. He hung up and looked at the others. "That was indeed our Embassy, seems they

had a call from London asking them to meet up with me in Sean's absence. I have to be there tomorrow at 2pm. They asked who the rude person was they just spoke to!" he winked at Joe.

There were stunned looks all round before Jack finally broke the silence, "seems as if our hopes and prayers have been answered. Damn that was quick work; Sean must have made a big impression."

"You've hit the big times now James; tea with the Ambassador," said Joe jokingly.

James was suddenly feeling sick. How on earth did he ever get himself into such a situation. What was he going to tell the Ambassador, or his secretary, or whoever met him, and would they believe him? It was one thing working with Sean and following the professional, quite another, taking the lead and being an equal. Everyone would be expecting him to perform, to use his powers of persuasion and his skills at speaking, to convince one of the most influential diplomats in the British Government, that the world was on the brink of two major events. Both could have disastrous consequences.

His eyes flicked over to the three sitting in front of him, "would either one of you care to accompany me tomorrow".

Three heads shook negatively. Hank spoke first, "must admit I'm impressed on several counts: firstly, that Sean has such power of persuasion, secondly, how seriously your government has taken these stories and thirdly, how quickly they've made contact. Wouldn't happen with us, that's for sure."

James looked worried, "I'm not sure I can do this. Way too big for my untrained skills. Thought Sean would be a better judge of character and more sensible, rather than to rely on an aging layman to handle such sensitive matters".

"Don't under-estimate yourself James, you'll do a brilliant job. It's not like you don't know what you're talking about; you've been with it

all the way. Just tell her, them, everything. Don't leave anything out and
don't embellish and you'll be fine. We all trust you." Joe spoke softly
and looked at James in way he hadn't seen before. It was as if Joe was a
father, encouraging his son.

The three Americans spent the next half hour cajoling and
encouraging their English guest before Hank held up his hand. "Guys,
I think we should leave it for now. James will be fine." Looking over to
the older man he carried on, "Joe will drive you and wait at the gates.
Once you're done, he'll bring you back here and we can have a debrief."

James thanked Hank and nodded to Joe, "what time is it in Hong
Kong? I would dearly love to have a few words with Sean before my
meeting".

Jack looked at his watch, "Its 6pm here so it should be 7am over in
Hong Kong, why don't you call him now?".

Hank picked up the phone and got the secretary to get Sean on the
line. As the connection was being made, they left James alone in the
room.

Sean's voice came through loud and clear, "Jamesie, nice surprise,
what can I do for you?".

James spoke quickly, giving Sean the run-down of the call he had
received earlier and expressing his reservations.

"That's first class; never thought London would act so quickly. For
sure indeed, you are the perfect man for the job; you know all about it
as well as I do. Be yourself and tell them everything I've told you. It'll
all be fine."

James grunted and tried to find excuses but, deep down, he knew
they were feeble and wouldn't wash.

"Now's not the time to chicken out Jamesie. If you had any qualms,
you should have walked away in London. Enjoy your cup of tea and don't
make eyes at the Ambassador's wife, I hear she's rather good looking."

"Shut up or I won't go. Wish me luck."

"There's my boy; give me a call once you're back. Keep smiling and think of Britain."

The phone fell silent and James was left looking into space. What a man! He could be rude, infuriating and sometimes tetchy; nevertheless he liked him even more because of that. He was happy to think he had him as a friend and was pleased in the knowledge that people like him were prepared to risk life and limb to protect the citizens of his country. He went to join the others in the corridor.

\* \* \*

## Wuhan

Ru and Mei Lien arrived at Chi Tao's office laden with files. They had commandeered a porter and loaded all the boxes onto a trolley before proceeding down the endless corridors. A few amused looks and wry smiles, as they passed other scientists hurrying to work. The secretary motioned them to wait and went to warn his boss the visitors had arrived. Ru quickly dismissed the porter and checked his pocket once again to ensure the two USB sticks were still there.

As they walked in, Chi Tao was sitting at his desk looking more like a tramp than the director of a research laboratory; unshaven, his usually crisp white shirt was crumpled, his tie loose around his neck. He noticed the look on their faces. "Excuse me but I didn't get home last night," he blurted out. He rubbed his eyes before pointing to a couple of chairs.

"I need you both to go over the entire project with me, take me through the calculations again as well as the data and your conclusions. Finally, what you, as scientists and individuals really think. I know you have reservations so want you to be honest and up-front."

Both nodded but Mei Lien was concerned. She was happy to spend as long as it took but did not think he was in a fit state to fully grasp the facts or consequences. She voiced her concern in a small voice. Chi Tao looked at her through red, bleary eyes before closing them. Putting his fingers through his thinning hair he agreed, and they got up. Leaving the room, they confirmed they would be back at 2pm. Soon after their departure Chi Tao left the office, locking it and instructing his secretary to clear his diary until further notice. The secretary watched his boss disappear down the corridor and inwardly smiled; unbeknown to the old man he had a key, had had one for some time, just for insurance as he justified it to himself.

Mei Lien and Ru made their way back to the lab along the now empty corridors. What to do? They did not really have time to go home or go anywhere and it would have looked bad to leave the centre early without official permission. On the way Ru asked if she had heard back from her "aunt".

"Sorry, with all that has happened since yesterday I completely forgot. She suggested we meet at the house on Saturday."

"Forgot! As if it was a small matter of buying a loaf of bread. Why Saturday? We may need to talk sooner; with things moving as they are, it could be too late."

"I said sorry. How long do you think it will take, going over things with Chi Tao?"

"We won't be finished today that's for sure." He thought a moment before continuing, "we don't have any excuses. Perhaps Saturday is the only day."

Halfway along the corridor she stopped and put her hand on his arm, "I'll go to the canteen and try to make contact with the old hag, ask her if we can change to an earlier day".

"You can try but it may be difficult if they are coming from the South". He looked dubious.

As they neared the laboratory, Lu Chin was sitting on the floor. He looked up and grinned showing a row of rotten teeth and the usual stubble. He got up and semi-bowed.

Ru looked puzzled, "what are you doing here? I thought the director told everyone to go home."

The man continued to grin, "yes, but I thought you might need help," he rasped.

"Help doing what? Everything has been done and is in the Director's office." Ru started to show his dislike of the man.

"Cleaning, I can help clean and perhaps move the animals," he replied slightly disgruntled.

Mei Lien stepped in. "Thank you, but we're fine. Everything is under control and the Director has asked specifically not to get anyone else involved."

Lu Chin looked back at her, disdain in his eyes, before turning and shuffling off.

"God I hate that man as much as you do," she said in a whisper. They watched him disappear down the corridor before letting themselves in to the lab and locking the door. Ru started to scrutinize the room, lifting phones and peering at the computers. He checked the lights and under the desks. "What are you doing, have you lost something?"

Ru shook his head. "Just checking for bugs," he replied looking more relaxed.

Mei Lien stared at him and shrugged. "Why? I don't understand. What's the problem?"

Ru pulled her over and sat her in the chair beside him. "You can never be sure. You know I don't trust people, especially officials. Now that we've finished our project and everyone has been sent home, you never know what they may do. Look at Lu Chin; what was he doing sitting outside? For all you or I know he may have been in here prying or bugging the place."

"That is simply stupid and paranoic. Like you, I can't stand the little man, but why should he bug an empty laboratory. No, it's ludicrous. Remember what you said to me when I did the same at home!"

Ru gave her a long look. "Perhaps you 're right; I am paranoic. The fact that we have such explosive facts is making me think funny." Tapping the desk, "Ok, we must organise that these poor animals are taken away and put out of their misery. You go and see if you can contact the cleaner whilst I talk to the vet."

* * *

To her relief Mei Lien found the cleaner mopping a table. She quickly made her way over to her and sat herself down. The old woman looked at her quizzically. Plucking up courage Mei Lien decided to come straight to the point. "We would like to postpone the meeting to Sunday, things have moved very fast, and we are tied up with the Director and may not be able to get away in time."

The woman looked around slightly worried. She nodded, "alright, 3pm Sunday, same place as last time. I will let them know". She left hastily and went to mop another table.

Mei Lien sat for a while watching the old cleaner, wondering who she really was, what her real job was. Leaving her tea half finished, she got up and made her way back to join Ru.

# CHAPTER 34

# Hong Kong

There was a brief knock at Jimmy's door before it opened, and David walked in. "Sorry boss, just had a message from Wuhan; seems the two scientists have asked to postpone the meeting until Sunday, something to do with them having a meeting with their boss. They are eager to meet, say things have developed faster than expected".

"When did you get the message?"

"Just now, came through the usual channels. Seems the girl was extremely anxious and insistent."

Jimmy asked him to call over Pearl and Sean. As soon as they were in the office, he relayed the message. "What do you want to do?"

"We certainly can't make it up there in time unless I go on my own. Sean's visa will only be ready late on Friday and valid from Monday."

"I would really like to be there," Sean said insistently. "Can't we ask them to wait."

David gave a little cough and they looked over to him. "The way the message was sent, it seems that time is of the essence. Why not let Tim speak to them, he's been following the pair ever since they left Beijing.".

Pearl butted in, "what about Sandra? She's been their contact and go between. They may be happier to talk to a woman and someone they know."

Jimmy thought for a minute before making his decision "No, I think Tim should be on his own. It will be safer for Sandra. Face it, these are amateurs and could compromise her." A further pause and he continued, "Tim's a good man, very adaptable and likeable, he'll be able to put them at ease. I do think however, that they should be warned you are not going to be there."

Pearl looked hesitant but conceded it made sense. It was never a good idea to expose an agent to amateurs; you never knew how they would react under pressure. They could easily let something slip inadvertently with fatal consequences. She nodded her agreement.

David left the room and immediately went to work.

\* \* \*

## Washington

Joe was sitting reassuringly in the back seat with James. "I hear your Embassy is very welcoming and has a lot of style. Unlike ours around the world, which are functional to say the least, you Brits know how to live. Home from home," he smiled. "You know the Ambassador is woman don't you".

James nodded slowly. "Yes, someone mentioned it yesterday; what's her name? Not sure I'm prepared or really want to talk to a woman; I feel more comfortable among men."

"Now, now, James that's not PC at all and very old thinking," he nudged his fellow traveller in the ribs. Kathleen Pringle, or rather Dame Kathleen Pringle, has been in situ for a couple of years now. From what I understand she's rather cute, both in looks and intelligence."

James smiled, "now who's not being PC. Thought you couldn't talk about women like that nowadays".

"Carter would sure have one of his fits. He and I are always clashing. Sadly, he is one of these modern kids who sees everything in black and white. Can't say this, can't do that, must be inclusive, a real pain in the arse. You can't talk without him pulling you up on something or another. I must say, I love to rub him up the wrong way." He shook his head and looked out of window.

The traffic was heavy as they made slow progress through the mid-day bustle of taxis, trucks and buses. James looked anxiously at his watch, "how long before we get there?".

Beth looked back through her rear-view mirror, "five, six minutes; we've just come on to Massachusetts Avenue".

Joe looked back at James. "Relax, it's going to be a picnic, no problem. As we discussed last night, just tell the lady exactly what we know and what our feelings are. She's old enough and experienced enough to decide what the facts point to and come to her own conclusions". He looked out the window again, "nearly there. Have you got your ID?".

James nodded and adjusted his tie. He peered out at the fast-approaching building and was slightly disappointed. "Is that it?" he asked nodding towards a large rectangular block with brick walls and banks of windows.

"Yep. Doesn't look anything from here but go round the side and it's a whole different story. This is just the working end of the building; doubt that you will be invited to the residence, even if you are James Horton esquire.

Beth was slowing down and pulled into a wide driveway. She stopped the car under the large canopy.

James took in a deep breath, adjusted his tie once again and fumbled in his jacket pocket for his passport.

"Good luck and don't worry, it will go fine and dandy. We'll be over there in the car park when you come out." Joe gave an encouraging smile and a wink.

As James stepped out of the car, he looked around him; now that he was standing at the door, the place looked huge. He made his way through to a vast hall and was immediately greeted by a guard who pointed to the security desk. His colleague beckoned him over and politely requested he emptied his pockets and put his briefcase on the conveyor belt, just as in airports, he thought. He then went through the Xray Machine and his belongings followed soon after. A third man asked for his ID and scrutinized it carefully before placing it face down to be scanned. A minute later the officer looked up and smiled, "Welcome to the British Embassy Mr Horton; I believe you have an appointment with the Ambassador, please follow this gentleman and he will show you the way.

They walked through the big hall, passing rows of painting and pictures of former incumbents. Past a bust of Churchill and numerous photographs of various dignitaries being greeted by Her Majesty the Queen. James was mesmerised by the grandeur and opulence. He looked out at the immaculately manicured gardens towards the elegant Ambassadorial residence. The smartly dressed man eventually arrived at a door and gently knocked before entering. He ushered James in and announced him to the secretary sitting behind a large desk. He left closing the door quietly behind.

The young lady got up and greeted James with a warm smile. "Welcome Mr Horton, thank you for being on time. Unfortunately, the Ambassador has a previous engagement, however her Deputy will be seeing you. Please take a seat whilst I let him know you are here."

James sat awkwardly in one of the large, plush chairs, looking around at his surroundings. On the wall behind the desk hung a picture of The Queen and in one corner stood the Union Jack. Two filing cabinets close to hand; three telephones and the obligatory computer screen on the desk were the only obvious signs this was a working, functional office.

The Secretary soon returned and requested James follow her. They entered a large bright drawing room with wonderful views of the garden and grounds. To his left was a one of biggest oak desks he had ever seen, two large, gilded armchairs placed in front of it. The room was ornate but not over ostentatious and had numerous paintings of past Kings, Prime Ministers and Ambassadors. A large version of Her Majesty hung on the wall behind the bureau and a Union Jack stood in pride of place, flanked by the flags of the four Nations.

As James was making his way across the room a medium built man in his sixties, immaculately dressed in a double-breasted suit, got up and came forward to greet him. He stuck out his hand and smiled broadly. "Welcome to a little part of Great Britain Mr Horton, I'm sorry if I kept you waiting." He then showed James over to one of the two large gilt chairs, "tea, coffee?" he asked.

James's mouth was dry as sandpaper and he managed to croak that tea would be lovely. The secretary departed and the two men settled down.

"May I introduce myself; my name is William Tindell and I am Deputy Ambassador. Sadly, the Ambassador has a previous pressing engagement but insisted you were seen as soon as possible." He leant forward, "we understand from London that you are here on behalf of MI6 and one of their agents; I believe he is presently in Hong Kong, am I right?" James nodded and Tindell continued, "I also understand that you have some rather important information to relay." He paused watching his guest. "You are not officially working for MI6, is that right?"

James was about to speak when there was a knock and the door opened. A footman, clad in white jacket and gloves, appeared with a silver tray. He placed the salver gently on a side table, bowed slightly, and left. William Tindell got up and went over to the side table, poured two cups of tea and offered his guest a selection of biscuits which James declined.

"As I was saying," continued the Deputy Ambassador, "we are very keen to learn what you and MI6 have to say. London told me their man, a certain Sean Docherty, is presently in China and you are deputising for him. He sat back and crossed his thin fingers.

James took a deep breath and begun his lengthy report. At first, he was nervous, wondering whether he was wittering on too much but as time went by, and his listener nodded and took notes, he relaxed and gained confidence. Finally, he had come to the end and looked over apologetically, "please excuse me, Deputy Ambassador, for being so long winded. I'm not used to giving such speeches on a subject which is so sensitive, and to be honest, is not my line of business".

William Tindell smiled nicely and inclined his head. "Please Mr Horton, there is nothing to apologise for, you have given a most clear and concise account of what you and the Agency have found out. I now have several questions if I may?"

There followed a long list of queries the Deputy had noted. He probed, asked the same questions in a different manner, and clarified certain points. James answered as well as he could and thought, all in all, he had done remarkedly well. Sean and the boys would have been proud of him.

It was past 4pm when William Tindell finally put down his pen and sat back in his chair. "May I congratulate you Mr Horton on the manner you have dealt with this entire matter. It is obvious you and Mr Docherty, as well as our counterparts here in Washington, have discovered something that could be extremely concerning, not only to the West, but to the world at large." He looked at James intently, "I'm not sure what our next move is going to be, but please rest assured I will bring the Ambassador up to speed and, if she deems it fit, will contact the White House."

James mumbled his thanks and was about to add something when he was interrupted. "As for the Hong Kong situation, this does sound rather alarming; however we cannot do much from here. It is for London, in particular the PM, to decide on the appropriate action." He rose to signal the meeting was over. "I look forward to meeting you again soon. In the meantime please keep us informed of any developments. I would appreciate it if you let my secretary know how long you are here for and how best to contact you." He accompanied James to the door and showed him out smiling broadly.

Back in the office the secretary heard the door open and pushed a buzzer, seconds later, and as if by magic, the same man who had led James to the office appeared and escorted James back to the main hall. "Do you have transport or would you like us to call for a cab?"

James thanked the man, nodding to the security guards and doorman as he walked out into the evening sunlight. Back at the car he slumped into the seat beside Joe and let out a long, deep breath.

"Hey, James, you took your time; Beth here was about to send out a search party. How did it go?"

"Fine, all fine. I didn't see the Ambassador as she was busy but spent all this time with her Deputy. He was extremely charming and listened intently. After I had finished giving him my report, he grilled me on many of the points, asking the same question repeatedly but phrasing it differently every time. Talk about inquisition."

"Was he convinced? What did he say? Come on James, put me out of my misery."

Beth interrupted, "where to now boss?".

"To the office, James is about to be interrogated a second time." He turned to the Englishman, "you thought the deputy gave you a hard time, just wait until Hank gets started," he laughed.

*     *     *

Back at the office Hank and Jack were waiting. Both jumped up when they walked in and bombarded James with questions.

James held his hand up. "Gentlemen, all in good time. First things first, I need a pee. After all the tea I've consumed I'm busting." A roar of laughter erupted.

Back in the room, feeling relieved in all senses, he settled himself down in what had become his seat. Before starting his lengthy account of the afternoon's proceedings, Sean came on the phone loudspeaker. "So, in conclusion, there's good and bad news. The bad news is that little can be done from here regarding the situation in Hong Kong. He was clear that it is a political decision which can only be made in London and by the PM himself. The good news is that he took the threat of the chemical or biological discovery very seriously and promised to have a word with the Ambassador and get her to talk to the White House."

Sean's voice came through, "congratulations Jamesie, sounds as if you did a fantastic job. Thanks a million, we really appreciate what you've done; it's a shame about Hong Kong but at least we've brought it to their attention. You never know, something may come of it. As for the chemical thing, I'm one hundred percent sure there will be action; London acting so quickly can only mean they're concerned on both fronts."

"Anything happening your end?" asked James.

"It seems that our two friends want to talk more, and very soon. We're setting up a meeting sometime over the next couple of days."

The call ended and the three men in the room thanked James for his time and effort. Jack suggested that they all went out for a meal to celebrate, but the idea was vetoed by Hank as too dangerous.

"What'd you mean too dangerous? Life must continue. The least we can do is to feed this poor man properly. Why don't we go to the Claret Jug, it's a posh place and somewhere that few of the political establishment frequent."

"Bloody expensive," muttered Hank. "Not sure it would be passed by finance."

"Ah c'mon Hank don't be a spoil sport and such a bloody miser. About time you stood your hand, especially since you've been banging on about being the boss." Jack winked at the others.

Feeling cornered Hank succumbed and reluctantly agreed. "Ok, you make the reservation Jack, but NO shop talk, understood."

# CHAPTER 35

# Wuhan

They were about to make their way to the office when Ru's phone rang. It was the secretary telling them that their meeting was postponed until 9am the next morning. At a loss and with time on their hands they headed for the canteen. They sat down at a window table far from anyone else and Ru tucked into a bowl of noodles with prawns; he was famished. "You look as if you've not eaten for a week," Mei Lien said looking at the heaped, steaming bowl. "You're not pregnant, are you?" she giggled. Ru immediately looked up, pasta dangling from his mouth. After sucking in the last piece, he managed to turn the question. She shook her head, "not that I'm aware, not yet."

Their relaxed conversation was interrupted by the appearance of the old cleaner who, as usual, busied herself by flicking the tabletop. She smiled and in a low whisper told them she had got confirmation of the meeting the following evening. One warning though, aunt and uncle would not be present, but a cousin would take their place. Not to worry, he was kind, very likable and would be able help, he was to be trusted.

After her departure Ru looked out of the window at the drab courtyard and grimaced. "Not sure I like talking to some stranger. I don't know, do you?"

"Do we have any choice, that's the question? We asked for the meeting, and obviously the foreigners can't manage it in such a short time; they must be working together. No harm in going, we don't have to say anything if we're not sure," Mei Lien said hesitantly.

Ru was about to say something when Mei Liens phoned pinged. She looked at it and opened the new message, it was from auntie. She showed it to Ru who nodded, "better delete that now," he mumbled.

"Well, that goes to prove they know this person and have arranged for him to meet us. I say we go."

Ru sighed and shrugged his shoulders. "Ok, if you say so. I trust your instincts; anything for a quiet life."

"Oh! don't be such a grumpy old man and don't be rude, I never nag you." She gave him one of her sweetest, sexiest looks.

"We better get back to the lab and arrange for those animals to be fed before they starve." He got up and started to make his way through the hall.

Mei Lien quickly caught up with him and whispered in his ear, "is it the real reason or have you got other ideas?" she giggled.

He looked at her and shook his head, "talk about me! No, you will have to wait until we get home," and he marched down the corridor.

They occupied themselves by feeding the animals, now looking rather sorry for themselves. None of them were well and all were stressed. Mei Lien took pity on them, "when is the vet coming to put them out of their misery?" she asked.

Ru immediately picked up the phone. He had completely forgotten. With all that had happened over the past twenty-four to thirty-six hours, it had slipped his mind. He spoke to the head vet who promised to send someone down within the next two days. Ru shook his head, "nothing is urgent in this place, where is the sense and professionalism, all gone nowadays".

He went over to the animals and started to look at them intently, turning to Mei Lien he shook his head. "Why don't we take a few more samples from each of them? The ones we didn't inject look as bad as the others."

Mei Lien came over and looked closely. "We don't have any of our equipment, it is all locked away for disinfection".

"Yes, but we still have keys and the cleaners haven't been. It won't take long."

She agreed and Ru went over to retrieve a few syringes and test tubes before donning his protective apron. Quickly and efficiently, he collected the samples whilst Mei Lien took the tubes to the centrifugal unit and started it up. Once finished they began to analyse the findings and put them through the computer. An hour or so later they both sat back, a look of despair and horror on their faces.

" What have we produced!" exclaimed Ru in whisper. "This is a total disaster; these results are a hundred times worse than we had first expected." Mei Lien remained silent, her face a blank and tears began to form in her eyes.

\* \* \*

Chi Tao was lying on the bed, his mind in a turmoil. His worries had started last night whilst going through the data with the two young scientists. At first, he was confident that the discovery would open a whole new world as well as exciting prospects for him. However, with time, he realised more and more the significance of the findings and the probable devastating consequences the discovery could have. As a scientist he knew the dangers, as director of the research Centre, he also knew what Beijing expected and what the future lay ahead for him if he did not let them know.

His wife was away visiting relations, so he had stayed in his office overnight going over and over the data. Now back home and exhausted, he still could not sleep. Eventually he drifted off into a fitful slumber. He woke with a start, listening. Was it the phone, the alarm clock or doorbell? It was dark outside and he shivered. He checked his phone and the door, no one was there as he had already suspected. He made his way to the bathroom and sat in the sauna for a while. After a cold shower, followed by a shave he felt more human, but his worries had not gone away; they were still in his head going round and round. His phone indicated he had a missed call from his secretary, probably worried his boss had not returned. With a sigh he called him back; never mind it was 9pm, the man wouldn't like it but so what. A grumpy voice replied but quickly changed to a reverent tone once he realised who the caller was. Chi Toa gave him a couple of orders, one to be done immediately, the other first thing in the morning.

Returning from the kitchen with a couple of beers, he settled down and flicked through the channels. Things would be better in the morning he hoped.

*   *   *

The secretary just nodded and pointed at the door not bothering to greet Ru and Mei Lien. They knocked gently and waited to be called in. After a while, the secretary rose and shuffled over shaking his head. He gave a loud rap which was immediately answered and jerked his head indicating they should enter.

The Director was sitting at his desk and looking his normal self again. He rose, greeting the young scientists with a smile.

"May I apologise on two counts," he began. "Firstly, for yesterday, I wasn't feeling too well and had had a sleepless night. Secondly, for cancelling our meeting and rescheduling," he motioned them to sit down.

Ru was about to speak when Chi Tao continued. "I've been thinking, this discovery of ours, are you absolutely sure you've got everything right. Have you checked and re-checked?"

They both nodded and again the old man butted in, "In that case we have a problem, a very big problem. I haven't gone through all the files; I hope and suppose you have all the information on a USB stick?"

Once again, they nodded, but this time Ru managed to get a word in, "yes Director, we have all the data on two sticks which I have here"; he pulled out the envelope and handed it over to Chi Tao. "We agree with you and, like you, we are extremely concerned. In fact, with nothing much to do yesterday we went to feed the animals and discovered they were all ill. After analysis we have concluded that what we have is for worse than we ever thought".

Chi Tao eyes narrowed and demanded to be updated. Passing over the data Ru went through the figures and results. When he had finished the director sat back slumped in his chair, his face bathed in sweat. It was a long time before he spoke.

"Has No 6 been deep cleaned yet as I instructed? And have the animals now been cremated?"

"No sir, the vet hopes to come by sometime within the next couple of days, until then we cannot arrange for any cleaning to be done; it would be much too dangerous. I am assured the animals will be taken away by Monday," he lied.

Chi Tao nodded, "why is it taking so long. I gave the order two days ago," he glared. "There's no time to waste, especially if this new data is correct."

Ru was going to say something but thought better of it. He remained silent and vaguely nodded his agreement.

Chi Tao moved his gaze to Mei Lien, "why don't you both come over to the computer", he moved across the room where he sat at a large desk and held out his hand, "USB please". Pointing to two stools, he motioned them to sit down. "Let's make a start; please be concise with your answers, we must go through this data from the beginning with a fine toothcomb."

For the next five hours they sat pouring through the figures, explaining the finer points of their findings and answered every question with precision. They refrained from giving Chi Tao any of their opinions. Both had decided that it was up to their director to make up his mind, to take whatever action was needed. They had warned him of the dangers, something he plainly understood, so there was no further need to expound on their fears. They had done as they were asked to the best of their ability, although they were very unhappy at the results, it was now out of their hands. The stools were hard, so by the end of the long hours both had back ache and pains down their legs. It was relief when, at last, Chi Tao sat back and thanked them. They had been extremely helpful indeed and most professional. He looked round at them getting up and beamed broadly. "Thank you both for your patience and for your excellent work. I will ensure you get all the credit you merit". He walked over to his main desk, "I am shortly going to Beijing for a few days, where I'll be presenting our work. I am confident our Centre will be well looked upon and will benefit from all this."

They both smiled back politely but he continued, "please ensure that everything I asked for is done by the time I return; no excuses". He signalled that the meeting was over.

On the way to the door Mei Lien plucked up the courage and turned toward their boss. "We are both glad you are happy with our work and explanations and delighted you will be presenting the findings in Beijing. We wish you good luck. Before he could reply she continued, "can you tell us when we can return to the capital, now our work has been completed we will need to make arrangements".

He looked at her over his specs and in a dismissive tone, "yes, yes of course, we will talk about that on my return, I am too busy now to think about trivial matters like that; goodbye". A sense of guilt came over him and he quickly added, "I will be away for a week why don't you both take a few days off, have a rest".

\*　　\*　　\*

Once alone in the corridor, they both exhaled deeply. Mei Lien leant against the wall, "wow, that was a few hours I shall not forget in a hurry. My bum is so numb I could sit on a cactus plant and not feel anything."

Ru giggled and had to agree. "How do you think it went? I'm happy at the way we handled all the questions, and you, you came over very professional and business like. Yes, I think we impressed the old goat. Not sure about you, but I'm dying of thirst."

They marched off down the corridor towards the canteen giggling as Ru started to massage her bottom. It was only once they had reached the hall, that both remembered their late afternoon appointment. The big clock indicated 4pm, only just enough time to get to their next meeting.

The bus trip took longer than ever, or so it seemed. They travelled in silence, both deep in their own thoughts. Mei Lien stared out of the window at the streets full of early evening citizens scurrying around doing last minute shopping, trying to dodge the traffic and bicycles. Ru was in a different world, a world he did not want to be in but was constantly drawn back to. He was scared and worried. They were so lost in their own thoughts that they almost missed the bus stop, frantically scrambling down the aisle, they stepped out onto the pavement and heaved a sigh of relief, "that was close" said Mei Lien. "Had it not been for that woman with the screaming brat bumping into me, we would have missed the stop."

They made their way a little further down the road before turning left into the dusty side street. A sense of edginess came over Ru, a tingle ran down his spine, he turned round but no one was following. Walking quickly, heads bent, they soon arrived outside the small house. They glanced at one-another, and he could see fear in Mei Lien's eyes but said nothing; just opened the gate pulling her gently behind him.

\* \* \*

Chi Tao carefully wrapped one of the USB stick in a new envelope and slipped it into his jacket pocket. The second stick was placed along with the two large manilla files in his briefcase which he carefully locked. Gathering his coat and suitcase he made his way out of his office to the waiting car.

The airport was busy with commuters and businessmen. Chi Tao had not flown much and was surprised at the size of the airport and the number of people travelling. At security he panicked when asked to take off his jacket and put his briefcase on the conveyor belt. He lost sight of both for a few minutes and was relieved when he was re-united with his belongings. He checked the briefcase was still locked and patted down his jacket pocket, smiling as he felt the envelope and its contents.

He spent the flight deep in thought, planning, mentally going over his presentation. The next couple of days, weeks perhaps, were going to be defining, make or break time for the centre and for Chi Tao Ming.

# CHAPTER 36

# Hong Kong

Sean was sitting at his bedroom window gazing out at the view over the bay; he was getting bored and edgy. Another day and he would hopefully get his visa, that was what Pearl had told him. He started to think about her. The more he got to know her, the more he liked her. A girl who knew her job, was dedicated and obviously had a hard streak in her. Just look at the way she disposed of that caretaker the first time they went to talk to Mei Lien; no wonder she didn't have a husband or boyfriend, or did she? She never spoke about anyone, so in his opinion, probably not. She was extremely attractive, fine legs too, and he had to admit he enjoyed being with her.

His mind drifted to Jimmy, another professional of the highest calibre. Now, there was a man he admired, a man who was at the top his profession, another dedicated, near fanatic, loving what he was doing. He had no idea if Jimmy had any field-work experience; probably not, but he was a master of his trade, and what he didn't know about eavesdropping and spying on other countries, could be written in a few lines. What he really liked about Jimmy was the way he ran his department, had complete control, and how he did not miss a thing. He had a certain way of putting over his orders as ideas which everyone automatically agreed with. The man's easy demeanour and friendliness just attracted you to being his friend. Sean wondered whether Pearl and Jimmy were anything more than just work colleagues. He doubted it;

both were too professional to know that personal involvement would not marry well with their job. Was Jimmy married? Not to a woman that was for sure, but to his job – most definitely.

He picked up his drink and gently swirled it around. Over the past eighteen months he had met a wide range of characters and made some good friends. He was pleased he had renewed his friendship with James after so many years. What a delightful, intelligent man, always wanting to help, his sense of fun matching his own. He was pleased he had given him some excitement and a new purpose in life, although he was concerned that things might go wrong and he had put his friend, yes, his best friend, in danger. Not being trained in the workings and minds of the underworld or criminals, he worried how James would cope with violence or even death. You never know what might happen, things seem to be going smoothly and to plan when, suddenly, bang, it all changes and you find yourself in a life-threatening situation or gun battle. In the world Sean lived in, violence was never far away, and he certainly did not want his friend to come to any harm. He would have to be alert.

Then there were the Americans. He never thought that he would be able to work with his counterparts over the pond. They worked differently, acted irrationally and impetuously some of the time, but this lot seemed different. Jack was smart, knew their world inside out and like him had been through many years of gruelling field-work in the most dangerous parts of the world. He thought and talked like a spy. Sean had noticed he remained constantly alert to danger, had that innate ability and instinct to smell it out. Same with Joe, another solid professional with a good sense of humour, which he liked. Joe was a ferret, digging up pieces of information with ease and once he got his teeth into something, would not let go. Easy going, with a friendly manner, he could charm anyone. Sean was sure that Joe was no saint, another hardened field-worker, no doubt seeing off many a criminal, and would not think twice before sending them to meet their maker.

Hank, well Hank was quite different, very insecure. He guessed he did not much like his job, never did. From what he had gleaned, Hank had spent a few years in the field but was soon moved to a desk. He suspected the man had not got the stomach or the natural ability, but he could be wrong. Hank was alright, in little doses, and he was well suited to his office role and paperwork.

His mind went back to James and his visit to the Embassy yesterday. He would have dearly loved to be a fly on the wall and watch his friend. He was sure James would have been petrified at first but once inside, his English public-school education would have taken over. He knew his subject and, like a true professor, had prepared well. Adding to that, his feeling of responsibility towards Sean and the Americans would have been immense. Sean bet that by the time he left the Deputy's office, James would have felt very much at home.

His thoughts were interrupted by the ring of his mobile. It was Pearl. Good news, his visa was ready to be picked up and she had sent the office boy to collect it. Would he like to meet her for diner later and she would hand it over to him? They could discuss plans for the visit to Wuhan. Putting down the phone Sean's thoughts returned to Pearl's legs. Would he make a pass? He shook his head; be sensible man, don't spoil a good friendship and you know your golden rule, never get involved with work partners.

\* \* \*

## Beijing

Chi Tao walked into the vast building that was the Government Centre for Scientific Research. He followed the signs to the conference hall feeling nerves coming on. After landing last night, he had made his way to the designated hotel just across the square from the Centre; the place was full of delegates. He didn't know anyone and didn't wish to mix, so spent the evening in his room going over, once again, his speech and what he had to say. He entered the vast hall, which was set out in a semi-circle, each place with a small table, a screen and earphones. In front, the stage was set with a central dais and microphone; on either side a row of tables with ten seats. A red curtain covered the entire wall behind. Chinese flags were everywhere. He was in awe and a huge feeling of pride came over him.

Showing his ID badge, he was waved through, and a young woman dressed in a crisp cream suit showed him to his place. He settled down and took out his papers. There was no one to his left so he turned and gave a bright smile and a polite bow to the woman on his right. She glared at him before busying herself with her papers. He picked up the agenda and read through it, it was going to be a long day. Turning over the page there was a list of all the speakers. He looked down for his name, but it wasn't there. He blinked, disappointed and surprised. He seemed to recollect that he had received a note advising him that he had been selected as one of the star speakers. Rummaging through his briefcase he found the note. Reading through it, he realised that his moment was not scheduled for the first day but for the following afternoon, to a much smaller and more select audience. Oh well! by next year everyone would know him; he wouldn't be sitting in these rows, but up there on stage. He smiled to himself, content.

The day was long and extremely boring. The speakers rambled on and on about the importance of working together, of working for the people but most of all, for the good of China. They were split about half and half between political and the military. Each one trying to out-do the other in rhetoric and enthusiasm. The politicians expounded the virtues of working for the economy, how science was putting China at the forefront of world economy. The military pushed for research and development to protect the people and the country from foreign enemies, in particular the West. The end of each speech was greeted by a standing ovation and broad smiles by the other dignitaries. Finally, the Chairman, a middle-aged man, stood up and thanked everyone for their contribution and for attending. Before closing the session, he reminded all the delegates to carefully read their invitations and to make their way to the correct hall the following day. This hall was not going to be used. Everyone stood up as the national anthem was played and rapturously applauded off the speakers.

Chi Tao did not bother looking at his neighbour but gathered his files and made a hasty retreat to the hotel.

\* \* \*

## Wuhan

Tim greeted his visitors with a warm smile and a bow. He pointed to a couple of chairs and offered them some tea. He noted both were nervous and trying hard to hide the fact. The girl's hands were shaking, and she tried to conceal her feelings by clasping them tightly together and occasionally wringing them. The man kept swallowing and licking his lips. Both were unaware of doing this and thought they were acting calm and collected.

Tim opened the conversation by thanking them for coming and apologising that their "aunt and uncle" were unable to be present. He continued, "my name is Ying Po, just call me Ying, I am your aunt's cousin. We are close but sadly cannot meet up very often. She tells me you have something you wish to ask; I am at your disposal." He smiled broadly and took a sip of his tea.

Mei Lien swallowed before speaking, "thank you for seeing us. I'm not sure if you are the right person we should talk to. Our problem is rather complicated". She hesitated and quickly continued, "not that you would not understand; you see, what we have to say is rather technical and involves our work".

Their host remained relaxed and continued to smile, "I understand, you don't know me and what you have to say is probably rather delicate. Please do not worry, I am not a scientist and have no knowledge of the subject, but I am a good listener." He sipped some more of his tea and seeing them still unsure continued, "why don't you give me an outline of your problem, I could then perhaps pass this on, or even make a few suggestions".

Mei Lien was looking at him intently, her mind racing. Ru scratched his chin before cagily speaking, "it concerns our research. We are scientists you see, and we have a problem; it is extremely complicated. It's more of a moral quandary rather than a technical one." He looked over at Mei Lien. "I'm sorry. We have wasted your time; we can work it out ourselves."

Tim remained impassive, "I fully understand, I would be the same. It is never easy talking to a stranger, especially when it involves personal feelings. Please don't worry, you haven't wasted my time. I did this for my cousin. I will let her know you would prefer to talk to her directly." He kept his voice smooth and friendly although inside he was disappointed. They were certainly very cagey, panicky even, and understandably so. He picked up a visiting card and handed it over to Ru, "here is my card and contact details. If ever you change your mind or need any help, just give me a call".

Ru glanced at the card and read – Ying Po, Director, Purveyor of Fresh Fruit and Vegetables to the Trade – he thanked Tim and put it in his pocket.

Tim rose and showed them to the door, "thank you for coming all this way; again I'm sorry I couldn't be of more help". He bowed and let them out, watching the couple walk hastily down the street.

Mei Lien looked round to make sure they were alone before turning to Ru, "what did you make of him?" she asked.

"Nice enough man. Think he was a bit put out by your remark and insinuation he wasn't bright enough to help us."

"Yes, it sort of slipped out. Did you notice anything about him?".

"No, can't say I did. Why?"

"I am sure we've seen him before. Not sure where or when but I'm convinced we have met him."

"You're probably right, but in a city of eight million plus, I doubt very much we have seen him. He supplies fruit and veg so possibly it was at one of the markets".

Mei Lien was not convinced but let the matter drop. She slid her arm around his waist and changed the subject; now was not the time or place to discuss what had happened.

Back at the flat she busied herself making dinner; Ru came through and leant on the counter. "I've been thinking about what you said, about Ying. I think you are wrong about seeing him. I know your female instincts are usually right, but he really doesn't look familiar at all." He went to taste a prawn from the pot, "keep your paw out of there, they're not ready", she slapped him gently on the hand.

Looking sheepish he continued, "now I've told you my feelings, what did you make of him?".

"Not a lot, but my instinct is that he was honest and wanting to help. He can't be too bad if he's related to auntie."

"Everyone can be bad. I can assure you of that! Not sure what they were thinking of when they suggested we meet him. What does he know – a fruit and veg man – to think he can help us sort out our problem?"

"That's very judgemental and not fair. You don't know the man, and because he is a merchant doesn't mean he has no brains. He looked intelligent enough to me. Anyway, I think it was very nice of them to offer his services."

Ru grunted. "Well, the whole thing was a waste of time and I'm disappointed. I wasn't convinced the two westerners would, or could help, now I'm sure. We're on our own from now on."

"Don't be like that. You never know. I trust them, and I think they were doing their best." She poured the steaming food into a couple of bowls. "Come on, time to eat."

\* \* \*

Ru woke up soaked with sweat, his heart thumping. He looked at his watch, 2am. He was in too much of a turmoil to get back to sleep so got up and went through to the sitting room. He remembered the nightmare vividly, a dream he had never had before and did not like. For the first time in his life, he had dreamt of his parents, they were calling him, faintly shouting at him to come and join them, their faces blurred but recognisable.

He sat in the sitting room shivering. What did it mean, why such a dream and why now? He remembered his childhood, his father coming home, beaten and half dead. He recalled how his mother had cried for days on end, the hardship and eventually how, because of him being in Shanghai, he never had the chance to say a last good-bye. He started to cry, he realised he had never really grieved.

After a long while he made his way back to bed and snuggled up to Mei Lien, her warm body comforting him.

\* \* \*

## Hong Kong

They were sitting at table by the window. Pearl had taken Sean to one of her favourite places. It was one of the dozens of restaurants and bars that lined the promenade, offering superb views over the bay. She liked this one especially for the fine seafood and friendly service. They sat chatting over a glass of wine waiting for the first course.

She had picked him up earlier from the hotel and Sean had been mesmerised by her appearance. A short black skirt that showed off her legs, those never-ending legs, a lowcut print blouse and a pair of high heeled shoes. Her hair loose down to her shoulders, was hooked around her ears that sported a pair of dangling earrings; a small pendant hanging from a thin gold chain lay just at the top of her small cleavage; she looked stunning. As they made their way to the waiting taxi several men looked round, envious, the women on their arms, jealous.

Enjoying each-others company, she asked him about his life, was he married? did he have any children? He kept his life story simple, omitting the more wild and gory episodes., telling her about his younger days and his renewed friendship with James. He felt embarrassed, he never really spoke about himself or his past; that was a part of him he normally kept secret.

In turn, she told him about her childhood and how she came into her career. Like him, she was not normally comfortable talking about herself but, tonight, she was feeling relaxed and enjoyed his company. Conversation flowed freely.

She filled him in about Jimmy and, as he had suspected, there was no romance, never had been, just a professional relationship and a deep trust between them. Both had similar backgrounds and reasons for joining the world of spies.

He paid the bill and they strolled along the promenade. She had slipped her arm through his and they watched the night life pass by, the young couple kissing, the older ones strolling along, content with life. As they stopped to watch one of ferries leave the pier, she moved her arm to round his waist and nestled into him. His mind was in turmoil, and he felt like a teenager on a first date; keeping her delicate body close to his, he breathed in her scent.

There was a loud ring from her bag and they both jumped, startled out of their dream. The spell was broken. She answered it in her professional voice, listened and nodded, before hanging up. Looking at him, a slight sadness in her eyes, she apologised. "That was Jimmy, he's asked us to meet him at the office in twenty minutes."

He sighed and, taking her hand, thanked her, "I will remember tonight for a long time; thank you for a wonderful evening".

She smiled before they turned and made their way to hail a taxi.

\* \* \*

As they walked through the door, Jimmy was standing in front of a screen busy talking to one of men. Both seemed serious and both wore worried frowns. They went over to join them and were immediately greeted with a jovial smile. "Nice evening?" enquired Jimmy. Patting the man on the shoulder and giving him a last comment, Jimmy turned and showed them into his office.

"Sorry about that; you came quicker than expected. Apologies also for cutting your evening short, hope you had a nice time".

Sean was about to speak but Jimmy continued. "Had news from Wuhan not long ago. Tim met up with the couple earlier this evening, but they basically refused to talk to him. He reported that they were both extremely nervous and anxious."

"Sure, that's a shame indeed. I had high hopes we would learn a lot today. I guess it makes our visit all the more necessary." Sean sucked on his pen, deep in thought.

"Now that you have your visa which is valid from tomorrow, Monday, I agree, you and Pearl should go up there and make contact." Jimmy looked at Pearl and reading her mind, "Ok, you did have your reservations, I must admit, but you shouldn't blame Tim. You know how people clam up and don't like change."

Pearl nodded, "I'm not blaming him, I'm sure he did his best".

Sean was about to speak when Jimmy butted in, "I've got you both booked on the 9.45am flight and have asked Sandra to make contact with our friends again. Perhaps you can try calling them Pearl?".

"It's a bit late now but I will first thing in the morning."

"Did Pearl give you your passport and visa?" asked Jimmy.

Sean nodded, "yes, all looks good, thanks".

"Well Mr Sean Docherty, is it nice to be travelling under your real name again?" Jimmy asked grinning widely.

Sean looked blank and kept a straight face. "What do you mean, my real name. You suggested I used another name, so, you have it."

Jimmy's grinned even more, "Sean, I made enquiries and knew all along that Mike Flannigan was a cover name. I didn't say anything, I was happy to go along with it."

Sean smiled, he had to give it to the man. "Oh, so you've been checking up on me have you, and what else have you found out?"

"That you have a distinguished military career, have served numerous tours in Northern Ireland as an under-cover agent and since you left the army, were recruited by the Firm. You have undertaken several assignments in South America, Africa and one in Thailand. Prior to being asked to investigate the current event, you were working on a drugs investigation and the possible links between the Taliban and our Triads." He grinned one of his cheeky looks. "Want me to carry on?"

Sean held up his hands, "seems you know me better than I do myself". Looking over to Pearl, "there I was telling you all about myself and you already knew".

She laughed, "it's the first I've heard of all this, promise; Jimmy never divulges things like that, do you?".

Jimmy got up, "sorry, can't help it. Now, it's late and we have a busy day tomorrow so, time for bed".

Sean was dropped off at the hotel and Pearl agreed to pick him up at 6am.

# CHAPTER 37

# Wuhan

Ru had been looking at his phone for a while before he spoke, "why don't we go to Yunyeng for a few days? It's not far, a couple of hours on the bus and I understand it has some lovely scenery and walks. We can find a small place overlooking Donting Lake and relax; after all, the old goat suggested we had a few days off."

Mei Lien agreed enthusiastically, anything to get away from this dump of a city with its noise and pollution. "When are you thinking we go?"

"Tomorrow; there's a bus at 9.30am and we should be there for just before 12noon, stay three nights."

She threw herself round his neck, kissing him all over before rushing off to pack. Ru shouted after her not to take too many clothes and to throw a few things in for him.

They were on the bus making their way through the out-skirts of the city; Ru was looking out at the distant hills. Mei Lien, her head resting on his shoulder, suddenly jumped and started to rummage through her bag. He asked her what she was looking for. "My phone. I must have left it in the kitchen charging."

"You don't need your phone; we're on holiday and who would call us anyway?" She agreed and settled back. "We're on holiday to get away from everything; I also left my phone behind. Nothing will happen until the old goat gets back, so relax."

Arriving at Yunyeng bus station, they hailed a taxi and gave the address of a small hotel Ru had found on the internet. Nothing was booked; he figured the place would not be busy in early November and he was proved right. They were shown to a nice, bright room overlooking the lake and, to Mei Lien's relief, it was clean. Leaving their bag still packed, they went to explore. They walked along the river, wandered the quaint old streets, saddened at seeing once fine buildings now falling into disrepair. They stopped often to taste one of the many lovely smelling dishes offered by the numerous stalls that lined the narrow lanes and sampled the various aromatic teas. It was night-time before they got back to the hotel and flopped down on the soft bed, exhausted.

Mei Lien woke to rain battering the window. She got up and looked out at the dismal, grey day and returned to bed. She snuggled up to Ru and the next few hours were spent making love, enjoying each other's intimacy. He told her of his dream and how he had never grieved properly for his mother. She held him, stroked him and whispered soothing words. They braved the cold and the rain for a short while before returning to the hotel soaked. That night over diner, Ru suggested they got married in March. Mei Lien eyes shone bright but suggested May – the weather would be better and the flowers in her parents' garden would be in full bloom. He agreed and they celebrated by having a few more drinks. The rest of the night passed making love, exploring, enjoying each other's body.

Their short break ended all too rapidly and soon they were heading for the bus station and back to the daily grind.

\* \* \*

Jimmy had arranged for separate tickets to be booked for both Pearl and Sean with reserved seats. The flight was only half-full and passengers had been spread out. With a spare seat between him and Pearl he had considered moving closer but, after consideration, thought better of it. He could still feel her body nestled into his and had the smell of her perfume in his nostrils. No, stay where you are, it's safer. He asked for an English-speaking newspaper but there were none, so he closed his eyes and drifted off. Pearl flicked through her magazine.

As they were making their way down the long corridor, he asked her to get a local paper, he wanted to know how or if, the demonstration in Hong Kong had been reported. After picking up a copy of the South China Post they made their way to the exit. They were heading for the taxi rank when a man came up to them. "You want taxi mister?" he gesticulated and repeated the question. Taken aback Pearl declined but he insisted. She suddenly realised it was Tim and nodding, she grabbed hold of Sean and they followed him to a private cab. No one spoke until they started to pull out, only then did Pearl ask him what he was playing at.

"Jimmy told me you were coming and asked me to meet you," he said in a business-like manner. "Sorry for the charade, no point in anyone knowing you were expected, and I didn't want to advertise the fact that I know you".

Pearl made the introductions and Sean asked what the plan was.

"We have a couple of hours yet before our young friends' return home from work. I suggest we wait until they get in before Pearl contacts them and arranges a meeting."

He dropped them off at the hotel and an hour later was back to pick them up. They made their way to a car park not far from the apartment and headed for a small tea house where they managed to get a table by the window. They watched as people came and went, chatting about life in general but always keeping alert. Time passed and it was getting late but still no sign of the young couple. Pearl started to feel uneasy and decided to have a wander up the street. Perhaps they had missed them. She returned twenty minutes later and signalled the two men to join her. Once outside she headed to the car park.

"What are you doing?" asked Tim.

Pearl was taking out her phone, "I went to the apartment and the caretaker said they had gone away, left this morning, early. She has no idea where they were heading for or for how long." She pressed speed dial on her mobile and waited. The phone rang several times before she heard the standard message that the recipient was unavailable; she hung up. "No answer, just the usual message."

Tim looked puzzled. "They didn't mention anything yesterday, no hint; wonder where they've gone." He, in turn, took out his phone and called Sandra. In a cryptic manner he asked her if she knew anything. Negative, she hadn't seen them today.

They sat in the car in silence before Sean spoke, "you don't think they've gone to Beijing?".

Both shook their heads. "No, they're not high up enough. Something has happened or they've been sent somewhere at the last minute." Tim's tone had changed to one of concern. "Sure enough they were scared and worried yesterday but not so much that they would have run away."

Sean suggested they return to the hotel and Pearl could try calling again later. Tim declined the invitation to join them saying he was going to try and find out their whereabouts.

"I'm really extremely sorry. We've been keeping tabs on them all this time and the day we want to talk to them they disappear. It's all my fault, I shouldn't have come to pick you up." He shook his head.

"Oh no, no! not at all. It is no ones' fault, it happens, and you certainly didn't know they would disappear." Sean's tone was reassuring and genuine. "Probably just gone some place for the day."

They were sitting in the bar when Pearl tried again but, again, there was no reply. She was perturbed, more worried than Sean, and started to blame her colleague. Sean came firmly down on Tim's side. Looking at Pearl he spoke in a harsher tone than he had meant, "you don't seem to trust him much; noticed that back at the office the other day".

She looked uncomfortable, "it's not that I don't trust him, I'm just not sure he's up to doing this kind of job. He's more used to going undercover than surveillance".

"It happens; I've been there. You spend weeks tailing a target, watching every move and suddenly you lose him, just when you least expect it. Ok If there are a few of you but, on your own, it's pretty damned hard to stay with them 24/7. Think you are being a bit harsh on the man".

She blushed slightly, "I suppose you're right. What's our next move?".

"I don't know about you, but I'm off to bed; I'll see you in the morning. Try giving her another call in an hour or so and then try again tomorrow first thing. She may have left her phone behind by mistake."

\* \* \*

Tim was late picking them up, he looked as if he hadn't slept all night which was indeed the case. After leaving them the previous evening he and Sandra had set to work trying to find out what had happened to their charges. It was only this morning, after visiting the airports and train stations that they had got round to checking the main bus park. Sandra, posing as secret police officer, had found a ticket salesman who recognised the couple. He had sold them two return trips to Yunyeng, a small town a hundred kilometres away. The return ticket was for Wednesday.

He greeted Pearl and Sean. "Very sorry I'm late; Sandra and I have spent the night trying to locate the pair. She has discovered they left for a small town not far away and have a return ticket for tomorrow. We can drive down now if you like."

Sean thanked him profusely and Pearl had to admit she was perhaps wrong. They agreed it would not be a good idea to make the trip as obviously the couple had taken a couple of days off and there was no point in disturbing them. They sent Tim home to get some sleep and arranged for him to pick them up the following morning. It was a grey, uninspiring day but they decided to spend it getting to know the city; not that there was much to the place.

*   *   *

## Beijing

At last Chi Tao's big day had arrived. He woke early, did his morning exercises, before padding into the bathroom for a cold shower. Feeling full of the joys of life he dressed in his best suit and knotted the red tie with care. He looked in the mirror and was pleased with what he saw.

He made his way over to the conference centre and to the correct hall. As the previous day, he showed his pass, went through security and was shown to his seat by a young woman. He looked at her and at her colleagues and wondered if they were clones out of the same laboratory, he couldn't tell the difference. They all looked the same, were dressed the same and all had that bland expressionless look. No smiles, no warmth, just robots.

He nodded to his near companions, who eyed him suspiciously, and made himself comfortable. He looked at the list of speakers, he was number seventeen. Each one was allocated twenty minutes precisely; it was going to be another long day. Sitting back in his chair he re-read his notes.

At precisely 9.45am a small parade of men dressed in dark suits followed by a handful of military officers came onto the stage and took their seats, busied themselves with papers and waited for an elderly man to rise and make the opening welcome speech. He took full advantage of his moment but finally, he called the first speaker to the rostrum and proceedings began.

Chi Tao sat half listening, half in a trance. The various orators before him outlined and promoted their findings and discoveries, all vying for the limelight and hoping their project would be chosen. Slowly he crept up the list until he was next. He started to feel ill, his mouth began to go dry, his stomach knotted. The speaker finished, turned to thank the panel before walking off. Chi Tao was about to get up, when the little man rose and announced the morning session had come to an end and requesting everyone be back no later than 1.45pm.

There was a mass exodus towards the canteen, but Chi Tao remained rooted to his seat until, one of the robotic girls, came over and politely requested he leave. He could not face mixing with the other scientists and making small talk, answering questions. He went outside and stood under the large canopy watching the rain fall and breathed in the cold air.

Once everyone was back in their seats and the dignitaries had taken up their positions. the little man stood up and announced the afternoon session open. Chi Tao made his way up on stage and stood on the dais. Looking out over the room full of his peers, he placed his speech on the lectern with shaking hands, cleared his throat and began his presentation. He was not sure whether he imagined it, but did he get as much applause as the others? He turned to thank the panel who nodded blandly, expressionless. He returned to his seat, armpits soaking and sweat trickling down his back. There were a few nods from his nearest colleagues but none of them showed any warmth.

He sat for the rest of the afternoon not really listening, his thoughts back at his centre and what he should do with his team in lab No 6. He had lost track of time but came back to reality when he faintly heard his name being mentioned and some muted applause. Looking up, he saw that the officials were standing, ready for the National Anthem; he followed suit.

No one was looking or taking notice of him so he assumed he must have been dreaming. He collected his papers, placed them neatly in his briefcase and followed the others out of the auditorium in silence. Yet again, he opted not to follow the crowd and decided to skip the official drinks reception. Instead, he headed for the exit and to the relative peace of his hotel.

He slumped down on his bed, exhausted and a feeling of disappointment drifted over him. After a while he got up and had a shower and suddenly felt famished. As he was dressing, he told himself to be realistic, why should a small director from a second-tier laboratory, expect to be listened to or be expected to come up with a revolutionary find. No, you must work your way up the ladder; just like in football, you start low and slowly get promoted up the ranks if you are good enough. He was pleased he was not attending the evening gathering, no one would miss him and the thought of listening to all those smug scientists, boasting about how good they and their institutions were would have depressed him even more.

Making his way through the entrance lobby, he was intercepted by a receptionist who handed him a large envelope. He took it, thanked the man, and proceeded to the restaurant. He ordered food and his favourite beer. He didn't like being on his own, so he busied himself with his phone. Should he just get up and leave? No, he was starving. Feeling awkward, he opened the envelope and took out the crisp headed paper. He had to stifle a yell of excitement. He read it twice, making sure he had not misunderstood, checking the headed paper, making sure it was not a ghastly hoax. He sat back in a daze and ordered more beer. Back in his room he consumed several more beers and even demolished four of the miniature whiskies from the mini bar. He got very drunk and eventually fell asleep.

# CHAPTER 38

# Washington

James woke with a feeling of unease. No one had heard from Sean for three days and all efforts to get hold of him had been in vain. He felt useless and a burden on Joe who, he was sure, had better things to do. The more he got to know the man, the more he liked him. He had a great manner and was attentive as well as amusing. The previous night Joe had regaled him with numerous fishing tales, of which many James suspected, were exaggerated; nevertheless, they had spent a fun evening with, perhaps, one dram too many. With nothing much to do and having been away a few days he wanted to get back to Claire, to the cottage and to his comfortable bed.

Jack had returned to London the previous day leaving him in Joe and Hank's care. The celebratory dinner had gone well until the time came to pay. Hank had gotten in a strop about the cost and suggested they split the bill which was promptly vetoed by Jack. They had left him sorting out the payment and muttering how he wouldn't get it passed Finance.

He walked into the kitchen and was greeted by Joe and Beth who were seated at the table, large mugs of coffee in hand and a box of pastries between them. He had got used to Beth and her cold manner. A woman of few words, he had wondered whether she was married but soon discounted that idea.

Joe looked up from his paper, "morning, how are you on this new day?". He pointed to the box of buns, "help yourself, Beth went out to buy them first thing; kept a couple for you," he grinned.

Sipping his tea, James selected a muffin and bit into it. "Any news from our wanderer?" he asked. Joe shook his head. Feeling slightly embarrassed he continued, "have you any idea how long I'm going to be here for?" then added , "not that I'm not liking your company, but I'm sure you have better things to do than to be my chaperone".

Joe shook his head slightly again, "don't fret, you're sure not a burden, it's a pleasure having you. I must agree though, you can't stay here forever and probably want to get back home". He offered James another pastry which he declined. "Let's talk to Hank and see what he thinks. Glancing at his watch he nodded to Beth, "better get ready, five minutes". He stood up and shoved the last pastry in his mouth.

The day had been planned the night before; to start with, the first of two daily catch-up meetings, followed by a tour of the Senate which Joe had managed to organise. It was going to be a private visit arranged through a friend of his who would then take him on a short sightseeing tour of the main city monuments. As he got into the car James was looking forward to his day.

*   *   *

Joes' friend dropped him off outside the office building and, after thanking him, James headed for the main door. Being a regular visitor now, he was immediately recognised, and the guard led him through to security without a question. He made his way up to Hank's office where the secretary greeted him with a smile and led him to her boss. Joe had already arrived and both men enquired whether he had had a good time.

After he gave a brief outline of his tour and what he had seen, Hank immediately took over. "I understand from Joe you are wanting to go home, and I don't blame you, I would also. We still have no news from Sean; just hope he is ok. You never know in those damned countries." He briefly paused to take a breath. "What about if you fly back tonight? There's a flight leaving at 20.45, so time enough".

James was about to agree when Joe butted in, "not that we are wanting you out the way, you can leave any time".

At last, he was able to talk. He looked at his watch, it had just gone 5pm, plenty of time to throw his belongings into his bag and get to the airport. He agreed that their suggestion was ideal and thanked them.

On the way to the airport Joe apologised for Hank's bluntness, adding, " he used to be a smooth talker but over the past years he's become a different man. Had a good sense of humour when he was young but lost all that of late". James assured him he had no problem and was only grateful for all their help. Before getting out, he asked to be kept updated on events, especially if they had any news of his friend; he didn't like to admit it, but he was worried.

*　*　*

## Wuhan

Ru and Mei Lien arrived back to the flat early afternoon; the rain had eased slightly but the weather was still damp with a chilly northerly wind; both felt relaxed after the couple of days away. Ru was sitting at the table when he heard a knock on the door. Puzzled he went to see who was there. He gasped in surprise as he came face to face with Pearl who was smiling broadly; Sean towering behind her.

In a croaked voice he invited them in, checking that none of the neighbours had come out, before quickly closing the door and calling Mei Lien. She came skipping out of the bedroom and stopped dead, jaw dropping open when she recognised the visitors. As she followed the other three into the small lounge, her composure returned, and she was soon busying herself making tea for everyone. Ru waved them to the settee and perched himself on the edge of the table. Finding his voice, he made polite conversation, telling them all about their last-minute trip to Yunyeng until his future bride returned from the kitchen.

After pouring and handing out the cups, Mei Lien made herself comfortable on the floor; she spoke for the first time. "How did they get in? What did they say to the woman at the desk?" She started to panic inside. Continuing in a flat monotone voice, she asked the purpose of the visit, her eyes moving constantly between the two guests.

Pearl picked up on her anxiety and spoke in a calm and gentle tone. She told them no one had seen them entering the building. They had used the rear fire escape which was open, by-passing the front desk and they met no one on their way up. She quickly told them that they had changed their travel arrangements after uncle had reported they preferred not to speak to him. She realised they had a problem which, understandably, they were not keen to talk about with a stranger. Ru relaxed slightly and his breathing slowly returned to normal. Mei Lien suddenly burst into tears, sobbing uncontrollably. Ru went over to comfort her, and she calmed down. Wiping her eyes, she looked up at him. Something passed between them, that something only intimate couples have, and soon both started to talk. The flood gates opened, and the couple poured out their fears and concerns. Sean and Pearl listened silently, not interrupting, not asking questions. They let the couple release the pent-up emotions which had been tormenting them for weeks. Any comments were soothing and reassuring. When Ru and Mei Lien finally finished, they fell silent, exhausted by the tension of the moment.

Pearl was the first to speak and, in a gentle voice, started to probe. Sean asked the more technical questions, while his partner tried to ascertain the finer points of the moral dilemma. It was past 9pm before they were both satisfied that they had the complete story and fully understood the scientists' concerns. Sean suggested they went out for a bite to eat, but Mei Lien declined telling them it would be too dangerous and that it would arouse suspicion; in their position, being with a foreigner was not a good career move.

Before leaving, both Pearl and Sean stressed that they should not hesitate to contact either of them if they needed to talk further. They also impressed on the couple that uncle was extremely trustworthy and that they should not think twice about calling on him. If they were worried about talking on the phone, they should make arrangements through the old cleaner at the canteen.

As they reached the top of the stairs, Ru came over and, in a hushed voice, asked if they were going to leave by the same door. Sean nodded and headed for the stairs.

Closing the fire escape door carefully, they quickly made their way round the building and exited into a dark alleyway. Carefully, they emerged into the street, turning right before crossing over and headed for the car park. Tim was sitting waiting patiently.

On the way back to the hotel they brought him up to speed and discussed their next move.

\* \* \*

Ru closed the flat door, careful not to make too much noise, and returned to the lounge where he found Mei Lien staring into space, deep in thought. He sat beside her and took her in his arms. They remained silent for a long time.

He was the first to break the silence, "well, that's it, no going back now. We rather walked into their trap".

Mei Lien shook her head, "no, not a trap. They were genuinely concerned about our whereabouts and then, we just gave them everything they wanted," she paused slightly. "I feel better, it's as if a heavy weight has been lifted from my shoulders; I feel so much calmer and my head seems clearer."

Ru did not answer for a long while. "What are we going to do? We cannot resign, the old goat won't allow it and probably would become suspicious. We continue as if nothing has happened? That's going to be hard for both of us." He fell silent again. He looked down at the love of his life and kissed her gently, "no, we are going to have to live with it, try to put it behind us and forget".

It was Mei Lien's turn not to say anything. Eventually she nodded slightly and after a heavy sigh agreed. "I know I would not be strong enough if I was on my own, but with you, anything is possible, you are my rock."

\* \* \*

## Beijing

Chi Tao woke with a thumping head, his mouth was dry and tasted as if had licked the backside of a panda. He tried to sit up but immediately felt sick so quickly lay down again. He groaned and tried to get his brain to work. When was his appointment? Not today, he was sure - tomorrow? Yes, that was it, Wednesday at 1pm, he relaxed a bit. He needed to go to the bathroom and gingerly sat up, head pounding and that feeling of nausea quickly returned. Bumping into a chair and clattering into the door frame he just about managed to reach his destination in time; he stayed there for a long while.

Back in bed, feeling slightly better, he picked up his phone; he had a missed call from his wife, well that could wait! He then checked that his meeting was indeed the next day and, with that confirmed, drifted off to sleep.

It was dark when he woke up and he lay in bed wondering where he was and why he was still in his pyjamas. He sat up and, apart from a vague ache at the back of his eyes, felt more human. The nausea had gone, in fact he was feeling a little peckish. He surveyed the room and cringed when he saw the amount of empty beer bottles and miniatures. What had got into him? He seldom drank more than a beer or two, and then only on a Saturday or if they had friends around. He could not remember the last time he had had a whisky; he did not really like the stuff. Feeling guilty he phoned his wife, apologising, but it had been a particular long and difficult day. He told her about the meeting the following lunch time and shuddered as her yell of excitement went right through his brain; he realised he was still in a delicate state.

Not wanting to go to the restaurant, he ordered room service and went to freshen up. After a shave and brushing his teeth several times, he had a shower, standing under the beating jet for a long time, slowly turning the temperature down. By the time the meal arrived he was sitting up in bed dressed in his kimono, feeling human again.

\*　　\*　　\*

## Wuhan

Mei Lien and Ru had slept like logs, the best night's sleep either of them had had for a long time. They felt a sense of freedom and renewed enthusiasm. The feeling soon waned as Ru sat at the table having his morning tea. What had changed? Nothing, all the facts were the same, the same problems remained, big decisions had to be made. He imparted his thoughts to Mei Lien who dismissed them and put them down to his paranoia and his fretting mind.

They entered lab No 6, now silent apart from the hum of lights and air conditioning, making their way quickly over to the glass screen separating the laboratory and the room housing the animals. The poor creatures were still there, the monkey screamed, the birds roosting on their perch, the cat looking longingly at its possible prey. The pair of mice and two chickens were more subdued, they hardly moved and none of them had eaten anything. Ru commented on how cruel they had all been. Firstly, they had placed a cat between birds and mice; secondly, and more unthoughtful, they had gone away leaving them unattended. That reminded him – they should not have still been there. Why had the blasted vet not yet removed them? He went over to the phone and dialled the extension. To his frustration and annoyance, he got the same lame excuse and a promise someone would come by between tomorrow and Saturday. He slammed the phone down and swore.

Mei Lien was watching the animals intently, giving special attention to the mice and chickens. Ru came over and vented his frustration, "if those animals have not been removed and this place has not been deep cleaned by the time the old goat gets back on Monday, we'll be in for it".

Mei Lien put her arm round his waist and nodded toward the animals, "those mice and the chickens look pretty sick to me. Monkey is not one hundred percent either, in fact, the only ones who look ok are the birds". After feeding and giving them fresh water, they sat watching their captives for a long time. Ru was the first to speak, "why don't we take fresh blood samples from all of them? We can then put them through the computer and get an analysis. That way we will know what is happening."

"We did that the other day; nothing will have changed. We haven't got time. What happens if the vet arrives any minute?" asked Mei Lien.

"The idle toads won't be doing that. I reckon it will take the boss to give the order himself before they do anything. Yes, we did test but I'd be happier if we repeated the exercise."

They put on their gowns, gloves and masks, before making their way to the room next door. Forty-five minutes later they had fresh blood samples from every animal.

They worked quickly and efficiently, both knowing what they had to do. Transferring the blood samples into test tubes, labelling them, before setting them into a specialised and sophisticated centrifugal unit for analysis. They recorded the data and printed the results before entering the findings into their computers. Two sets of results to be analysed by two different computers, just to make sure.

It was nearing 8pm when they sat back and compared the results. Both showed identical readings. Ru's demeanour darkened and all his worries returned. The tests had just re-confirmed the last findings and his worst fears. Mei Lien tried to cheer him up, but it was pointless, her boyfriend was in a world of his own and they remained silent for a long while. Finally, he sighed a deep, long sigh before swinging round to his computer. Taking the required and necessary back-ups he copied the findings onto USB sticks. He didn't put these in the safe but placed them in separate envelopes, then sealed them before slipping them into Mei Lien's bag. She turned to him puzzled, "why are you not putting them in the safe? I understand you are giving two of them to Chi Tao when he returns, that's normal, but why take a third copy".

"He smiled, a thin and sad look on his face and put a finger to his mouth, "insurance". Patting his pocket, he continued, "this is to protect us, just in case anything bad happens. If anything should happen to either of us, we should hand this over to the foreigners. As for putting them in the safe, they are better with us; think of the likes of Lu Chin."

She looked at him, suddenly scared. He went over and put his arm round her shoulder. "I'm sure nothing bad will happen; I'll make sure you are safe. You never know what might happen, I might be run over by a bus, or one of those mad taxi drivers; you can relax, I'm not aiming to go soon." He kissed her gently and wiped away her tears.

It was late evening when they returned home exhausted and drained.

\* \* \*

# Beijing

The sky was grey with low clouds scuttering overhead, and a thin drizzle fell over the city. Chi Tao busied himself preparing for the impending meeting. He sat in the hotel lobby watching the comings and goings of delegates, some taking the week seriously, others, simply happy to be away from the daily grind. He checked his watch several times; he did not want to be late.

Making his way across the vast square, he entered the imposing conference hall that had been recently rebuilt. The usual security checks done, he went over to the main desk and asked for directions. An older clone came over and signalled him to follow her. Arriving at a small lobby, she pointed to a corridor and instructed him to wait on one of the chairs he could see in the distance. He made himself as comfortable as possible and looked at his watch; ten minutes early, perfect. He waited patiently until it was well past the hour and began to wonder if he had got the time wrong. He was about to check his official paper when the door opened, and a young woman walked out. She looked stern and ignored him. What on earth is a child doing here and how did she get herself invited he wondered.

He waited patiently for what seemed ages. At last, a secretary beckoned him forward. Taking a deep breath, he adjusted his tie and smoothed his jacket; he entered a small conference room devoid of any warmth. He was confronted by a long table set at an angle, behind which sat five middle aged men. A single chair, also at an angle, was placed in front of them. He made his way over to the empty seat, bowing reverently before settling himself down. Three civilians and two military made up the panel.

One of the civilians, a small man with a straggly beard and thick glasses, cleared his throat and made the introductions. Niceties completed, he started proceedings. "Please give your full name and date of birth."

"Chi Tao Xing, fifth of May 1949".

"Name of laboratory and position?"

"Director at the Chinese National Institute and Research of Virology & Microbiology in Wuhan."

The man nodded. "Can you pass me your copy of the research and findings please?"

Chi Tao fumbled in his jacket pocket and handed over his USB stick praying he would get it back. All six turned to the large screen and the meeting began. They trawled through the findings, every word, every sum and every small detailed scrutinised and questioned. For just over four hours he sat through the grilling until, eventually his inquisitors were satisfied.

The little man cleared his throat again, "excellent work and most interesting. We will now adjourn to discuss today's proceedings and will get word to you of our decision. Please ensure you are available". He nodded signalling that time was up.

Chi Tao made his way back to the hotel, exhausted and drained. He had no idea how things had gone, there were no indications, no expressions, just the last few words which, he was certain, were said to everyone. All he could do was wait.

# CHAPTER 39

# West of England

James was happy to be back. He had to admit he had enjoyed his last trip; the meeting with the Ambassador's Deputy had, with hindsight, gone better than he had expected. Sitting in the kitchen with a mug of tea and one of Claire's scones, he gave her a full account of his movements over the past week. She loved listening to his enthusiasm and his stories, regaling her with his rather poor imitations of the American accent. She was proud of him, proud of what he was doing, although she would never tell him. She knew that had she done so, he would have blushed and felt embarrassed and that was something she would never do; she loved him too much.

He was busying himself in the greenhouse a few days later when he heard Claire call him. There was a phone call and, as he hurried back to the house, she told him it sounded like the American in London. He picked up his mobile panting slightly. "Sorry to disturb you James, but I thought you would want to know, I spoke to Sean earlier, all is well. Asked me to tell you he will phone tomorrow and report back to you."

James thanked him and asked if he knew why his friend had not been in communication. No, he had not said much except that he had a whole lot of important information; and that, as usual, he could not say anything over the phone. Just before hanging up Jack hinted that they may be meeting up soon in London.

He was rudely awoken at 5.30am the next morning by the buzz of his phone. He turned on the bedside light and rubbed his eyes. He should have known - Sean. He picked up."

"Morning Jamesie," came the breezy voice. "Yes, I know it's not your usual hour, but could you do me a favour and nip up to town this morning and meet my boss. He will put you and Jack in the picture. He's expecting you at 11.30am at HQ. Ask for Patrick Flynn, he will be waiting for you at reception."

"Good morning, or is it good evening? Glad you're ok and kept in touch. Yes, I'm fine thanks and yes, all is well here," he replied sarcastically.

"Oh no! Don't say I've upset you now. I certainly didn't mean to do that; guess it's been pretty hectic around here and it's not easy phoning from China." He paused for a few seconds, "Jamesie, are you still there?".

"Sorry, guess I was worried about you." He felt bad. Yawning he continued, "I'll be there. What's you man's name? Any idea when you're coming back? I have loads of things I want to bring you up to speed with."

"Tell Patrick what you have to say, he's fully in the picture. As for when I'm back - no idea. I'll be in touch soon. Be good and give Mrs H my love." The phone went dead.

After stretching and gathering his thoughts, he got out of his bed and dressed. Blowing a kiss to his wife, he placed a note on her side table before letting himself out.

\*　　\*　　\*

He took a taxi to the vast, imposing building of MI6 on the Thames, and was paying the cab driver when he heard Jack's unmistakable voice just behind him. They greeted like old friends and made their way into the lobby. Jack turned to James, "into the lion's den," he grinned.

"Not often that an American spy is invited to visit the nerve centre of British security".

After passing through the usual radar check, they went over to the large imposing reception desk to announce themselves. It was not long before Sean's boss appeared, hand outstretched and introduced himself. They proceeded to a bank of lifts, soon stopping on the 6th floor before emerging into another reception area. They were guided to a large conference room overlooking the river.

Their host explained in detail what Sean and his Hong Kong office had sent earlier. He answered several questions from Jack before turning to James.

"On behalf of myself, my department and the British government, I would very much like to thank you, Mr Horton, for all your hard work and input in this case. Mr Docherty - I believe you know him by his real name - has spoken enthusiastically about your contributions. Just a shame we didn't know you twenty years ago," he smiled broadly. James was about to reply but he turned to Jack, "I must also thank you and your agency for your great support in this matter and for looking after Mr Horton whilst in the United States".

Jack nodded, "it's only natural. We all work for the same cause, although sometimes in a different manner. I firmly believe this situation is one of the most critical we have seen in years, even in these times of terrorism and world tension. As for looking after Mr Horton, it was a pleasure, we respect his contribution and thoughts." Winking he added , "not to mention also, he is a very charming person and has become a good friend." James cheeks flushed and he tried to hide his embarrassment.

The head of the Far East desk turned to James once again, "do you have any update on the financial transactions of these... so called scientists?".

James shook his head, "none since the last time I spoke to Sean. Having said that, I only got back a few days ago. I will get to work immediately I return home."

"No need to apologise, it's quite understandable. Perhaps if you could let me know once you have checked, I would appreciate that greatly."

"Ok, what now..." Jack was about to ask when he was interrupted by the ring on the phone behind his host. There was some head nodding, a yes here and there, followed by more head nodding before the phone was replaced.

"That was one of my men on the Hong Kong desk. He tells me Mr Docherty has spoken to one of your men, a Joe Briggs?" He looked up queryingly at Jack who nodded. "It seems that Mr Horton's visit to our Embassy has produced some rather rapid results."

James blushed slightly again.

"We understand the Ambassador has a meeting with your Vice President sometime in the coming days. Apparently, it was questioned why the head of your agency has been bypassed. You must have done a good job, Mr Horton, of impressing the delicacy of the situation."

Jack was surprised and delighted. "Gee, you people don't hang around, I'm impressed. What would you say is our next move?"

There was a slight pause before the MI6 man continued, "I really don't want to impose any further demands on Mr Horton, we have asked a great deal from him already". Looking over to James he continued, "having said that, I would like you to find out if there have been any further financial transactions. Once that done, and whilst Mr Docherty is in Hong Kong, I feel it is important we have someone in Washington. Could I impose once again and ask if you could go back, Mr Horton?" There is little we can do from here apart from emphasising to the PM and the Government the urgency and dangers of the situation".

Jack agreed instantly. "I will stay here and try to impress on our Embassy with, hopefully your help, to take the situation seriously; the forthcoming meeting with the Vice President should focus some minds. It occurs to me; would you be happy coming over to Nine Elms and talking to our ambassador; he might take things a little more seriously coming from you".

"Well, that's sorted. I suggest you plan to return to Washington on Saturday or Sunday Mr Horton, if that is ok with you," quickly adding, "please make sure to keep all your receipts and tickets so that we can re-imburse you; first class travel does not come cheap". Smiling at Jack he nodded his agreement, "just let me know when you want me over, I would be delighted to help".

James signalled his agreement and asked Jack to make the necessary arrangements with Hank and Joe.

They were escorted back down to the main hall by their host. Once outside Jack suggested lunch and they made their way to a small café. Over a Caesar salad and glass of sauvignon they discussed the meeting. "I can't say how much l, also, appreciate your help, James. Like our man, I feel pretty guilty sending you back to Washington so soon. I fully agree that it is essential you are there ready and prepped, if called by your Embassy. I just hope your wife is ok with it.".

James assured him there was no problem although he had to admit, he had never travelled so often or so frequently.

∗　∗　∗

## Beijing

The following day was a free day for all delegates. Chi Tao had decided to go shopping, he needed a new suit and he thought that his wife might like a new dressing gown or slippers. The weather had not improved, so he jumped into a taxi and asked to be taken to the Central Business District where all the top shops could be found. There were a couple of Malls to shelter in if the rain came on too hard.

As he sat back, his thoughts drifted to the previous day. Had he projected himself well enough, had he spoken clearly and, most important of all, had he answered all the questions with confidence and knowledge. It was out his hands now, only time would tell. He checked his pocket for his mobile and looked out at the skyscrapers, the bustling streets and the extraordinary buzz of the city. He hoped one day soon he would be part of all this. Neither his wife nor he enjoyed Wuhan. They were northerners and had spent their younger years in Shanghai before he was posted to his present job. Yes, it had been a big honour, but he always felt he had been given a bad deal, he deserved better, and it irked him. In a way he felt he had been banished, had lost his close friendships and contacts. He was jealous of his childhood friend Tao Wey-Ming who had been given a similar job but here, in Beijing. The man was never as good a scientist but spoke better, had an easy way and was a magnate to women and men alike. They still spoke, occasionally, but typically, since he arrived in town Tao was too busy, or too snooty-nosed, to meet up with his old friend. Well, all that was going to change he hoped.

He spent hours browsing, comparing prices, and haggling, before he opted for two suits which, he thought, would reflect his impending new position. Even if nothing came of his hopes, the suits would send out a message back home, that he had achieved heights that few could imagine possible. He moved on to a large department store where he selected a couple of shirts and a new tie before turning his attention to finding an adequate gift for his wife. Tired, his feet aching, and his wallet considerably depleted, he made his way back to the hotel.

He opened the bedroom door and found an envelope lying on the floor. Sitting on his bed, he ripped it open; he glanced through it and yelped with joy. It was an invitation to attend a panel meeting the following morning at 9am to further discuss his presentation.

He had slept like a log and awoke early, full of the joys. The weather had cleared and a pale, watery sun peeped through the late autumn clouds. Arriving in plenty of time he was again directed to the same drab room and sat on the same hard chair waiting to be called in. His stomach started to knot, and he realised, too late, that partaking of a large breakfast had perhaps not been a wise choice. He was called in.

The same expressionless men greeted him with a nod, before he was pointed to the single chair. The old man cleared his throat and questioning began. After three hours of gruelling interrogation one of the Generals stood up and started to pace. Everyone was silent apart from the constant throat clearing, all eyes followed the prowling man. He had said nothing, had shown no emotion. Finally turning to Chi Tao, he asked him to wait outside.

Once back in the corridor Chi Tao let out a sigh of relief. He was bursting for the bathroom and debated a long time before nature decided for him. He had just returned when the door opened and he was waved in.

The General did not wait for him to sit down and immediately began his speech, leaving Chi Tao standing aimlessly in the middle of the room. "May we congratulate you and your team on the most interesting work, one of the most revolutionising and, most important discoveries of recent times. This will most certainly help China regain world power, both in military and economic terms. It will not go unnoticed; I can assure you."

Chi Tao was unsure what to do or if he was expected to say anything. The decision was taken out of his hands by one of the civilians who continued. "As the General said, it is a most significant find and one that China can be proud of. However, as you yourself have warned, it is a highly dangerous and potentially lethal discovery, so all precautions must be taken. Please explain your thoughts on what to do with the scientists involved."

Chi Tao cleared his throat; it must be catching he thought but instantly focussed back on the question. "I was thinking of redeploying the six members around different laboratories and would prefer if they could be sent to different research centres. Although each one worked on a specific aspect of the project, they only got a brief outline of the outcome not long ago. My feeling is that it would be best to ensure separation." Four heads nodded in unison. "I feel confident none of them fully understand the implications or dangers relating to the findings."

The second military, a Major, looked up queryingly, "why do you suggest they are split up then?".

"Precaution, just a precaution sir."

The old man cleared his throat before telling them that he would get to work immediately and arrange for the transfers to be done forthwith.

The General nodded his approval and continued, "what about the two young scientists, Mr Nuang and Miss Chow?".

Chi Tao paused in thought for a second or two before answering. "I am totally confident they are trustworthy. Both fully understand the implications and were the ones to express their concerns. I am certainly more than happy they will not talk, and equally as happy to have them remain in Wuhan." He was pleased that he had managed to get that last point across.

One of the civilians butted in, eyebrows raised, "you are expecting a great deal. To have two such eminently important scientists kept in such a secondary research centre is a big request. Do you not feel that they would better serve the country being here or in Lanzhou? Why not send them to different establishments like the others?".

Chi Tao hesitated before giving his answer; a lot depended on it. "They are young and enthusiastic but still need a steady hand to guide them and help them blossom to their full potential. Yes, they were instrumental in finalising this project, but our other scientists in the team did most of the work. I am certain a spell in a lesser important research centre like our ours, would be beneficial to them. I also understand the two are to be married next year so I would not like to split them at this stage."

The man looked at him intently, "am I to understand that you are proposing to guide and develop their careers? Are you sufficiently qualified?".

He was about to answer when the Major interjected, "in my opinion, if Professor Xing is confident he can help develop these two then, we should give him a year to prove it. I must add however, that if a project occurs where we consider their expertise is required, then he will have to agree to release them immediately".

"Sounds very fair," said the General.

"That is settled then. The young couple will remain in Wuhan under the professor until such time as this panel decides otherwise." He paused and smiled for the first time, "I must say General, I'm a little surprised you are giving your blessing to these young lovers; not normally your style".

Chi Tao crossed the square in a daze; he could not believe his luck; everything went as he had hoped. Back at the hotel he flopped into a chair and closed his eyes. He came to with a jolt; panic set in. Where were the two USB sticks? Had they kept them, his only copies? He had no way of getting them back. He remembered handing one over the first day in the conference hall but had completely forgotten about their request to use his second copy two days ago when he made his presentation. What a fool. Would Ru or the girl have kept a copy; he doubted it. It was policy not to allow any scientist to hold on to any of the information; then he remembered with relief that everything had been backed up on the computer which was back in his office. He breathed a sigh of relief.

Sitting back, sipping a cup of herbal tea he reflected on the meeting. He was elated that the programme had been accepted; that they had produced something that would help the National cause. He felt proud that he had been congratulated but, at the same time, a sense of disappointment descended upon him. There was no mention of promotion or a move to Beijing, no hint at being invited to meet the President or given an honour. He had managed to keep the young couple, that was a victory in itself. Once the work had been publicised and everyone had recognised what a major contribution they had made, he felt confident that the reputation of his centre, as well as his own, would grow. At last, he would be recognised, he would be someone. He ordered a beer in celebration.

\* \* \*

Once professor Xing had left, the two military and civilian counterparts departed leaving the old man to finalise the paperwork. They were swiftly driven to another meeting taking place in a secret location. Apart from them, the President and his closest aides, there would be a handful of military, economic and scientific experts. The topic – how best to use this new discovery to help China gain world ascendancy and to boost the flagging economy.

# CHAPTER 40

# Hong Kong

Following the meeting at the flat, Pearl and Sean had brought Tim up to speed. They had agreed that he should continue surveillance and had warned him that the young couple might perhaps try to make contact. They were highly emotional; their minds were in turmoil so he had to take precautions and remain alert.

They were now sitting in Jimmy's office giving him the same account, expressing their fears and concerns at what the young couple might do next; it was anyone's guess.

The situation in the city was deteriorating and further massive protests were planned for the coming weekend. Beijing was making threatening noises and there were rumours of Chinese troops moving towards the border. Jimmy now had a dozen agents in town, mingling with the leaders of the protest movement as well as in government circles. Reports were coming in hourly, so much so, that he had to bring two more aides in to cope with all the extra work. He was sending four, if not more, despatches to London every day with the up-to-date situation, all of which were taken seriously. Since changing the encryption system, he was feeling more confident his messages were not being picked up by Beijing. He turned to Sean, "I must thank you for your help in letting London know what is happening here. I doubt there would have been much urgency if you had gone back and spoken to the boss".

Sean shrugged, "for sure I didn't do much, it's good however, to see that the government has taken things seriously. I had hoped for a stronger condemnation but, I'm certainly no politician, they work in a very different way. They all laughed.

"I must say," he continued, "I'm chuffed to hear about the developments in Washington, that's a real step forward; especially after what we have just learnt".

"So, plan of action?" asked Jimmy.

"Not sure, I sort of feel in limbo. Part of me tells me I should stay in case something happens; the other part says I should go to Washington. What do you think?"

There was a long silence as all three tried to decide what the best option was. Eventually Jimmy spoke, "Pearl is here, and I think her task from now on will be to keep 24/7 tabs on what is happening in Wuhan. You, my friend, would probably be of more use in the States. We can keep you posted of any developments."

Sean had to agree; he had been thinking along the same lines but needed confirmation. A few hours later he was heading back to the airport.

\* \* \*

## Beijing

After receiving the call, the woman quickly put on her coat and left her home. She hurried along the side street and emerged into the main artery where she battled her way through the crowd and morning traffic. She headed for a market on the north side of the city, a place she did not know well and usually avoided. It was known to be a rough district, populated with a large share of the city's drug gangs and dropouts. She always felt uneasy when going to a place she did not know for the first time, where escape routes and the lie of the land were unknown.

Stepping down from the bus she pulled her coat round her tightly and adjusted her scarf; the thin easterly wind was cutting. Following the precise instructions that she had memorised; she made her way across the market and reached the building marked with a vivid green door. Looking up at the crumbling walls and peeling paintwork she navigated her way through a stall selling pots and pans, stopping once inside to check no one had followed her. She let her eyes adjust to the dim light before climbing the rickety wooden stairs. She stopped on reaching the second floor and looked back; no one had followed her. Opening the only door, she peered into the broom cupboard and found a dial. Turning it as instructed she waited until she heard a low creek and saw a hatch in the floor slowly open; she walked through into a dark passage. She lifted the short ladder before pressing a button close by and watched as the hatch clicked shut. Turning, she shuffled a few feet, her hand brushing the wall where she felt a switch which she flicked; a dim light glowed somewhere further down the passageway. Proceeding along a narrow corridor, feeling her way down some more stairs and shuffling through the tunnel she eventually came to a sharp bend. Turning the corner, she saw a faint chink of light on the ground indicating she had reached her destination. Cautiously she knocked on the door and slowly pushed it open, blinking several times and squinting in the bright daylight. She found herself in a small parlour, a man in his mid-forties sat at a table facing her. He rose from his seat and greeted her. His expressionless eyes bored into her, and there was no warmth in his demeaner.

She looked round at the sparse room; it was lived in but had been neglected. Little time was spent tidying and no effort had been made to put things away or make it look homely. She took the chair by the small stove and watched whilst he poured her a cup of tea.

He settled himself across the table from her and spoke in a low hushed tone, clearly, distinctly and with no frills. She listened intently not interrupting. When he had finished, he rose and made his way to a dresser from where he retrieved a book and handed it to her. Taking it, she placed it in her bag and got up to leave. He showed her to the door taking her back up the dark corridor and thence to the broom cupboard. Leading the way, he checked all was clear before she made her way down the main stairs and out into the street. She had not said a word.

Back at her small apartment, she took out the book, retrieved the machine from under her bed and got down to work. Several hours later she had completed her task and sat back to check everything was correct. Finally, content, she opened the box and sent the message.

Picking up the book she went over to the small stove and tossed it in, watching until it turned to ash.

* * *

## Washington

James had made his way to the immigration queue and stepped up when he was called. The officer took his passport, flipping through the pages he looked up at James, "Mr Horton, it appears that this is your third visit to Washington in just over a month; please tell me the purposes of these trips".

James had been expecting this and Jack had warned him. "On business – my company is in the midst of a very important deal," he replied smiling.

The officer was not convinced and continued questioning his motives. Reluctantly James pulled out a letter Jack had given him and handed it over the officer. The man looked at it dubiously before pressing a button and requesting James to move over to one side until his colleague arrived; he beckoned the next traveller.

He did not have to wait long before a large woman appeared dressed in full uniform and sporting a rather lethal looking weapon strapped to her belt and a pair of handcuffs. She had a few words with the immigration officer and took the passport, letter and retrieved his briefcase before ordering James to follow her. He could not but notice several other passengers staring at him suspiciously. He was shown into a small office where he was ordered to sit; his briefcase and documents disappeared along with the officer, through to another room. As he settled down the door behind clicked and he was locked in.

He lost track of time but eventually the woman reappeared holding his passport; she smiled and apologised for the wait. He was free to go on his way and she escorted him through to the baggage reclaim where he found his bag waiting on the carousel; all his fellow passengers had left.

Silently thanking Jack and relieved that whatever he had put in the letter seemed to have worked, he made his way to the exit when he heard his name being called. He turned to see Sean coming towards him, hand outstretched and a broad grin on his face.

"Good man, you made it Jamesie. Heard from the boss that you would be flying over today or tomorrow, how are things?"

James was delighted to see his friend, "yes, all fine, just had a spot of bother getting back in; seems I've been visiting too often, but Jack had given me a letter which luckily did the trick. Didn't know you were going to be here".

They entered the large arrivals hall and immediately came face to face with Beth. She smiled broadly and welcomed James before greeting Sean. Both men noticed she was dressed in a suit which fitted her a little too tightly, the bulge of her gun under her arm not helping; both smiled knowing they were thinking the same thing. As they exited into the cool air Sean indicated he was going to take a taxi, swiftly silencing his friends' protests. "All arranged Jamesie, don't you worry. I'll make my way to my usual address, have a long shower followed by a much-needed sleep. Twenty-six-hour journey with two changes of planes has taken its toll and anyway, I wouldn't want to poison your air which my BO." He laughed and clapped his friend on the shoulder, "see you tomorrow partner"; turning to Beth he continued, "make sure he behaves and don't let him lead Joe astray," and he winked.

James spent the evening alone; Joe was in Texas and returning the following day. He agreed to let Beth get a carry out and made sure she bought something he could eat, not that he was all that hungry.

*   *   *

## Hong Kong

Jimmy received the message later that afternoon; he had been following developments in the streets and the ever-growing number of protesters. As always, the official figures put out by the authorities differed vastly to the actual numbers. His people on the ground along with the organisers were quoting twice the official figure which he could well believe. He would have loved to be there, protesting for his rights and the rights of his fellow citizens but he had work to do.

He picked up the transcript and immediately called Pearl to come and join him. Handing over the paper he sat back and put his feet on the nearby chair. Pearl read it carefully, turning to the previous page to re-read a passage before continuing. She looked up, "that is one scary report and one that confirms we have a major problem. If all of that is true, no wonder our two lovers are worried".

Jimmy grimaced, "oh, I'm sure every word is true and yes, it only confirms our worst fears".

"I must give it to our people in Beijing, they have done a fantastic job. Has Tim been advised?".

There was a silence before Jimmy nodded, "yes, and he's very concerned for his charges safety. You know how Beijing are paranoic about people knowing too much. He's suggesting we get them out as soon as".

"Sean – he knows also?"

"No, not yet. I've asked London to forward it on to him; he'll get it the minute he arrives in Washington."

"You want me to go back and help Tim? It won't be easy to persuade them to leave."

"I would leave it a day or two; you can go back but use a different identity for travelling. We can't act hastily; we need time and a plan. We'll only get one shot."

They sat staring at the TV, both far away, deep in thought, both planning how best to proceed. They were brought back to earth by a knock on the door. Tony marched in and handed his boss another report, "just received this, thought you would want to see it soonest".

Jimmy took the proffered papers and read through them before, again, handing them over to Pearl. He looked over to his senior man, "what do you make of it?" he enquired, interested in getting the man's take.

Tony scratched his chin before answering. "Well boss, I certainly don't like it. Those bastards in Beijing are going to use this to their advantage no matter how much devastation it causes. They will see this as an opportunity to re-set their flagging economy and advance their ambitions. Not sure how to stop them though. They have the world by the short and curlies and won't stop until they get what they want."

Jimmy sat shaking his head, "I tend to agree with you. They're obviously planning to wage one big devious war on the entire world. If they get away with it, God help us!".

\*     \*     \*

## Wuhan

On the flight back, Chi Tao sat deep in thought. Having put his disappointment aside, he now had to plan for the future. On the one hand he had to accept the fact that he was going to be stuck in Wuhan and that he would not really get the recognition he deserved. There were positives to the situation, not massive but he would have to make the best of what he had. The first was that he had secured the stay of his main assets, at least for a while. He would have to get them started on a new project as soon as possible and would have to ensure the powers in the capital were fed positive news on a regular basis. To do that, he would have to find himself a new secretary; he did not trust the one he had, slimly, slippery little piece of work. He was sure the man was snooping and listening in, probably had seen certain private files. Only the Jade Emperor knew if he understood what had just been discovered. No, he had to go and go fast. He would replace him with his niece, a good girl, attractive but not overly endowed with brains or curiosity. So long as he paid her well, she would do what she was told.

He would then have to start promoting himself; make sure people knew and understood what he had done and how he had catapulted the city and the research centre to the forefront of Chinese technology. It would take time, but he had time, he was a patient man; the end result would be worth the wait. He smiled to himself, content.

\* \* \*

Ru and Mei Lien made their way to lab No 6 on Monday morning. They checked the animals and quickly realised they had got worse. The birds were sitting on the floor of their cage, huddled together and breathing rapidly. Monkey was silent and looked glum; he kept scratching at his ears and his chest. His breathing was rapid and faltering. One of the mice was dead whilst it's companion cowered in the corner constantly rubbing its little red eyes. Cat was not faring much better either, also showing signs of breathing problems. The only two that looked half content were the chickens.

Mei Lien took pity on them and asked Ru to phone the vet again. After what seemed ages, he returned to tell her that he had got the same answer, someone would come when they had time.

His mobile buzzed, it was Chi Tao asking – no – ordering them, to come over immediately to his office. They were surprised not to see the secretary at his desk and waited patiently for his return. Sensing something untoward Ru went and tapped gently on the door. The director's voice called them in.

Chi Tao apologised, saying his secretary had been taken ill and his replacement had not yet arrived. He then recounted his week in the Capital at great length and the great honour of having their discovery accepted by the Chinese Government. Triumphantly and with great glee he told them that he had managed to secure them a permanent place with him and the centre.

Mei Lien recovered first and congratulated the director on the wonderful news and told him how proud they were for him. He beamed broadly and immediately launched into explaining his idea for a new project. When, at last, he had finished Ru pulled out one of the envelopes.

"Sir, you may wish to take a look at this. We run a quick blood test on the animals last Thursday and the results are all on here. Perhaps you may wish to send these to Beijing."

Chi Tao took the envelope and looked at his young protégé with a worried look. "I don't like the sound of this young man." Removing the stick and making his way to the computer he continued, "and why were the animals still there? I thought my orders were clear".

"Yes sir, very clear; I have now asked three times for them to be removed but each time I am told they are too busy and that it will happen soon."

Chi Tao scowled; his jaw clenched tight. He sat down and started to look at the data. A few minutes later he rose and looked at the two young people in front of him. "It certainly confirms our findings, and that this new discovery is much more serious than previously thought. You were right to proceed in the way that you did, although it does not excuse ignoring my orders."

Mei Lien chipped in, "we were not ignoring orders, Sir; the vets were ignoring us. Just to point out that all the animals except for the chickens have greatly deteriorated since Saturday. We came in to check on them and feed them".

Chi Tao looked thoughtful. "I know, and I I'm sorry; it's not your fault. I would like to go and see for myself." He pulled out the USB stick and placed it with the second one in the envelope before heading for the door. He locked his office and followed the two down the corridor.

He inspected the animals with great care, making comments and asking a few questions. Satisfied he turned and headed to a desk and picked up the phone. After waiting to be put through he barked several orders, gave whoever was at the other end an ultimatum and returned the receiver with a crash. "Someone will be here at 5pm to remove these poor creatures. I would like both of you to supervise the removal and ensure the place is locked up until the cleaners come to disinfect. I suggest you get them to do this twice and not to forget fumigation."

# CHAPTER 41

# Washington

The four were in the conference room with Jack online discussing events from London. Sean gave a detailed account of events and read out the two new messages he had received via London. There was a long silence whilst each member digested the facts. Hank was the first to speak, "what a bloody mess. I just can't see the White House getting involved in the Hong Kong crisis. The President is sure no lover of the Chinese, but he will not want to be seen to be meddling. As for our other problem, that is more serious; I just pray your guys at the Embassy have impressed on the VP how important and urgent this case is."

Joe then briefed everyone on his trip to Texas and his visit to SACS Laboratories. It was a large organisation with, it seemed, excellent facilities. Everything was bold and in your face. He did not manage to get to talk to anyone and, despite his insistence, was not granted an interview. He admitted to being disappointed as he had hoped to talk to someone in management and get some idea of what they were working on.

It was James' turn and he also had little to report. After returning home from the London meeting, he had contacted his friend at the bank. The man had reported that activity on Professor Howard's account had slowed down, unsurprising since his client was dead and buried. The last transaction had been a couple of weeks ago for three hundred thousand dollars. It came from HSBC in Beijing and the amount was transferred out to a company in Panama. The order was given by Freeman.

Having covered everything, they decided to finish the meeting. It was a wet, cold day so Sean and James decided to stay where they were and catch up. The other two left them, but not before reminding them to meet in Hank's office at 4.30 later that afternoon.

The banter was relaxed, Sean recounting his latest visit to Hong Kong and Wuhan as well as the meeting with the young couple. "You should really take Clare to Hong Kong, it's a great place, lots to do and see. Best make it sooner rather than later; if China gets its way things will change dramatically."

They were about to go downstairs when Joe burst in followed by a puffing Hank. He thrust a sheet of paper into Sean's hand, "read it, it's just come in from Jack," he exclaimed. At the very same time James' mobile began to ring. He looked down and his eyebrows raised in surprise; he answered.

Sean took the sheet of paper and read through it quickly, a broad grin came over his face and he looked up at the others. James was nodding and agreeing, thanking the person at the other end as he terminated the call. All started to speak at the same time.

James did not stop, "that was the Embassy; the Vice President is visiting tomorrow afternoon to discuss the situation in Wuhan and Hong Kong," he smiled. "They want me to attend and have asked if one of you could accompany me."

Sean showed him the note advising that a meeting had been scheduled for tomorrow and suggesting James attend with, if possible, another member team. There was whoop of joy from all four and they slapped one another on the shoulder. Hank was the first to recover, "right guys, who should it be, me or Joe?".

Sean was quick to reply, "no offence Hank but I personally think Joe should go. He knows James better than you and they seem to make a good team. As much as I would love to go, I feel that it should be someone from your side".

There was a silence, Hank looked disappointed but eventually had to concede Joe was the better negotiator and had a slightly more polished way. There was a silent sigh of relief from the others. The telephone rang on the desk and Hank picked up. It was Jack; had they got the note he had sent? They told him about the call James had received a few minutes earlier and the decision that Joe should join him. Jack winced imagining how Hank was feeling but, from his tone, the man was ok with that. Like Joe, he knew it was going to rankle and gnaw at his boss but, hey, that was life, and he should be old enough to put his vanity and feelings aside. He congratulated them, wished them well and suggested they went out for a celebratory drink on him.

\* \* \*

When James appeared in the kitchen the next morning, he was surprised to see Joe already dressed in a suit and tie. "Thought I'd put on my Sunday best seeing as we are meeting some high-powered politicians," he smiled.

"You certainly scrub up well I have to admit, not sure that tie is the best of choices." He heard Beth stifle a giggle. "I have a more appropriate one if you would like to try it."

Joe feigned surprise, "what's wrong with my monkey tie?". Looking down at it he continued, "perhaps it does give out the wrong impression, not sure your guys would approve. Go get yours then."

\* \* \*

It had just gone 2.30pm when Beth swung the car into the car park and pulled up out-side the main doors. Joe gulped hard, adjusted his tie and took a deep breath. He turned to James, "what do I look like partner?"

James patted him on the arm, "just relax, you're looking very much the part", then "what did you say to me? Ah, yes, it will be all right, everything will be fine and dandy," he nudged Joe in the ribs.

The two men were met at reception by the same man who had led James the first time. They walked along the corridor, James pointing to the bust of Churchill and to a couple of paintings depicting past Kings. The young Secretary welcomed them before leading them through to the lounge where the British Deputy Ambassador and Vice President were standing chatting amicably. Both turned and William Tindell came forward to greet them. After introductions they were ushered to four chairs and discussions begun.

Over the following hours both James and Joe were grilled by their hosts. The politicians were given the latest news from Hong Kong and Wuhan and stressed the critical and perilous situation both crises had become. James was amazed at how Joe expressed the situation, not once swearing or getting uptight with any of the questioning. He was clear, precise, and forceful. For himself, he thought he had complemented his partner well and felt far more relaxed than that the first time. He did not hesitate to give his views or to expand on Joe's answers. At long last the conversation turned to what should be done. The Vice President was adamant that, despite the President's total loathing of China, very little could be done to help defuse the Hong Kong situation. He would certainly advise that the USA make the strongest representation to the UN and ask them to condemn China's actions in the strongest of manner. He would also seek urgent talks to take place between Britain and his country to see what could be done.

On the subject of the chemical or biological threat, this was a whole different ball game, and he promised his government would do everything possible to condemn China and get them to halt production. He fully agreed that the dangers were immense and the future of the world and its economy was at stake.

William Tindell stood up signalling the end of the meeting. Both men thanked their guests for the hard work and excellent cooperation and asked them to ensure they were kept posted. Before leaving, the Vice President added that he was more than concerned about the idea that several of his top Civil Servants might be implicated in a sordid plot. He would brief the President immediately and asked both of his visitors to remain on standby.

The air was icy and as soon as James and Joe stepped outside, and they realised how much they had been perspiring. The cold sweat quickly stuck to their shirt making them shiver. They waited until they had got into the car before shaking hands and letting out a huge roar. Beth looked back into her rear-view mirror, "guess by the sound of it, things went well".

"They certainly did Beth. That was an experience; gee, those guys are hardened interrogators, I felt I was back at training camp except there was no physical abuse." He lay back before continuing, "I didn't really believe you James; thought you were exaggerating the last time. I take my hat off to you; for an amateur, it must have been hell".

"All in the course of duty," he smiled.

\*　　\*　　\*

Sitting in Hanks office with Sean, Joe related what had happened and what was said. Jack again was live online and joined in with the praises. "Sounds as if things went very well; great to hear you have both been put on standby. If you think that was tough, wait until you're grilled about our two moles by the boss. I sure don't envy you."

There was more discussion before Jack asked if they had gone for that drink yesterday. No – both Joe and James wanted to be cold sober so it was agreed everyone would have an early night. "Right, why don't you guys go out tonight and celebrate, Hank is happy to pay."

Hank swallowed the bait and loudly protested; he had paid last time and had enough trouble getting the bill passed by finance so, no he was not going to be bludgeoned into it this time. Jack roared with laughter and suggested to Sean that they both shared the bill. He agreed, "we'll drink a toast to you Jack".

# CHAPTER 42

# Wuhan

Ru and Mei Lien had little to do apart from wait for someone to come and take the animals away. Chi Tao had not yet decided what project to give them, nor had he gathered a new team. Over the past couple of days, he had busied himself writing reports on the old crew, making sure he gave them glowing references, but not too glossy so as not to arouse suspicion. His niece, the new secretary was slow and not particularly good, and he admitted to himself his decision to employ her had been a mistake. Give it a few weeks and he would find a more competent aide.

His mind drifted back to the last findings the young scientists had shown him. Every time he thought about it a feeling of foreboding took over; what kind of horror had they discovered and what would the people at the top do with it; he shuddered. With little hope of promotion or a move to the Capital perhaps it was time to retire, go to the country or even, God forbid, to Hong Kong; he put that thought out of his head immediately.

\*    \*    \*

There was a loud knock on the door and both scientists jumped, startled by the sudden noise. Ru went over to see who it was. He took a step back and his jaw dropped as he saw Lu Ching standing there, grinning his semi-toothless smile.

"What do you want" asked Ru.

"I am here to remove the animals," he took a pace forward.

"You're what!" exclaimed Ru baring the way. "You have no knowledge in handling them and are not a veterinarian so, sorry I can't let you in".

Lu Ching grinned and fumbled in his pocket for a note which he thrust into Ru's face. "See, it is a direct order from the Professor and signed by him."

Ru could not believe his eyes, "wait here and I'll go and check". He went to turn but Lu Ching barged in.

"I think it best for your career if you just let me in and allow me to do my job."

Mei Lien shrugged and went over to join her future husband. "Where is your protective gear and where are the boxes to put the animals in?" she asked in a harsh tone.

"Just let me do my job." He went over to look through the glass panels into the animal room before turning and snorting, "Seems you let most of these creatures die; they certainly don't look healthy".

Mei Lien's hairs on her neck bristled, "we asked over a week ago for someone to come and collect them. We are the only ones to have fed and watered them, so don't blame us".

They watched as Lu Chin went to collect a couple of large boxes and a crate from the trolley he had left in the corridor.

"You can help, it will be quicker if all three of us get to work."

They shook their heads, "no, you are in charge, and it is your job, so you just go ahead". They watched in horror as he went through with only a pair of surgical gloves as protection. Mei Lien turned away; she couldn't stand watching the hard and cruel way he was handling the poor creatures.

The mice and birds had died, monkey was on his last legs and even the chickens were now looking the worse for wear. Finally, he slammed the ape crate shut and heaved it onto the trolley. Not a word had been said as Lu Chin rolled his trolley into the corridor and off around the corner.

Mei Lien and Ru exhaled a long sigh of relief and looked at each other. Ru was the first to speak, "I think we should go and report to the professor. I really don't like what just happened". With a final look round to ensure nothing of importance remained they left, locking the door firmly.

On the way they stopped by the janitor's office and requested laboratory No 6 be deep cleaned, disinfected, and fumigated as soon as possible, as per the directors' orders. The woman told them she would get a team started in an hour or so and took the key. Before leaving Ru suggested her cleaners dressed in full protective gear and be careful. The woman gave him a withering look, "thank you, I know my job," she replied scathingly.

Arriving at the directors' office they asked to be seen and were immediately shown in. Chi Tao smiled and waved them over, "what can I do for you?" he enquired in a jovial voice.

"Sir, we have come to report the animals have been removed and that we have instructed the cleaners to commence their work."

Chi Tao looked puzzled. "The animals have been taken away you say, very odd. Just an hour ago the director of the veterinary department called to say it would be first thing tomorrow morning."

"Well sir, Lu Chin did it himself; he showed us a letter signed by yourself giving him the order".

Chi Tao exploded, "what! what letter? I never gave him a letter or any consent. Have you got it?".

Ru fished it out of his pocket and handed it over.

"That's not my signature! I've never, and would never give such a letter, how can you be so stupid?" He called his niece in, "what is this?".

The girl took the piece of paper and looked as if she was going to be sick. "I gave it uncle. I knew you wanted the animals cleared as soon as possible and this man came saying he needed a letter signed by you so he could do the job done."

"You did what!" yelled Chi Tao. "What did this man look like? Was he dressed as a vet?"

The girl shook her head and gulped, "he was thin, a bit rough and with bad teeth. Said he was a vet porter and his boss ordered him to come, said the letter would be waiting." She started to tremble, "I thought I must have forgotten, so found a spare sheet of paper, typed it out and copied your signature. I didn't want to disturb you."

The room was deathly quiet as the director sat there trying to control his temper. Eventually he turned to his niece and in a low monotone voice pointed to the door, "get out of here, get out of my sight and never come back. You have let me, our family, and the centre down. Out, now!" he yelled. As the door closed, he looked over to the young couple, "apologies, it is not your fault, you could not know, that I employed a cheating, useless niece who is capable of fraudulently forging my signature". He fell silent for a while before suggesting they take a week off. With no new project signed off and the lab being cleaned, there was little point in them hanging around; they should go and relax, take a rest; something they both deserved.

Mei Lien looked surprised and cleared her throat, " Professor, that is most kind of you, but you gave us a few days off last week, when you were in Beijing. We can't possibly take more time off."

Chi Toa nodded and smiled, "I know, I know but there is nothing to be done for now and I need to get a new team together so, my orders are for you to relax, take some rest, plan your future".

\*    \*    \*

They were enjoying the break, two days of lying in, lounging around and not doing or thinking about work. Ru had wanted to go to Shanghai to visit his parents' shrine and catch up with his mentor at the University.

Mei Lien, although not keen, urged him to go but he didn't want to leave her on her own. A major factor in his decision which he did not mention was the cost; flights were expensive, and he could not warrant the expense. He would need to get permission from Chi Tao and a special pass, but he did not want to disturb the old goat, so in the end he shelved the idea. The weather was cold with a persistent drizzle, giving them the excuse of staying in bed and hanging around the apartment. They went out for a couple of meals, visited the new mall, and browsed the stores for a potential wedding dress.

They had returned from a food shop and had settled down to watching the news on TV when the presenter dropped the bomb shell. A crew and reporter were on the banks of the river and pictures were beamed of a body being retrieved from the river. It seemed the victim had jumped off the Yangtze River bridge and committed suicide. Police announced that first indications showed it to be the body of professor Chi Tao Xing, Director of the Chinese National Institute of Research of Virology & Microbiology here in Wuhan. That it was too early to confirm the cause of death or why he should take his own life. The Professor had recently attended a national conference in Beijing where he and his centre had been praised for a new revolutionary discovery which would help put China firmly on the world map. The reporter continued to say that the professor was admired and much liked by all at the centre, as well as being highly respected among his peers. They showed a brief clip of him welcoming the American party who had recently visited. There was no mention of his wife or family.

Ru and Mei Lien sat glued to the screen, stunned, unable to take in what they had just heard. Mei Lien slumped back on the sofa, a tear running down her cheek. "I can't say I liked the old goat, but he was harmless; why should he go and jump off a bridge, it doesn't make sense," she croaked.

Ru took her in his arms, "it surely can't be because of what his niece did. Ok, forging his signature wasn't nice but it wasn't as if she had committed a heinous crime; having said that perhaps he felt his honour had been compromised. No, it must be something else; surely the knowledge of what could happen if their discovery was misused would not push him to take such a drastic action. He seemed happy enough the other day, it must be something secret we don't not know about."

She wiped her eyes, "wife problems? Or had he been caught with a concubine?" she asked.

Ru shrugged, "perhaps money troubles – we don't know if he was a gambler, perhaps he owed a small fortune. Whatever, it is sad and being selfish, it leaves us in the lurch; what's going to happen to us?"

Mei Lien suddenly looked happier, "does this mean we can leave this awful dump and go back to Beijing?".

The rest of the evening was spent in a haze. They discussed different possibilities and options but, in the end agreed it was out of their hands; they would have to wait and see what conclusions the police would come to and what was going to be decided for them.

* * *

## Hong Kong

Jimmy had taken to sleeping in his office, deciding that it was not worth the hassle of going home only to be called back in at some un-godly hour. The office was at full capacity with three extra people on day shift and two on at night. The situation in the city was getting worse and more volatile by the hour. Developments in Wuhan worried him intensely. He had put Pearl in charge of keeping tabs up there but had turned down her offer of joining him and staying over as well.

He was about to lie on the camp bed he had installed when the phone rang; it was Tim.

"Sorry to disturb you cousin at this late hour, but I thought I should tell you, the factory manager has been found dead. It seems he committed suicide earlier this afternoon."

Jimmy was stunned, "what's going to happen to the goods. Will they be in good hands?"

"The goods are fine; I'm just not sure what will happen to them and when they will be released. I will try and find out more and get back to you soon."

Jimmy nodded to himself, "thank you for keeping me abreast of the situation, and I look forward to hearing from you soon. Please give grandma my best regards."

After hanging up, he quickly texted Pearl with the news and followed it up with the same message to Sean.

# CHAPTER 43

# Washington

James walked into the kitchen and immediately felt tension in the air. Joe looked up and smiled as he greeted his friend. "James, meet Carter my aide and trainee. Carter, this is James Horton from England, I've told you about him."

The two men shook hands and James went over to make himself a cup of tea. Carter was about to speak when Joe interrupted, "Carter here thinks I should not have asked Beth to go and get your favourite bun, says she is not my slave". He was about to continue when Beth appeared brandishing a bag of pastries. "Hope you got some of James's favourite fancy pink dodgers," he asked with a grin.

Carter could not contain himself any longer "I think you should have more respect for women and not talk the way you do. It is most offensive and inappropriate. You can't treat people like slaves; you can't just order Beth to fetch things for you and you should respect people's feelings."

Beth shrugged and offered James a bun which he took, thanking her. Carter continued, "you can't wear that tie sir, it is offensive and disrespectful".

Joe looked down at his tie, "what the heck is wrong with my tie? What's so offensive; it's a tie that I've had for years - it was given to me by my niece as a Christmas present."

Carter shook his head, "it has monkeys on it; it is totally disrespectful and sends out the wrong message".

Joe was losing his cool rapidly, "it's only bloody caricatures of monkeys, they don't represent anyone or anything, they don't even resemble the darned animals. Ok, a couple are swinging from a branch, and one is eating a banana; so what? I've seen you eat plenty of bananas; doesn't mean you are being disrespectful or rude."

"That is not the same thing. Why do you have to say fancy pink dodgers? That's rude and derogatory too, you are alluding to and insulting the LGBT movement and implying they are different."

Joe exploded, "Just fucking grow up Carter and stop making a complete ass of yourself. Have you really listened to yourself; you are just talking crap and a whole lot of balls". He got up and slammed down his mug, spilling half of it on the table, "right, leaving in five minutes". As he reached the door he turned round and in a calmer voice said, "I'll clean up when we get back Beth, you fetch the car". Beth smiled and wiped the table and looked at the young man. "It's ok, it's not beneath me and I am doing it of my own accord; you heard what the boss said, get moving."

Carter was about to take the driver's seat when Joe bawled, "Carter, out of there and get in beside Beth; she is the driver as you well know". The young man was about to reply but thought better of it.

They drove in silence for a while before Beth turned to him, "how long you been in the service - one, two years? Think it's time you grew up and changed your ideas".

Carter was sullenly looking out of the window and turned round to look at her, "why does he think nothing applies to him; he seems to be living in a different world. Look, he orders you to go to the shops, to drive, to do this and that and has no regard for you."

She looked over at the young man and shook her head, "I think it is you that is living in a different world. You don't worry about me, I'm old enough to look after myself and, to be frank, I find it disrespectful that you think I'm too weak to speak up for myself. As for all this bullshit about his tie, it's baloney, just your warped idea of the world."

"No, I respect you Beth, I respect women and yes, I take offence to heart. He should know better than to spend his time being rude and derogatory."

Joe had been listening and decided it was time to speak, "I am not rude; brash perhaps, but I respect women as much as men provided that everyone does their job. I've been in this business since before you were born, faced death more times than you've had a cold shower and fought more bad guys than you ever will, so stop being so bloody sanctimonious and get off your high moral ground".

Carter was about to reply but Beth interrupted, "listen, our job is to look after our guest and to defend our country from a bunch of terrorists and subversives, hell bent on destroying our world. My job now is as a driver and bodyguard and I take my orders from my boss who, in this instance is Joe. What he says, I do, whether I like it or not; that is what I am paid for and what I signed up to."

"Still, you don't have to accept that kind of behaviour. There are rules and people you can go to report such things."

Beth took a long deep breath, "how many people have you killed? How many people have saved your life when you thought the chips were down and you were toast?" She looked and waited but he remained silent. "I've killed over fourteen people in this job, protecting my fellow citizens, and Joe back there has probably shot more doing the same. We live in a different world, we have different criteria; we don't live like normal people, and I sure don't care what he tells me and how he talks to me. We have worked together for a very long time and all I know is that I owe him my life, twice in fact. Without him I would be six feet under. Both times he shot the bastard who was about to blow my head off so, forget telling me about complaints departments, my rights, or my feelings because honestly, you don't know nothing." She glanced into her rear-view mirror, "what time do you want to be at your next appointment?" Before pulling into the car park, she turned one last time to her fellow passenger, "if you don't like what you see or can't cope with the heat, I suggest you get out".

\* \* \*

They were about to enter Hank's office when Joe put his arm on Carter's shoulder, "you stay here boy, this meeting is not for you".

Once inside and the door firmly closed, he turned to James, "really sorry for all that James, not a scene I wanted you to witness. I promise not all our youngsters are like Carter".

Sean was quick to give them the news of Chi Tao and his presumed suicide. He had received the message first thing and was disturbed. He was certainly not convinced the man had taken his own life but, not having met the professor or known much about him, could not be sure. The others remained noncoital. The discussion moved on to the forthcoming meeting and the potential consequences.

The two Americans had another half hour before leaving to join John Pintaro, head of the CIA. The afternoon was going to be long and difficult. Before leaving, Hank made a couple of phone calls and after putting down the receiver pressed the intercom and asked his secretary to send Carter in. The young man nervously looked round at the four seated around the table. Hank waved him in.

"Just had a call from one of the foreign heads of departments, asked if I had someone spare to help out. I volunteered you, Carter; guess that's ok?".

The young man was about to speak when Hank continued. "Much appreciate your help over the past few months, but it's time you moved on so, I'm sending you down to the Africa section; seems they need someone in Angola. Had trouble there last week, had two of their guys killed and need someone urgently. I said you would be glad to help."

Carter half nodded and cleared his throat, "that is very good of you sir, but l...."

Hank interrupted, "great, you're leaving immediately so I suggest you get downstairs pronto, make yourself known and get your orders. Good luck". He nodded to the door and waited until the man had left.

Joe shook his head, "that was a bit harsh Hank. I know the guy is useless and an idiot but to send him to Angola, of all places..."

Hank smiled, "he won't go. Bet he's on his way to personnel to hand in his resignation. No great loss and we're doing him a service."

Sean had to agree with his two counterparts. By the sound of what had happened earlier that morning, the man would be killed or get someone killed. You were either made for the job or not.

Before parting company Sean turned to Hank and Joe, "are you sure it's ok for James to stay here a few more days, just until we get a conclusion of this afternoon's outcome. I'm sorry I can't stay but I should fly back to Hong Kong tonight, I just have a feeling I'll be needed." Turning to James, "happy with that Jamesie? If all goes well, you can fly home on Thursday".

They all made their way down to the car park. Hank and Joe were greeted by the huge officer who had taken care of Maggie and drove off to their appointment. Beth drove Sean to the airport before taking James to the safe house. On the way she looked back at her guest, "apologise for this morning Mr Horton but I just couldn't stop myself".

James smiled back, "no need to apologise Beth and, please, call me James, it's not as if we don't know each other. I understand Mr Carter has been sent to Angola, leaving very soon".

Beth laughed, "not surprising with his attitude. My guess is that he won't go, will hand in his resignation and try and get a pay-out for unfair dismissal, that's the sort of person he is, totally useless to the service and the Nation."

"That is exactly what Hank said, reckons it won't be long before he joins one of these left-wing anti-establishment groups and leads protest marches."

"Well I hope to hell he doesn't come face to face with me." They both laughed.

James hesitantly asked Beth if they could go out for a meal; he didn't like the house much, it was so cold and soulless and, the longer he spent time there the more he felt edgy. Besides, he'd had enough of carry out meals and burgers, he longed for pasta or a good steak. She agreed and suggested a small place close by which offered half decent food and a good Argentinian Merlot.

*     *     *

The car entered a leafy suburb and proceeded along a wide avenue flanked by trees and glowing in autumnal colours. They turned into an entrance and stopped at the wrought iron gates; a few seconds later the gates swung open and they proceeded up the drive way. The grounds were immaculately kept with borders and neatly trimmed hedges, something you would expect to see in England. They stopped outside an imposing door covered by a portico, steps leading up to the main entrance.

Joe and Hank go out and looked around. They had heard about this place but never actually been here. It was little known to the general public and to the media, only used occasionally by the President when entertaining foreign dignitaries or for special meetings. Many countries had such retreats where leaders and close advisers could meet and discuss sensitive matters. The mounted the steps and were about to press the bell when the door was opened. They were greeted by a couple of Marines and shown to a large ornate table which served as a desk. They were instructed to leave their coats, phones and politely asked to empty their pockets of all keys and coins before being led across the hall. The Marines marched briskly down a short corridor and knocked at a door, immediately opening it and ushered them through. Four men were standing huddled in the middle of the room, and all looked round at the new arrivals. The head of CIA went over and greeted them before turning to the others. "Mr President may I introduce you to Hank Gobolski and Joe Briggs who are working on the case."

The President nodded and shook hands, a firm grip which surprised Joe. John Pintaro then went on to introduce his two men to the Vice President and to Frank Campese, Vice President of the Senate Committee for Research. The introductions were barely done when there was a loud rap at the door and Brian Milento was shown in. The Vice President then indicated towards the conference table and invited everyone to take a seat.

The President cleared his throat, a loud raspy sound, before addressing the company, "thank you for coming gentlemen, I know you are all very busy, but I believe recent developments in Hong Kong and China are very serious. I understand from the Vice President that he has had a couple of meetings with the Deputy Ambassador of Great Britain and both our countries agree this is a major crisis." He paused to look round the table, "I will now let the Vice President continue".

Over the next hour the group discussed the situation in Hong Kong and China and what action, if any could be taken.

The President looked thoughtful before speaking again. "I will start with the situation in Hong Kong; it is clear, after discussion with the Cabinet, and in particular the military command, I don't see what we can do, other than to raise the issue with the United Nations. We could impose sanctions but, in reality, our hands are tied. We do not want to be seen to be interfering in China's internal affairs although, technically, Hong Kong is semi-autonomous. I must admit I am frustrated; you know how I distrust that shower and I am absolutely convinced they know what they are doing. So, for the time being, we will take it to the

UN Council next month, raise concerns in the press and wait and see. I believe the British are taking a more pro-active approach; they can do that, as they have historical ties and many of Hong Kong citizens can claim UK citizenship."

There were nods all round and a murmur of approval. As an afterthought the President continued, "I want all agencies to keep a close eye on developments and to work closely with the Brits on this, understood?". More nods and murmuring confirmed his order was understood.

The Vice President moved on to the second and, in all their minds, the most important crisis; that of the production of the new chemical weapon which had been brought to their attention by the CIA and MI6. Hank and Joe were grilled at length; they were requested explanations and their take on how they, as well as Jack and the British team, saw the situation.

Joe finished the synopsis with the last update Sean had received and the reported suicide of the director of Wuhan's Research centre. There was a long silence before Brian spoke. "Is that the guy who welcomed the American party a few weeks back?"

Joe nodded, "Sean is not one hundred percent sure it was suicide. In my opinion it could be, but he sure knows more about that than I do".

The discussions went on for a long while before the President closed the subject with no real conclusion. Thanking his CIA team, he intimated his scepticism, he did not believe, or wanted to believe, the Chinese would use such a weapon unless it was against certain internal dissident groups. He asked to be kept up-dated daily and advised immediately of any changes. Looking at Hank and Joe he continued in his monotone voice, "gentlemen, I much appreciate your hard work and especially, the report you handed in to John. I am delighted our two nations are working together; keep up the good work. Now, may I ask you to leave as we have a private matter to discuss." He rose and shook their hands.

Once outside they both let out a huge sigh of relief. Hank was the first to talk, "not sure about you but I'm certainly in need of a beer. That grilling, gee, did they not go over things with a fine-tooth comb. Must give it to you buddy, you did great, had an answer to everything."

Joe smiled, happy that his boss was satisfied and appreciative of his contribution. "What do you think they thought of the second report? Guess that was the private matter."

"I sure wouldn't like to be in Brian and Frank's shoes; just hope they get what they deserve."

* * *

The next morning Joe was nursing a sore head, he looked awful; sick as a parrot on a snowy day as James put it.

Beth came in clutching a handful of newspapers. "Take a look at these, never seen such a thing before," she exclaimed, tossing the pile on the table. Joe picked up the top copy and looked at the front page; the headlines screamed out at him. **Vice President of the Senate Committee for Research & Second Director of the CIA Arrested.** The papers then continued to announce that following an internal CIA investigation, both Frank Campese and Brian Milento had been arrested on counts of treason, fraud and money laundering. Nothing was mentioned about China but a whole page was taken up reporting that the Chinese owned three of the main pharmaceutical companies in America in which Mr Campese was involved in. It was claimed that he was being paid indirectly via a Panamanian company. It was also alleged that Mr Milento was involved in arranging access and visas as well as facilitating hiding these facts. He was also accused of receiving undeclared payments. They indicated that an internal source had brought the facts to light and that they were ready to testify in court. Both men had been arrested early the previous night and were being held under tight security in a secret location.

Joe let out a whoop of joy and punched the air, "one nil to the goodies," he exclaimed. He was about to call Hank when his phone buzzed. It was Jack - he sounded excited and congratulated Joe for his first-class work. "Where is James, is he still with you?" Joe agreed with whatever was said and hung up. He looked across the table, "Jack has asked if you could stay on a couple more days, he's flying out first thing in the morning and would like you to be here so he can thank you".

James reddened slightly, "certainly, but I'm not sure what I've done to deserve any praise".

"We'll get you booked on a flight mid-morning on Friday if that's ok. Oh! and he said he had let Sean know via his boss in London." He then dialled Hank. Both men had a long discussion and sounded extremely pleased with themselves; they confirmed that they would be meeting up later the next day to brief Jack. Joe looked at James and Beth, "damn, I suddenly feel a whole lot more human. What about we go and get us a late breakfast and then we can go watch the Redskins. I have a mate that can get us some tickets. Show you James, what a real sport is," he winked and gave a big grin.

\* \* \*

The next day they all met up in Hanks' office as agreed. Jack sat and listened to both men excitedly relate their meeting with the President and Vice President; just like kids he mused. He thanked James for the invaluable work he had carried out. The phone on the desk rang and they all jumped, startled by the loud buzz. Hank picked up, listened and nodded before replacing the receiver. "That was John, wants us to go across to see him." Looking over at James, "and that includes you James".

The air was full of speculation as they talked animatedly between themselves, wondering what this rare summons was all about. Hanks decided that it was to fill them in on the details of the previous day and how things were going to proceed. Deep down he hoped that he would be promoted by way of thanks for what he had done. Yes, he deserved it, he had been around for a long time and now his boss was going to be sent to jail, he was the obvious choice. He was careful to keep this thought to himself, he certainly didn't want to look too presumptuous.

They were shown into the conference room and John Pintaro soon joined them. They took their places round the table, Hank making sure he sat next to the big boss.

The Head of CIA looked round the table and smiled broadly. "Well gentlemen, I must first thank you all for the excellent work. Your expertise and determination paid dividends and you have managed to expose two very unsavoury characters. I just hope our main witness won't change her mind or get scared," he continued to look at the four men in front of him. "You do realise that you will be called to the stand as prosecution witnesses, don't you? It won't be easy; many allegations will be thrown around and your past will be dug up." He looked over to James, "just to reassure you Mr Horton, you will not be expected to testify; this is an internal affair and as a foreigner and someone who is not employed by our agency, you are not expected to attend. Having said that, we greatly appreciate your help and contribution," he grinned easily showing a very white set of near perfect teeth.

Jack took the pause and butted in, "what is the time scale John?".

"I guess between four to six months. You know what lawyers are like and the US Department of Justice is not known for its speed. We need to ensure we have a watertight case; I'll make damned sure nothing goes wrong. We must absolutely get these guys behind bars. Bloody Press are having a field day, accusing us of incompetence and being rotten, chucking us all in the same basket. We must make sure they go down big time."

Joe raised his hand to speak, "did they admit to everything? Tells us what happened".

"Yes and no. They started to confirm certain points but then clammed up, I guess they suddenly realised whatever they said would incriminate them and be used against them. It ended up by them answering every question with "a no comment"; I would have done the same. Further interrogation is taking place today with their lawyers in attendance. We let them go after about an hour, telling them we would talk to them at a later stage. It had already been planned to arrest them early that evening at their homes. Of course, we have been keeping twenty-four-hour surveillance on them."

"Where are they being held?" asked Hank.

There was a shake of the head, "can't tell you that I'm afraid. What I can say is, it's in a top security site and that they are being kept in solitary confinement for their own safety."

John Pintaro took a long sip of water before continuing. "Right, there is another big question we have to discuss, and that is who will be taking over the role of my second in command." Again, he took a sip of water before looking at his men. There was a palpable tension in the air as the three men tried to avoid full eye contact with their boss.

James watched with interest. To his untrained eye, he detected a glint in Hank's eye and, was it his imagination, a quickening of his breathing. Jack remained calm; his demeanour unchanged. As for Joe, the man seemed to be taking everything in his stride, he was certainly a cool customer. Knowing the man as he did, he decided that Joe would be happier going back to Maine and to his cabin. Had he been a betting man, James decided that it would be Jack.

"It's not an easy decision and not one I relish. You all three are first class men, reliable, hardworking, and extremely experienced so, you see my dilemma." There was a long pause, the world seemed to have stopped around them and you could practically hear the hearts beating in the three chests. Eventually, rising from his chair John Pintaro spoke. "My mind is made up and I'm offering you, Jack, the post of number 2 of the CIA."

There was a silence whilst everyone digested those words. Hank visibly shrunk in his chair, his jaw tightened, his fists clenched white.

Joe was the first to speak, "congratulations Jack, you deserve it and are certainly the man to sort this mess out. Look at what you've done in London, well done". He beamed and stuck out his hand.

Hank pulled himself together quickly and croaked his congratulations and echoed Joe's words.

Jack was blushing slightly as he stood up and went over to his boss to thank him. "I will do everything in my power to ensure the agency gets back on its feet and comes out of this crisis a stronger and more resilient organisation. I thank you John for your trust, I will make sure it is well placed." He looked at his two colleagues, "and with these two giants I'm confident we will go from strength to strength".

Joe shook his head, "sorry boss, but when everything is wrapped up with the China thing, if ever it is, I'm off back to my cabin and fishing. I was only brought down here under duress, and I am sure you don't need an old, cantankerous and, as Carter would say, rude and derogatory, dragon like me around. Not good for the image." He chuckled.

Jack shook his head and looked at Hank, "looks as if it will just be the two us which is fine by me; unless James would like to join?" he said teasingly.

*   *   *

They were making their way back to the office when Joe suggested they should all go out and celebrate. Jack was quick to agree. Hank followed along but said he would join them in a while, he had something important to do first.

# CHAPTER 44

# Hong Kong

Sean checked into the hotel and took the elevator up to the sixteenth floor where he found his way to his room. The receptionist had greeted him warmly and proudly told him he had managed to secure his usual room. Long-distance travel was not easy and never got easier; he flopped onto the bed and fell asleep immediately. The next thing he knew was the sound of the phone, his wakeup call. It was the first of three he had booked, the memory of the first visit still very much in his mind.

He made his own way to the office as he did not want to disturb Jimmy more than he had to; with the number of visits he had recently made, he knew the way. Throwing his rucksack over his shoulder he hopped off the tram and made his way along the busy streets, stopping to buy breakfast at one of the many stalls.

The office, as usual, was a hive of activity; TV screens giving out news, operatives sitting at desks with earphones on or working on their computers. Jimmy was standing behind one of the girls, a new one, pointing at something on her screen. He turned round and waved as he heard Sean enter, indicating he should go through to his office. Pearl came over to greet him and they made their way into the glass screened room.

Sean pulled out a neatly wrapped parcel from his rucksack and handed it over to her, followed by a bottle of malt for Jimmy.

Embarrassed, both thanked him, Jimmy promising he would not open it without him.

Sean then updated them on events in Washington and could only surmise what effect the earth-shattering developments would have on the CIA and American politics. He had been pleased to hear of Jack's promotion, although he would miss his new friend when he returned to London. One positive was that he now had a close contact and ally at the very top, in case of future need.

Both Jimmy and Pearl gave him the low down on events in Wuhan. Both felt sure Xing's death was not suicide; their man on the ground was convinced it was a killing, but by whom? That was the question. None of them believed the official line, and the more the Chinese confirmed it was suicide, the more they had other ideas. Tim was working hard to find out; it was a risky business but knowing him, he would be ferreting around until he got an answer.

Sean stretched and yawned, a good night's sleep still did not help the jetlag or ease his muscles. "Do you think our two lovers are safe?" he asked.

Good question and one that neither Jimmy nor Pearl could be sure of; It was concerning. Jimmy's gut feeling was that they were safe for now; whoever killed Xing did not necessarily want to see off two prominent scientists; they would be useful in the future, and it would look much to obvious. The powers in Beijing, if they were responsible, would not want to be seen to be undertaking the systematic killing of two prominent scientists at this stage; no, for the present he thought they were safe.

Sean was not so convinced. He agreed that, if it was ordered by Beijing, they may be alright for the present, but nothing stopped them being transferred to some outback place and then disappearing. If it was simply a contract killing by the Triads for a debt or the likes, then, yes, they were ok. Jimmy did have to admit he had considered the first point as a highly likely possibility; he however discounted the Triad theory.

Pearl remained sceptical of either of her colleague's theories and was more in favour of the suicide version. They knew about Xing's ambitions, that was clear from the report they had received from their contacts in the capital and from Wuhan. Perhaps he had counted on his discovery propelling him to great hights and receiving the promotion he had dreamt of. The loss of face or shame of not being recognised sent him over the edge. Perhaps the knowledge of what they had discovered, whatever that was, had panicked him and, realising what damage it could do was too much for him. As for the two youngsters, well, they would probably be sent to Beijing or Lanzhou where they would be put in charge of a new project and kept under strict surveillance.

Both men were dubious but did not contradict her. Jimmy however, suggested she went up to Wuhan to help Tim keep an eye on both youngsters until such time as Beijing had decided where they would go. Whilst there, she could try to make contact with them and find out if they knew what plans had been made. It would be interesting also to have their take on Xing's fate. She agreed and suggested she flew up the next day.

\* \* \*

## Wuhan

It was still cold and drizzly when Ru and Mei Lien decided to have a walk round the market; they were feeling hemmed in and the novelty of not having to go into work had worn off. Mei Lien suggested they called by the laboratory and have a tea in the canteen; she wanted to see the old cleaner and find out if she knew anything about Chi Tao. Ru was hesitant but relented for a quiet life.

They entered the large hall which was full of lunch time dinners, a buzz of conversation and laughter; life seemed to have carried on as before. Just shows, Ru commented, that no one is indispensable. Mei Lien felt a sadness come over her, she did not particularly like the old goat much, but the thought that no one really cared or appreciated what he had done, saddened her. They looked round for the old cleaner but couldn't see her. On the way out they asked another of the staff of her whereabouts and were told she had left for health reasons. Neither believed the excuse but kept silent until they were outside the gates.

"What do you make of that?" asked Mei Lien.

Ru shrugged, "not surprising; probably thought with the professor no longer around, and us away, there was no further need to stay".

"You really think she was just here to spy on us and him?"

"And to help us, yes. I'm convinced she has something to do with the foreigners, working for them."

Changing the subject slightly she continued, "I wonder if that slimy Lu Chin is still here. Hope he got thrown out or sent to Mongolia," she shivered.

They made their way to the market and took time strolling round the hundreds of stalls. Mei Lien was struck by the amount of tat and rubbish on sale and the prices. How could anyone want to pay good money for such cheap and shoddy goods. Despite the cold, they meandered through the aisles until they reached the food section. Now, that was worth spending time in. The smells of steaming pots tickled their nostrils and started Ru's stomach rumbling. "You can't be hungry again, you only just had breakfast," she giggled pulling herself closer to him.

They stopped to buy some fish before moving on past the array of fresh vegetables. Ru suddenly stopped and, nudging Mei Lien, nodded ahead. "Is that Ying Po, over there, by that stall with the blue awning?"

Mei Lien peered in the direction he was pointing. "Yes, certainly looks very much like him. He must be a trader as he said he was."

Jostling through the crowds, they headed in his direction but had to stop suddenly to let a van through. When it had passed, they could no longer see their man. Walking over to the stall Ru asked where he could find Mr Po. The stall holder simply shrugged, he had left after delivering the load of vegetables and pointed to half a dozen sacks. He would be back in two days' time at about the same hour if that was any help. They thanked him and moved on feeling disappointed. Both felt better, especially Ru, who had not bought his story of being a purveyor of fruit and veg but now, he had to admit he had been wrong.

Cold and wet they decided to go home. They wandered back through the market and were passing a stall selling chickens when they came face to face with Lu Chin. All three froze, startled, and stared at each other icily. Lu Chi was the first to recover and quickly gave one of his toothless grins; rubbing his bristly chin he bowed sarcastically and asked what they were doing here, at the market. Ru chose to ignore the man and started to walk on. Lu Chi called after them. "See you lost your protector," he sniggered. "What you going to do now? Reckon you'll be sent to some backward dump, just like the prof was going to be," he let out a low gritty laugh.

Mei Lien shivered and both she and Ru picked up their pace, not looking back. They felt his eyes bore into their back and it made the hair of Mei Lien's neck stand up. She started to sob.

Before reaching the apartment, they stopped off at a tea house. Both were shaking, cold from the rain and from the recent encounter. As they sat down Mei Lien dried her eyes and took hold of his hands; they were freezing but comforting. They were silent for a long time before Ru spoke.

"That was the last person I would have expected to meet. He gets nastier and uglier by the day."

Mei Lien felt her eyes moisten again, "do you think he knows something we don't?" she asked. "He seemed pretty sure."

Ru shook his head, "no, don't worry, he was just being spiteful and nasty. He wanted to upset us and, in his warped way, thought he would get one over us."

"Well, he certainly succeeded with me," she sniffed.

He squeezed her hand tighter and tried to comfort her. He tried to change the subject but even talk of a trip to Hong Kong to buy a wedding dress could not comfort her.

\* \* \*

Ru had slept badly once again; he had not had a good night for some time now. He kept having the same recurring dreams about his parents, his childhood and his mother, and they disturbed him. Last night they were intermingled with images of Lu Chin and his gritty laugh kept echoing in his head. He got up early and got dressed before going through and making breakfast which he took through to Mei Lien. She woke, stretched, and asked what time it was in a drowsy voice. She moaned when he told her it had just gone 7am. She pulled him on to her and kissed him passionately; he let himself be undressed; all thoughts of breakfast banished. After making love he fell asleep, a deep and peaceful sleep, the best he had for some time. When he woke, she was sitting by his side, fully dressed, stroking his cheek. Looking at the clock he grunted and smiled, he had been out for the count for nearly three hours. He rose to kiss her, but she got up and started for the door. Looking back, she called out, "breakfast in fifteen minutes". She blew him a kiss and went through to the kitchen.

\* \* \*

Having landed in Wuhan, Pearl went through her usual routine of changing her looks, making herself look plainer, more Chinese so that she would better blend in better with the locals. Making her way to the hotel she pondered on how best to contact the two scientists. She would have to meet up with Tim but did not relish the thought. He was nice enough, harmless, certainly good at his job, but she did not really like him. She couldn't put a finger on it. Perhaps he was too Chinese, had been living too long in this complicated and dangerous country; she should really cut him some slack and make the effort. She had never met his partner, Sally, and wondered what she was like. She was brought back to earth by the taxi driver telling her they had nearly arrived. He dropped her off a block from the hotel and she watched him drive off, weaving is way in and out of the traffic.

After checking in she made her way to the apartment block but having reached the door, changed her mind and retraced her steps. Her intention was to call on them and have a chat but, at the last minute, she decided not to spring her presence in the city on them. She would call and arrange a meeting somewhere neutral and in a public place. Better all round and safer for her charges.

Back in her room she called Tim but there was no answer; she cut the phone, annoyed at not being able to talk. She turned on the television and sat glowering at it glumly.

*    *    *

Tim had met up with his partner, now no longer a cleaner at the research centre. They had spent most of the past seventy-two hours trying to find out what had really happened to Chi Tao Xing. Neither of them believed the official story of suicide. Tim worked the market whilst Sally went in search of the professor's friends and family. It was not an easy task as she did not wish to raise suspicion, and few would be willing to talk. Even in this day and age, it was not good to talk, especially to strangers.

Tired and slightly despondent, they had met back at the flat to exchange findings. It was a small, one bedroom place, in a grey depressing high-rise situated not far from the research centre. Certainly not cheap but ideal for what they wanted.

After having had something to eat, Sally checked her watch before going over to take out the old suitcase from the cupboard and set up the machine. She put on the headphones, switched on the unit and waited. A few minutes later a voice came on and started to read a children's story. A slow clear voice, each word precise, monotonous, certain words ever so slightly stressed. Sally was taking notes in shorthand, ignoring the tale but concentrating on certain passages and sentences. At last, the voice stopped, wishing the listeners good night. She removed the earphones shaking her hair to loosen it and replaced everything neatly back in the case and then back into the cupboard.

They put on their coats and were seen leaving the building, arm in arm, a couple going for a night out. They smiled and nodded to several of the other residents who liked this middle-aged couple, good, hard working people. He supplied fruit and vegetables to the market and she, well no one was sure, except that she was always out. They got on to a bus and headed for the other side of the city, to a small house halfway along a dusty street. Once inside they settled down and Sally opened her notebook and read the transcript aloud, there was nothing new or exciting to report. Exhausted they went to bed.

# CHAPTER 45

# Washington

The evening was noisy and raucous. Hank joined them at the restaurant; no one knew what he went to do that was so important but whatever it was, it had made a difference. He was in great form, laughing and cracking jokes which only he laughed at, the others politely going along with him.

Jack sat back and watched; Joe was his usual self, making rude comments and feeling at ease with life. James was joining in, enjoying the banter and Jack was impressed at how this seventy-year-old Englishman had adapted to his new life and friends. He remained a gentleman at all times, very little seemed to fluster him. If only he was twenty years younger, he thought. He looked round at Hank. Hank troubled him, there was something going on and Jack had this feeling, a feeling he got when his instincts told him not all was well. Hank was an oddball, a man who never really fitted in, was never happy with life or his lot. He had always been like that, an outsider, never being a team player. He wondered what Hank thought of recent developments; had he been friends with Brian? He doubted that, more like the opposite he thought.

It was late when the evening broke up; the long-suffering Beth taking Joe and James back whilst he and Hank were driven home by the colossus. After dropping his colleague off he let out a long sigh, in a couple of weeks he would be back to take up his new position; he would then have to tackle the Hank problem head on.

The following afternoon Beth drove him and James to the airport. James had been remarkably perky after the previous night and was in good spirits, clearly happy to be returning home. They had arranged for them to return to the UK on the same flight and have adjoining seats; the least they could do after all James had done over the past year and half.

*   *   *

## Wuhan

Refreshed from a good night sleep, Tim was up early and busied himself preparing for the day ahead; his mobile rang, and he picked up. Pearl tried to be light-hearted and not show her feelings; but she was still upset that he had not answered her call the night before, even after he had told her they had both gone to bed exhausted after a two-day shift. She told him she was back in town and would like to see him, sooner rather than later. They agreed to meet at the market just after 10am, he had to be there to drop off a delivery; she would have no trouble finding him. After hanging up he looked at the phone and shook his head, funny one that one, he thought to himself. He had barely put the phone down when it rang again; he picked it up and growled wondering what she wanted now. His tone immediately changed when he heard the caller. "Sorry, I thought you were one of my customers," he lied. "She's very difficult and has been on twice this morning."

Ru accepted the apology and asked if they could meet later in the morning. "Of course, delighted. Why don't we meet at the market, you know where it is and it's easy to get to and, although crowded with thousands of people, probably more private. Meet me at my main client's stall – it's in the fruit and vegetable section, one with a large blue awning, you can't miss it." Just before hanging-up he added, "it will be easier if you entered the market at gate 16, that way you will avoid having to go through all those awful clothing stalls," he joked.

There was never a dull moment he thought. First the princess wanted to meet up, most likely to check on them, then one of his charges; it was going to be an interesting and busy day. He wondered

what Ru wanted that was so urgent and whether his girlfriend would be there. What was the reason? It wasn't like the man to come voluntarily; he always had the feeling the scientist distrusted him. Oh well, he would find out soon enough. He called out to tell Sally and they discussed a plan of action.

* * *

Ru had decided to call Yin Po, he wanted to ask him about Chi Tao and what his thoughts were about his death; he also wanted to tell him about their encounter with Lu Ching the other day. In fact, he wanted to have a good heart to heart with a man, to talk about his fears and concerns of the discovery. He had no friends. Yes, they had spoken at length with the foreigners and had opened up, but he needed to talk to someone, man to man. They had been in the city for six months now and knew few people apart from the people they had worked with. He certainly still did not entirely trust Yin Po and wondered about the wisdom of meeting at the market, but he had no other option, and it was too late to change his mind; he had no one else to turn to. After thinking hard and long he had decided to make the call and now it was done he felt better.

Going over to Mei Lien, he told her what he had done. She looked surprised but didn't say anything. He asked her to accompany him, but she declined; no, she would only hinder him and anyway, she didn't want to return to the market ever again and feared bumping into the creep, Lu Chin. Deep down he was relieved, he wanted to be alone and not have to worry about her. She handed him his jacket, wrapped a scarf round his neck and kissed him lightly on the cheek. She watched him emerge from the building and cross the street before disappearing down the busy road, swallowed up by the crowd. Turning towards the small hall she noticed his keys were still in the door. She shook her head, when would he not forget them, the number of times he had locked himself out or relied on her to take her set. She went into the bedroom and striped the bed.

*     *     *

Pearl made her way through the crowds and spotted the blue awning. Making her way along the crowded path she reached the stall; Tim was nowhere to be seen. She browsed whilst waiting, eventually spotting a man and a woman wheeling a load of crates towards her. They greeted her before unloading the goods and suggested she accompanied them back to the van. She followed feeling uncomfortable and conspicuous. She realised that she had been desk bound too long, had lost the art of mingling and acting like a native. It had been what, ten years since she had last worked in the field. She didn't miss it, some were born for that kind of job, others like her, were more comfortable doing the thinking and the plotting. She never liked the killing, still disliked it even though, like a few months back, it had to be done.

They took her into a large, noisy tearoom, which was seriously in need of a clean, and found a table along the back wall. Once Tim had settled down, he looked up and asked what she wanted. They discussed Chi Toa's death and he gave her all the details they knew. By the end of it, she had to agree it looked very much like a killing and not suicide. They told her about the call this morning and the meeting with Ru.

Pearl was surprised and worried. What did he want, why now? She wasn't convinced meeting at the market was a good idea although accepted it made sense. They agreed she could be there but only if she stayed in the background, out of sight. He wanted to speak man to man and, as he did not know she was in town, seeing her unannounced might spook him.

Ru had made good time but, as the market got closer his pace slowed; a feeling of anxiousness came over him and he began to wonder if he had made the right decision. He arrived at gate 16 only to find it closed. Following the throng, he went to the next entrance and entered the crowded market heaving with traders and shoppers. He pushed his way through the bustling crowd, narrowly avoiding being mown down by a van until he spied the top of the blue awning. He stopped to buy some fruit and proceeded to amble his way to his rendezvous.

The woman had been waiting, pretending to busy herself with her shopping. She had clocked him as he came through the gates and followed at a discreet distance. She saw him nearly being mown down by that idiot, stood next to him whilst he bought the grapes and had vanished into thin air once her charge had met up with the trader.

Tim was quick to spot Ru and came over to greet him.

"Mr Nuang, welcome, please follow me to my van where I can show you my goods," he smiled politely and led Ru down the alley between dozens of smaller stalls. Ru had trouble keeping up and was unable to speak a word. Finally, they arrived at the vehicle where Ying Po ushered him into the back; he followed his guest and closed the door.

"So sorry to rush you like that, I didn't want you to talk about anything out in the open; we are safe here and out of ear shot".

Once his eyes got accustomed to the semi darkness, Ru made out another person, a woman, dressed in plain country clothes and wearing an apron. He recognised her immediately as the old cleaner at the canteen and acknowledged her presence. She smiled back at him and gave a little bow. Ying Po settled down beside her and encouraged his visitor to say what he had come to tell them. Ru had wanted to be alone with the man but decided he had little choice but to proceed. Conversation was stilted to begin with but as time went by, he relaxed, he got more animated and poured out his concerns. The two listened quietly, not interrupting, occasionally nodding, or asking for clarification. A sense of relief came over Ru as he finally came to the end and fell silent. Ying Po and the woman showed concern and asked what they could do to help. They were both stunned at the revelations he had told them, shocked at what they had learned but showed sympathy and in soothing voices helped calm the young man down.

Ru did not know what he wanted nor the kind of help he and Mei Lien needed. He knew he wanted a quiet life, a life where he could enjoy his work and be with his future wife, but he did not know what this couple could do to provide it; all he wanted them to tell him was that all would be well.

Sensing the young man's thoughts, Ying Po earnestly told him all would be fine, that with time things would change and that he could look forward to a happy and fruitful life. When he felt the moment was right, Ying Po got up and opened the back door of the van, daylight came flooding in making them all squint. Jumping out, he beckoned the young man to follow him. They were making their way back toward the stall when the trader stopped and turned to the scientist, "tell me what you want me to do. If you want my assistance to move to Hong Kong, say so; anything is possible, I am here to help". He looked earnestly at the young man and saw the uncertainty and fear in his eyes.

"Thank you, but I don't really know what I want or, for that matter, what you can do for us." Hesitating he continued, "the only thing I wished you could do, is to make sure our discovery never sees the light of day; but that I know is impossible". He looked as if he was about to burst into tears. "I have not slept properly since the day we handed the results over; I will never rest in peace and will carry the guilt for the rest of my life".

Ying Po felt pity for the young man, sympathy as well as a deep sense of helplessness. They shook hands and in a loud clear voice thanked him for his order and the confidence he showed in this humble trader.

Before parting company, he whispered, "you have my number, call me any time, day or night". He turned and left Ru looking after him.

He watched the man disappear before turning to make his way back; he felt exhausted. His mind was a million miles away when he heard someone calling out to him, "hey, young man, you want chicken?". Looking up, he stopped dead in his tracks. There, in front of him was Lu Chin, same stubble and same sneering, toothless smile. Before he could move the man had caught him by the arm and was dragging him towards a stall crammed with cages full of birds of all kinds. He tried to pull away, but Lu Chin's grip tightened.

"Don't be so stuck-up scientist, you're no better than me. Where is that pretty piece of fluff of yours?" he asked in an evil tone.

"What do you want? Take your hands off me," Ru twisted and tried to untangle himself from his grasp.

"C'mon, buy something, buy a lovely chicken. Here, this one, comes from a good home, in fact it is well educated, It's been in a laboratory for the past three weeks." The snarl got uglier as he continued, "what about a bit of monkey, lovely juicy leg, that also comes from a good home".

Ru looked at the man horrified. "What do you mean they came from a laboratory".

"You heard me. They come from your laboratory, lab No6. These are the creatures you wanted the vet to put down and burn. You are so stuck up and used to your bourgeois ways you did not see the opportunity - well I did".

Ru could not believe his ears. Had he heard right? Did Lu Chin actually say he had some of the test animals? No, not possible, he was winding him up. "You're talking rubbish and winding me up, now let me go."

Lu Chin's grin got wider, "oh no I'm not. I never joke when it comes to my livelihood. Thanks to you I lost my job. Old Xing refused to give me a new posting or give a reference so I have to make a living as best I can."

Ru didn't know what to do or say. At last he spluttered, "have you just said, admitted, you killed the director?".

The grin vanished instantly, and two cold eyes bored into Ru, "that is exactly what I said. The pompous bastard deserved it, and so do you if you aren't careful".

He shuddered involuntary and he felt the blood drain from his face. He remained silent for a moment starring at the man standing in front of him. "You realise that those animals, if indeed they are the ones you claim, are infected and could kill thousands, possibly millions of people?"

Lu Chin stood there and simply shrugged, "what do I care, it's not my doing; you are the one who is the killer, you and all your lot; you and them made it, have got the congratulations, the honours. You sound just like the old man".

Ru could still not fully comprehend what he had heard. He wished he had never come, never set eyes on Wuhan. Lu Chin continued, "you don't believe me, do you? think I'm making it up," he pulled Ru over closer to the animals. "Look, they still have the ring tags and batch number. Now, are you going to buy one? They have your name on them, fitting isn't it?" he laughed that raspy noise.

With a surprise wriggle Ru pulled away from the monster and made for the busy alley, turning back he shouted out, "leave me, leave us alone or I'm going to the police".

He hurried away, bumping into people, tripping as he went; he couldn't get out of the place fast enough. A large truck came rumbling past, its cargo swaying perilously and honking its horn. He stopped and watched it pass, stepping back to avoid being hit. He felt a sudden terrible pain hit him in the lower back followed a few seconds later by a second one, he gasped and let out a low moan before sinking to his knees. In the distance he heard screams and voices shouting; soon someone was leaning over him. He felt cold and his whole body started to shake, the pain intensified, excruciating. He felt someone lift his head and hold him. His eyes went hazy and through the mist he saw Mei Liens face smiling at him before fading away to be replaced by his father and mother, they were calling him.

*   *   *

Tim had returned to the van and was sitting in the front seat with Pearl. "What do you make of all that?" he enquired.

She was silent and grimaced, "couldn't get a more detailed account if we wanted. The lad certainly poured his soul out. Thought he had told us everything at that last meeting." She looked over before he could interrupt, "yes, I got everything on tape".

"It looks as if Sean and the Americans were really on to something and by all accounts this stuff really does exist. Scary, to think man can manufacture such lethal weapons, if you can call it a weapon."

She agreed, "let's hope for all our sakes the people in charge realise how dangerous it is; it's worse, or at least as bad as the atomic bomb".

Their conversation was disrupted by a commotion and shouting voices in the distance, people were running and calling for an ambulance; curiosity got the better of them and they went to investigate. Approaching the scene Tim spotted Sally, she was kneeling on the ground comforting someone, cradling them on her lap; he moved closer. When he got to her, he noticed she was crying, stroking the head of a young man dressed in a blue jacket and wearing a scarf; the man they had spent the past hour with; he gently helped her up. Someone came with a blanket and covered the body. Un-noticed they slipped away from the scene and returned to the van before driving off to the high rise.

They dropped Pearl off close to her hotel and arranged to meet later. Just as Pearl was getting out, he leaned over and reminded her not to call Jimmy, phones were listened to, that they would communicate the news through the usual channels. She gave him a withering look but said nothing.

By the time they had reached the grey building Sally had calmed down and was back to her normal, professional self. "I don't know what happened; one minute he was there, the next he was bleeding to death." She went over what she had seen, the truck rumbling past, the young man stepping back then crying out in pain before collapsing. She had seen a man walk away quickly but only saw his back. She felt terrible, her job was to follow and protect, and she had failed. Tim tried his best to console and re-assure her, it was just something no one could foresee, unfortunate but she should not blame herself.

Once in the flat, he went over and took out the suitcase and placed it on the table. Sally busied herself setting up the machine, put on the headphones and started her work. Meanwhile, Tim cleaned the minute bedsit thoroughly, wiping the tops, door frames, handles. Every small crack was seen to until he was happy no traces were left. When they had finished, they made a final check of the place before closing and locking the door. It was only once they were back in the van that they took off the protective gloves they had put on before entering the flat.

\* \* \*

Mei Lien was worried. It was dark now and Ru had been gone for hours. She had tried phoning his mobile several times with no reply. Looking out the window every few minutes she was getting more and more agitated as time went by; where was he, what was he doing? She would have gone to the market looking for him, but she did not want to leave the flat just in case he returned and couldn't get in.

She tried his phone again, returned to look out, panic setting in. She went through to the kitchen and boiled the kettle when there was a loud knock on the door; startled she yelped, burning her hand with scalding water before rushing to the door to greet him.

Her face froze as she saw a woman and a man dressed in police clothing. They asked to come in and made their way into the small hall. The young woman then gave Mei Lien the terrible news that her boyfriend had been stabbed at the market. There had been an altercation between him and one of the stall holders but that was all she could say at present. No, they had not arrested anyone although they did have a vague description of a suspect.

Lu Chin! She knew it, she had felt it deep down, and that was one of the reasons she had decided not to accompany Ru to the market. She did not want to meet the man again but now, she blamed herself. Had she gone, she may have been able to diffuse the situation or protected her man.

She showed the two officers out and closed the door; tears started to well up and soon flooded her cheeks, she sank to her knees sobbing uncontrollably.

# CHAPTER 46

# Hong Kong

Sean was sitting at Jimmy's desk flicking through his phone messages. Nothing new from Washington except that Jack and James were heading back home. He wished he could. Matters in the US were taking their course. Hank and Joe were helping their boss prepare a watertight case against the two rogue men so, nothing much he could do there. Back here, things were also progressing; they knew the Chinese had invented a lethal chemical weapon however, no one really knew much about it. It was now up to the agents in Beijing and Wuhan to find out as much as possible and try to get to the bottom of it. Pearl had been placed in charge and he had confidence in her. As for his part well, it was pretty much over. He had taken the vague idea and rumour, dug around and through hard work, with a little help from his friends, had taken matters up as far as he could. So, a couple days and he too would go home; thinking about it got him excited.

Jimmy strode in suggesting he would go home for a few hours, "I haven't been back in five days and I need a shower and some fresh clothes. You want to come along?" he asked.

Sean agreed instantly and helped his friend bundle up his dirty clothes and place them in a black bag. Before leaving, Jimmy clapped his hands and demanded every one's attention. "Guys, I'm going to go home for a few hours but will be back before the next shift change. Anything happens, anything at all, call me, understood?" He looked around and grinned, "right I 'm off for a shower which I guess most of you will be pleased to hear". There were smiles and a few chuckles.

Before boarding the tram, they stopped by a laundry where the bag was handed in. Jimmy spoke to the plump owner in Mandarin, and they laughed. She bowed and gave a broad smile as they departed. "Use this place pretty often, it's handy and she's happy to deliver the clothes to the flat or the office; she even gives me credit so I can pay her monthly."

Getting off twenty minutes later, they proceeded up a steep street for a couple of blocks, finally entering a tall residential building. Jimmy hit the button for the thirty-fifth floor out of forty. Sean watched as they shot up, the green numbers flicking past rapidly. The flat was small but airy with two bedrooms, a bathroom, and a small kitchen off which there was a cosy lounge offering superb views across the bay. Sean went to the window and looked out. You could see over the flat roof of the building in front, in the distance the sparkling sea and slightly to the left, the tall office buildings of the city centre.

"Make yourself at home; there's tea, coffee and biscuits in the cupboard, and milk in the fridge, although better check it's alright, I think it's been sitting there for a week," Jimmy grinned. "I'll just have a shower, won't be long."

Sean made himself a coffee and opened the fridge; he smiled; it was just like his. A few bottles of beer, a couple of eggs, a piece of sad looking cheese and a quart carton of milk. He opened it and sniffed, curling his nose up at the smell; he poured the thick gunge down the sink. He went over to the big window and looked out at the view, no comparison to his back home. He settled himself into the sofa and looked around. There was a photo on the side table, and he picked it up. The picture was of a twenty something girl, dressed in summer t-shirt and shorts, hair tied in a ponytail. She was laughing at something, showing off an even set of white teeth. His thoughts were interrupted by Jimmy returning looking much more human and sporting a fresh pair of jeans and a crisp yellow shirt. He replaced the photo feeling slightly embarrassed at his intrusion. Jimmy went over to the fridge and took out a couple of beers.

"Cheers, welcome to my humble pad," he said waving the bottle and smiling broadly. "Must say I enjoyed that; surprised you sat next to me on the tram, you must have a problem with your sense of smell," he laughed.

"Nothing wrong with my nose, I had to chuck the milk". He took a swig of his beer, "drinking on duty, not like you Jimmy," he said winking.

"Think I deserve it, spending the past five days in the office, eating tepid noodles and not having a proper wash or shave, yeah I sure need it".

Sean turned to the photo and nodded towards it, "who's that, a girl friend, wife?".

Jimmy suddenly looked sad and shook his head, "my sister, taken about six months before she disappeared and was killed. She had just got back from Uni in Melbourne, studying law. We were up at the top of the cable car celebrating her degree and the placement she had been offered in one of the big law firms in town." He gave a big sigh, "went to visit our mother's aunt up in Shenyang who was dying; my mother was ill herself and couldn't travel, so she offered. Two days in and she was arrested on suspicion of being a subversive and thrown in jail; the rest you can guess". He looked thoughtfully before continuing, "the bastards tortured her for four days before she died; I have never forgiven them and never will". He went over to the fridge and took out another couple of beers.

Settling himself in the swivel chair he looked at Sean, "ever been married?".

Sean shook his head, "no, not that I didn't want to but the way my life has panned out , there was no real opportunity. Spent my whole life fighting baddies, travelling around the world being shot at – not a great prospect for any woman." They were silent for a while before he continued, " funny how your life is shaped by events; mine reflects yours in many ways. Parents and sister dying at the hands or through the deeds of the IRA pushed me to my career. All I wanted to do was to punish the evil bastards and anyone who causes death and mayhem in the name of a warped ideology."

"When are you going back, have you decided?" Jimmy asked changing the subject.

"Yeah, I was thinking about that back at the office; think I might go home on Sunday if that's ok with you. Not much else I can do now; it's up to your people in Beijing and Wuhan to ferret out as much info as possible and feed it back to us. Why don't you come back with me, stay a few weeks, visit your old haunts? It would do you some good".

Jimmy shook his head, "not the right time now but, yes, I would love to one day". He looked at his watch, "come on, time to get back, don't want to be late". He got up and went over to pick up his jacket, checking his phone before he slipped it in his pocket.

They arrived back at the office just before change over to the night shift, Jimmy's laundry had already been done and delivered which surprised Sean; that didn't happen back home. A young woman, the new one, came up and handed Jimmy a sheet of paper; he glanced down at it briefly and read. Instantly his expression darkened, his jaw clenched before he exploded. "What the hell is this?" he roared, "why was it not sent to me? You heard what my last words were – to contact me immediately anything important came in". He glowered at the girl before continuing, "when did this come in? Three hours ago, three bloody hours ago and no one thought to let me know". He thrust the sheet of paper into Sean's hand and stormed out into the main office, the girl following hot on his heels.

"I didn't want to disturb you, did not think it was really that important," she whimpered.

"Not that important, not that important! It's the most serious and important thing that has happened, can't you see that?" He went over to Tony, "did you know about this latest report".

He shook his head, "No boss. I did tell her to make sure anything that came in be passed on to me, this is the first-time I've heard of it."

Sean handed over the paper to Tony who looked down at it, his mouth gaping wide open when he had digested the news. "Really sorry boss..." but Jimmy cut him off.

"Not your fault, if you're not given information and orders not followed you can't act on it. Make sure the girl is paid off immediately, I don't want to see her in this place ever again, understood?"

Sean had never seen his friend in such a temper, nor did he suspect, had any of the others . There was a deathly hush in the room as everyone kept their heads down, studiously looking at the screen in front of them or listening into their headphones. Jimmy shook his head, "what in the name of God, Buddha or Allah was she thinking, I just don't understand it," he was working himself up again.

Sean put a hand on his arm and nodded towards his office, "we need to think, and think fast, at what we are going to do next, c'mon".

They sat down and Jimmy took a deep breath, "sorry for that, not often I lose my temper, generally I can keep it under wraps but, this, this..." he pointed to the report. "I just don't understand people". He picked up his phone to call Pearl but thought better of it. "First things first, we must make contact with our people in Wuhan and find out what happened; then they must ensure the girl is kept under surveillance 24/7."

Sean was pleased that Jimmy had returned to near normal and put on a cheery voice, "good man, for sure the priority is to protect the girl. Can we get her out and bring her back here?".

"It will take time, even if she is willing; not easy, but possible," he mused. "Quickest and safest way is by private plane; costly, but I may know someone who would be willing to help with that." He called Tony over and motioned to close the door.

"We're thinking of getting the girl out by plane. Can you contact Tim and let him know. Probably best to get them to talk to the girl first and persuade her it is in her best interest and the safest option. It's clear they want all the top people silenced and she is, in my opinion, the next in line." He looked over at Sean before continuing, "first and most important of all, they must keep her under surveillance and protection 24/7 starting this very minute, tell them to let Pearl know and she can help". As Tony was about to leave, he called over, "ask Bingo to come over".

Sean looked quizzically and smiled, "Bingo, why Bingo?"

"He's addicted to the game, spends every hour of his spare time and most of his salary playing."

Bingo knocked on the door; a small dumpy man with thick glasses and a ponytail stood hesitantly waiting to be called in. Jimmy waved him in and immediately spoke to him, "have you still got that friend of yours, the one with the private jet?" he enquired. The man nodded his face expressionless.

"Good, can you ask him how quickly he can get to Wuhan? We have an urgent package and a passenger to pick up and bring back. Try to keep the cost as low as possible; tell him it's for the good of Hong Kong." The man nodded again and left.

"A man of many words," commented Sean.

"Guess it's spending hours gawping at cards and listening to people, not much cause to talk in those places; I must say, he is really good at his job, switched on, unlike some around here." He sucked on his pen, "if the plane is free, I guess they can be up there by tomorrow night or early morning on Saturday; I would prefer night but..", he shrugged, " beggars can't be choosy".

"What do you plan to do with her once she's here?"

"We have a safe house, seldom used; in fact, I had thought of offering it to you, but it went clear out of my head."

"Oh no! I'm perfectly happy at the hotel, loved being waited on and having my bed made, towels changed, minibar stocked," he grinned.

"We would have to get her new ID, a new life. That could be tricky; in my experience people don't like changing who they are and there's always a risk they make a mistake; the first six months are the most crucial." He gave another big sigh, "that is if she wants to leave China, we don't know if she has family or where she is from; she might just want to take the risk".

Sean looked thoughtful, "she may have had a big enough fright to persuade her it's not good to stay. My thoughts are to get her back here, then see what she wants to do; guess it wouldn't be too difficult to spirit her back if that was her final wish." Jimmy was deep in thought, so continued, "what about sending her to the UK? She knows the place, speaks the language and with her expertise would not find it hard to get a job. HQ could easily get her a passport and citizenship as well as help on the job front."

Tony came back and tapped on the door before popping his head round, "I've sent the messages but not sure if they got them. There's been no reply through the usual channel so I coded a text message, we'll have to wait and see." He was about to leave when Bingo joined him, "Ok, my friend could go up on Friday any time you want, needs to be back latest Saturday evening as he has a client first thing Sunday morning".

For the first time since they had got back to the office Jimmy smiled, "good work boys and thank you. Can you put your friend on stand-by, the minute we hear back from Tim or Pearl we'll let him know; did he mention how much?"

"No problem I'll tell him. Where is he flying to? I did ask for a ballpark figure, but you know what these people are like, they never commit."

Jimmy looked at Tony before answering, "tell him Jiujing airport, I know it's a fair distance from Wuhan but It has a small private jet section and I hear it's busy, so they won't arouse suspicion. Wuhan International will be too obvious if they start looking for her."

Both men agreed and headed back to their desks. The night shift had taken over, yet Tony remained, he wasn't happy walking out and leaving unfinished business, he also felt responsible for not letting his boss know in the first place. The more he thought about it, the more he worried; it was unlike Tim not to reply but he kept his thoughts to himself. Jimmy, in his office, was also uneasy, he never liked silences and agents not responding, in his experience it never boded well. He picked up and dialled Pearl's number which rang out; concern began to creep in, and it showed in his expression.

Sean, sitting across the desk, noticed the change and tried to re-assure him but it did little to help ease the feeling of foreboding. "I wouldn't get yourself too worked up, they'll be out keeping an eye on the girl, and you know how difficult it is; I certainly never appreciated being called when I was in the middle of an operation."

Tony came back in and stood looking worried, "I've tried contacting them again but still have no reply; I'm getting concerned boss, it's not like them, they're normally so quick at getting back," his voice trailed off.

Jimmy looked up and thanked him, "better go home, I'll be here, I need you fresh for tomorrow".

His office manager hesitated, "if you don't mind, I'll nip out for half an hour and get something to eat but then come back, I won't be able to sleep anyway so may as well stay over. You want anything?"

Both men shook their heads.

\* \* \*

## Beijing

The men gathered in a little known palace, seldom used apart for entertaining foreign guests who needed to be impressed. Situated in a secluded suburb of the capital it was a throwback from the time of the Qing Dynasty and dated to the early eighteenth century and used by several Emperors as a summer residence.

The eight men were all in the highest positions of their government and used to taking important decisions. The President and his closest aide were surrounded by two top military Generals, the Secretary for Economy, the finance minister, the Head of Security and the head of Scientific Development; the President's trusted secretary hovered in the background. Apart from the Generals, all were dressed in immaculate suits, crisp white shirt and red ties. The President motioned to the gathering to take a seat around the large ornate table.

He opened proceedings after thanking everyone for attending. Looking over at the Head of Scientific Development he requested a full and clear explanation of what the new discovery from Wuhan was all about and what potential use it could have. Following a lengthy narrative, punctuated by questions from all the men around the table he concluded, "as you see Gentlemen, it is not a chemical weapon but rather a biological weapon. It has the potential to cause unimaginable damage and millions of deaths."

"Have we got any antidotes?" asked the President's aide.

"No, not yet. I would strongly suggest we start work on finding one. We could use the scientists who developed this virus as they have the knowledge."

The older of the Generals shook his head, "not easy and probably not possible as I understand the two main people are dead. Professor Xing committed suicide, which I am dubious about, and the very bright scientist who finalised the discovery was stabbed twice in the back yesterday," he looked glaringly at the head of security.

They all looked at the security chief waiting for a reply; he looked around the table gathering his thoughts. "It was certainly nothing to do with us; the first we knew of either death was when my men were alerted by the local police. It seems this could be the work of one man, a loner who has a grudge against these scientists." He paused and shuffled in his chair, "I am told that there was some disturbance at the time of the stabbing and that several stalls were looted when their owners went to see what had happened. One was the stall of the man we think may have been responsible for the killing."

"And who is this man may we ask".

"We think he worked part time at the laboratory and did not take it too well when the Director didn't give him a placement elsewhere; seems he was a strange sort of man and that he may have forged Professor Xing's signature." He didn't feel comfortable at what he was going to say but, with the President staring at him had little choice. "We understand that there was an argument between him and the victim and that he had told the scientist that he had some poultry on sale which came from the laboratory."

The scientist looked up instantly in shock, "did I hear you correctly? Did you say this man was selling poultry coming from this latest project?"

The security chief nodded, " yes professor, and I believe, there was a monkey also".

"Are you absolutely, one hundred percent sure of this or is it merely hearsay?"

"I can assure you these facts are correct. It seems the man had just recently started in the market and was trying to make a name for himself, boasting that he had these "special" live animals and birds."

The second General butted in, "you said that a couple of stalls were looted, was one of these his?"

The scientist was getting more and more agitated at what he heard, "this is terrible news, in fact this may signal the beginning of something we cannot stop. Can I ask you again, are you absolutely certain these animals came from the laboratory?" He looked the man straight in the eyes.

"From all the statements we have, I can almost guarantee these could be the ones."

The finance minister was the only man that looked sceptical, "what proof have you that he was telling the truth; if he was bragging, then we cannot be sure".

"We have spoken to the veterinary department at the laboratory, they have confirmed that they never gave the order to this man to collect the animals. It appears he managed to persuade the professor's secretary, at the time his niece, to forge the signature. The girl was new and scared of asking her uncle or disturbing him. So, to answer your question, we are adamant these are the creatures."

There was a long silence before the President looked at the scientist, "what does this mean, what could be the outcome?".

The man remained silent whilst deciding how to reply. "Well sir, the situation could be catastrophic. You see, all the animals were heavily infected by a microbe, germ if you prefer, which causes breathing difficulties; it has the symptoms of flu and mainly attacks the lungs, it will most probably cause death among the older population and people with existing health issues. As this is a new and very virulent form of the disease it could spread like wildfire."

The President looked glum, "Can I ask why such a project was sanctioned in the first place; it seems it has little use apart from spreading mayhem".

The scientist cleared his throat, "I understand sir, that the military had requested that the laboratory worked on inventing a biological weapon to counter the Russians who are well advanced in this form of warfare. It seems this just developed as it went along, no one really understood what was being produced until near the end. The young scientist, Mr Nuang and his assistant, Miss Chow were sent down to finalise testing when the Professor in charge fell ill."

"But surely someone would have realised this was not just a run of the mill discovery. Did Professor Xing not have any concerns?"

"From what I understand, they did tell him and expressed their concerns, but they were ignored. The professor recently came to Beijing and presented the findings, I was one, along with the General," he nodded over to the shorter, squatter man, "who selected and singled out this discovery as being revolutionary".

The General nodded, "Yes, it fitted our brief perfectly and was, by far, the most interesting and cheapest to produce".

The President sat back; concern etched on his face. He leaned over and looked at the scientist, "professor, in your opinion, what are the chances of this illness getting out?".

The old professor rubbed his eyes and pursed his lips, "it is, as I said very virulent; we are not one hundred percent sure how easily it is to get infected from being in contact with animals but, what we are sure of, is that once it starts it will spread quickly".

"You have not really answered my question. What are the chances of this illness spreading?"

" Mr President, I' afraid I cannot tell you. It could be out now, next week or it may never be; it depends on who and how many people have been in contact with the infected animals."

The head of Security turned to the military and asked why and to what purpose they had wanted to get their hands on such a weapon apart, from trying to get one over the Russians.

The younger of the two looked at him in puzzlement. "We need a weapon to use in case of war. We have the bomb, but we all know that is a theoretical threat and will never, well by us anyway, be used. The devastation caused and the lasting damage does not warrant it's use. No, we need something that will incapacitate a country on a short-term basis, make it easier for us to overcome the enemy and, at the same time, cause it untold economic and financial damage."

The finance minister looked up beaming and turned to his President, "Sir, this could be exactly what we are looking for, the answer to all our problems".

"I am not sure I fully understand, please explain yourself."

The Minister looked over to the secretary, then back to the President, "do you think we could ask the secretary to leave; there are some highly delicate things to be discussed and I don't think it wise to have outsiders present".

The President shook his head in disagreement and motioned to the secretary to remain. He looked over to his minister, "the man stays, say what you have to say or don't say it at all".

Sheepishly the man mumbled his apologies, he clasped his hands tight together and cleared his throat. "We all know that our economy has been struggling over the past couple of years. The only sector which is excelling is the electronics sector, but we cannot rely on that for ever. Already we are seeing the likes of the Americans and British putting difficulties in our way, blocking deals, being protective and stopping us rolling out our new products in the name of safety; no, it won't last so we must find another way". He looked round the table before resuming, "Our only hope is to go about it in a more subtle or devious way, by wrecking our enemies' economy and forcing them into such a perilous financial situation, they have no other option but to come to us".

There was a long silence as the other members let his words sink in. The little General was the first to speak, "and how do you propose we do that?" he enquired.

The Minister's mouth twisted into a crooked smile, "by unleashing this virus in several countries and letting it spread. I understand from the professor, that there is no known cure yet however, I'm sure with the head start we have and the knowledge we have gained in discovering this virus, we can come up with an antidote or vaccine. We would then score twice. We would have to be prepared, firstly to help and bail out the western economy and secondly, we could be seen as the saviours of the world by supplying a cure."

The scientist sat with his mouth open but managed to splutter, "that's a terrible idea and I'm ashamed to think our country could even entertain such a thought. You do realise that it could come here and cause us much suffering and damage as well, viruses do not recognise borders?"

The finance minister ignored the comment and continued, "we must ensure we have a huge stock of medical equipment, syringes, gowns, gloves, masks all that sort of stuff. With some good media and PR work we could let it be known that these are absolutely essential necessities in the fight of this infection and offer to sell our supplies. In my mind it's a fantastic opportunity." He was on a roll and seeing everyone remained silent pressed on, "a further benefit would be that it would cause unrest among the populace; you know how the west loves to be free, well, we could promote the idea that restrictive measures on movement would be necessary to stop the spread of the disease. This can be done here for a short while to prove this works. As said, they like to be free and won't take kindly to being kept locked up, unable to work and play. With some well-timed words and media influence we could encourage civil unrest which we can use to our advantage."

The President held up his hand to silence his minister, "I understand and appreciate your thoughts as well as everyone's comments and concerns; this is a very big decision which will have major consequences and repercussions whatever we decide. It has some great merit and, on the face of it, would help us greatly. However, I suggest we sleep on it for a few days and reconvene in a few days' time. In the meantime, I will ask the finance minister to put some figures together, the Secretary for the Economy to start planning production of this medical equipment and you sir, I require you to set in motion a programme to finding an antidote or cure for this illness". He stood up, thanking everyone before leaving the room, closely followed by the secretary.

\* \* \*

It was dark when the man made his way towards the small, run down flat in the northern part of the city. As he walked briskly along the busy streets, he made a brief call; after speaking to the recipient, he changed direction and headed for a small restaurant where he found a secluded table and ordered a chicken noodle dish. It was not long after he had finished his meal that the woman come and sat across the table from him; they spoke in hushed tones. He handed her a note that he had scribbled while waiting and watched her place it in her bag. They left together but headed in opposite directions.

# CHAPTER 47

---

# Hong Kong

It was 1.20am when Jimmy was rudely awoken from a broken sleep; through bleary eyes he made out Tony standing at the door, a worried frown across his brow. "Sorry boss, but this just came in and does not make nice reading."

Jimmy got up and stretched, giving out a yawn, "how do you do it Tony, you haven't slept for what, twenty-four hours?" he enquired. He took the sheet of paper and read it before re-reading it a second time. Looking at his aide, "is this for real, are you absolutely certain you got this right? Who took it and deciphered it?".

"Absolutely certain, I know it sounds like some Sci-Fi story, but it has come direct from our man in Beijing; he was sitting in on the meeting".

Jimmy went over to the phone and called Sean; a sleepy voice came on, "think you better come over asap, do you want us to pick you up?". The drowsy voice had changed instantly into a sharp, alert voice; yes, that would be fine, he would be ready in twenty minutes.

An hour later the three men were discussing the situation. Sean shook his head, "unbelievable, are you sure your chap got this right? I just cannot accept that they would stoop so low."

"You don't know these people; they're capable of anything," Jimmy snorted. "I believe it was discussed; whether they will decide to act on it only time will tell. Seems we'll know in a few days."

"Have you told London and Washington? If not, that's a priority whether you trust the lines or not."

Jimmy smiled for the first time, "that's another thing I forgot to tell you, I was wrong, communications are safe although we have changed codes and tightened up procedures. We've told London but not Washington."

"Any reaction?" asked Sean.

"No not as yet but it will come, and I bet it will be laughed at and not believed."

"Ok, I'll send a message and explain how concerning the matter is, might even get James up to London and stress the urgency; they'll listen to him as much as to me." He got out of bed and made his way over to one of the desks, "I'll let Washington know and inform Jack as well".

Jimmy turned his attention to Tony, "any news from Wuhan". A shake of the head was all he got, he grimaced and screwed up his nose. "Try to contact them again but not too often, we don't want any prying ears or eyes picking up on the tries."

Tone nodded and made his way to his desk.

\* \* \*


## Washington

Hank and Joe were going over their report and putting the final touches to their case against Milento and Campese when there was a knock on the door. A secretary came in and handed her boss a file, not waiting to be told to leave she made her way to the door and closed it silently. Hank opened the brown folder and read through it; it was from Sean. He let out a whistle and passed it over to Joe.

Both men looked stunned and were silent, letting the information sink in. Joe was the first to react, "gee! you think this for real? It's fiction stuff" he exclaimed. "I know we can't put anything past the Chinese, but this, this is beyond belief."

Hank was about to reply when his phone buzzed, it was Jack from London. "Hey, have you seen Sean's report? Unbelievable but I don't doubt it for a second."

All three chatted for a while, each one giving his take on the report before Jack took over. "I've sent this to John just now, I think it's essential he, you, get this over to the White House asap. This is way too important to delay advising the President. James is on his way up to see me, and I think Sean has made an appointment for him to meet his boss later this evening. I'm meeting the Ambassador tonight; it's all go on our side of the pond."

Hank confirmed he and Joe would go see John Pintaro immediately and they would arrange to get the news delivered to the President. The call ended and Hank sat back, a feeling of emptiness settled into him. He resented that Jack, not yet his boss, was ordering him about but he kept his thoughts to himself, his time would come.

\*   \*   \*

The next twenty-four hours were hectic, with communications criss-crossing over the Atlantic. In Washington as well as in London meetings at the highest level took place and Cabinets were hurriedly assembled for special meetings. The British Prime Minister spoke to the President who agreed that this development was highly toxic. Despite their agreeing the situation was extremely serious, both men had very different ideas on how to tackle the matter. To the Englishman's surprise, it seemed that his counterpart would take a rather more relaxed attitude to the whole affair and did not seem to fully comprehend the possible chaos that could befall them. Life would continue as normal, and he made it clear that he considered the Prime Minister was overreacting. They parted but not before he had given reassurance that America would fully support Britain once it had left the EU.

\* \* \*

## Wuhan

Pearl had tried to call Mei Lien five times that day with no success. She was getting annoyed at the silence until Tim suggested that maybe Ru had taken her phone and it was now in some police station along with his possessions. He suggested that it would be a good idea to stop trying before it aroused suspicion and put them in danger. They did not know how Mei Lien had entered Pearl's details and none of them wanted to be contacted by the local police.

She was not happy but admitted he had a point. Sitting in her hotel room later that night she decided to try one last time, but still she was met with a continuous ring. She then called Jimmy to report their failure and to get orders as to what should be done. To her surprise, her partner sounded slightly annoyed at being asked what he considered to be a silly question. She was on the ground, she was surrounded by two of his best people, so it was up to them to decided how to proceed. Before hanging up he told her in coded language that they had a plane on standby that would come and collect her and her charge at Jiujing. He hung up and looked puzzled. What had gotten into her? Pearl was normally a cool, calculating and professional agent but now, he got the very strong feeling all was not well and that the three seemed not to be on the same wavelength. That wasn't good; it was at times like this, when personal egos or characters came into play, that people were more likely to get harmed. He told Sean of his misgivings, and both agreed that the problem would have to be tackled head on once the operation had been completed. Sean smiled over at his friend, "oh! the fun of being a boss," he grinned.

# CHAPTER 48

---

# Wuhan

Mei Lien had not left the flat since she had been given the news; she could not sleep and couldn't stop crying. She sat for hours staring out of the window hoping to see Ru walk down the street although she knew he would never do so again. She heard her phone ring but ignored it, she didn't want to talk to anyone, didn't want to be nice or hear nice things, she wanted to be left alone with her memories and her thoughts.

She went to the fridge only to find it practically empty, a bag of rather tired stir fry, a piece of dubious looking chicken, some bread and a couple of eggs. She felt her stomach rumble but could not summon up the energy to cook anything so went back to the window and continued to stare out. Her mind wandered back to the few days in Hong Kong, the proposal and the happy celebrations that night. She recalled the recent break they had, the love making and all the plans they had made. She shivered and started to cry again; oh, how she missed his calm voice, his joking, his sometimes-annoying mannerisms, and the feel of his warm, strong body when he lay next to her. She sighed a deep, long sigh and pulled a throw around her tightly.

She had no plans, did not know what she was going to do or where she was going to go. Her mind was a blank. She curled up and lay on the floor and cried herself to sleep.

She woke with a start the next morning; she was feeling cold and shivery even with the blanket round her. The day was bright with a watery sun trying to break through the autumn clouds. She went to have a long shower, got dressed and returned to the window. Looking out she watched the morning rush of people and cars. She noticed a green van parked up on the other side the street, she stared at it a long time. Had she seen that before? Was it there yesterday? She couldn't say for definite. Her phone rang and she reached over about to answer when she changed her mind; once it had finished ringing, she looked at the number but did not recognize it. Mei Lien was still sitting at the window a few hours later, and the van was still parked in the same spot. She decided to go out and get some food, an excuse for walking past the vehicle and having a look to see who was inside. She was adamant someone was there – were they watching her, waiting for her? First the old goat had supposedly committed suicide, then Ru getting stabbed, she was sure it was Lu Chin in that vehicle. Well, she wasn't going let him scare her into being a prisoner in her own flat; time to confront him even if it meant he killed her also. She had lost everything so she didn't care, she just wanted to look into his eyes for the last time and remind herself how evil he was; she would carry his image forever and would look him out when his day came and he joined, her and Ru on the other side. She would make sure the dragon of retribution engulfed him in flames and he would be reincarnated as a dung beetle.

Walking out into the street, Mei Lien made her way towards the van, as she got level to it looked in. She was surprised to see it was empty, instantly looking behind to make sure he wasn't creeping up on her; her breathing steadied when there was no sign of him, she relaxed slightly. Keeping alert, she made for the local supermarket and quickly bought a few essentials before making her way back towards the van; it was still empty. As she entered the apartment block, a sudden thought came to her and panic set in. Was he waiting upstairs, had he been waiting for her to leave the building so that he could gain access and kill her where no one could see? Her legs trembled and she started to shake uncontrollably. She inserted the key and opened the door gingerly, all the while checking that he was not hiding in a dark corner of the hallway. She let herself in and quickly locked the door. Breathing heavily, she made her way round the small flat looking everywhere, behind curtains, under the bed and in the main closet. Finally, she relaxed and let out a slow sigh of relief. Making her way over to the window she, looked out; it was still there and yes; she could see someone sitting in the front seat. She rubbed her eyes and shook her head. She picked up the phone and rang the police; they weren't interested.

After returning from her inspection and shopping Mei Lien had spent a long time sorting out Ru's clothes and his books. She went through his drawers and put his personal treasures such as his diplomas and a couple of photos of his parents in a box and placed his passport along with them. She found a USB stick and quickly remembered this was the copy of the last findings they had made. He had taken three copies of the research and results; two had been handed to Chi Tao for his trip to Beijing, the third he had kept. She recalled Ru had said that it was an insurance policy just in case something happened to one of them. She had not understood at the time what he meant but now, all was clear. Picking up the stick, she replaced it in the envelope and slipped it in her bag. Once her tidying had been done, she carried through the box and her bag to the small lounge and set them on a table. She had to decide what to do with them.

\*    \*    \*

Darkness had fallen and Mei Lien was sitting, curled up on the sofa watching TV when there was a sharp rap on the door. She jumped, startled at the sudden noise, terror flooding back instantly. She went over to the window; the van had gone. She looked up and down the street but could not see it. A second knock, more insistent this time. She went over and asked who was there. "Police, we need to speak to you Miss Chow."

Holding her breath, she decided instantly that she would tell them about the van and Lu Chin. She had barely unlocked the door when it was violently pushed open and two masked individuals hurtled in knocking her to the floor. The door was immediately closed and a hand was quickly put over her mouth and nose; a strong smell filled her nostrils and she lost consciousness. The two worked efficiently and silently, the smaller of the assailants took out a syringe and injected the limp body with a strong sedative before placing tape over her mouth. The larger one went in search of a couple of blankets. They expertly rolled Mei Lien up and tied her into a bundle making sure of leaving space for her to breath. They then scoured the small flat looking in every cupboard and every drawer before turning their attention to the box and the handbag. They went through the belongings carefully, retrieving the envelope containing the USB stick and passport; the slighter of the two intruders slipped it under their shirt. They placed Mei Lien Chow's passport in the box and sealed it before placing the two items in a large rucksack. The task completed, they made a second inspection ensuring nothing of importance had been missed or forgotten. Satisfied, one of them went over to the window and slightly opened the curtains. He was looking for something or someone. He made his way back and, for the first time spoke in a hushed voice; they conversed in Mandarin in a clear educated manner and typical of urban Beijing. An hour elapsed before they looked at their watches and nodded.

The larger of the two picked up the bundle and put it over his shoulder, Mei Lien was petite and weighed nothing for a man of his size, while the second slung the rucksack over a shoulder and went to the door. Turning off the light, they ensured no one was out on the landing or in the emergency stairwell. Silently they made their way down, cautiously checking each level before reaching the ground floor. Again, a quick check, a nod to signal all clear, and they hurried noiselessly to the fire escape and made their way out into the dark alley. Making good time they soon emerged into the deserted side street and the waiting van. The back doors swung open, and the bundle was carefully placed inside along with the rucksack; the smaller person got in and sat by Mei Lien. They drove off in silence and headed South.

Outside the city limits Pearl started to take off the police suit she was wearing. Bundling the clothes into a second rucksack she turned her attention to Mei Lien; she untied the bundle slightly and checked her breathing and pulse. Tim had also taken off his uniform and had handed them behind to be placed in the hiking bag. They carried on in silence until they reached a bridge spanning a fast-flowing river. The van stopped and the three passengers got out to stretch their legs; they breathed in the cold night air. Tim took out the large rucksack which had been filled with rocks, it weighed a ton and he had trouble hauling it to the side of the bridge. Checking no other vehicles were in sight, they all three heaved the bag over the side and watched it splash into the river and rapidly sink to the bottom. They returned to the van, Tim taking over the driving.

Two hours later the lights of the airport came into view. Pearl checked on Mei Lien one last time, gave her a further small dose of sedative before tying her up again in a bundle. Arriving at the private plane entrance gate they pulled up at the booth and presented the documents Tim had printed out. The guard scrutinized the papers and enquired what was in the bundle. Satisfied with the reply he did not bother to check, he had been on duty all night and was scheduled to finish in fifteen minutes, so wasn't interested in delaying matters. He handed over two passes and pointed to a Learjet parked half a mile away. The gate opened and they drove through.

Stopping at the foot of the plane the three got out and were greeted by the pilot who stood at the top of the steps. Tim went up to introduce himself and hand over the documents. He briefly explained to the pilot what the special delivery was; the man nodded and smiled, satisfied. The bundle was gently lifted aboard and placed on the floor. Before he left, Pearl thanked him and Sally for their help and wished them a safe return to base.

As the car pulled away the jet engines came to life and the plane slowly made its way to the end of the runway; a few minutes later it was airborne leaving the ground disappearing below them. Pearl went up to the cockpit and requested the pilot came out into the cabin, she did not wish the co-pilot to hear what she had to ask. She returned and sat back, closing her eyes; she suddenly felt drained and exhausted.

She was woken by the appearance of the pilot by her side. He confirmed that he had advised her people in Hong Kong of their ETA and that they had thirty minutes before starting their descent. Pearl thanked him and got to work. She untied Mei Lien and released her from the straps they had put on her. She took off the gag before taking down the emergency oxygen cylinder. She then gave her charge a further injection and waited. A few minutes later she saw a flicker of Mei Lien's eye lids followed by a low groan. She applied the gas mask and slowly brought her charge back to life. She massaged her wrists and ankles and, struggling, managed to sit her upright in a seat.

Mei Lien's head was throbbing, her mouth was dry and eyes bleary. She tried to focus but her brain could not seem to pass on the messages it wanted her body to do. She sat, slumped in her seat, staring at a face she recognized but could not yet put a name to. She did not know her surroundings, everything was un-familiar, she had never seen this place before. The humming noise rang loud in her ears and they too, began to hurt. She was given a glass of water but couldn't hold on to it, her hands were numb, her wrist and ankles sore. She tried to rub her eyes but spilt the drink over her blouse instead, the cold-water biting into her stomach. The woman next to her fussed about and dried her, she then held the glass to her lips and Mei Lien managed to have the much-needed drink.

The plane started its descent and a bell pinged. Mei Lien looked around, she seemed to be on a plane but had no idea how she had got there. Suddenly feeling tired, she closed her eyes and drifted off.

The plane touched down with a thud and Mei Lien jumped, startled by the sudden jerk. She opened her weary eyes and looked out the window at the glittering water close by and the outline of skyscrapers in the distance. The plane taxied along, weaving its way to the stand before it came to a halt some way from the main terminal buildings. As soon as the engines had been turned off the door was opened and Mei Lien was hit by a fresh salty smell of sea air mixed with kerosene fumes, she wrinkled her nose. She was still feeling sleepy, her limbs ached but her head had cleared slightly although she could still feel the thump of her blood being pumped round her body in her ears. She rubbed her eyes and temples and ran her fingers through her knotted hair. Looking over at the woman sitting across from her, it slowly began to dawn on her where she had seen the face before. She tried to speak but her mouth was dry and her throat sore - nothing came out. The woman smiled gently and handed her a bottle of water. She started to speak, "welcome to Hong Kong Miss Chow, you are safe and in good hands. I'm sorry if you feel a little shaky and sore but will explain everything once we get back to my flat."

A car pulled up at the foot of the steps and a slim man dressed in jeans and a white shirt got out, He made his way up and entered the plane. He spoke a few words to the pilot before greeting Pearl and Mei Lien. He helped them down the steps, practically carrying Mei Lien whose legs felt like jelly. She was placed in the back of the car and Pearl settled in beside her, the young man taking the driver's seat and they made their way to a gate far from the main terminal buildings. They were waved through without a stop and headed for the city.

They drove in silence, Mei Lien just sitting staring out at the looming city skyline and increasing traffic. Her brain was beginning to function once again, and she slowly began to remember the sequence of events. The knock on the door, the voices announcing the police, being knocked over and a hand smothering her mouth and nose; after that, a blank.

* * *

Pearl's flat was on the twenty ninth floor of a modern tower block just a short walk from the centre, it was modern and airy. She didn't need a big place as she lived alone and spent most of her life at the office or away on a mission; it was simply furnished and minimalistic, just how she liked it. Standing in the middle of the living area, Mei Lien looked around, she liked what she saw, not unlike her own taste, it was decorated simply. There was no view except on to another tower block which was separated by a busy street.

She was still drowsy and her head begun to hurt once again. Pearl produced a couple of pain killers and suggested Mei Lien went to lie down for a while. She took her through to the snug bedroom and gave her a bathrobe, closed the curtains and showed her charge the bathroom. Mei Lien flopped onto the bed and fell asleep immediately.

She was woken by a wonderful smell of cooking and looked at the clock by the bed; 5pm, she must have slept most of the day. She got up and went to have a long shower, enjoying the strong hot jet needle her body. Well rested, her headache gone, she felt human again. The wonderful aromas coming from the kitchen made her realize how hungry she was; it must have been nearly two days since she had last had anything to eat, her stomach started to rumble. Immediately memories flooded back of her beloved Ru, his belly always grumbling, always hungry; she sighed and went through to the bedroom where a pair of jeans and a t/shirt had been laid out for her. Both were too big, but she took them thankfully.

She went through to the kitchen where she helped Pearl finish preparing the meal before they made their way into the living area;

two men were standing chatting, backs turned towards them. As they entered, both men turned round, and she remembered the smaller one who had met them off the plane. He greeted her with a broad smile and introduced himself as Jimmy Wong; the larger man she also recognized immediately as being the foreigner. Ru had been right, they must be spies and she was now under their control; she shuddered inwardly.

Over a meal of pork and noodles Jimmy and Sean explained to Mei Lien how and why they got involved and the events leading up to the other day. Jimmy looked over at her and spoke in a soft voice, "I must apologise and stress you are not a prisoner here; after careful consideration we decided the best and safest thing was to get you away from Wuhan as soon as possible".

Mei Lien was silent for a while before thanking them for their explanations, she felt calmer now she had got some background. She had been puzzled at the events and asked if they could tell what had happened.

Jimmy took over and spoke in their native tongue, "after Professor Xing went to Beijing and presented your discovery to the National Committee, he returned to Wuhan. It is understood that the powers in the Capital did not trust him to keep this mouth shut and ordered that he be dealt with. I can assure you he was murdered, and it was made to look like suicide. They then worried that, as he was extremely lax with security, other scientists would talk loosely so they arranged for all your team to be dispersed to far corners of the land and given very menial jobs. The two people they feared most were you and your fiancé."

Mei Lien was sitting silently; she had stopped eating and feared what was coming next. She nodded for Jimmy to continue.

"Your intended decided to speak to our agent, Ying Po who, incidentally, has been following you since you left the Beijing; he and his associate travelled with you on the train."

Mei Lien gasped in surprise, "was the cleaner at the canteen also one of your agents?".

"Yes, in fact she was the same person who was on the train. As we've told you, we had been tipped off that you were going to be working on a highly sensitive project, we understood it was a chemical weapon. We decided to keep watch and, yes, to try and gain your confidence; sorry". He looked apologetically at Mei Lien. "Your fiancé had arranged to meet our man at the market that fateful afternoon; he was taken to his van where they sat in the back, out of sight. Ru talked freely and gave us a clear insight as to what had been produced, he expressed his grave concerns if this fell into the wrong hands or used in the wrong way. I don't need to tell you how panicked and distressed he was. Pearl here was also in the vehicle, she recorded everything he said."

Mei Lien's eyes darkened, "what happened after he had finished?".

"They left the van and Ru headed off back towards the exit. Sally, the cleaner, was going to follow him while Pearl made her way to the main gate where she would take over. Unfortunately, Sally had barely left when a large cart bumped into her and she momentarily lost sight of your intended; when the path was clear she saw him move to avoid a lorry bearing down on him and that was when the killer struck. As your fiancé stepped back, he was met by the man who stabbed him twice in the back",

Mei Lien was on the verge of tears; she took a large sip of water, sniffed and with a set expression nodded for him to continue.

Jimmy confirmed if she was alright and getting her reply continued, "Sally was there instantly but it was too late, she blames herself for his death, but she could do nothing about it; it is just how things happen sometimes. I am truly sorry for your loss, we suspected something like that might happen and tried our best". He looked up at the sad face with damp eyes. "We knew who did it, it was an agent from Beijing – he worked in your laboratory and was planted there by the security forces in Beijing to keep an eye on you all and report back. He was the same man who killed the Professor."

Mei Lien spoke in a soft tone, "Lu Chin, I knew it all along. Neither of us liked or trusted him, he was evil. A few days before, we were at the market and he had a run in with Ru, taunted him that he was going to kill him and wreck our lives. Ru had threatened to report him," she mumbled.

Jimmy was about to speak when Mei Lien continued, "I knew it was him, when Ru did not come home, I sat for hours looking out of the window and I watched a van parked just up the street. I couldn't see inside but it remained there for almost two days. I even went out to confront him but when I got there he had gone. On my return to the flat I phoned the police to report him but they said they couldn't do anything. Just before you came to abduct me I noticed the vehicle had gone so thought that they had acted."

Jimmy looked over at Pearl and Sean before resuming, "it was him alright, you were right. We had caught up with him and kept a 24-hour surveillance on both of you. We saw you coming out of your flat and were worried he might decide to attack you, so, just before you arrived, we managed to lure him away. We got lucky and managed to listen in to his phone and picked up a call from the police warning him you had called them; that's why we told you it was the police at the door."

Mei Lien looked visibly shaken, "do you think he would have come after me? Where is he now?". She spoke in English, so Sean picked up the conversation.

"Most definitely, his orders were to eliminate you and dispose of your body." He looked at Jimmy who continued, "he won't harm you or anyone else, that I can promise you."

"Do you know where Ru is? I tried to ask but no one knew or would tell me."

"No, I'm afraid we don't. We've checked the hospitals and morgues but have found nothing. They may have taken him and buried him in some small rural cemetery." Jimmy did not want to say that they had probably disposed of the body immediately.

"How did I get here? I remember opening the door but that's all."

"Yes, I'm sorry about that; it could have been done a little more delicately, but the situation was urgent, and we weren't sure you would have come had we asked. Pearl and Tim were the two who came to your door, they had managed to get a couple of police uniforms - no don't ask! I'm afraid they drugged you. They carried you to a vehicle where Sally was waiting before they drove you to an airport about 250km away and put you on the private plane we had hired. I just hope we didn't hurt you too much; it is not easy carrying a dead weight, even someone as slight as you."

Mei Lien nodded and thanked him his for his honesty and for telling her what had happened. She rose and went over to her bag but remembered she had not seen it and started to panic. "Where is my bag?" she enquired about to burst into tears.

Reading her mind Jimmy went over to his jacket and retrieved the envelope and passport. "Are you looking for these?"

Mei Lien relaxed and nodded. "You'd better have this; Ru had made an extra copy in case things went wrong, it's the complete workings, calculations and findings we carried out and the reason he died, as well as the professor. It will confirm what Ru told your man in the back of the van."

"Are you sure?" it was Pearl who spoke first. "As much as we appreciate you giving us this, are you absolutely certain you want to..., well betray China?"

Mei Lien nodded, "absolutely sure, after what they've done it is essential you have it. Just make sure whoever gets it finds an antidote". She looked at the three of them with worried eyes, "what are you going to do with me?".

Jimmy was the first to speak, "what would you like us do?" he enquired. As I see it you have three options: firstly, you return to the mainland, we can arrange to get you back so no one will suspect anything. Secondly, you can stay here and thirdly we could arrange for you to live in the UK. It's up to you. I must add however, if you decide to return to China, we will not be able to guarantee your safety."

There was a long pause before Mei Lien replied, "thank you, can I think about it or do you need a reply now?".

"A couple of days at the most would be best, especially if you wish to return home."

Jimmy rose from the table, "well, I think Sean and I will be on our way, leave you two to get some rest". Turning to Pearl, "you don't have to come in tomorrow, perhaps take Mei Lien to do some shopping. Call me once a decision has been made."

The two men arrived back at the office; the night shift had recently taken over, but Tony was still prowling about, making sure everyone was up to speed. Jimmy waved him over and all three went into his room. He glanced through the reports on his desk before turning to his office manager, "get word to Tim and Sally to stay in Wuhan a few days longer, tell them to keep a low profile. Once we know what the girl wants to do, we will send further orders. Also, send word to Beijing to keep their ears and eyes open. We need to know what is planned, if anything, but everyone's safety is a priority."

Tony was about to disappeared when Jimmy stopped him, "and make sure you thank Tim and Sally for a great job done". Once the door had closed Jimmy pulled out the envelope containing the small stick with the priceless information. They sat down and waited to see what appeared on his computer screen. They gawped at symbols, graphs and calculations; none made any sense to them, especially to Sean as it was all in Chinese. They turned to each other and laughed.

\*    \*    \*

The girls stayed up until the early hours of the morning talking; Mei Lien poured out her heart whilst Pearl listened, taking in everything she heard. At last, they decided it was time to get some rest; Mei Lien asking if she could share the bed with Pearl, she needed comforting and to be close to someone. It was not long before she was asleep, leaving Pearl to lie and go over all she had been told. The poor girl was certainly distraught at the loss of her fiancée, they had had something special, intense; her plans and hopes now extinct.

# CHAPTER 49

# Beijing

The President had called an emergency meeting in his office; yes, he had initially given everyone three days but the report he had received earlier that morning meant an urgent change of plan.

Seated around a large table, his secretary discreetly positioned in the corner, he surveyed his aides with small hard eyes. He had accepted that the finance minister's idea would benefit China and put his country in an extraordinary position but, deep down, he had major reservations and was not keen to go down that route. The men all sat in silence, showing calmness on the outside but inside each man there was in turmoil. None liked these last minute , rushed meetings, they normally signalled bad news. Turning to his head of security, the President bored into his target. "General, a couple of issues have arisen which disturb me. You told us at our last meeting you had no idea who had killed Professor Xing and the young scientist, is that right?".

The General nodded and gulped slightly; he felt a bead of perspiration trickle down his shirt.

"So, tell me how come the man who killed these two scientists was personally appointed by you and instructed to spy on all the employees at this laboratory?"

The head of security was about to speak when the President continued, "unless he went rogue on you and, in that case, you didn't do a very good job in vetting him, I must presume you ordered him to eliminate these two people".

The General remained silent and just nodded. "Sir, I admit that I sent this man to spy on the scientists; it is standard practice and is happening throughout all the laboratories, factories and places where national security is paramount. His orders were to report back to myself and my department. He found out Professor Xing, although excellent in his job, was lax with security."

"Who gave the order to kill them both?"

" Not me Sir, as you said earlier, he must have done this off his own bat. We had arranged for all the other researchers to be placed in various laboratories across the country but had accepted that the best course of action was to keep the two youngsters and the professor in Wuhan in case they were needed. This does not explain why he decided to kill the professor. May I add that our man had been very strictly vetted and has been one of our top spies."

The President grunted and showed little of his feelings. He continued, "1 also understand from a report this morning, that the young woman has vanished, is that true?".

The General's breathing quickened, and he felt more sweat trickling down inside his tunic. He nodded, "yes, it seems that after our man had eliminated the young scientist, he himself was killed; we found him in a bin with his throat slit; the girl has indeed disappeared. We have a nationwide search for her ongoing, every avenue and every possible place is being investigated."

"You think she did it, a simple scientist, slitting the throat of one of our top men?"

"It's certainly a possibility, but unlikely."

"Well make sure we find her and find her fast and alive. We need her to talk and tell us what happened. No more mistakes General." The President's icy eyes remained on the man for what seemed like an eternity.

Finally, he glanced round the table, "now let us debate the merits of the proposal made by the Finance Minister". Everyone in the room had an opinion and a vested interest, opinions differed. The military and economists supported the idea, both were adamant this was a god-send and would propel China on its way to being a global superpower that would rule the world for many years to come. The scientist, was totally opposed to the idea, pointing out, yet again, that the disease could, would, probably hit the country and that they would suffer as much as the rest of the world. The head of security was not convinced either; he sensed his boss's hesitation and after the dressing down he had received earlier, decided it would be best for his career if he sided with the President. A major, but little known, power struggle had developed.

On two points all agreed, whatever the decision. Firstly, the WHO would have to be dealt with and their silence bought by giving them massive financial support. They would encourage them to point the finger at the western laboratories, or even better, to Russia. Secondly, the world press and media had to be fed fear and disinformation stories and to expound the willingness of China to co-operate with the rest of the world. It was massively important for the future of the electronics industry and the economy that China was shown in a better light.

*   *   *

## Hong Kong

The next morning Pearl took her protégé to do some shopping, the girl had absolutely nothing apart from the clothes she was wearing when they abducted her; the ones she had been lent were far too big. They were sitting at table in one of the department stores having tea, when Mei Lien looked at Pearl and smiled, "thank you for this morning, I've really enjoyed it. Thank you also for looking after me, I didn't realise what dangers you have all gone through and want to say I don't blame any of you for Ru's death; I'm sure the woman at the market did her best." The sadness in her eyes was there, plain for all to see.

"I've been thinking, now that Ru has gone, there is nothing for me back in China; my job prospects are bleak, and I will be looking over my shoulder for the rest of my life." She looked around at the other shoppers, "I like it here in Hong Kong, but it holds too many memories so, I've decided, I would like to take up your offer of moving to Britain".

Pearl was surprised at how fast she had made up her mind, thinking she would have taken much longer. She took Mei Lien's hand and looked her in the eyes, "you do know that there is no returning, no changing minds, the move will be final. What about your parents? You don't have to make a decision yet, give it a few more days."

Mei Lien nodded, "I understand, my mind has been made up, I want to start a new life in a new country. The sooner the better".

Pearl took out her phone and called Jimmy. After a brief conversation she replaced it in her bag, "you're leaving in two days' time with Sean, he will fly back with you and help you settle in. We will have a new passport and identity ready by tomorrow."

Mei Lien beamed, "thank you! There is just one more favour I would like to ask. Can anyone let my parents know I'm alright?"

Pearl promised she would try her best but could not guarantee it, she did not want to put their or her agents' lives at risk.

Mei Lien nodded, "I understand; time to celebrate, but sadly I have very little money so I'm unable to buy you champagne".

\* \* \*

After saying their farewells, Sean steered Mei Lien down the aisle, boarding the plane last. Jimmy had arranged for the pair to be allowed to by-pass security and all the formalities; he had also managed to get two secluded seats in First Class and ensuring both were treated as VIPs.

As the plane trundled down the runway and began its climb Mei Lien looked out of the window. In the distance she saw the hills behind which lay China, below Hong Kong was disappearing under clouds. She wiped away the tears forming in her eyes and turned to Sean. He smiled and held up his glass, she did the same, "cheers to a new life".

# Epilogue

## China - Beijing

The virus made its appearance in Wuhan a few days after the meeting; all worries of an internal power struggle vanished. The President and his closest aides had been taken by surprise and set about a limitation exercise. The publicity and national PR organisation went into over-drive with many actions taken which could only take place in a totalitarian state. Every move, every decision and every news bulletin ensured that China was shown up in a good light, was depicted as a decisive and strong country, not afraid of taking draconian action when needed.

Millions of dollars and hundreds of hours were spent "educating" the foreign press and media on how wonderful China was and how the world should act if the virus struck elsewhere. Once these information centres had been softened up It was followed by a sustained campaign of instilling fear, and whipping up a frenzy of panic which, in a very short space of time, would shut down entire nations, causing tremendous financial harm.

The world press and media were continuously fed fear stories which, the Chinese understood well, would help sell papers, fill news programmes and spread panic throughout populations. Over a period of six months China controlled the world media ensuring they did not point the finger of blame at them.

The supply of protective garments and medical supplies were offered to the poorer nations. Advice was given to all those affected and who cared to listen.

All the while a small amount of the war virus was produced, unsuspecting mules were sent around the world to spread it; nothing could stop a world pandemic; the devious war had begun.

\* \* \*

Whilst most were happy and satisfied with developments, the security department was not. The bad and more serious news of the disappearance of the young woman had major consequences for the General and his department. Miss Chow had seemingly vanished into thin air. Extensive door to door searches, checks at train and bus stations as well as at airports and border controls had come up with no leads. Enquiries in her hometown and at her parents' home had proven fruitless. The Hong Kong police had been alerted, but they had not come back with anything. The head of security was under enormous pressure; his career was about to come to an end.

\* \* \*

## Wuhan

Lu Chin had been sitting in his van watching his target's apartment. He had no real plan how to deal with her and his task had been made more difficult by the fact she had locked herself away. The killing of the boyfriend was easy, kids' stuff, but the girl, she was not playing ball. He was sitting staring across the road when there was a tap at his window; he looked up and his eyes were greeted by the sight of a young woman smiling warmly. He wound down the window and she asked him for help, her car would not start, could he help? Bored and confident his target was not going anywhere, he agreed and followed the attractive body round the corner. He had barely passed a narrow alleyway when he felt the blade of a knife across his throat, he gasped and gurgled, hardly feeling the final thrust of the weapon sink deep into his neck. His body was placed in a large bag and bundled into a bin where it would be collected by the refuse truck soon after.

A few days later the first confirmed victim of a new virus had died in the main city hospital. The body was that of a trader who had stolen a chicken from a neighbour's stall during the recent murder of a young man at the market; he had eaten it that night. A monkey from the same stall had also been taken by a looting shopper, and soon after three members of his family died of a mysterious new flu-like disease.

Ying Po and the canteen cleaner, otherwise better known as Tim and Sally, followed orders and remained in Wuhan, just getting out before the authorities closed the city to the outside world. On orders from Beijing, no one was allowed in or out, a 6pm curfew was initiated. That situation would last several weeks. It was widely reported that the new virus had struck a vast number of citizens and that the lockdown was to save the illness spreading across China. Very few of the Wuhan residents had actually heard or knew of anyone with this disease, but most agreed the authorities had done the right thing. Foreign correspondents, under strict police and military control, were invited to film the near deserted city and fed the agreed stories.

As the quarantine came to an end and restrictions were lifted, the same journalists and TV crews were invited back to be shown how China had managed to contain and beat this new, deadly virus. Only a handful of top political members knew the four initial deaths were to be followed by thousands more. Thanks to the propaganda machine they were not reported. To the outside world, where the disease had started to take hold and spread, it gave a clear indication on how to deal with the situation. With a compliant and besotted media, ever eager to set panic across the population and undermine their home governments, the world slowly came to a halt.

* * *

## Hong Kong

Jimmy Wong was a happy man well, for a short time anyway. The fact that he had managed to get one of the scientists out pleased him, but he was sad at losing Ru. He did not blame his agents; they had operated under extremely difficult conditions and had shown some rapid thinking. Even Pearl had to admit she had been impressed at the quick planning and execution of Mei Lien's extraction. She still did not care for Tim, still thought he was arrogant but, as Jimmy reminded her, they lived in very different worlds, constantly in danger and always having to think on their feet.

He worried about his agents in Beijing. They were in the thick of it; one slight slipup, one moment of inattention and they would be caught, he shuddered at the thought of their fate if caught.

He was pleased at the success they had and the new friendship he had made with Sean. A man who thought like him, who had the same work ethics, a man he could trust.

One of his first tasks after the Irishman and Mei Lien had left for Britain was to put Pearl in charge of the China desk; from now on she would be responsible for the well-being and control of his agents across China. It was a huge and delicate job but one she was well capable of. After deliberating a long while she had decided it was too dangerous to send someone to visit Mei Lien's parents; later perhaps when the dust had settled. She also made up her mind to cut Tim some slack, as Jimmy had rightly pointed out, he and all her agents, lived in a very different world.

The second thing he did was to promote Tony to be his number two. The man deserved his promotion and he was delighted to think he had such dedicated back-up.

Once the re-organisation had been sorted, Jimmy turned his attention to the now main, and most important task, that of trying to help Hong Kong stave off China's subtle, back door takeover.

\* \* \*

## Washington

The news of events in Wuhan and of Ru's death came as no surprise. There was relief that Sean and the British had managed to extract Mei Lien and that she was now safe in Hong Kong. Daily meetings were taking place to keep the President and his aides up to date with the situation in China and Hong Kong. It was clear no one was interested in the latter, they washed their hands of the situation, even when explanations were plain for all to see; the administration had a blank spot. As for the rapidly spreading disease, this man-made illness spread by China - that was something different; the US were not going to let themselves be bullied into closing down the economy. They quickly understood what the Chinese were trying to do and were not about to be influenced by the poisoned press and media. They knew all too well about fake news and their left-wing, anti-American agenda; resist, deny and resist again, that was the President's motto.

Hank stuck at his job for a couple of weeks, long enough for him and Joe to finalise the case against the two clowns they had caught. The case had been handed over to the lawyers and the courts and was making its way through all the usual long-winded processes; it was expected that the two accused would stand trial sometime within the next ten months.

Not wanting to wait for Jack's return and take over as his boss, Hank had handed in his notice, the very notice he had written out before joining his friends on that last night of celebrations. He left his office and desk late on the evening of December 15, closing the door he made his way through the empty reception area and down to the main hall. He nodded at the security guard one last time but said nothing. The next day he drove up to his retreat, a small house in the middle of a forest in Georgia; he was a free man.

Joe Briggs had been persuaded to return to Washington after news of Hanks departure. Initially he had refused point blank, he had been retired, brought back to help with the latest US/British case involving China and various dubious laboratories; now it was all over he wanted back to Maine, to his cabin and to is fishing. That was until Jack had called him and asked him to hold the fort until he returned from London. Reluctantly he had agreed, but only for six months, to help, short term. Deep down he was under no illusions, he knew it would be for longer.

Jack Warren finished up in London, he was sad to leave the old city. He liked it there and the move was made more difficult by the fact that he had made new friends. In particular, a certain Irishman, with whom he had a great understanding and affinity. Their mirrored lives, shared experiences and their mutual respect made for good friendship. He had also gotten to like James, found him amusing, a typically quaint Englishmen, well read, enthusiastic and a quick learner with a wonderful sense of humour, something he particularly enjoyed. He would miss their lunches and his visits down to the West Country. After welcoming and over-seeing his replacement, Jack returned to Washington to take up his new position as second in command of the CIA. It was going to be a tough job but at least he had great back up; without Joe he doubted he would have managed.

As for young Carter, he was spotted several times leading various demonstrations in New York, Chicago and in LA. Luckily for him, he never came face to face with Beth.

\*  \*  \*

## England

After the plane carrying Sean and Mei Lien landed at Heathrow, they were met by several MI6 officials and spirited through emigration. The following days were taken up with debriefing sessions and for Mei Lien, endless form filling relating to her new identity. Once all the formalities had been completed they had made their way down to Devon and spent a week with the Hortons, relaxing in the cosy home and going for long walks in the cold and wintery countryside. James was curious to find out all the details and listened to his friend recount the story. He was never quite sure how much was true and how much was made up; he could never tell once Sean had lapsed into his Irish imagination.

After returning to London, Mei Lien, now known as Miss Iris Zhu, was found a job in a laboratory on the outskirts of Oxford. Her job, and that of a select few of her colleagues who she had working under her, was to find an antidote to the new flu-like disease that was spreading like wildfire across the world. She did not know that her new workplace was, not so long ago, where Sean had first raised his concerns and voiced his suspicion. Later the creator of the laboratory had been found dead in a carriage at Euston station.

His partner and close friend had now been appointed head of SAGE, the governments advisory body, tasked to advise the Prime Minister and the cabinet on the best way to handle the pandemic. Un-beknown to his employers, the man was still in the pay of the

Chinese government, something that would come to light months later to the great embarrassment of the British Governments.

Mei Lien or Iris Zhu was continually contradicted, her research hampered, by the man she and Sean had warned was a traitor. No one apart from James, and MI6 believed them, yet nothing could be done without proof. They spent days worrying about the sensitive information on the USB they had extracted from China and went to great lengths to keep it secret. Eventually, reports from Jimmy and his people in China, had persuade the head of MI6 that they had sufficient evidence that the man was a traitor. After advising the Government, he was arrested. The British press and media were up in arms, accusing the secret service and the Cabinet of being incompetent. At his trial a few months later, it became evident that he had made a fortune being paid by his paymasters on the other side of the world to supress and hamper any discovery of vaccine for the virus. During the trial, in the hope of getting a softer sentence, he dropped a bombshell accusing the second in command of the CIA and a senior American politician of being his paymasters. No one believed him until it was reluctantly confirmed by the U.S. They were all sent to jail for life.

James Horton resumed his quiet life in the country. During the long winter days, he often thought about the buzz and excitement of the past couple of years, he missed it. His plans to visit Washington and Hong Kong were put on hold due to lockdown and he was sorry he could not introduce Claire to his new American friends. Thankfully, he was able welcome Sean and Iris occasionally for brief visits. Both were busy but always enjoyed their friend's hospitality. He had not been asked to help Sean with his latest operation.

Sean had been moved back to his initial investigation on drug links between the Taliban and the Chinese Triads. With help from his new friends in Hong Kong and their agents on the ground, a major operation was set up in co-operation with the Dutch anti-drug squad. A year after he had resumed his investigation the news was announced that the largest haul of drugs the UK had ever seen had taken place. Thirty-nine foreign and British nationals had been arrested and a major network had been dismantled.

Semi-retired, Sean retreated to his small apartment in the country but quickly became bored and soon resumed part time work for MI6. In his time off he would make frequent visits to the West Country along with his protégé. At last, he relented to their pressure and was persuaded to sell his flat and buy a small cottage not far from his friend Jamesie Horton.

# Notes

Thank you, dear reader, for staying with me throughout this story. It is my first book and I enjoyed every minute I have spent writing it. Like all authors I have had my ups and downs, my frustrating days and those when inspiration came easily.

It is not intended to be anything else other than light reading, a story based on existing circumstances - but what it is not, is an exposé, or actual truths about facts on what has recently happened. All characters are fictional, any names or resemblances are purely co-incidental. Likewise, some places are known to many, and I have deliberately made their description loose and inaccurate; others come from my imagination.

I must thank my wife for her encouragement, her comments and her critique, she has been an invaluable help and ally. I would also like to thank my Publishers and in particular Diane for her great help and advice.